Feel free to put your initials on
this card to show that you
have read this book.

A Golden Bond

Elaine Jannetides

Blue River Press
Indianapolis

A Golden Bond - Copyright © 2015 by Elaine Jannetides

Published by Blue River Press
Indianapolis, Indiana
www.brpressbooks.com

Distributed by Cardinal Publishers Group
2402 N. Shadeland Avenue, Suite A
Indianapolis, IN 46219
317-352-8200 phone
317-352-8202 fax
www.cardinalpub.com

ISBN: 978-1-935628-57-6

Cover Design: Phil Velikan
Book Design: Dave Reed
Cover Photo: iStock.com, photo iStock ID _000016240947
Editors: Brenda Robertson Stewart, Holly Kondras
Copyeditor: Liz Evans
Author Photo Credit: Marissa Doherty

Printed in the United States of America

10 9 8 7 6 5 4 3 2 1

This story encompasses a collection a different characters all
of which are an invention of the author's imagination. Any
resemblance of anyone living or dead is purely coincidental. All of
the characters are purely fictional born of the author's imagination.
The small town in Indiana where a few of the characters lived
does not exist in reality only in the author's inventive thoughts.

Dedication

This book is dedicated to my loving husband, Nick, whose patience, understanding, and endless encouragement meant the world to me.

Contents

Salute to the Veterans

A BIG SALUTE TO ALL THE ARMED FORCES OF THE UNITED STATES OF AMERICA SERVING IN PRESENT OR IN PAST WARS. WE LIFT UP OUR HEARTS TO ALL VETERANS!

A small portion of this book is dedicated to the end of World War II and the beginning the Korean Police Action (Conflict). The world was in confusion. Their heads were spinning in fear and uncertainty, from the joy of a victory to fear of a new war. We were welcoming our armed forces back home after serving on the front lines only to find that there was a new challenge facing them. Everyone was hoping against hope the inevitable would not happen. These were indeed dark times.

Without these brave men and women in the armed forces, who knows what the future might have brought.

They entered the armed forces as young and unexperienced men and women and returned as mature people ready for the challenges of life.

We thank them for their service.

Prologue

Life for a teenager in the 1950s was quite different than life for teens today. Music was different; activities were different; entertainment was different. Tradition in the Era was held in a position of importance and honor, and families observed it together.

The school year always began the day after Labor Day and ended the first week of June. That was also the month when graduations took place. Swimming pools opened on Memorial Day, May 30th, rain or shine; cold or warm, the pool would be ready. Conversely, the pools all closed on Labor Day, once again, rain or shine; cold or warm.

Music from the 50s is considered the Oldies nowadays with a strong influence from World War II. It was not till late 1959 that Rock and Roll came upon the scene with the introduction of Elvis to the world. Little things were very important to everyone, such as the cap and gown for graduation ceremonies and the class rings, which were a long-time tradition. Let us not leave out bobby socks worn in the style of the school a person attended.

The Korean Police Action had a very huge impact on both young and old. Young men were being drafted just as they were beginning their adult lives.

Public schools did not have buses to transport students; instead, they walked to and from school.

Most families owned one car and one black and white television set.

You are about to be introduced to Angie, her brothers Joey and Sammie, and how they faced life's trials and overcame them.

We first meet a few of the girls walking to school with a song in their heart, full of excitement and looking forward to their senior year. They are talking about selecting their class rings. The senior students all wanted to buy their class rings and enjoy wearing it the entire year. The female students would usually enlist their mothers to help with selection. Angie's experience with her class ring became a real adventure, nothing at all resembling anything her classmates and friends would experience. Unknown to Angie, her journey with the ring would have many unexpected twists and turns as she embarks on the plan she has set out for herself—a journey that spans over many years. A common bond is formed that connects six very different women in *A Golden Bond*. Read and enjoy this amazing story of hope, caring, and love.

A Golden Bond

Chapter 1

Summer's End

The last day of summer vacation in 1954 was a typical Indianapolis summer day: sunny, green, and hot. Angie Demetrious and her best friend Barbara Clark rode their bikes to the neighborhood swim club. The annual end-of-season swim and picnic party was in full swing. Every year the club held the event to thank the member families for their support; however the children believed the party was just for them–one last big celebration before the return to school. The younger members always called it their back to school party, but the high school kids, paraded about as if it was just for them and were prone to believe *they* were the focus of the day. *Everyone* was ready to have a wonderful time.

The trees which encircled the club house shone brilliant green in the bright sunlight, creating a breath-taking sight. The girls looked forward to seeing their friends from school today. Angie and Barbara parked their bikes in the bike rack and began walking across the lawn to size up the action. Familiar faces were everywhere as the two girls walked around the grounds. On the way they passed the tennis courts, which were located close to the large pool, the centerpiece of the club. The pool was big enough to accommodate water polo and swim laps. Parents could even play with their children at the same time. At the far end of the grounds was a gigantic above-ground diving tank with large portholes in the wall. Spectators watched the divers as they cut through the water after their plunge. Some of them would swim up to the windows and wave. It was fun to watch. One of the main attractions was the tall slide, close to the center of the pool, where a very long line was forming with both adults and children waiting for their turn to take the thrilling ride down the slide.

The girls were looking forward to seeing their friends from school at the pool today. Of course everyone was included—all the junior high and elementary school kids were there having a wonderful time. That did little to divert the seniors from feeling really special today. Angie had to smile at this thought for she knew that it was a family pool, and the party was in honor of all. It was a great back to school celebration. Even with all these activities going on there was still room for mothers and fathers to play with their small children.

Angie and Barbara stepped out of the bright sunlight and into the dimly lit locker-room to change into their bathing suits. They chattered away excitedly without a care in the world at the moment.

At first glance, one would see two lovely girls talking and laughing, the makings of a pretty picture. Barbara was tall and slender. Her face was framed with shoulder-length blond hair that showcased her lovely blue eyes and perky mouth and nose. Angie, in deep contrast, was a petite girl with dark brown curly hair which had a mind of its own, always dancing around freely forming waves and curls on her forehead and falling about her face. Of course this was not the intended plan for the hairstyle yet it ended up forming a beautiful border for her delicate face. Her expressive brown eyes gave away feelings she would rather keep hidden. The girls had a beauty that caused heads to turn wherever they walked.

Dressed and ready to head for the pool, they walked toward the exit but halted quickly as the dreaded footbath sanitizer stood in their way. Everyone had to pass through it to cleanse their feet before entering the pool area. It was made extra big to insure all would walk through the ice cold disinfectant. What a joke. Instead, everybody walk around the edge as if it were a tight rope. No one wanted to step into the freezing water. Barbara stopped at the footbath and shook her head. "I'm not going through it."

"Me either." Angie laughed and the two stepped around the edge re-entering the brightness of the outdoors.

They immediately ran into five of their friends and joined them on the deck. They were not there for long before one of the girls shouted out, "Let's play water polo!"

"Sounds great," another one said, jumping in the water.

"Let's do it. I'll get the ball." The pool became a hot bed of activity with all the swimming and water sports under way. More kids joined in the fun as the games began to get more exciting.

After all that playing the kids got hungry and were ready for lunch. It was about that time that music began to play though the loud speakers that were placed around the pool area, filling the air around with the sweet sounds of songs they loved. They all began to drift toward the lunch room near the deep end of the pool; melodies played continuously, and everyone was swaying to the pleasant sounds that filled the air. Before long they were all dancing and singing along in between eating lunch. When they got too hot to keep dancing, they jumped into the pool to cool off and went right back to dancing again. This went on for hours. Dance, sing, and jump into the pool. The order of the day was *fun*, and they were all having a great time.

The day flew by as all good things do, and the time for drying off and going home was close at hand. The water in the pool was so refreshing that Angie was finding it very difficult to get out. The pool was still packed with many of her young friends. Angie still could not make herself get out of the water. This scene had been repeated many times over the entire summer, but today was the last day of swimming before the pool closed for the season— Labor Day, September 1954. Tomorrow would be the first day of school for Angie and her classmates—marking the beginning of her senior year. Everything was exciting and full of hope and wonderful plans for the future.

The two girls dried off before getting dressed for the ride home and chatted away. As far as they were concerned, they would be best friends forever. "We better hurry so we can ride our bikes home before it gets dark," Barbara remarked as they were changing into their dry clothes.

"I really hate going home." Angie groaned. Barbara nodded knowingly. "Athena, my stepmother has been on the war path for days, making life in the homestead very unpleasant. I can't seem to do anything right. I wish I could figure out why she hates me so much. Even when I try to do something nice for her she seems to resent it. I wish I knew what would make her happy besides my leaving home and never coming back again."

"Why does she have it out for you?" Barbara asked, knowing that Angie would not know the answer. Angie just shrugged her shoulders.

***

Rebecca Demetrious

Basil was a hardworking man who left Greece and came to the United States with his father when he was a young man. His father was a Greek Orthodox priest sent to the United States to help establish churches in various communities so that the newly arrived immigrants would have a place to worship. Basil had discovered in the United States there were many opportunities to find work and earn enough money to financially help his family in Greece. His dream did not stop there. He wanted to return to Greece and find a good woman and marry.

He returned to Greece some years later, a handsome and successful business man happily reunited with his family. However, in the back of his mind he still carried a desire to find a bride and have a family he could call his own. He was ready to fulfill this dream. When he met Rebecca, he knew she was the love of his life from the moment he saw her sitting in the flower garden at her parents' home. She was his dream come true. They married and came back to the United States as husband and wife. Life was good for both of them. After two years, their first child was born, a son they named, Joey; two years later, Angie, a darling baby girl was born. Several years later, Sammie came along. Their home was filled with happiness and joy. Rebecca was always baking cookies and creating wonderful meals. She delighted in taking care of her family. There was joy and laughter throughout their home all of the time. The home always welcomed family and friends. Basil's dream had come true.

Angie was now seventeen years old beginning her last year in high school, her big brother Joey was nineteen years old and a freshman at Yale University. On the other end of the spectrum, her kid brother Sammie was eight years old and in third grade at Public School #61. The siblings were very close and had grown even closer after Rebecca's death, two years earlier.

Sammie was just a little guy, almost six years old when she died. Angie and Joey did their best to help him deal with this tragedy, but they were devastated from their own loss and could not offer as much comfort as the small boy needed. Confused and troubled, they desperately tried to understand why she died. Poor little Sammie never understood what had happened. The children watched her suffer throughout the entire illness but always believed she would recover. They stood at the ready anytime their father needed them to step up and take care of things when he had to take Rebecca to the hospital. He had put all of his available energy into getting excellent care for his wife. He took her to Mayo Clinic to obtain a second diagnosis for her condition. It was there that a team of outstanding surgeons performed her surgery. She appeared to be improving when she return home. The family was sure she would be alright after seeing her increased energy. Sadly, a short time later, as fate would have it, she began to slip deeper into her illness once again.

There were moments when Basil, in his solitude, would slip back in his thoughts to happier times when he met Rebecca and fell hopelessly in love with her. She was like a flower, fresh and beautiful. Everyone adored her but none as much as Basil. Then the unthinkable happened; Rebecca became ill. Basil was beside himself. He could still see her standing before him smiling and telling him not to worry, everything would be fine. These flashbacks troubled him very much, and he became afraid that he might be losing his mind and tried to block her from his memory.

***

Sitting on the sofa in the living room with her Bible open, Rebecca called Angie to come and sit with her. Her voice was weak but her Greek accent was familiar and comforting to Angie. She was reading the Bible almost all the time lately. The sunlight poured through the front window. Angie plopped down on the couch next to her, picked up one of the pillows lying in the corner of the sofa, and hugged it against her tummy. "It's pretty out today, isn't it, Mom?" Rebecca nodded, a tear rolled down her cheek.

"Honey, I know you and the boys don't realize that I'm very ill." Angie's smile faded. "The treatments aren't working, and…"She took a deep breath. "I'm very sick." She struggled to get the next words out. "I don't want you to be upset, and I don't want you to cry. I'll be leaving this world to go to a better place in heaven."

Angie shook her head. "No, Mom, no." Rebecca took her hand and nodded weakly. Her hand was so fragile. The words she spoke were beginning to sink in. "Listen to me; you are the only one I have to put in charge of the boys." She put Angie's hand to her mouth and kissed it as another tear streamed down her face. Quickly she brushed it away. "I worry about Sammie. He is so small, and I won't be here to raise him. There are some things I failed to teach you and the boys." She picked up a notepad that was setting on the end table and tore the paper from it. Angie stared at it, trying to read through the blur of tears that formed in her eyes. "Keep this paper with you. These are some of the things I want you to be watchful of. This list will serve as guidance for you."

Angie swallowed the lump in her throat and pinched her lips together to keep from crying. She tried to be strong to show her mother that she would take care of the family, but she didn't think she was capable of doing a good job. She looked into her mother's comforting hazel eyes and broke down, crumbling into her lap and crying hard. "Now, now, Angie, it's going to be all right. You are stronger than you think." She stroked her daughter's back trying to comfort her. Angie took a deep breath and looked up with tears streaking her face and hair falling in wild waves over her eyes. Rebecca tore off another sheet of paper. "I regret that I never taught you how to pray. Here are three prays. Keep them with you and never stop praying them."

Angie stared at the prayers without really reading them.

"This has been so hard on Daddy, Angie, be patient with him."

Maude, the maid Basil hired to help with the housework walked through the dining room into the living room carrying two glasses of lemonade. "Here you go, Missy." She understood the seriousness of Rebecca's illness. Handing Angie her lemonade, she said, "Your mama is a good woman. You help her when she needs it, you hear?"

"Yes, Maude," Angie replied, wiping her face with the sleeve of her dress.

Maude was coming to the house every day to help clean, cook, and do the laundry. It was a few weeks later when Rebecca became too weak to even get out of bed. There were many trips to the hospital, but when she was leaving on what would be her last trip to the hospital, she took Maude's hand into hers and said, "I am leaving now, Maude, but this time, I will not be coming back. Please take care of my babies for me."

With tears in her eyes, she said, "Don't worry, Missy, you get well, and I'll take care of your babies for you."

As Rebecca had predicted, she did not return. She had lost her battle.

The child was confused. All through his wife's illness, he never once discussed or divulged the name of her illness. When his wife died there was little to no discussion with the family of the illness that took her life, nor was her death which impacted the entire family, ever discussed.

After Angie received the news of her mother's death, Angie found solace in her bedroom. She had never felt lonelier. How would she grow up without her mother? Mom won't be there when I graduate, she thought. Her lip quivered. Who would step in and give her advice about what to wear or make sure everything was taken care of in the house? She missed her mom. Placing her hands to her face, she wept. She wanted her mother back. Think good thoughts and happy memories, she told herself as she got up the grab a tissue to dry her tears.

***

A fond memory came back to her of the wonderful Thanksgiving dinner she and her mother cooked together just this last year. Rebecca had sat down by the kitchen table wrapped in a shawl for warmth. She was too weak to do the cooking, so she directed Angie through the entire process of making the dressing, cooking the turkey, mashing the potatoes, and best of all, creating the perfect cranberry sauce and pumpkin pie. Angie didn't realize that Rebecca was training her to assume the responsibility of preparing a meal. Now that her mother was gone, all the lessons were was gone as well. She began to look franticly around her room for a piece of paper and a pencil to write all the directions down so she could remember exactly how to cook the Thanksgiving dinner next year. She would have to remember that entire lesson on her own and must hurry or she would forget something. Once again she felt very alone. She took a deep breath realizing she was going to be the mother of the household now. Making matters worse. Basil could not bring himself to even say Rebecca's name. The family had never experienced death before, and he could not bear to talk about the loss they had suffered. His grief was deeper than anyone understood, and he dealt with it by acting as if their mother never existed.

At Rebecca's funeral there was weeping and mourning. Sammie was confused. He stood in his Sunday suit, looking like a little man and staring up at all the adults wondering why they were all crying and all dressed in black. His aunt, in order to help the child, took his hand and rushed him by the coffin without a word. No one thought about explaining things to the puzzled little boy.

Immediately following the funeral, Basil took the black dress which Angie had worn to the funeral out to the incinerator in the back yard and burned it. With that done he turned to her and said that he never wanted to see her wear a black dress again. The color black was a symbol of death, and Basil did not want to see his wonderful daughter have to bury anyone ever again. He wished Angie to have a happy and carefree life not burdened with sickness and death.

She blinked back the tears and nodded her head. Though he seemed harsh, she understood her father's heart. He had lost the love of his life, and his center was gone, never to return. From that day on the children never heard their mother's name mentioned again. No memories, no more tears—just a looming nothingness. Everyone grieves in his own way, but this was the grieving of a broken heart, of love lost, and a very lonely, bewildered man. The only thing that pulled him through was his faith in God. In his grief he was unable to share that faith with his children. His pain was deeply felt. Somehow the older children knew that, but poor Sammie was unable to understand any of the events that had transpired. He was simply too young.

When Rebecca had become so weak, she would ask Sammie to open the drawers for her to retrieve a sweater or other piece of clothing. This became his job. After the funeral, he waited by the bedroom door to hear her voice call his name so he could open a drawer for her. But she never called.

Sammie was looking for his mother everywhere. He would sit on the back doorstep of the house for hours waiting for her to come to the door. When Maude realized he had been outside for so long, she called him in to have lunch. She never thought that he could be out there actually waiting for his mother to come home.

One day, a neighbor brought Sammie home to Maude.

"Maude, he goes to the bus stop every day." The neighbor explained. "I asked him why he waits there and he said..." She put her hand across her mouth and shook her head. "You know the boy doesn't talk much." Maude nodded. Sammie hardly spoke. Since Rebecca died, it was rare if he opened his mouth. "He said that his mommy has been gone a long time, and he was waiting for her. Someone had better sit down and talk with this child."

Many of Sammie's adventures to find his mother led to great panic in the household. One day, Maude couldn't find Sammie anywhere and scoured the neighborhood looking for him. She finally found him ten blocks away at the corner grocery store looking into the window where he and his mother would walk every day to pick up items that she needed for dinner. His nose was pressed to the window and tears were streaming down his face. "Sammie, what are you doing here?" Maude asked.

Face still pushed against the window, he answered, "Waiting for my mom."

Maude gently took him by the hand and walked him home, hiding her own tears.

When Angie heard this, she cried. For the first time since the funeral Basil became concerned. It was a house in chaos because the main character was gone.

Joey was older and able to understand the tragic event that had taken place but not old enough to realize just how difficult it was for Sammie and Angie. He knew he would not have his mother's guidance and advice that he had depended upon throughout his years, and that crushed him, though he did his best to hide it. Rebecca had understood that, although Joey was a brilliant student, he was not able to make good judgment calls on personal decisions and what course to follow concerning his career and future. He was now on his own and would have to decide what course of study to take, not only his own career choices, but also how to help his siblings. He was great on the academics but short on common sense: the exact opposite of Angie. He was also very impatient, and he would get angry, especially when Sammie would withdraw into television programs and not hear or see anyone or anything around him. Angie tried to talk to her father, but he was almost as bad as Sammie when it came to solving any problems.

**

This was the state of affairs for the first year after their mother's death. Then without any warning, Basil announced that he was going to get married again. His brothers in Greece had found a bride for him. This seemed to him a good solution since he was not one to get into the dating game. He was to leave the next month and travel to Greece to meet this potential bride, and if she was acceptable to him, they would marry and return to Indianapolis. This is when Athena, their stepmother, entered the family's life. Unfortunately for the children, Athena had her own ideas as to what direction would be taken in the Demetrious household.

**

"What are you wearing to school tomorrow?" Barbara's question snapped Angie's thoughts back to the present. "I'm wearing my broomstick skirt and yellow blouse," Barbara was saying

"I love that outfit," Angie commented. "I haven't even thought about that yet. I'd better get on it right away, or I'll be in some deep trouble in the morning. Well, we're home. I'd better get inside, or I'll miss dinner. It's been a great day I had so much fun," Barbara said as Angie started to walk her bike towards the door.

"I did, too. It was one of the best days I've had this summer. See you in the morning," Angie said as she waved goodbye to Barbara.

What am I going to wear tomorrow morning was the question that ran through her head as she was getting ready for bed. She decided to think about it in the morning.

**

At 6:30 a.m. the alarm called out loud and clear. "Not yet," Angie moaned.

"It's time to get up, time to get up in the morning," Joey yelled from the hallway outside Angie's room.

Angie hopped out of bed and began her ritual of getting ready for school. "Let me see," she thought, "what I am going to wear today? I know my peasant blouse, my full skirt and, my stiff full slip..." Saddle shoes, and don't forget the all-important bobby socks always worn straight up, never any other way. This was very important; it was like an unwritten law of identification. Every school had a different way to wear bobby socks, and heaven help you if you didn't comply with the rules. If she wanted any breakfast, she had to hurry before Barbara got to her house to pick her up, Angie thought as she ran downstairs.

"Oh what a beautiful morning, oh what a beautiful day, I've got a wonderful feeling everything's going my way!" sang Angie as she met Barbara outside her home. She was full of excitement and could not wait to share it with everyone around her. A group of her girlfriends were walking to school with her, and they were all equally excited and joined in song with Angie. Everything's going my way—the Graduating Class of 1955.

"Can you believe it?" asked Carol.

"It sure went by faster than I thought it would," said Barbara.

The fall air was brisk and felt great as they made their way to Circle City High. The walk to school was about a mile, but it never seemed long to the girls. They talked all the way there and all the way home. It was amazing that they never ran out of things to say, but they never did.

Kathy was the quietest because she was just a junior this year and would be left without her group after the school year was over. She was not in any "it's a wonderful day" mood today for sure. Who would she have to walk with when they were all gone to whatever college or university they had been accepted to attend? They were all in the same neighborhood, and for all the years they had gone to Circle City High, they had walked down the street together. Barbara would pick up Angie and then the two of them would pick up Carol then Kathy. A little way down the street they would stop and pick up Sharon. After school, if there was no after-school activity, they would all meet and walk home together, rain or shine. It was always fun. Today was special for the seniors because the class ring information was to be distributed. They would have the jeweler's brochure in their possession by the time they were walking home from school and discussing their choices with their families that very evening. Kathy, however, only had the joy of studying for her English Six Test which would start tomorrow. Everyone knew if they didn't pass this test, they wouldn't be able to graduate the following year. It covered a basic review of everything that was taught over the past two years of high school English. It was a high stress situation; the biggest test of their high school career. It was bittersweet because once she completed the test, she too would be preparing for higher education just as her friends were. It was also sad because her best friends were going in different directions after graduation. She still would have their company till the end of the school year. Everyone knew this day would come; it just came up sooner than any of them thought. Everyone walking together made the time go much faster.

After school they all met and began the walk home, with books and brochures in hand. The girls were filled with excitement now that the ring information was in their possession.

"Which rings did you like best? I can't make up my mind. I haven't really picked any one ring out yet. I love them all. They're so neat. What do you think?" They were so excited that they all talked at once.

"I'm just like you. I still haven't made up my mind yet. My mom will help me make the best pick," Barbara said thoughtfully.

Angie gasped for a moment as the word *Mom* struck her heartstring and sadness rushed through her. What a special word, she thought. It's always taken for granted, but when your mom is gone forever, the word becomes almost sacred. The word *Mom* was only uttered with the deepest love and respect.

"You know me," Barbara, continued, "I like big and bright all the way."

"I wish my mom was still alive." Angie sighed. "She always loved to help me pick out clothes and shoes, and I know she would love helping me make the right choice." Athena had never shown any interest in any of her school activities. Angie felt uncomfortable asking her for any advice. As for her dad, he was no help. He didn't understand class rings. He would probably get impatient; he had become a different man since he married Athena.

"Don't worry; everything will work out just fine. Joey will help pick out the ring," answered Sharon. "Well here is home. See you later, alligator."

"After while, crocodile," they all replied and continued on the way to their homes. The next home was Angie's.

"I'll see you guys later. Call me if you want to get together after you finish your homework."

Angie ran up the steps to her home and entered the front door. "Hello. I'm home, anyone here?"

"Back here in the kitchen," came a reply. "Your dad and I are having a snack," Athena answered. "Come on back and join us." Athena sounded strangely welcoming. Angie shrugged, realizing that she was ready for a snack. But was it the time to break the class ring news on the parents or should she do it later? Athena must be in a good mood since she just asked her to have a snack with dad and her. She usually didn't like to share dad at snack time. Well there's no time like the present.

"Hi Athena; hi, Dad, how is it going? Boy it sure smells great in here."

"Would you like some hot chocolate, Angela?"

"That would be great." The unusual climate of joy was more than she could ever hope for—the exact right time to ask about the class ring.

Athena set a cup of hot chocolate and a slice of cinnamon toast in front of Angie and returned to her seat.

"Sit down, Angie. Athena and I have some news for you," Basil began. "We just got the report back from the doctor this morning and he confirmed what we had hoped. To put it as simply as possible, Athena and I are having a baby. In eight months you will have a new little brother or sister. Isn't that great news?"

As the words rolled off his lips, Angie dropped her toast into her hot chocolate and looked up in disbelief. How embarrassing. I'll be the laughing stock of all the school. Parents of high school kids aren't supposed to have babies, Angie thought to herself. Now don't blow your cool—stay calm, Angie told herself. "Do the boys know?"

"Not yet. We're going to tell them when they get home," Dad replied.

"I suppose this is not a good time to ask if I can buy a class ring, is it?" Angie ventured.

"I should have known better than to talk to you about something as serious as a new baby blessing our family," responded Athena. "I actually thought you would be mature enough to understand the importance of this wonderful event, but NO! Not You! You're never happy for anyone else's joy. You're plain selfish," she replied angrily.

Angie fought back. "What am I supposed to say? I can't believe any of this. I didn't think parents your age who have teenagers even had sex and now you're having a baby." Angie was in tears.

Basil had reached the point of anger. "That's enough. You crossed the line."

Athena stood by and coldly said, "You'll get used to it soon enough. This is a fact of life, and you will have to accept it. As for a class ring, you can do whatever you like as long as you pay for it. No money is going out to you for a silly class ring. Go to your room and move all your stuff into the small room down the hall. We'll need that room for the baby, and I want to get started as soon as possible. Now go!"

"Dad, Athena, I'm sorry. I didn't want things to go this way. Please don't make me move my room. There isn't enough space in the small room for me. I'll be leaving for college at the end of the school year, and you can have the room then."

"Stop the drama, Angela. You have to learn to give and take a little. I understand that you are surprised, but a new member is coming into the family, and we have to prepare. I am asking you to help by cooperating. There isn't going to be any college for you. We will be educating two boys, or maybe three. We'll know when the baby comes, but we will not throw our money away on a college education for a girl who will end up in a kitchen being a housewife. Find something else to do, and you better start before you graduate from high school. Buy your own ring out of your allowance if you want it that badly," replied Athena, standing red faced in front of her.

Angie stood up with her books and walked upstairs to move her room and to rethink all the plans she had made for her future. This was all too much. She knew things had been very tense in the household, but never did she dream that it would reach this point. She loved babies. Heaven knows she'd been looking after Sammie since Rebecca died. Maude did what she could, but she wasn't there all of the time. Basil made sure there were meals cooked, but that left her to see to it that Sammie took baths, brushed his teeth, did his homework, went to bed, and got up for school the next day. She didn't mind because she loved Sammie and knew he missed their mother as much as she did. She thought things were good and everyone was getting along. Dad missed mom and was lonely when he married Athena. She appeared to be a caring religious person, but she never liked the kids very much from the beginning. They were too independent and didn't seek guidance from their father concerning their school schedules, majors, career choices, or what after school activities they participated in. Athena didn't have any understanding of Joey, Sammie, or Angie from the beginning. She didn't approve of the decisions they made. Basil was happy not to have to worry with their decisions. After all, he had been dealing with a dying wife, and the children had proven themselves to be very self-reliant and trustworthy. It was a huge help to not have to deal with the additional burden of school. Athena, on the other hand, was horrified they had been permitted to function in such an independent way. The whole situation was one that she was determined to reverse. She wanted the children to receive permission from her for every move that was taken. Needless to say, this made for enormous conflicts every day. Athena was forever reporting to Basil that one of the kids did not follow the rules of her house and had to be punished. The only one who escaped punishment was Sammie who was too young to have reached this level of independence.

Joey had spent the entire summer break facing the rage and

disapproval of both Athena and Basil. If she wasn't complaining he was sleeping too late every day, it was the friends hanging out with him at the house. The way he ate irritated her. In fact, there was nothing that pleased her about him. He would blow it off, looking forward to the end of the summer break. There was never any mention of how proud the father was of his grades and accomplishments, such as making the dean's list and having his scholarship extended to next term.

While Angie moved into the smaller room, she thought about which ring she could afford. One thing was for sure, the big expensive ones were out. That left three rings. That certainly narrowed the selection way down. Joey would have to help her choose which one of the three was the best.

"Joey!" Angie called out. "Joey, can you please come to my room." Oh my gosh, she hoped Athena and her dad didn't get mad because she called Joey. Angie was already beginning to feel the full force of what had happened between Athena, her father, and herself that afternoon. She didn't want to rock the boat any more than it already had been. She wished today had never happened and they could start over. Ha! Like that could ever happen. Basil would never change his mind, and Athena would encourage him 100 percent. The real question was, what was she going to do? Her career plans had been made. One year of college pre-nursing and then get accepted into the nursing program at the Medical Center and apply for a specialty as a surgical nurse. If that didn't work out, then emergency room was the next choice. That was the plan which now had to be modified. She would have to figure out how to do all that and pay for it at the same time. Working her way through school wouldn't be an easy task. All of these thoughts were running through her mind as Joey came into her room.

"What's up, Angie?" asked Joey as he entered the room, completely unaware of the events of the day or what Angie wanted.

"Help me pick one class ring out of these three rings," was the reply he got. "OK, let me look at them." He looked over the pamphlet Angie had brought home from school. "Gee whiz, Angie, why did you pick these three? I always thought you loved the blue stone rings. These are all just plain gold and kind of flat looking."

"The average ones are the only ones I can afford. Please don't make this any harder than it already is. Which one do you like?"

"Get the gold one with the blue trim and Circle City Indianapolis written around it. That way you can pretend the blue is the sapphire you always wanted."

"That's it! That is exactly what I will order tomorrow. It's twenty-five dollars, and I can afford it, and it will remind me of all the great times I have had in high school. Thank you for helping me, Joey. Can you help me carry this box of things to the small room down the hall?"

"I'm afraid to ask why you are moving all your stuff to the small bedroom."

"I'll explain it all to you tomorrow when I have had a chance to pull myself together. I promise. There is no reason to pull you into this mess."

The ring was selected, and the move to the new room had begun. Angie began with the closet. She moved her wardrobe into it. Needless to say the closet filled up very quickly. There was room for everything with the exception of a small cardboard box that contained a few of her mother's things that she had managed to salvage before her father had given everything away to the shelter for the poor. He believed that it was good for the soul of the deceased to give their clothes to the needy which was the last act of charity the deceased person could do.

Her father permitted Angie to keep just a few items—a handbag which her mother loved to carry; a few pieces of jewelry, nothing valuable; her favorite earrings; a necklace; and a long braid of her hair. After victory was declared and World War II ended, Rebecca and Angie's Aunt Julia fulfilled a promise they both made to have their very long hair cut immediately. That braid of hair meant a lot to Angie. Laying the two sheets of paper her mother gave her with instructions on them next to the other prized possessions, she closed the box. Since there was no room in the closet, she carried the box up to the attic and stored it there. The rest of the items were moved and placed in the new room.

It was all in a day's work for the young girl who was trying to figure out her future education and comply with the wishes of her father and stepmother. Now all she had to work out was how to pay for a higher education and her class ring.

It was really nice of Joey to stop his packing and come and help Angie pick out a ring. He was leaving on Saturday. His summer vacation was over, and his fall semester was about to begin. Registration at Yale University was Monday and class started on Wednesday. Fortunately he was able to preregister earlier in mid-August when he went out East to visit his roommate Digger who lived on Long Island, New York. He seemed to love Yale and was trying to decide if he really wanted to continue with the pre-law. To say that Joey was a very good student would be putting it mildly. Due to his academic record he earned a very good four-year scholarship that paid his way through school. It was a great opportunity for him. Angie was never that kind of a "good student." She managed to get very good grades for the most part but never reached the level that Joey had and never would. It was very difficult for Angie to follow him in school. All the teachers expected the same kind of work from her. Try as she did, she was never able to reach the high level he had accomplished. The good thing for Sammie was, by the time he got to Circle City High School, the expectations of anyone reaching Joey's level of scholastic brilliance would have faded into a dim memory. Lucky guy.

Chapter 2

The Road Is Set; The Decision Is Made

It was Saturday and all her chores were done, so Angie went to Barbara's house to hang out a while and just talk. This was her free time, and she was anxious to get out of the house. Barbara seemed upset and wanted to talk. She and her mother were always fighting about something, usually about her doing more and more of the housework that her mother didn't want to do any longer. Barbara thought this was unfair, but it was nothing new. All her friends had to do chores to help around the house. Not many had the good fortune to have someone like Maude coming every other day to clean, wash clothes, and help with the cooking. When Basil married Athena, the kids thought that Maude would not be around as often, but Athena enjoyed having a maid doing the housework for her. Maude was a big help and whatever she did not do, Angie would finish. Actually Athena was lucky. With that much help she had a lot of free time.

Lately, in anticipation of the new baby, she had taken up knitting and was busy making sweaters and booties.

The girls were looking out the window and saw Barbara's next door neighbors. They were a handsome young couple who had been married for about two years. They had just bought the house next door to Barbara's parents' home. Angie was thinking out loud when she said, "They must be very happy."

"Don't envy them too much," Barbara added. "Chuck has been really sick. He lost half his stomach. Jill is afraid he might die. She told my mother if he dies she would not be able to support herself. She has no skills or training. She wouldn't be able to get a job anywhere other than working as a clerk. That kind of job would never pay enough money to support her and a family if they have one. Mom told her she needed a trade."

A trade! A light bulb went off in Angie's mind. That's it; she needed to research trade schools. If she had a trade she could get a job and pull in a decent salary that would help her pay tuition for college and nursing school. True, this was a whole new way of thinking. She had set her path with the end result being becoming a nurse. Now she had to take a detour. The outcome would still be nursing but getting there would have to take a little longer. First thing she needed to do was make a list of all the possibilities available. The most important thing on the list would be a timeline to keep track of the change of events in her plan. All these thoughts were racing excitedly through Angie's head like greased lighting. She could leave school at the beginning of the January semester. She had all the courses and requirements for college entry already, or at least she would have enough credit hours at the end of the fall semester. She had made sure of that when she planned her course of studies. The whole last semester she had planned to take only elective courses anyway. She could come back in June for commencement. It could work out perfectly. What a great plan.

Barbara judiciously watched Angie as her face changed radically. "What's going on in that brain of yours? You look as if you jumped into a fire and found out it burns," Barbara remarked with narrowed eyes laid questionably upon her friend.

"Don't tell anybody, but I think I have solved a problem. I have to go home and do some research and do it quickly. I'll see you later." Angie ran out the door and headed for home.

"What?" standing with her mouth hanging open, Barbara watched Angie run home. "Strange."

Angie ran home in record-breaking speed. Joey had already left for Yale so she really had no one to talk to about her solution. Barbara would not understand what she was thinking not in a million years. That's okay, I'll figure it out on my own, she thought as she entered the front door. She pulled out the telephone book from the top of the refrigerator where they kept it and sat down at the dining room table to look up trade schools. No luck. Why don't they place the listings in a more logical way? The way things were listed it is a wonder anyone can find anything. I'll check schools; it's got to be there, thought Angie. Dental Hygiene (this is a maybe). Barber (this is a no). Cosmetology (what's that?). Wait a minute, she thought as she read enticing headlines: GET A LICENSE IN SIX MONTHS. "This is interesting. I'll check it out,"

Angie said with satisfaction.

Maude walked into the dining room; quickly Angie shut the book and smiled up at her innocently. "What are you doing, Babe?"

"Oh, nothing." Angie said jumping up from the table and putting the phone book back. Maude watched her suspiciously as she went to her small bedroom to think privately. All the rest of the schools required too long of a commitment to complete. The license in cosmetology would take six months, meaning that the course would be finished just in time for high school graduation. She could work the whole year and maybe make enough money to pay for college for a year and still work and go to school. What a plan! I'll call this number in the morning and get all the information I can before I say anything about this to anyone, she thought. This could work for me. I really think it will. At just that moment it came to her what a cosmetologist was—a beautician. This was even better. Sharon's mother has been doing people's hair for a long time. She could tell Angie everything she wanted to know and also recommend a good school!

As life would have it, there were a few kinks in the plan. First of all, Angie had never been in a beauty shop in her life. Her cousin had always cut her hair, so she never had the need. She had no idea what to expect. It never occurred to her that she would not like the trade. Liking cosmetology should have been one of the first considerations on her list along with her father's approval. Those were two big hurdles to jump. All she cared about was that the course took six months and at the end of that time she could be out making money. She had no idea what it would take to make money in the beauty business. What unexpected surprises were awaiting her?

Chapter 3

Breaking News

"Be cheerful, be controlled, don't lose your cool, and whatever you do, don't be demanding." These were some of the many thoughts running through Angie's mind as she prepared to share her plan with the family. She had not told anyone yet and had no idea how it would be received.

The class rings were delivered that morning at school. Angie tried hers on and was the admiring how it looked on her finger. She just loved it and smiled as it dazzled against her skin like a golden bond. It was not exactly what she wanted, but it was the one she could afford and she was more proud of it than anything else she had ever purchased on her own. The ring became a symbol of the achievements she made in her four years of high school. She beamed with pride. What lay ahead was going to be entirely different from anything she had done up to this time. It might sound silly, but as she gazed upon the golden bond it became a symbol of both the past and the future

As she approached the house she was thinking of how she should present her proposal of attending the University of Cosmetology. Many hours were spent talking to Sharon's mother and Angie's cousin, who was also in the business. He rented booth spaces out to beauty operators. They both said that this was one of the best schools in the city. She called and went to visit the school. She toured the facility but still had no idea how to judge if it was good or not. They were all very nice to her, showed her around, and told her about the program. There were a lot of students working in an actual beauty shop which was in the facility and opened for business. The instructors called this practical training. She felt that this was a good starting point and with the endorsement of both Sharon's mother and her cousin, she was ready to forge ahead with the plan.

She took a deep breath; her heart was beating like a drum, her knees were shaking, and on top of that, her mind became a total blank. None of this was a good sign. Get a hold of yourself, she chided. Maybe she should not do this today. Maybe tomorrow would be better. NO! Today was the plan and today is the day and that is that. To say she was nervous would be putting it mildly. She was in an all-out panic mode. Angie hesitated as she approached the steps that led to the house. She swallowed hard. It's now or never.

"I'm home," she called out." Is anybody home?"

"We're back in the kitchen," the reply came from Athena. "We're having a cup of hot chocolate. Would you like a cup?"

"No, thank you," answered Angie, as she made her way to the kitchen. Last time she had a cup of hot chocolate with them everything went badly, and she definitely did not want a repeat of that. Besides, she was too nervous to drink anything. Stay focused she kept telling herself.

"You're home early today. Did you skip a class?" asked Athena slyly. Her father looked up quickly waiting for an answer.

"I didn't wait for the girls today. I came straight home because I wanted to talk to you about something. I'm a little nervous about this so please give me a chance to explain my idea." Angie struggled to get the words out. "I know that things have been strained between us, and it hurts me as much as I am sure it hurts you both. I've been trying to make some kind of plan for my future education that will be satisfactory to you and help me also reach my goals. I don't want to create any hardship on anyone in the family by making unreasonable demands. I just want to have a meeting of the minds as to what direction I'm leaning. I hope you understand and realize that this is all I want." Finishing her monologue, she took a deep breath.

"I already told you, no college for you. I am not paying for you to go play and party with your friends, and that is final. Don't you understand anything?" Her father was already getting worked up. Angie's cheeks reddened and hot tears were forming in her big brown eyes. She was trying very hard to stay calm, but her composure was slipping fast.

She held her head up high and continued. "I just wanted you to know that I have decided to leave school at the end of the fall semester. I have enough credits I need to graduate. I also have all the requirements and grade point average needed to enter college. After much consideration and research, I decided that it would be a practical plan to enter a trade school and learn a skill that would enable me to earn enough money to work my way through school. I thought that I could enter the University of Cosmetology. It requires one thousand hours of classroom and practical training to qualify to take the State Board of Cosmetology examination to receive my Cosmetology License. After I complete the course of study, I would be eligible to take the exam. It would be a trade that I could use to work my way through school and go on to nursing. The course costs one thousand five hundred dollars. That's all I will need, and a white uniform is required." She stopped and gasped for air.

"Boy, you never quit do you, Angie? I told you, you're on your own and here you are trying to get one thousand five hundred dollars out of me," Basil shook his head in agitation. He had heard enough of the pitch and was finished listening to any plan Angie had cooked up. He really had not paid any attention to anything she had said. He just gave his ever ready answer, which was no.

"Calm down, Basil!" Athena said putting her hand on top of his. He sank into his seat and gave her space to speak. "It's actually not a bad idea. Surely you can see that Angie is for her future." Athena looked at Angie and asked. "Have you even gone to visit the school?"

"Yes, I went downtown on the bus and visited the school and interviewed with the head of the school. She gave me all the information. She said that I could start as soon as I finished Circle City. I checked with the school, and they said that I could come back for commencement in June. That way I could graduate with my class."

Why was everything always so difficult to discuss with her father and Athena? Her friends had problems with their parents but could still have a reasonable discussion to resolve their issues. Athena's intervention on her behalf was a totally unexpected surprise. It made her feel a little uneasy when she should have felt good about having the support.

"Angela, I know I am not your mother, but I feel I must say this to you. If you leave school in January, you will miss out on a lot of your senior activities and parties. These are things that you can never have again. Think about this very carefully."

"I know that, but surely they will include me. I'll still be in the neighborhood and will continue to keep in touch with everyone."

"Look, Angela." Basil had calmed down and was thoughtful as he spoke. "I love you, but you know that we are not financially able to educate everyone in the family. I am sorry it looks as if I am picking on you, because that is not true. We love you very much." He used his hands as he explained. "You simply cannot continue driving a point until you make us all crazy," he said, trying to get Angie to understand why he was refusing to help her. "We just want what is best for you. Why did you pick Beauty School, when you never even go to a beauty salon yourself? I don't understand any of this. What kind of counseling led you in this direction?" He finished with a deep sigh. "You are still young and should enjoy your high school years."

"It's been fun, but I must think of the next step for my life. I can't count on getting married, having children and being a housewife. Look, Dad, there is nobody exactly breaking my door down to take me out. I haven't had a date since Homecoming and that was a fix-up. I need to be able to support myself, and this is the best solution that I can come up with. The course will take about six months if I can go every day and some weekends. I have to work in their shop a total of 1,000 hours and should be able to finish in time to attend commencement with my high school class. If you pay the one thousand five hundred dollars, I promise I will try to pay you back as soon as I start to make some money."

She could understand that money was short, but she did need some help. Even if she could go into the job market in January, the best she could hope to get was a clerk in a grocery store or department store. She had elected all college entry courses, absolutely nothing as far as a trade. The only thing close was typing and shorthand. But she was not very good at either, especially shorthand. That was the only course she dropped in all of her high school years. She couldn't go back and change anything now. Besides, she had made up her mind she wanted to be a nurse. She had sweet memories of how wonderful the nurses took care of Rebecca when she was in the hospital. She wanted to do the same for someone else's mother. She missed her mother more on days like this when she was fighting her battles alone. Her desire was to help people who were sick. She looked determinedly at Basil. Now tears were streaming down her checks at the thought of her mother sick and dying.

"Please, Dad, loan me the money, and I will promise to pay you back. I'll work at the supermarket at night and pay you all I make until I pay you back. I bought my ring by saving my lunch money. I know I can do it." This was the final plea to her father.

"OK, OK, I'll give you the one thousand five hundred dollars, and you do not have to pay it back. I don't want you working all night and going to school all day; you're too young to do that. We are not that short of money. That settles that. Now where is this ring you bought?"

"This is it." She held out her hand. "Isn't it beautiful?"

"It's beautiful," Basil said as a tiny grin turned up his lips. "You did a good job."

"Thank you, Dad. Thank you, Athena. I'll try to make you proud." Angie nearly skipped out of the kitchen with excitement. Heading up the stairs to her room, she stopped suddenly.

Something wasn't matching up. Athena was always very critical of everything Angie asked to participate in with her friends, which wasn't all that often. She acted as if everything Angie wanted to do was a sin against God. She always made the accusation that her activities were evil and Angie had no fear of God. Athena would warn her that she would pay the consequences for her evil doings. For Athena to be nice was odd. Puzzled by Athena's concern, she worried that Athena might look upon this move as an opportunity to get Angie out of *her house* once and for all.

She was going to miss her senior activities. The truth was that she really hated that part of the plan. She had elected to take some classes she had always wanted to take but never had time on her schedule and now that was out. This was not the time to look back or to hesitate. It was full speed ahead at this point.

Chapter 4

The Plan Begins

Christmas break was just around the corner, and Joey would be coming home. Angie hadn't told him about her plan yet. The time to start her new venture was getting closer and closer, and as the days drew near, Angie's mood became bluer and bluer. Although she hated to admit it, Athena had been right about her missing all the senior activities. Pointless as it might seem, the thought of not being present for senior skip day, or senior dress down day, not to mention the turnabout dance, made her feel sad. After all, just because she was leaving school in January didn't mean that the rest of the school would change the activity calendar around so she could be part of all the senior activities.

The winter had started out with snow that just kept coming. The walk to school was hard, but the girls made the best of it with each other's company even when the wind would whip around their skirts and freeze their legs, which were always cold. The school dress code didn't allow the girls to wear slacks to school, making it even more difficult to keep warm.

The girls were aware that Angie was graduating midterm and were very disappointed that she had not changed her mind. This made her decision even more agonizing. The class ring, however, was a welcomed reminder of all that she had achieved and the future that held great promise. Angie wore her class ring all of the time. She never took it off; she loved it so. It had become an old friend and the last link to Circle City High School. Basil, showing warmth and kindness, gave the twenty-five dollars to cover the cost of the ring. She really did love him very much even though they were both too much alike to get along without an argument.

Joey finally came home for Christmas break, and it was great to see him again. Now that he was away at school it was impossible to visit except on holiday breaks. Yale University was located in New Haven, Connecticut, and it was too far a distance to go for just a weekend visit. The only way Angie would be able to travel to Yale would be by train and that was out of the question. Anytime the mention of a visit to Yale came up a small war would erupt. Basil reminded her about his good name, and he would not allow any daughter of his to humiliate him by traveling like a common streetwalker to a university campus and have the whole community talking about her. No Siree, this was not going to happen, NO absolutely NOT!

She pretty much got the message that she would not be going on any visits to Yale. Still, she had always wanted to go to an Ivy League campus to see what it was like, but it was not worth the drama.

Joey had always wanted to attend an Ivy League school. When he received the scholarship it was his dream come true. It should have made Basil proud, but he really did not grasp the magnitude of what an accomplishment his eldest son had made. He set the standard in high grades, and Basil had become so accustomed to them that he expected the same excellent marks from the others. When they did not reach that level of academia, Basil was disappointed in them. It's strange when Angie thought of it. For anyone to think that this accomplishment could just be an ordinary expectation. Nevertheless, Angie was very proud of Joey and boasted of his accomplishments whenever the occasion arose.

The first afternoon Joey was back, Angie made hot chocolate for her brothers. As a special treat, she squirted whipped cream on top of the drink. Athena was out with friends shopping for baby items. Soon the new baby would be there.

Joey sat at the kitchen table sprinkling cinnamon on top of the whipped cream in Sammie's hot chocolate. "I don't want that," Sammie said with a wrinkled nose.

"Trust me, you'll like this."

Angie pulled up a chair next to him. "Oh, put some on mine."

Joey shook the spice on his sister's whipped cream. "I wish you would have talked to me before you jumped on this decision to go to cosmetology school," he said.

"I needed to make a plan quickly." Angie shrugged.

Sammie took a careful taste of the whipped cream and lit up. "This is good, Joey."

"I told ya." He looked back at his sister. "Well, it's too late to disapprove now. I wish you the best, kid."

"Thanks." She smiled. "I can't wait for all the Christmas festivities we're going to."

"Yeah, we're glad you're home, Joey." Sammie chimed in. "You make Christmas break so much more fun."

Joey smiled at his kid brother and ruffled his hair. He was much more patient since attending Yale.

Joey made Christmas break a great time with all the Christmas festivities. There were a lot of parties to go to. Between his friends and Angie's there was a lot going on. Everyone loved to hang out together, and it was always fun. Joey and Angie were only eighteen months apart and most of their friends were mutual ones. Joey's time was very precious, and he went out with his girlfriend as often as he could. Since Angie did not have a real boyfriend, her male buddy, Jimmy, would be her date by default which made it more fun for everyone. Jimmy was not only a good friend but also good company. He was her secret buddy that came along with them to all the festivities. Of course there was the ever present class ring which had become more and more important to Angie the closer the school year came to an end and cosmetology school came closer to becoming a reality.

Christmas break was filled with so many activities that before anyone realized it, the time had come for Joey to go back to school. All were saying goodbyes again. Just like that, he was off to Yale. There were no horrible fights this time with Athena and Basil. Athena was too pregnant to keep law and order in the house her way. She would never have allowed all the parties and comings and goings that went on the whole Christmas season. Now with the Christmas break over, Angie went back to school to take her finals. This would be the last hurdle determining if she could in fact graduate in January. There was no reason to think that she wouldn't do well, and her final grades were excellent.

Next week the new semester would begin, and Angie would start her first day at the University of Cosmetology. She had to buy two white uniforms for the new school's classes, and she was beginning to get very nervous.

Monday morning, she stood in front of a small mirror that sat on top of a chest of drawers. She tugged her uniform straight and nodded in satisfaction. Angie put on her coat and was on her way to the bus stop. The number 6 bus was the one that went downtown. She was on her way to a brand new adventure.

Chapter 5

The University of Cosmetology

The building which housed the University of Cosmetology was in fact an old rundown mansion that had been converted into the school. It would have been an old deserted haunted house if it had not been rescued by two older ladies who, as beauticians, decided it would make a great location for a beauty college. There were three floors in the house, not counting the basement. It actually was very clean inside, but no matter how clean it was, it still looked dreary. The first two floors were used for the school, and the top floor was the dormitory where the girls from out of town lived.

Angie knew that this would be a very different experience than high school, but she didn't expect quite the mix of people that she found. They ranged from young girls to older women and a few men—none of them were what you would call kids. She was the very youngest student there. Not exactly what she had expected. She had always attended school with people her own age. This was completely different. In all of her school experiences, the adults were the adults in charge. These adults, however, were on the same level as she, and the atmosphere was entirely different. At first glance there were not many students that she felt she could be friends with. She decided to go slowly and get herself oriented before she jumped to any conclusions or friendships. There were a couple of girls she felt she might be able to buddy up with. Before she did anything she thought she should go to the orientation and the first class and maybe then see how things went. One thing was for certain, with the exception of two other girls, all the rest were older well-lived adults.

One girl in the orientation with her was a little older than Angie. She was friendly and must have sensed that she was still wet behind the ears and decided to take her under her wing. She approached Angie and introduced herself.

"Hi. I'm Jenny. It's my second day. Would you like to sit together?"

"Sure. I'm Angie. That would be great. I'm not sure what I'm doing. This is all new to me."

"Angie, we'll struggle through together. Come on, let's get to our seats." Just like that a new friendship was born.

"Hey, Jenny, did you realize there would be so many older people in this class?" asked Angie as they walked to the next session.

"Not really. I know that a lot of them are divorced or separated. The guys are all right, but watch out for Frankie. He's a ladies' man and loves to chase the young ones. Then there's Steve. He's gay, and Julia is a nymphomaniac. She'll screw anyone." Jenny said as Angie's brown eyes grew round as saucers and cheeks turned a beautiful shade of crimson. Angie was still too naive to comprehend that there were actually such people she would be exposed to every day. Most of this conversation was taboo and embarrassed her. She never heard any woman expressing herself in such a crude manner. Half the time she didn't understand what Jenny meant by some of the things she said. True she was older than Angie, but not that much older. She was twenty and Angie was eighteen. Still she was very different from all of the girls she had ever known before. She couldn't quite put her finger on it. From the beginning Angie decided their friendship was one at beauty school only. No other social events outside of the school. There was something about Jenny that made her very uneasy. She decided it would be best to just be friends with her at school only until she got to know her better. There would be little time left during the day anyway for extra activities. If she did have extra time she wanted to spend it with her high school friends.

The courses were really easy and did not require much studying. The hardest part was the practical work.

Class and work would start at 8:00 a.m. and did not quit till 6:00 p.m. It was nothing but work or being worked on. Angie must have had twenty different hair styles the first week.

The ring was right there with her the whole time. The people at the school were "the stuff of great stories," the kind that were so interesting you could write about them. Betty was the most outrageous one of all. Every lunch hour she would be out in the car with a guy doing more than just kissing him. Later, someone let the cat out of the bag that the man she was meeting with was her ex-husband, and he was paying her for sex. Angie was shocked. The women were always throwing out unforgettable comments about each other. The one that stuck in her mind was: "There she goes again," one woman would say to the other. The reply would be, "All I've got to say is, it's a pretty poor chicken that can't scratch for herself." Angie had never been exposed to these kinds of situations. It was all new and a little frightening to her. This might be something witnessed in a movie but never in real life. Most of the people there were desperate and vulgar. She was sure they were down on skid row, but this wasn't skid row. "What am I doing here?" she asked herself. This was a regular soap opera. Frankie was out after every girl that lived upstairs in the dormitory. Angie plugged along praying that June would come quickly, and it was still January. Winter was going to be very long. Spring was all Angie could think about.

It was not all bad, and Angie was actually learning a lot of new things about hair care and beauty tips she had never known. As an added bonus she was also learning a great many life stories. There were a group of the girls from the dorm who were dating guys from the Mortuary School. "Hey, Angie," one of the girls said when they were in the restroom powdering their faces. "We might do the hair and makeup on the new corpses that come in over there at the mortuary school. Isn't that keen?"

"Keen?" Angie replied, keeping her face from contorting into complete terror.

"Yeah. There's good money in it. What's the matter? You look like you've seen a ghost. Ha ha- no pun intended."

She left Angie standing in front of the mirror with her mouth ajar. It was challenging enough working with so many different kinds of hair that living people had; she didn't want to add corpses to her list.

On the week the class was learning about permanent waves, they actually wrapped the perms. The chemicals in the solution were very strong and got trapped under Angie's ring. Her skin was irritated and blistering. She had to take off the ring until she was finished working with the solution. She laid it down on the vanity and completed wrapping the perm. As she finished with the solution, she rinsed her hands and turned to pick up the ring. It was gone.

"Oh no, I can't find the ring." She dropped to her knees looking across the floor desperately. Grabbing a broom, she swept the area but the only stuff she brushed into the dustpan was hair. She retraced her steps, but could not find it anywhere. Tears were welling up in her eyes. Her ring was gone. If she had lost a hundred dollars she could not have been any more upset. How could this be? She had it right beside her.

Jenny was working at a work station close by. Maybe she saw the ring. "Hey, Jenny you didn't happen to see my class ring around here did you?"

"No, I didn't see it. Where did you leave it? I'll help you look for it."

"I took it off while I was wrapping a perm. When I finished, I went to put it on and it was gone."

"Don't worry, Angie, we'll find the ring."

And the search began. They looked in the sink, the waste basket, the laundry basket, and last of all, the entire storage closet where all the supplies were stored. The result was zero; the ring was gone. This was so disappointing that Angie began to cry. It was the one thing that had kept her connected to her high school class. The link between her high school life and her beauty school life was gone.

She sighed, "How could it just disappear?" She shook her head and took one last look around. "I have to face that the ring is lost and this search verifies it," Angie's voice was burdened with disappointment. "I'm going home early tonight. See you tomorrow."

Jenny watched Angie as she left the room. With silent disenchantment, she put on her coat and went out to the cold winter air and waited at the bus stop.

The wind blew Angie's waves out of her face as she waited for the bus. She looked at her ring finger still red from the chemical burn and wished she would have never taken that ring off. The University of Cosmetology was taking up almost all of her time.

She was fast reaching her thousand hours of practical work. In a month she would be able to take her State Board exam, get her license, and begin working in a salon. Keeping her mind on that helped her keep it off of the treasured ring she just lost.

Chapter 6

What About Jenny?

Jenny was still standing at the door watching Angie head for the bus stop. "Boy, that girl needs to chill. She's got everything anyone could want and more," she thought with disdain. Jenny would love to have her life for just one day. She didn't have a chance to get a class ring. The real truth was that she never made it far in school, let alone to the senior year. Her only chance was to find herself a rich guy and nail him before he knew what hit him. Glancing around, she pulled the ring from her pocket where she hid it just after stealing it off of the vanity. That serves Angie right for leaving it in plain sight and being so trusting. She had every intention of returning it as soon as she got what she wanted. The ring was going to be on her finger when she went out with Eddy tonight. She'd drive the old jalopy home to the small town where she lived. She always thought it was full of nobodies, which included her family. Everyone who lived there thought that hanging out at the drive-in restaurant was a great night out. Not her. She was determined to never be held down to a mediocre life, as was true of most of the population in that town. She was going to be somebody. She'd be rich and beautiful, the envy of everyone around her.

Poor girl didn't even know that she was already pretty as a picture. She didn't need to prove anything, but all she ever thought was that she'd show those hikes a thing or two. Angie was nothing but a loser, thinking nursing is so great. Ha! That's a laugh. Work your ass off emptying bed pans and cleaning up after sick people and doctors, making peanuts in return. What a joke. She'd be lucky if she could just make a living after getting out of Beauty School.

Eddy was her ticket out. Tonight he'd find out what a great catch she was. She would show him this ring and tell him what her future plans were. She'd talk about all the colleges and universities that were offering her scholarships. Of course, there was no need for him to know anything about the University of Cosmetology.

He was always talking about his sister Irene and how smart she is. When he sees this class ring and Jenny tells him about what a great career she has ahead of her, he'll really be impressed. Up to now she hadn't made any moves on him. All these thoughts were whirling around in her head. She was desperate and willing to do almost anything to change her circumstances.

Enough of the daydreaming, time to hit the road and start getting ready for the big date. She really kind of liked Eddy. He had always been nothing but nice to her. Nice is easy, and there are a lot of nice guys around who are nothing but losers. Eddy, on the other hand, had a used car lot and a future if she could get him out of this dead-end town. Every time they went out, he picked her up in a new fancy car. He was also promising her a new car. Well it was time for him to come through with his promises.

Jenny lived at home with her father and mother and three brothers. Her mother worked like a dog, but no one in the household respected her. She had a sweet disposition and would get taken advantage of by her family. Her life had taken a turn toward total servitude. It was the easiest way to avoid the disagreements, arguments, and fights which seemed to erupt at the drop of a hat in Jenny's household. She had been a very religious person before she met and married Jenny's intimidating father who would threaten her with her life if she even tried to go to her church and would kill her if she tried to take any of their children. Allowing Jenny to go to the big city for beauty school was a huge battle. Her mom really fought hard for that. She realized that Jenny would not have any chance without some means of supporting herself. Jenny, however, had her own plan. When Eddy came knocking on her door at 8 o'clock sharp, Jenny was more than ready, but she made her mother answer the door.

As Eddy and Jenny drove away from her home together, she began to tell him how wonderful he was to pick her up and take her from that horrible home. She told him that her parents were abusive. He strained a bit at that.

"Your mother seems to be a very sweet woman," he said.

"Oh don't let her fool you. That sweet woman cusses me out if I ever do anything she doesn't like. I can't wait to be completely free of them."

"Wow, Jenny, I had no idea," Eddy said pulling into a drive-in restaurant and ordering dinner for them.

"It's worse than all of that," she said, telling more lies about her mother and father. Some of what she said about her father was true, but she always made each situation worse than what it really was. What a fool this guy was. He didn't know the truth from a total fabrication. The whole evening was one big sham, and Eddy was totally taken in. He believed her one hundred percent, and his heart went out to her. He wanted to be her knight in shining armor and rescue her from this terrible situation. He took her hands into his own, looked lovingly into her eyes and asked her to marry him. "I want you to have the dark green Jaguar sports car," he said, pushing a stray hair from her face. "Think of it as a pre-engagement present; the engagement ring will come later. I want you to pick it out, Babe." He leaned in and kissed her in a way that almost made her fall in love with him. He had no idea what he had gotten himself into.

Wow! Fantastic, this was easier than she had hoped. She looked at Angie's ring on her finger. This class ring of Angie's was a good luck charm, and there was no way she was going to give it back. She was keeping it forever. Now all she had to do to keep the goodies coming was to keep this fool happy. This should be as easy as pie. She'd have him eating out of her hand before the end of the week.

"Would you like to see my apartment?" Eddy asked. "Do you have to be home any special time; do you have a curfew?"

"Yes to the apartment, and no to the curfew."

"Great. Let's go."

Eddy's apartment was state-of-the-art with all of the latest features and appliances available. His large brown leather sofa sat in the middle of the living room with a high polished wood coffee table in front of it. Finishing the room off in a perfect square were two matching leather chairs with wood end tables on either side of them. The rooms were small but tastefully decorated. It was very impressive, and that was exactly what Eddy wanted—to dazzle Jenny and prove to her how lucky she was to be with him. Not exactly the typical bachelor pad Jenny was accustomed to. Most of them were messy dumps. This was so much nicer, and she was impressed.

The evening started slowly. Although shy at first, it was not long before some heavy petting was going on and continued for a long while. At one point Jenny was wondering if this guy was ever going any further. Slowly and very gently, Eddy's hands began to move ever so slowly until they were under her sweater and even more gently his hands were playing with her breasts. When there was no objection to his action, he unhooked her bra with one swift movement, freeing her breasts. His other hand never stopped stroking them and caressing her nipples and she had begun to moan and sigh. His kisses were hot, and she was really taken aback by his gentle touch. She loved it; it felt so good, but she hated it because she was losing control. He pulled the sweater over her head, and his mouth was on her freed breasts, sending sensations all over her body. She was breathing deeply now. She had never expected this from Eddy. She reached for his trousers and unzipped them. His manliness aroused her beyond belief. He was ready and so was she.

"Take me," she whispered as they got lost in the grandness of the moment. When it was over he kissed her gently and lovingly cradled her in his arms. She would never forget this moment, but she knew she would never be able to relive it again.

She was getting pretty tired and thought she should get control of the situation or she might end up falling asleep on the spot. "I really better get home. It's late. You have to be at work in the morning, and I'll have to be in class. I need to go and let you get some sleep.

Eddy, you have taken me to a place I have never been, and I never knew I could be as elated as you have made me tonight. I will always remember this night for the rest of my life."

Eddy stood up and looked down on her face. He kissed her gently and said, "I'll remember everything about this evening. I love you very much. I'll drive you home, and you can pick up the car tomorrow."

"I've got a better idea." She said getting up and stretching. "I'll drive myself home in my new car, and I'll come by at 8 a.m. and pick you up for breakfast." She picked up her sweater that had been tossed carelessly onto the coffee table earlier and put it on. "Then I'll drive you to the lot and you can pick up another car. I'll leave my old car for mom to drive when she's running her errands. Now isn't that a better idea?"

Eddy shrugged a bit uneasily. "That sounds good to me. I'll see you tomorrow."

She raced out of Eddy's apartment so quickly that she had forgotten to put on her coat. The night air greeted her with a cold sting. She hoped the car would start. To her satisfaction, the car turned over. She began the drive home and replayed the evening over in her head. Everything was perfect— the evening, the proposal, and the sex was great. He was not her first partner but was by far one of the most skilled—definitely a breast man, and she loved that. Most of the guys she had been with were only concerned with satisfying themselves and not taking the time to get her aroused. Eddy did both, and he was good. Tonight gave her a great deal to look forward to.

Chapter 7

The Sports Car

Jenny drove to class in the morning still on a high from the night before and was excited to show off her new car. "Just wait till everyone sees the Jaguar," she thought. "They will fall over with envy. If Angie could only know what good luck her class ring brought, she would never believe it. It's better for her to stay as innocent as she is. You could tell her anything, and she would believe it. Poor fool. She would never believe that anyone could possibly tell anything but the truth, and she sure would never suspect that anyone would ever deliberately take it. It's best for her to believe the ring is lost. What she doesn't know won't hurt her. This ring is working for *me* now, not her. She wouldn't know what to do with a lucky ring anyway, and that kind of enchantment should never go to waste. She's never known anything but the straight and narrow, what a poor fool. She has no idea what she's missing in life." Jenny's deceitful narcissism convinced her of a greatness in herself that did not exist.

When she pulled into the parking lot at the university, the girls there swarmed the car. "Where did you get that car? It's a beauty. Don't tell me Eddy came across with it?" They were all talking at once.

"Yes, yes, and yes" was her reply. "He loves me, lucky guy. He is just crazy about me. And you know what else?"

"What?"

"He asked me to marry him."

The girls squealed the news and started chattering about celebrating.

Angie watched the show at a distance. Why in the world would any guy just hand a car over to a girl? Jenny never said anything about Eddy that indicated she was in love with him. Here she just had started going out with him and now they were getting married? She didn't get it. Angie's dad would never allow her to accept a car from a guy.

"What's the matter, Angie, jealous? I can't help it you don't have a boyfriend. You need to make yourself over and stop being such a plain Jane," was the cruel remark from Jenny. Shocked and hurt that she would be so insulting, Angie smoothed dark brown curls from her face and turned away from the group. She thought they were friends. Well, now she knew better. Who cares about nasty cracks and all of the silliness being slung around out there by the car? There was something fishy about this whole thing.

Angie recovered, turned back toward Jenny with a smile, and said, "Enjoy it in good health and congratulations on your engagement."

"Angie, I'm sorry! I didn't mean to hurt your feelings."

"Oh, you didn't. I've got an appointment and have to go." She turned and went into the school. For sure things are getting sticky around here, she thought as she went inside the door. June cannot come soon enough. If Jenny thought a Jaguar made her a big shot, she had a lot to learn. Even so, the last thing Angie expected was to have the plain Jane comments thrown at her. It did hurt her feelings. She never thought of herself as a pretty girl, but at the same time, she didn't think she was plain. It is funny how one little statement can cause so much hurt. She smiled remembering how Rebecca and Maude used to tell her what a pretty girl she was, how her deep brown eyes shown of beauty, and how the waves of her hair were like a midnight waterfall. She rolled Jenny's words off of her back.

Jenny continued to show off her car. She took everyone for a ride, one by one. She had one of the girls who lived in the dorm cover for her by signing her in on time so Jenny would not lose any hours. Otherwise, she could not graduate on time to take the spring State Board examination. Jenny had promised her a date with Eddy's best friend if she made sure that the instructors had no idea that she was outside riding around in her new sports car. After manipulating so many people, she was sure she could get away with murder!

At lunch time, Jenny showed up to make sure the instructors saw her working.

Everything went backwards that day for Angie. Not a single client was satisfied with her work. Everything was a redo, and the clients were not nice about it. Thankfully, the day finally came to an end. Angie closed up her station and was getting ready to go home. Jenny stopped her suddenly.

"Did you hear about Frankie?"sShe asked breathlessly.

"No, and I don't want to hear either."

"I think you will want to know because it's about *you*."

"What are you talking about? I don't even talk to Frankie except for hi and bye."

Several students had stepped in closer to listen, including Frankie.

"That's not the way the story is coming out. His wife was here raising hell with Mrs. Hall, the dean of the school, today. She told the dean that *you* told her, Frankie and Jill were messing around. She was ready to close the school down if Mrs. Hall didn't do something about it."

"That's not true! I don't even know Jill that well, and I sure don't know Frankie's wife or what goes on around here after hours. What's going on? Who's trying to get me into trouble? I have been minding my own business ever since I started here. I don't know any of these people beyond the front door of the school." Would Jenny be so cruel as to start this rumor, Angie wondered suspiciously.

It was a nice speech, but it didn't hold any water as far as everyone was concerned. Angie was the stool pigeon and no one else was going to take the heat for it. Frankie glared at her. "You're toast, girly. If you see me coming, you best get out of the way." Never in all of Angie's life had anything like this ever happened. He was so angry that he raised his hand and was about to hit her when Mrs. Hall stepped in. Frankie scared Angie. She was so upset; she didn't know how to defend herself. Tears were in her eyes, but she blinked hard to not allow anyone see her cry. This was humiliating. First Jenny makes a fool of her for no good reason, and now Frankie verbally and almost physically assaulted her, and she had no idea what was going on. Would June ever get here? She hated everything about this place and the people here. No one was nice, and none were like her dear friends from high school. The thought that this might continue into a work situation was insufferable. Angie told herself to calm down. Tomorrow was another day. She assured herself that there were a lot of very nice people in this profession, but she had not met them yet. On top of everything else, there was, Jeff, the number two Casanova of the school who wanted to date her. She could just see the fireworks if she was to waltz up to her house with him. One look at him from Basil and Athena and the police would be at the door with guns drawn. This was so awful it should be a tragic comedy.

Completely downhearted, Angie left the school and walked home. She could not face the bus ride tonight. It was a cold day, and the nightfall came sooner than expected. Entirely misjudging the distance and the weather, she shivered. She wasn't just cold; she was frightened as darkness closed around her. Why had she decided to walk home? She thought to herself, more proof of just how stupid she had been all day. Worst of all, the buses had stopped running every fifteen minutes and now were running every hour. The last one had passed her five minutes ago. She was now hurrying to the next stop before the bus arrived. When she reached the bus stop she still had twenty minutes wait once she got there. This was the worst night ever. Hugging herself against the cold, she watched strange people pass by. She quivered more. The minutes seemed to be an eternity. Oh how she longed for the days when she and her friends were walking home from school. Those were carefree days—just school, home, and studies to worry about. The sound of the approaching bus drew her attention out of thoughts of good times with her friends. The bus pulled up to the stop, and the door flipped open. She leaped on as if it were her refuge. It felt good to be safe in a warm bus. Bed really sounded good to her now.

When she opened the door to her house, Angie entered into a whirlwind of confusion and anxiety. "What's going on?"

"Angie! Good, your home. Athena is having the baby tonight. I have to take her to the hospital. Get some dinner together for Sammie and yourself. Here are the keys to the car. Get it out of the garage and bring it around front. I'll help Athena out. Grab that bag and put it in the car."

That was just like her dad. He already had three children and still fell apart as soon as it was time for the fourth baby to come. He was almost in panic mode, she was thinking as she backed the car out of the garage and drove down the alley to the front of the house. Out came Athena and Basil and into the car they went.

"I'll call you as soon as I know anything. Bye. I love you," he called as they pulled away from the curb.

"I love you, too," she answered.

Angie went into the kitchen and searched for something easy and quick to make for dinner. Five hours later the phone rang, bringing the news that Athena had given birth to a baby boy— little Bobby.

The next day Angie helped Sammie get ready for school. Maude would be there shortly, and Angie should be able to get to school on time. There was no way she would share this news with anyone at school. She was going to have enough trouble the way things were without the razzing of having a baby brother added to the mix.

Thankfully, very little was said to her at school. She made sure to stay out of Frankie's way and did not even try to talk to Jenny. The days passed, and June arrived at last. Now it was on to the State Board of Cosmetology and the test for her license.

Jenny had taken and passed the board exam. She was busy planning her wedding and had little time to make more trouble. As her school friends wished her well, she gave credit to the good luck ring she had, and it wasn't the engagement ring either. Jenny's relationship with Angie had not improved since that fateful day. Aside from the occasional "hello" in the halls of the school, Jenny kept her distance, which was quite fine with Angie. She had had enough of the vulgar ways of most of the women there. Jenny boastings of a magic ring was just plain dumb, but those comments made Angie feel uneasy. She hadn't been comfortable with Jenny from the time her class ring disappeared. She acted mean and conceited since its disappearance. Their stations were next to each other, giving her access to the ring. Angie would arrive at the conclusion often that Jenny stole her ring, but always dismissed it thinking she was overreacting. Soon this whole thing, cosmetology school and all the Jennys and Frankies, would be behind her. She was going to move on, and they would become a dim memory.

Chapter 8

Back to the Plan

The State Boards went well, and the next event was graduation. Angie had prepared and studied for the test. Barbara was her model for the practical part of the test, and she passed with flying colors. Thank God for that. There was no way she wanted to go back to Beauty School for a one week refresher which was required before you could take the test again.

It was time for her to go to Circle City High School to get fitted for her cap and gown. Going back to high school after attending the University of Cosmetology made Angie feel like a stranger who did not belong. Was this the school she had spent four years of her life attending? Why had it seemed so large at that time? Now it seemed as if she had never been there at all. The students seemed so young, and she felt out of place. All the seniors were lined up alphabetically. As she approached the table she saw some of the students from her homeroom. They were all very nice to her, but she definitely felt like an outsider. Some asked where she'd been. They hadn't seen her around. She was actually sorry she even decided to come back for graduation. It sounded good at the time, but now, as the big plan began to unfold, it didn't seem to be exactly what she had anticipated. She had never counted on feeling so disconnected from everything.

Barbara came over to talk to her. "Hi. Why didn't you call me? We could have walked over together."

Even she seemed different. The intensity of trying to get through the courses at the university as fast as possible had caused Angie to mature much faster than she had expected or even dreamed. She never realized that she had cut herself off from all her friends because her time was all taken up by trying to make up all the hours she needed to finish beauty school. She finished all right, but she also lost all the fun of her senior year. She now realized she had lost out on a lot. Her ring had disappeared, and so had her senior year.

"Do you have a date for Grad Dance?" asked Barbara. "If you don't, there's a great guy who would love to go with you. You know him. It's Jimmy Jordon. He saw you coming into school today and asked if he would have a chance with you if he asked."

"Oh Barbara, I feel like an outsider. He'd probably have a better time with someone else."

"If he wanted someone else he wouldn't have asked me to help him ask you," she said, giving Jimmy the come on sign.

Jimmy stepped up to the girls. "Hi, Angie, you look great. It seems like forever since I've seen you. Have you been alright?" he began. "I don't want to sound bold, but will you go to the Grad Dance with me?"

"Yes," Angie replied and for the first time since she entered the school, she smiled.

"Great! We'll double date with Barbara and Chris, OK?"

"Yes, again," she laughed. It could be that things were not as bad as they had first appeared to be. I'm going to the Grad Dance with Jimmy. She smiled and was at peace for the first time in a long time. What a great feeling to have—your mind clears and all the pieces fall into place.

Something kept coming back in her mind. She couldn't understand what was bothering her, but for some reason, her class ring kept coming up in her mind. Now that she was at Circle City, it bothered her more than ever. It was the way Jenny was acting ever since the ring disappeared. Besides the clients, she was the only one around when it went missing, and Angie didn't think one of the clients would have taken it. A lost-and-found note was posted, but no one responded. The ring was lost as far as Angie was concerned, but that crack Jenny made when everyone was wishing her good luck about "the good luck ring" that wasn't the engagement ring either had always bothered her; what did it mean? She hoped this subject would not continue to come up and haunt her for the rest of her life. What a scary thought that Jenny and her crazy ways would haunt her forever.

Chapter 9

The Grad Dance

Time to pick out a dress for the Grad Dance. Angie might have missed the last semester of senior year, but she was going to senior prom, and she was going with Jimmy. Even Basil liked Jimmy. First she checked her closet for any dress that would work. There was one, but she had worn it several times already. Maybe Barbara would have something that would work. Before Angie could call her, the doorbell rang. She hurried to answer it, and there was Barbara with a dress bag in her hand.

"Look what I found in my closet," Barbara was saying as she came into the house. As she opened the bag she uncovered a beautiful white dress. Angie was taken aback as she looked at it.

"Aren't you wearing this dress?" was all Angie could get out.

"It's the perfect dress for you. I hope you'll wear it."

"It's beautiful. I can't believe you've brought this dress over to see if I would wear it," Angie uttered in shock.

"Don't be silly. I have a great dress already, and this dress would be sitting in the closet collecting dust if you don't wear it." Barbara rambled on. "If you don't take it, I'll be very upset."

"Oh thank you, Barbara, you are really my best friend. I've missed you more than you can imagine."

"OK, OK no more fuss. Just put it on and let's make plans. The dance is in three days, and we have to hustle to get everything ready."

The dress looked great on Angie, and the girls were busily making plans for a special night. The graduation ceremony was Tuesday at 7 p.m., and the Grad Dance was being held on Saturday. Angie's choice to leave high school mid-year had cost her the feeling of excitement which the others had for graduation, and for her it had lost a lot of its sparkle. Barbara's family was having an open house, as were many of her other friends. They were all being held on the same day, the day after the graduation. It would be a busy week of congratulations and good luck parties. She was really looking forward to it. She had missed so many events that this would be a real treat. Now the prom would be the grand finale of the week. Wow, what a week. The excitement was growing.

"Alright, Barbara, what kind of planning do we do for the dance?" asked Angie not sure if she had any responsibility for making plans.

"All we have to do is look pretty and be ready when they come to pick us up. I believe that we're going to either the Parkmore or the Tee Pee."

These were the favorite hangouts of the high school kids. They were drive- in restaurants, but on special occasions the girls would wear a dress and the guys a jacket and dine inside the restaurant. It was perfect. You had to be dressed up to eat inside and that would certainly not be a problem since they would all be dressed to the nines. The band was Les Brown and His Band of Renown. The event was to be held at the City Ballroom in the downtown area. The more Angie heard, the more excited she became. "It's going to be a great time, I'm sure, and I can't wait. Thank you, Barbara, for making it possible for me to be a part of this."

"Angie, we all have missed you since you left for beauty school and want you to at least enjoy this last event of the class of 1955 ."

"I can say thank you over and over, but this means a lot to me. You know that I lost my class ring at beauty school, and after that I felt that I had lost my connection to this class."

"You're as much a part of this class as anyone is and don't forget it. OK, I think we've got it all under control. Will your parents be taking you to the graduation ceremony, or will you need a ride?

"They'll bring me, but thanks for the offer. See you there."

The graduation ceremony went smoothly, and the grad parties were fun. Angie saw many classmates and felt their excitement of stepping out into the world and spreading their wings in college and some were entering junior college. It was exciting to hear their plans. She really wanted to caution them about what was out there but decided not to say anything. Everyone has to find out for themselves what it means to spread their wings and fly. She did and found out that many times disappointment is what you run into.

Jimmy took her to most of the parties. He was such good company— always cheerful and full of fun. He was liked by everyone, and it felt good to be escorted by him. There were great spreads and wonderful music. Just being there was exactly what she needed to make her feel a part of it all. The biggest event was yet to come this weekend.

Angie styled her hair like a pro. What else would you expect from a pro? Barbara came over to get styled along with four of their friends, which turned out to be great fun with everyone critiquing each other's hairdos.

This is the most fun I've had in a long time, Angie thought. When I finally get to campus and stay in a dorm, I could give the girls staying there haircuts to manicures to facials or whatever they need done. That would be a great way to make some extra money. I could make money and friends at the same time. I'll have the whole summer to start working and by enrollment time I should have enough money to make a down payment on tuition.

By the time all the girls had their hair done, it was time for them to hustle home and get dressed and wait for their dates to pick them up.

Angie hurried and cleaned up the mess from all the hair products and rushed home to get ready for Jimmy to pick her up. It had been a fun day, and the best was yet to come. She liked being with Jimmy because he was always so much fun.

At 6 o'clock on the dot the doorbell rang. Basil answered it and welcomed Jimmy into the house. He called to Angie, and she came into the room. Jimmy had a beautiful white wrist gardenia corsage, and Angie gave him a white rose boutonniere. Basil had tears in his eyes as he watched this sweet moment taking place. He stood there for a moment and suddenly said, "Picture time." He posed the couple, whipped out his Kodak, and snapped away. It was not his personality to do that, which made it all the more special. Angie had always thought of Jimmy as a buddy and tried very hard to keep any romantic thoughts about him out of her mind. At this moment, however, she would have liked to freeze time and forget the buddy stuff. It was a safe way to handle male friends, but she had been safe forever, and this was senior prom. She wanted Jimmy to like her as the girl she was. They said goodbye to her father and set out to pick up Chris next then Barbara. When they arrived at Barbara's house there was a lot of picture taking and joking going on. If this was an indication of what the evening was going to be like, it was going to be a wonderful one.

***

The ballroom was wondrous. The Grad Dance committee had done an amazing job decorating. The room would have been beautiful even if there had not been any decorations. The ceiling was an unbelievable sight of delicately painted moving clouds, stars, and moonlight. The magic in the room was everywhere. It was the most beautiful sight Angie had ever seen—completely breathtaking. The committee had small flowing trees set in different locations on the dance floor, completing the magic. Grad Dance night was the night that Angie and Jimmy discovered that they could have easily become more than buddies. This unearthing was a bit of a problem since he was going to attend the University of Illinois in Springfield, Illinois, and she was planning to attend the local university branch and live at home. She did not want to complicate her life with a long-distance relationship which would end up not working out anyway. Joey had always said that as soon as a couple went their separate ways they began to drift apart, and it would end in a breakup and someone would always get hurt. She was sure this would happen with Jimmy and her. Enjoy the evening she told herself and let well enough alone. They had a wonderful time. Les Brown and his Band of Renown made beautiful music. Jimmy was a wonderful dancer. The night was magical, and the event would always be filled with good memories along with the hope that the buddies would go on being buddies. At the end of the evening, Jimmy leaned over and gave Angie a sweet kiss on the lips filled with innocent affection, but it made her heart stand still. It could not have touched her more if it had been a hot passionate kiss that knocked her off her feet. It was a sweet ending to a wonderful night—one night that they both would treasure forever.

Chapter 10

What About Jimmy?

Jimmy Jordon was an all-around good guy. He was very responsible and had taken care of his brothers and sister, helping out his mother after his father was killed in an automobile accident. It was a time when the world had stood still for the family, and they were all in a daze as to where to go from there. Their father had taken care of everything. Now he was gone and had left his wife, Mona, in a state of panic with four children to bring up alone. Jimmy was the oldest child in the family and felt a strong responsibility to step up and help in any way necessary. Mrs. Jordon had to seek employment in order to support her family. Therefore, Jimmy had to take charge of the children after school while she was still at work. Jimmy was on the football team at Circle City High; he was entering his senior year at the time his father passed away. Angie and Jimmy had known each other for years. They both attended the same church. He had already graduated and completed three years at State University. Angie had seen him off and on over the years, but since he was four years older than, he had felt he was too old to have any interest in her at that time. He and Joey were friends but had lost touch with each other when they went to different universities. They had run into each other at the Tee Pee and when they were home on school breaks. It was during one of the spring breaks that she caught his eye. They were all at the Tee- Pee. Jimmy had come home for Easter, and he and Joey had gotten together. Angie was always hanging around with her brother and the Circle City High crowd. He really liked her and she looked great that night. He had always thought that he was too old for her, but he didn't think so that night. In fact he thought he would really like to get to know her a lot better. Unfortunately, he did not get the opportunity that evening, but he did run into her friend Barbara and got the latest scoop on her. He mentioned that he would really like to get to know her better. That was when Barbara told him that she was sure that Angie did not have a date for the Grad Dance and maybe she could arrange a double date. That was why Jimmy happened to be at Circle City High that day when Angie was getting her cap and gown for the graduation ceremony. Barbara was the go-between and had a lot of fun arranging this unforgettable evening for the two of them. Angie was totally in the dark about the entire conspiracy. She always thought that it was just very fortunate that Jimmy had happened to be at the school at the time. There was a time or two that she wondered why a third-year college student would be hanging out at the high school, but she dismissed it as a stroke of good fortune that he happened to be there and actually wanted to take her to the Grad Dance. Little did she know the amount of planning it took to accomplish that meeting.

Jimmy had worked hard to get to state university, and his mother had worked hard to keep the family together. She was very proud of all her children. Unfortunately, life had taken a lot out of her and left her a very weary and lonely woman. Her children were growing up, and her youngest was about to begin high school. This was about the time that she began to go out on dates. She was an attractive woman, and it was easy to see why men would be attracted to her. She never got serious about any of them but was merely a good friend and companion. She never married again because she had seen too many bad results from second marriages, especially where children were involved. She was content with life as it was. She had loved her husband deeply and knew she would never have that kind of feeling for anyone else .

Chapter 11

Jenny's Wedding

Jenny was busy with her wedding plans. She and Eddy went into the big city to select an engagement ring. Of course this was very difficult as nothing seemed to please her. Jenny finally settled on a two carat diamond emerald cut with a matching wedding band. The ring was quite expensive, five thousand dollars and some change. It had to be sized to fit her finger. The jeweler told them he would call them as soon as the ring was ready.

The wedding dress became another ordeal of never-ending complaining. She had told Eddy that there was no place in this small town or Indianapolis that had any dresses she would ever consider wearing. They were all strictly for the birds. She needed to go to New York City to find the dress of her dreams, and off to New York she went and bought a two thousand dollar lace and beaded designer gown which was over budget. Eddy was more than a little upset. He was beginning to think that he was marrying a gold digger.

Her parents were not interested in paying anything for the wedding. For some reason they thought he was a money tree. He really loved Jenny, but he could see that she would have to be roped in on the spending. Every time Eddy tried to discuss money with her, she would cuddle and make up to him, and he would melt. What happened to all the plans for her career, all of the scholarships she had been offered? He seriously doubted that there was any career or any additional money that would be coming in from any promised profession she had talked about.

Jenny continued to believe that the class ring was truly her "good luck" charm. She never was without it.

"Eddy," called Jenny from the other room. "I just got the best idea. You're Irish, and you have never been to Ireland have you? I thought it would be great to go there for our honeymoon and visit the land of your roots. What do you think?"

She rambled on without waiting for an answer.

Eddy stood in front of the window struck speechless. What was going on here? What started out as a simple wedding had turned out to be a nightmare and he was left holding the bills.

"I talked to your mother, and she thought it was a great idea. I called a travel agent to see if I could arrange a trip to Dublin, and it's no problem. I think this would be a great time for us to consider getting one of those new credit cards that everyone is talking about. What do you think?"

"I think you are out of your mind. What do you think we're made of— money?" With that said he stomped out of the house and went to the car lot. He had better sell everything on the lot or he would never make it.

Where did Jenny ever get the idea that he had endless wealth? He never indicated that he was able to pay for all these expensive things. The engagement ring was one thing as it would be something she would wear forever, but the dress was for a one-day event—never to be seen again, and it cost two thousand dollars! He had seen beautiful dresses for two hundred dollars that would have made her look amazing. He had to slow this spending down. Maybe a credit card would be a temporary solution. Sure that it was all just the result of the excitement of planning the wedding and the furnishing of the new house and everything else that was going on, Eddy decided to move into the house and save the rent on his apartment. However, Jenny moved into the house, and even though they had made no secret of sleeping together for quite some time, it didn't stop her from wanting to play it coy and pretend that she was still a virgin. The truth was that most everyone who lived there knew about her many sexual exploits with numerous young men in her beloved hometown. Many thought Eddy was out of his mind for marrying such a woman. Nevertheless, she was concerned about what people would say and told Eddy that he had to wait until after the wedding before she would allow him to live in the house with her. As a result, poor Eddy now had two payments and utilities to deal with—his apartment and the new house to say nothing about the new furniture. After the wedding he thought things would return to normal, whatever that used to be. The more he thought, the worse he felt. What was going on with this whole irrational thing? He was wondering if every new couple went through all this craziness. He decided he'd have to call his father and ask him to have lunch so maybe he could lend his wisdom on these matters.

After his lunch with his father and a long heart to heart talk about his problems with Jenny's spending habits, his father understood Eddy's concerns, but also realized that Eddy loved Jenny very much and nothing would change his mind about that. His advice to his son was to table some of his concerns about the bills and try to enjoy the moment and worry about the bills one at a time, to avoid becoming overwhelmed. His father knew it would be futile to suggest that the two postpone the wedding until they both got to know each other much better. For that reason he avoided saying that and prayed for the best outcome.

Maybe a trip to Ireland would do us both some good was Eddy's conclusion. The confusion and the bills only got worse the more he tried to unravel the problem.

The phone rang. Eddy hoped it was a customer as he answered in a very businesslike voice, "Eddy's Cool Deals. This is Eddy. How can I help you?"

"Hi, sweetie, it's me. How are you doing?" It was Jenny. "I wanted to remind you that we're going to pick up the rings tonight. We have an appointment with Evan's Jewelry Shop at 6 o'clock. Don't forget. Love you!"

"Oh, alright," his response was unenthusiastic. "I'll see you there. Bye." Why did I say I would let her pick out any ring that she liked? With a deep sigh he set out to organize his desk. His hope for a busy day came to pass, and he sold two cars and had five customers who would be back later to test drive.

As luck would have it, Jenny was at the jewelry shop and had already picked up the expensive ring. True it was beautiful, but the price was colossal. The next day Eddy applied for a credit card.

The wedding reception was going to cost another five thousand dollars. This was so far out of control that Eddy was having nightmares. As if this were not enough, Jenny's parents refused to take part in any of the wedding responsibilities. Eddy was Irish Catholic, and the wedding was going to be at the Catholic cathedral.

Jenny's father was furious at the thought of entering any church let alone a Catholic cathedral. Her mother had long since given up trying to go to any church for fear of the consequences. They had made it very clear to all that they were not going to take on any responsibility for the wedding and were even indicating that they would not attend the wedding at all. Jenny was not troubled in the least. As far as she was concerned, she was glad not to have her loser family there. They would just be an embarrassment to her. She was getting away from them and all that they represented. The last straw was when the bill arrived for the flowers which came to two hundred dollars, and she was told that it was the responsibility of the groom.

The one question that Eddy asked himself over and over again was, how will I ever be able to pay for all of this?

The end result was a beautiful wedding, which her parents did not attend. They begged off, saying they had no money with which to buy clothes to wear and were not interested in some "snooty event filled with all that phony baloney." As a result, Jenny's father-in-law walked her down the aisle. Eddy was in such a nervous state that he never even knew what was going on around him. Jenny, on the other hand, was in seventh heaven. The wedding was her dream come true.

Chapter 12

The Trip to Ireland

The honeymoon was to be a wonderful experience, but it got off to a rocky start. Jenny had never flown in an airplane and was terrified. In her fear, she blamed Eddy for everything from the long lines to the luggage not being nice enough and how embarrassing that was. Finally they boarded the plane which only gave Jenny something else to complain about. The seats were all wrong. Why had he been so cheap and hadn't bought first-class seats. After all it was their honeymoon, and they deserved the best. When they finally sat down and settled into their places, her fear had subsided and she began to be much more reasonable. The surprise of the day was that they arrived without any incident and were met by Eddy's cousins. After all the hugs and introductions, they retrieved their luggage and stepped out of the airport into what looked much like an ad to tempt you to visit this beautiful country. It actually took both Eddy's and Jenny's breaths away. Eddy's relations were very amiable and hospitable people. There was so much to see and so little time to see it all. Jenny was extremely pleasant to all the cousins, telling them about the wedding and their new house. The ever-present class ring was with her every step of the way. By this time, Jenny was convinced that it had magic powers and that nothing could have come to pass without the ring's presence.

The drive to the hotel where the couple was staying was short. A very pleasant place, it offered many amenities. The cousins dropped the couple off and encouraged them to relax from the long trip, suggesting they should take a nap. They would return with the rest of the family and take them to dinner around 6 o'clock.

Eddy had decided to relax and enjoy the trip no matter what it cost. Taking his father's advice, he would concentrate on one bill at a time. Of course the credit card he had just acquired had made him breathe a little easier. In the meantime, he would live in blissful ignorance and enjoy the honeymoon.

The honeymooners both thought the best way to see the main sights was to book a tour. They had a week, and it would be gone in a blink of an eye if they didn't take advantage of tours which would take them to the most important sights.

Eddy had heard about Ireland all his life, and this was the first opportunity he had to actually see it for himself. He was happy to finally meet his cousins because he had heard so much about them and was pleased to know that they also were excited to meet him and his new bride.

Eddy stopped worrying about the expenses since he had opened his new credit account, but he had yet to receive a bill and was unaware of the interest that was already accruing on it. He and Jenny had decided to book tours that would take them to the most important sites of Ireland so they would be sure not to miss anything. Who knew if they would ever be able to visit again?

The week went by in a flash. On the final day of their trip, the couple was scheduled to visit an historic Irish castle. It was something they had both been looking forward to all week. When they left the hotel that morning, they brought their baggage with them to store with Eddy's cousins while they took the tour, so they could go straight to the airport for their evening flight.

They had a wonderful time at the castle, which ended with a stop at an Irish pub. The lounge was actually a large reception room which had been transformed into a cozy Irish pub. There was a roaring fire in the huge fireplace and everyone was served Irish coffee. Suddenly the whirring sound of a helicopter rose above the chatter, and everyone rushed to the window to see what was happening.

"What's that?" asked Jenny.

The helicopter descended onto a landing pad in an open field outside. It must be someone special to make such a grand entrance, Jenny thought. After the blades stopped rotating, out jumped an extremely handsome gentleman. He was accompanied by an entourage of equally handsome people. From the moment the group stepped into the pub, the staff fussed over them to make sure they were well taken care of. He looked familiar to Jenny, but she couldn't place him. She thought he might be a movie star but decided it could not be him because that actor was in Hollywood making a movie.

"What a wonderful life, to be rich and famous. This is the life I want," Jenny said with envy. "Eddy better get busy and sell a lot of cars." Finally, the tour guide began to gather the group for their return bus trip to Dublin. What a grand ending to a wonderful trip.

In the rush to get to the tour on time, Jenny forgot to pack the class ring in the suitcase. Instead she hurriedly placed the ring in her small carry-on case.

She would feel more comfortable with the ring right by her on the return trip home.

She didn't want to take a chance on losing the ring in a piece of lost luggage.

Meanwhile, at Eddy's cousin's house, Molly the maid was busy cleaning and tending to her daily tasks when she came upon the luggage in the hall. Curiosity had gotten the best of her for she had seen Miss Jenny place something into her carry- on case. What could it have been? She approached the case looking at the beauty of the luggage. She had never seen such perfectly matched luggage. It was without a doubt the most beautiful matched set she had ever seen. Her mistress had lovely luggage but even that baggage was not as beautiful as Miss Jenny's and Mr. Eddy's. As she was admiring the suitcases her eyes caught something sparkle on the floor close to the smallest case. Molly bent over to look more closely at the shiny object and saw the magic ring. She had heard Jenny talk about all the good luck the ring had brought her. She said she was never without it. Perhaps if she just slipped it on her finger for a wee minute, she would feel the good luck herself. Very carefully she picked up the ring up and slipped it on her finger. The magic ring slipped right on as if it were made for her. At that very moment she heard the front door open and the voice of her mistress calling for help with the groceries which she was trying to carry into the kitchen. Molly rushed to take the ring off but it was stuck on her finger. She pulled on the ring, but it didn't budge. She had to answer her mistress or there would be a price to pay. "I'm coming, madam, I'm coming." By this time she was certain she would be discovered to be a thief. "Oh my, oh my, what should I do?" She ran to help her mistress with the packages in the kitchen. When the groceries were put away, Molly headed straight to the sink to use some soap to loosen the ring. As the ring came off Molly began to enter the hallway where the luggage was. She reached the area just as Miss Jenny and Mr. Eddy came through the front door filled with excitement over the castle tour. Hurry, hurry, thought Molly as she raced toward the luggage. But as luck would have it, Mr. Eddy had already reached the luggage and was carrying it toward the door to the waiting car.

"Hello, Molly," Eddy said when he saw her in the hall.

"Let me help you, sir," Molly said, in a futile effort to return the ring, but it was too late. Eddy was already out the door and had placed the luggage into the automobile and was calling goodbye and thank you to the rest of the family who were standing there saying their goodbyes. They were on their way to the airport. Molly was unsuccessful in her attempt to return the ring. No matter how much Molly regretted it, the ring was still in her pocket, and the owner was on her way to America. How would she ever get the ring back to Miss Jenny?

13 Chapter

And so It Goes

Jenny and Eddy were heading for the airport in total ignorance of the missing piece of precious jewelry. Jenny was not thinking of the ring right then as she was sure it was in her carry-on case. A new plan was forming in her mind. What plan could she possibly be cooking up now? Poor Eddy was exhausted but had enough energy to feel proud of himself for maintaining his composure and not worrying about how much everything cost. He was actually ready to take a nap, he was so relaxed. But Jenny's mind was working overtime. What was it that had her so excited? The next step to be taken in Jenny's quest for greatness, an event to make her socially desired and the envy of everyone she knew.

Poor Eddy was so small time. He would never be able to pull off anything like what she was thinking of. He was just an ordinary car dealer, and that's all he would ever be.

Was the ring really a lucky charm or was it merely a coincidence that Jenny had what she thought was good luck?

Molly had overheard the conversation Jenny had with the family concerning the power of the ring. She gave all the credit for her good fortune to acquiring it. She had made the comment that Eddy, poor man, had no idea of the ring and its power.

Now perhaps it was Molly's turn for good fortune. She had been a servant all her life as was her mother before her. It was time for her to change directions and have a chance for the "good life." Didn't she deserve an easier life as much as anyone did? Molly was a good girl, always loyal to her employer. True, they had been good to her and very fair. They paid her a good wage, and in return she had given them an honest day's work, but this was not about that. This was about her rising above this position and into a higher station. What was wrong with that? As she thought about it, she had a terrible attack of guilt. What was she thinking? How would this happen? She would sleep on it tonight and see how she felt in the morning. As for now, she felt guilty and ashamed.

The next day Molly went about her morning chores. First stop was to be the Butcher Shop. Molly didn't always shop for the household, but today Mrs. O'Donnell was a bit weary from all the activities with the American relatives and asked Molly to do the shopping for her.

"Top o' the morning, Miss Molly, how you be this fine morning?" asked the butcher as Molly entered the shop. "What can I do for you?"

Molly pushed a stray golden-red strand of hair from her freckled forehead and gave the butcher her order. Not a very thrilling start for the day so far. She said her goodbyes, left the Butcher Shop, and headed on to the O'Donnell home to begin her day.

"Who would that beautiful little lady be that just left the store?" asked a young man who was standing close by while Molly made her purchase. "She's quite fetching, wouldn't you say? Quite a little lady, I do believe." The young man inquiring about Molly was the butcher's son. He was helping his father prepare the meat for the day as he did almost every morning. "Tell me, Pa , would all your patrons be as fetching as Miss Molly?"

"Mind your manners, Mr. Mick, Miss Molly be a lady. I respect her like me own daughter. She's not like all the others you see coming and going these days."

"Aren't you showing too much concern for the wee lass? Don't worry about her. I see she is a quality girl. No doubt about that. I want to meet her nice and proper. Please introduce her to me next time she comes into the store. Or even better, next Sunday after Mass. I promise not to be an idiot, but a proper gent."

"Now how would you be knowing that Miss Molly goes to St. Patrick Cathedral?"

"Well truth be known, I've seen her there the last three Sundays I've gone, but never had the good fortune to get close enough to meet her. With your help, next Sunday I think you could make the introduction happen. What do you say?"

"Oh me lad, I do believe you're smitten. Between the two of us we can make this happen. Saints be praised."

Chapter 14

Back Home Again

The flight home was uneventful, and Jenny and Eddy landed in New York City with a four-hour layover. This will be great, thought Jenny— four hours in New York. I'll shop to my heart's desire. She quickly turned to Eddy and announced that with four hours to wait, why didn't they just go into the city and do some shopping. The announcement of nonstop shopping was like a blow to the stomach. It knocked the wind out of him. Not only had Jenny purchased everything she wanted in Ireland, but had totally drained him of all his cash. How was he going to stop the craziness before it put them in the poor house? The charge card was full, and he had just enough cash in his pocket to get them home.

"Absolutely not, and don't ask me for one cent. I'm done with all this madness. We are waiting here in the airport, getting a bite to eat, getting on the plane when it arrives, and going home, and that is that. We are out of money."

"What do you mean out of money? You told me you had all kinds of money," she shrieked in near hysteria. "You deceived me when you told me you were rich. What you told me was a lie! How could you do this to me? You no-good bum, you tricked me into marrying you, and now you're telling me there is no money. What kind of man are you? You are a lowdown liar." At this point she was making a spectacle of herself.

"Calm down, you're making a scene. Everyone is looking. What's wrong with you anyway? All this bad temper over shopping. Are you out of your mind?" Eddy said, his voice was a loud whisper, and his face was turning red. He was ready to walk away.

"You're not going anywhere, you jerk. This is still our honeymoon, or did you forget? This is outrageous. I can't believe you could treat me this way." She was trying very hard to cry but only anger would come out.

"You had better prepare yourself because when we get back you are going to start the great career you were always talking about; you are going to work."

"Eddy, what are you saying? I can't work. I think I'm pregnant. How can I work in my condition?"

Eddy wished that he could be happy about this news, but all he could think about was how trapped he was. He had not expected this in his wildest dreams. What happened to "the catch of the year" he thought he'd gotten? He felt sick at heart.

On the rest of the trip home they barely spoke to each other. The only communication was the necessary words which needed to be said.

All at once, the home life in their hometown became black and white, no color, just a very grim and sad beginning to their new life together. Jenny began unpacking and putting away everything when she realized that the ring was missing. Her heart started to race, and she felt faint. Where could it be? She was sure she had put it into her carry-on bag, but it wasn't there. She checked every nook and cranny, every luggage pocket; she even checked Eddy's pockets. All she found there was a lot of charge card receipts—nothing important and certainly no ring. Where could it be? Could Eddy have taken it? No, he wouldn't do that. It's lost, and she had no idea where to look for it. "Think, think, when did you have it last," she asked herself non-stop? "It was on a chain around my neck when I left for the castle. Then I thought I should put it into my carry-on so it wouldn't show through my sweater. It must be there." She ripped through the carry-on ten times, checking and rechecking the pockets and the lining of the case. Nothing, nothing at all. Someone at the house must have taken it. That is what must have happened. One of those sweetie-sweet relatives of Eddy went through the carry-on and found the ring and took it. The story of the power of the ring should not have been mentioned. What a fool, what a fool. By this time Jenny was sobbing. The luck was gone, and Eddy was very angry with her for the hideous display of public anger that went on at the airport. All of the awful things that were said. How would she be able to make things right? He left this morning without even saying goodbye. In fact, now that her attention went back on Eddy, he had not spoken a word to her from the time they left the airport. How was it that she had just now discovered this and had not noticed it at all yesterday? Had the fact that the money was running out and that she had put them both into debt overshadowed the fact that her husband was not talking to her. Not on the airplane, not on the ride home from the airport, and not in the house. He did not even try to make love to her last night. When she woke up this morning he was not even in bed with her. When he finds out there is no baby on the way, he'll think she devised the story to hang on to him. The truth is as of today there is no baby, but it could be the truth. They did have a lot of sex on the honeymoon. It could very well have been true. A pregnancy could be real this very minute. It could happen in bed tonight if she could get him in the mood. She had to do something to salvage this mess. As for the ring, it was gone and with all this financial trouble it would be too risky to make a stink about his relatives and accuse them of stealing the ring. They did treat them very well. They had invited them to stay in their home for the week. Even though she and Eddy had begged off on the offer, it had been made with great kindness and good intentions. The ring had to be forgotten for now. The problem at hand was to undo the damage that had been done by her horrific fight and disruptive manner at the airport last night. First things first—a call to Eddy's Cool Deals and sweet talk herself into Eddy's good graces. It certainly wouldn't be easy. He had never just up and left without a word. She walked over to the telephone and dialed the number. After several rings, an unknown voice answered the phone. "Eddy's Cool Deals, may I help you?"

"Who is this?" inquired Jenny, as she was taken by surprise when she heard the woman's voice on the other end of the phone. There was no receptionist working at the lot as far as she knew.

"Maria. I'm the receptionist. How may I direct your call?"

"Direct my call. There is only one phone in the whole place. What are you talking about?" Jenny shouted indignantly. What was going on; what is happening? "Let me speak to my husband immediately."

"I'm very sorry, Mrs. O'Donnell, but Mr. O'Donnell is not available. He left orders not to be disturbed."

"What!" Jenny shouted. "I am his wife, and I insist you put this call through to him."

"I am very sorry, but I have my orders, and Mr. O'Donnell said no calls no matter who it was. I do apologize, but this is my job and I have my orders and I will not bend the rules when he specifically said that you were no exceptions. Would you like to leave a message?"

"No. This is an outrage, and I will take care of it myself." By this time Jenny was beginning to feel very shaky. What had come over Eddy? This was not his usual way. He was always excited to talk to her. Why the change? This was not good.

Running up the stairs, she quickly got dressed and headed toward the car to go to the dealership in person. She would get to the bottom of this. Strangely, she was not as angry as she was afraid. Had she gone too far, was their relationship unable to be saved? What if this was true? What could she do? How would she proceed in her mission to undo what damage she had done last night at the airport? Don't worry, she told herself as she began to formulate a plan on her way to the lot.

The car turned slowly into the traffic and made its way down Main Street. As Jenny drove towards Eddy's Cool Deals she passed the Stop and Eat Here Family Restaurant and immediately remembered that they served Eddy's favorite roast beef sandwich and root beer. She slammed on the brakes, pulled into the parking lot, jumped out of the car, and ran inside before you could blink an eye.

"Welcome back, Mrs. O'Donnell, how's the new bride today, and what can I do for you?"

"Hello, Mr. Roberts. I'm great and thank you for asking. I'm just trying to feed my hungry husband, and I know how much he loves your roast beef sandwiches and ice cold root beer. Do you think that will make him happy on this beautiful day?"

"Can't miss. I'll add a kosher pickle and these deep-fried onion rings, and it will be irresistible."

"That will be exactly what the doctor ordered. Let's do it, and thanks for the delectable tips," and with that the plan began to take shape.

Jenny got back into the car and continued on her mission to once again govern the situation which had spun out of control last night. This was one time when she had to admit that she had gone way too far and needed to be more careful going forward in this marriage. She made one more stop and picked up a little gift for him for the office. He had always wanted a golfer paper weight for his desk, and she intended to fill the order. She completed the purchase quickly and continued to the lot. All she had to do was get to him before this new receptionist put the halt to her entering the office. Let her, if she wants to see some real trouble. She was Eddy's wife, and she was bringing him lunch, and no haughty receptionist was going to stop her.

She pulled up next to Eddy's Corvette and parked the Jaguar. Grabbing the bags she ran inside and into Eddy's office before the receptionist knew what happened.

Eddy's Cool Deals was an attractive and inviting building. The sign was bright red and white and gave a welcoming appearance. Eddy basically ran the used car lot by himself. He made all of the deals, did the bookkeeping, and knew enough about motors to do repair when needed. His dream had been to hire on a fulltime mechanic and office assistant. It seems that he just took the first step by hiring an office assistant today. There were two small offices, and she could see Eddy sitting alone in his as she made her way inside.

"Hi, Sweetheart," she sang as she glided into the office. "I've got a surprise for you just to show you how much I love you." It was a great entrance if she had to say so herself. She carefully laid the sandwich and the onion rings on the desk and handed him the small package and smiled sweetly. All of this attention was orchestrated to soften him up and melt his heart and prepare him for the rest of the plan.

Eddy was so shocked that he was at a loss for words. "What are you doing," he stammered. "I thought that you were gone."

"Silly man, why would I leave the man I love? I'm sorry I was such a witch last night. I don't know what got into me. It must have been the long trip home. Please forgive me, Sweetheart" she sighed.

What could the poor fool say? He was taken completely by surprise and was shocked by the whole display of kindness. He wanted to believe her and forget the ugly scene which took place last night. Did he dare to doubt her or should he forgive her and try to make this marriage work? He had to think of the baby that was coming. It was coming much sooner than he would have liked, but if they loved each other they could work it all out. Maybe he should give her a chance to prove herself. After all, there was a lot at stake.

"The sandwich looks great. Thank you for thinking of me. Would you like to split it with me?" he asked hesitantly, for he was still trying to put all of this together.

"Oh no, no, this is all for you, my sweet love." I better back off on this before I get too gushy, she cautioned herself.

"I guess I am much hungrier than I thought," Eddy said as he dove into his sandwich.

"I'll just sit here and keep you company. I hope you like the little present I bought you." She continued with the butter would melt in her mouth sweetness. He better like it; the golfer cost her two hundred dollars. There was no time to bargain; besides, he really deserved something he really wanted no matter how much it cost. Everything seemed to be getting back to normal, at least for the time being. Eddy loved the golfer paper weight and would never find out how much it cost, not if Jenny had anything to do with it.

Chapter 15

The New Budget

That evening, when Eddy arrived home, he was greeted with a hot meal on the table accompanied by fresh flowers and lit candles. The house was tidy, and all the clothes were unpacked and put away. Was this Eddy's house or had he wandered into the wrong house by mistake? Just then Jenny came out of the kitchen dressed in a very attractive pair of slacks and top. One of many things she had purchased in Ireland. Eddy was truly speechless.

"Sit down, darling, and I'll get you a drink after such a hard day at work," Jenny said as she poured a stiff drink for Eddy and herself. The evening continued in the same calm manner throughout the dinner and beyond. It was a dream come true.

Then Eddy dropped a bombshell. He felt that all was well, and it was a good time as ever to discuss the plan he had worked out to pay the bills. "We have incurred a lot of debt, with the wedding, the new house, and all the new furniture, and we need to start paying it down," he began. "I've decided to extend the car lot hours." Jenny was stunned by his announcement.

"What are you saying," she asked.

"I am saying that we need to start paying this debt down. We cannot continue to carry such a large balance on our charge card account. At the rate we're going I will lose my credit rating for my business."

"Are you saying we're poor?"

"No, I'm saying we are going to have a budget." He reached into his shirt pocket and pulled out a folded sheet of paper with an itemized list of all their bills. He showed her the list. "The cost totals seventeen thousand six hundred dollars, and, on top of that, a house payment of one hundred and fifty dollars per month and all of the new furniture payment of two hundred dollars per month. Of course there are all of the utilities for the house—

another one hundred fifty dollars per month."

Jenny just stared with her mouth hanging open. "What are you saying?" she asked again in disbelief. She was struck dumb by the very thought of an evening designed to lure Eddy into bed and have her way with everything she wanted turned into a budget talk where she got the short end of the stick. "What do you think I am going to live on, and why did you let your spending get out of hand?" She fired back at him.

"I'm going to extend the hours at the car lot to catch more customers," he continued. "You will have an allowance for household things. No more credit cards in your name. If you overspend your allowance, no more money till the following month."

"That's the last straw. I will not be on a budget. If I run out of money there will be no more till the next month?" Rage was beginning to rise within her. "Who do you think you are to treat me like a spoiled child that doesn't know when to come in out of the rain?" By now she really did not care if he liked what she said or not. She was furious and was about to unleash the wrath of God on him. "You promised me you had plenty of money and that we would have a good life together. Now you are saying that I am to be on an allowance and must live within it. You lied to me, and I will never forgive you for that as long as I live. You are a loser and always will be. I hate you!" Eddy was taken aback with the anger which Jenny exhibited.

"What are you saying to me? Are you saying that you don't love me and all of this was a front to fool me into thinking that you were going to be reasonable and try to work with me while we attempted to pay down our debt and work our way out of this hole we're in?"

"Oh, no, Sweetheart, that's not what I intended to say. I was just surprised that you were so concerned with the bills that you did not trust me to monitor my own spending. You were sounding a little unreasonable that's all. Please forgive my misunderstanding." She said in her fake sweetie voice.

"That's not what I heard. I heard you say that you hated me and would never forgive me. That's what I heard, and I'm sick and tired of your playing this game. Nothing is ever good enough for you. You didn't even want your own parents to take part in the wedding. You must really think that everyone believes all this bull you've been throwing out. What do you take me for, a total fool? I've been running a business which I stated from the ground up for the last four years. I'm a respected member of the community, which you bad mouth every chance you get. I'm the one who has been hoodwinked, not you."

Jenny could not find an answer for what he had said. What could she possibly do to get this relationship back on track? This was the big question. Her temper had gotten the best of her again, and now there was a price to pay. Up to this time he had not brought up the baby. Could he have guessed that this too was a lie? She had to get him into bed, and there she would convince him that she loved him and get pregnant. It was close to that time of the month, and she should be able to work it if he would cooperate

"Please, Eddy, darling, don't be this way. I am so new at this marriage game, and I know that I have made mistakes. The debt was absolutely as much my fault as yours. I didn't understand that you were really serious about all this money stuff you were complaining about. Let's start again and erase all the things we've said to each other tonight. Let's go upstairs and sleep on it." This was her last ditch effort to avert further damage to their relationship as there was already plenty damage done.

The wounded couple went slowly up the stairs and prepared for a good night's sleep. Jenny put on her honeymoon nightgown, which was very erotic. This should do the trick, she thought.

Eddy got into bed completely exhausted. It had been an emotionally challenging day. None of the challenges were as difficult as Jenny. She was a mystery and completely unpredictable as to what to expect. One minute everything seemed fine; then in a split second she would change and become a tyrant. He loved her, but he wished he had never married her. She seemed to only want a meal ticket and not a husband and family. Just maybe he was more captivated by her than in love with her. Whatever it was, he was not happy. In the mist of all this she slipped into bed and was all over him. She, and her very erotic honeymoon nightgown, had gone completely unnoticed. She was about to start making magic to lure him into her trap. She turned on her side and very skillfully exposed most of her breast just short of the nipple. He always went nuts when she did that; he did love the nipples and was definitely a breast guy. He loved to touch, kiss, and suckle them with great skill, and she had to admit she really looked forward to that part of the lovemaking the most. Something wasn't working because he didn't respond, so she began to slowly kiss him on his cheeks, then his nose, the forehead, and finally the lips. Still no reaction except to push her away; this was not the plan at all. He finally said to stop; he was too tired. She became even more aggressive and mounted him and began to gyrate slowly at first then increased the movement in an effort to stimulate and excite him. She felt the erection begin and at that she removed his tee shirt and next his undershorts. She was now moving with an added frenzy as she felt herself becoming more and more excited and could feel her body responding.

Suddenly, in the midst of this excitement, Eddy pushed her off, saying not too kindly, "I told you to knock it off. I'm not interested in any kind of sex tonight. I'm tired; leave me alone. I'll let you know when I'm ready to make love to you, and it won't be soon." With that said he reached for his shorts and shirt, put them on, turned on his side with his back to her, and went to sleep. She was stunned and hurt at the same time. This was not her first rodeo, but it certainly was her worst. He didn't even try to take off her gown or touch her except to push her off. She felt tears burn her eyes as total humiliation came over her. Sleep didn't come to Jenny that night. Sunrise was very slow to come. It was one of the most miserable nights of her life. This was a side of Eddy that she had never seen. It was also a side which she hoped she would never see again. Thankfully, sleep did come to her at morning's first light.

Eddy woke up, took a shower, dressed, and went to work without a sound.

Chapter 16

Let's Not Forget Angie

Angie's life had become frantic. Between night school and working all day at the beauty shop she had very little time for socializing. She was out in the real world now. While she was in beauty school, every student there was led to believe they would be making one or two hundred dollars a week. The problem was this was only a half truth. Unfortunately, by the time you made your guarantee, which meant if the beautician was making one hundred dollars a week she had to bring in revenue of twice the salary, which was a minimum of two hundred dollars. If you had no following, there was little to no money left for a salary. They encouraged all the new operators to not get discouraged. As soon as they built up a following, they would be in good shape. However, at the rate Angie was going, she wouldn't be able to pay for her next night school class. Her father told her to slow down and make some money first and then take the night school class. Angie, however, had other ideas and was unwavering in her plan. Needless to say, there was very little time for fun.

The lost ring was becoming a dim memory, though from time-to-time she would look at her empty finger where the golden ring once shone and wonder what had really happened to it. She was haunted by the same suspicion, that someone at the beauty school had taken it. At the time it never entered her mind that anyone had stolen the ring, but now it seemed to be the only realistic answer to the mystery. It never made any sense. One second it was on the vanity, and the next it was gone. The only person in the room besides the client was Jenny, and she swore that she didn't see it anywhere. Logic made her think Jenny picked it up. Since the day she spouted off with that hateful comment about Angie being plain, she had acted as if she was an enemy. She invited all the guys and girls from the school to her wedding except Angie. It had really hurt her feelings at first, but she found out later that most of them didn't bother to attend. They all thought Jenny had lost her mind and should see a shrink.

That was the great thing about the people there at the school; they called it the way they saw it. They had seen a lot and could spot a phony right away. The Frankie's and Jenny's of the world just wanted to be someone they were not. Frankie's wife divorced him and ended his dream of a string of beauty shops and spas all over the city. She did it on her own and was very successful. She had a good partner, and they branched out into beauty schools. As for Jenny, no one had heard from her to get any updates on what she was doing. All of the new beauticians who graduated with Angie were having the same struggle. No two stylists ended up in the same salon. As a result they were all solo on the work front. Angie slowly built her customer base in a very nice department store. It was hard, but Angie discovered that she had to sell herself and convince the client that she was confident and capable of cutting their hair and styling it in a flattering way. That was really all the client wanted. Putting it simply, they wanted to look as good as possible, and her job was to accomplish that. It was a service which she was providing. Why the instructors at the school did not spend more time on this phase of the career was a mystery to her. The stylists in this salon were all adults in their thirties, forties, and fifties with a wealth of life's experiences. It was an education just listening to them. Angie was once again the youngest member of the crew. Not only was she the youngest, but she looked like the youngest which inevitably left her with the problem of proving herself over and over again. She was always given the leftover clients when everyone else was busy. They weren't the once-a-week shampoo and set and comb out patrons, but more like the special occasion type of customer. This made it a struggle to make her guaranty and less money , but the tips were good. She knew that eventually she would get that following if she kept plugging away. All of her clients always requested Miss Angie whenever they needed an appointment. This was a very good sign and was definitely the road toward a following.

The talk in the breakroom, when things were slow that is, was about rotten marriages, awful boy- and girlfriends, and where they were going to go after work for Happy Hour. There were those who didn't take part in these conversations and were happy with where they were and what they were doing. Very few were thinking that this was just a temporary stop on their way to something better.

Jill Birdy was one of the younger ones in the crew and decided that Angie needed someone to take her under their wing to teach the ins and outs of the real world. She approached Angie one morning and asked her if she had any appointments for the next half hour. Angie looked up puzzled and answered, "No, not till 10:30."

Jill motioned to her and said, "Come on. Let's take a coffee break." Angie looked up in surprise and said, "I didn't think you could leave the floor until your lunch hour."

"Follow me. I'll show you how it's done." They made their way to the front desk. "Hi, Pam, is there any action?" Jill asked the receptionist.

"Nothing for the next hour. Good time for a break."

"Good, mark Angie and me out for a break." With that the two were on their way to a coffee break.

"You know, Angie, you would get more action if you looked a little more stylish. It wouldn't take much—a pair of flashy earrings, some hair accessories, some beads or scarves to give the plain white uniform a little pop. You don't need to spend a lot of money, and you have a discount in this store. The junk jewelry is very inexpensive. Let's go to the jewelry counter and see what we can find."

Angie was surprised but also grateful for the help. She had known she was definitely not in step with the crew. The receptionist was all decked out with makeup, jewelry, high heels, great dresses— the whole works. Not that she wanted to look that way, but she didn't want to look like little orphan Annie either. In less than fifteen minutes, Angie had picked out two pairs of earrings and some other accessories which she was very happy with.

"You know you don't need to wear a white uniform here, don't you, Angie? You can wear regular clothes, just nothing over the top. Only the shampoo girls wear the white uniforms."

"I was wondering about that. Pam more or less indicated that I should wear a white uniform. That's why I wear it," Angie was saying.

"All I have to say about that is lose it and lose it quick. One more thing you have to do. Make up to Pam because she's the one that has the power to send the clients to your station. If she doesn't like you, no good clients will be sent your way. Get my drift?" That was Jill's last piece of advice. "Now let's get back before we're missed."

Angie was amazed that Jill had taken the time to "mother hen" her and try to give her good advice as to what would help her get ahead with this new career.

The next morning, a new and improved Angie showed up for work. She had taken Jill's advice and was warm and friendly to Pam who became one of her best friends. She was making a huge leap into a new and improved Miss Angie, her professional name. Things were actually looking up in the beauty shop.

Angie still had her friends from the neighborhood and would spend some time with them when they came home for school breaks. It was great to have such friends. Whatever happened to her class ring didn't matter now anyway. Circle City High School was behind her, and she was more interested in her future. She was sad when she thought of how difficult her great plan had turned out to be. Even so, the graduation was a wonderful memory, and if it had not been for Barbara, she would not have had a date for the Grad Dance. She still went out with Jimmy when he came back to town, but they were just good friends.

Those fun days were replaced with hard working days. The sad part of the whole plan was that she really never liked being a beauty operator. That was one thing she had not factored into the equation. She was determined to work hard and make a success of it all, though. Angie had a lot of hard experiences in the overall adventure into the adult world. All of the gang that Angie hung out with were enjoying the activities and the atmosphere that school offered. They all knew that if they blew it, the chances of going on to college or the university and having a good career would be gone. Most of the people at the University of Cosmetology had already blown most of their opportunities or worse still, never had any opportunities at all. They had made bad choices, and in a last ditch effort they were trying to get a trade in order to make a living and make a better life. Not all of the students were that way, but a large population was. There were some great stylists who were doing quite well. They were so good that they actually had appointments and made big tips. The rest were trying very hard to get a following.

Angie had never frequented beauty shops before she went to beauty school, so she never knew that clients actually tipped you. What a dummy she was in those days. It was all behind her now, and she was still working and still depending on the tips to help pay for the night school class.

Some nights she was so weary she would fall into a sound sleep on top of her homework papers. All her friends were rooting for her to succeed. The only big bonus was that Angie always had a great hairdo. The fact she was dealing with all kinds of people and temperaments was another problem she had not anticipated. It was really good training, not only for the beauty shop, but as she discovered, it was also a good asset for nursing. This was all part of business.

***

Baby brother Bobby was a lot of fun to play with, but Athena still acted as if Angie was an intruder in the house. Athena thought since Angie was working now, she should be moving into her own place or at the very least paying room and board while she was living in the house. No matter what Angie did, it was never quite enough for Athena. She was really looking forward to the day when she could be on her own and not have to hear her stepmother's constant nagging. In a matter of time, she would be able to save enough money to move on campus and work in a shop closer to school; then everyone could be happy. Angie vowed that once she moved, she would never come back to this house again. She could never understand why Athena was always after her no matter what she did and how much she tried to help and take care of the baby. She saw no reason to return only to see her father. There was no way Angie could pay rent and continue with night school. She came home late at night after her class, sometimes ten o'clock, sometimes later. This relieved some of the pressure at home, but she really missed seeing Sammie and Bobby as a result. She would see them in the morning at breakfast, but even that was a touchy time. Things were getting tense between her stepmother and her father. Athena would always find something to say that would upset Basil, and the kids would get tense. Angie decided it would be best if she left the house before they all came down for breakfast to avoid any unpleasantness for everyone's sake. She always had the hope that things would be different. It was a mystery as to what actually was driving Athena's unreasonable attitude. She was totally unreasonable about everything when it came to Joey, Sammie, and Angie. It was almost as if she were jealous of the memory and any connection to the first marriage. Angie was not going to leave Sammie in that house alone. As long as Athena knew that Angie was coming home, she would lay off Sammie. Basil was getting older, and the pressure of all this tension was very hard on him. Angie tried hard to reassure him and let him know she loved him very much, but Athena didn't like it when she tried to speak to her father alone. In a few short months, Joey would be home for Christmas break, and that was something Angie would be looking forward to. At this time, her only goal was to keep the household at a low stress level. Other than a few letters, she had not heard much from Joey this semester. She imagined that he was busy trying to survive the pressures of school just as she was herself. No one could possibly have imagined how challenging the work load was in higher education.

Chapter 17

What of Molly in Ireland?

Molly, sweet thing that she was, decided that the ring was with her and unless Mrs. Edward O'Donnell inquired about it, she would keep it. After all, what else could she do? If there were mystical powers in the ring, she would be happy to use them for her own good fortune. She was not a greedy woman, but she had been a domestic servant all her life. As she got older, she became the upstairs maid. By that stage she was a full-fledged maid. It was time for her to make some changes. Perhaps she would meet the love of her life and live happily ever after.

Molly was singing a little Irish tune as she walked to Mrs. O'Donnell's house. Today she didn't need to stop at the Butcher Shop to pick up anything. She was going directly to the O'Donnell's so she could get started with her chores early. As she approached the house, she saw workmen about the lawn, which was very strange indeed. The mistress hadn't told her anything about expecting workmen.

"Good morning to you. What are you doing here this fine day? My mistress didn't speak of any work being done here."

The workmen looked up at her. The older of the two stood up and walked over to Molly and began to explain. "I fear there is a problem in the pipes, miss," he explained. "We were called to fix it for Mrs. O'Donnell. You go on about your chores and leave us to do our jobs. We'll be calling you as soon as it's fixed."

Molly nodded her head and went into the house. She hung up her cloak and went about her work. As the day went on there was still no word as to what the problem was, nor had Mrs. O'Donnell returned to the house. She must have gone to tea with her friends, thought Molly. Her thoughts were disturbed by a loud knock on the door. She opened it to find the older workman. "Sorry I am to disturb you, miss, but we be having a serious problem. All the pipes need to be replaced, and I need to talk to Mrs. O'Donnell."

"I'm sorry sir, but I don't know where she is. Can you leave a bill, and she will call you when she returns?"

"I'll do that, but no water till herself makes the call. "

Molly continued with her work. When her mistress arrived home, she gave the workman's message to her and she made the call. Molly was finishing up her work when there was a knock at the door. This time the younger worker stood on the other side of it. She was greeted with a bright smile and a single rose. "Hello, young lady, for all the trouble caused by no water, methinks yourself deserves this beautiful rose."

Molly was so taken aback that she stood there frozen, then out of nowhere the words, "now do you now," came out of her mouth much to her own shock. He proceeded to place the rose into Molly's hand. "Go on with you now. I think this special treatment is for my mistress, not for me."

"I saw you yesterday at the Butcher Shop, and today, here we are together working at the same address. I think the Saints are smiling down on us this very moment. They call me Mickey, and you are?"

Molly could not believe her eyes, or her ears. This was indeed the most unusual introduction she had ever heard.

"I beg your pardon, sir, but what do you think you are doing? I am at work, not at a pub asking for a pint!" She fired back at him. "I am not that kind of girl. What an idiot you are, and my mistress in the next room. Now go along with you."

Mickey bowed grandly and put her rose back into her hand with a tiny smile on his lips. "We'll be together; it's in the stars." He jumped up and clicked his heels and walked away none the worse for the tongue lashing he had received from the beautiful Molly. Under his breath he murmured, "Now that is some woman, and she's the woman for me"

Molly was totally flustered. How dare that common laborer be so bold? She was mortified. She was a lady, not some street walker. She threw the rose into the trash and continued her work. The workmen returned and finished the job, and the water was working once again.

The next day Molly was very careful going to work, but she did have to stop by the Butcher Shop to pick up some meat.

As she passed through the threshold she was greeted cheerfully, "Top 'o the morning to you, Miss Molly." She gave a start to see the fresh young worker that had given her a rose yesterday. Giving a nod, she focused on the floor to avoid meeting his eyes for fear she would lose her temper or betray her true feelings of joy at receiving a cheerful greeting. In spite of all her efforts, she was unable to hide her pleasure in the attention she had received.

"You still are angry with me, my lovely Miss Molly? Had I not hoped you'd be over it what with me having a hot cup of Irish coffee waiting for you?"

"How did you know that I would be here and not my place of employment?" she managed to say. She was surprised he knew where she would be.

"Ah, my lovely Miss Molly, 'tis me heart you've stolen with your lovely face and every step you make. You come here twice a week. 'Tis happy I am to see you today."

"Mr. Mickey, it would seem you'd have better things to do than check on my comings and goings. Thank you very much for the Irish coffee. It's a good way to start a day. You're a man of many surprises, you are. Yesterday it was a rose and this morning a heartwarming cup of Irish coffee. Me heart can't take on this charm."

"All this is done to win the heart of my lady, and I hope it is working. It's magic, it is."

"Go on with you now, stop this sweet talk. It's working magic making me doubt your intentions. Now go on with you before you go and break my heart." Molly even surprised herself with her answer. She turned hastily and walked out of the butcher's shop.

"Miss Molly, Miss Molly, wait you've forgotten your packages," Mr. Patrick called, but she was gone.

"Tis quick she is; quick as greased lighting. Don't trouble yourself. 'Tis my pleasure to fetch the parcel and deliver the same to her."

"Much obliged there, Mickey. I can't leave the store to deliver it to Mrs. O'Donnell's house."

"Tis my pleasure." Mickey picked up the package and started out the door.

Molly sprinted with record-breaking speed to get away from the Butcher Shop. As Mickey started down the street, he couldn't even catch a glimpse of her. She seemed to have disappeared. That was one unpredictable heartbreaker, if I say so myself, Mickey was thinking as he proceeded on his way to the house.

Molly was breathing hard not just from hurrying to the O'Donnell home, but also from the second encounter with Mickey. What was going on? Never in her life had anyone showered her with so much attention. It was enough to make a person go crazy. What did it mean? She was rude and acted disinterested, and still he persisted. This was too strange to understand. Surely he was just poking fun at her. To see what would happen. It was too much to bear to think that anyone would be making sport of her just to amuse himself. As these thoughts came to her mind her eyes began to fill with tears. The doorbell rang.

"Oh!" Molly said with a start. "Who would that be?" she asked, quickly wiping the tears with her apron.

Saints be praised ! It is him as big as life. He followed me home to torment me out of my mind.

Sensing trouble, Mickey knocked gently on the door and said, "Miss Molly, Miss Molly? You forgot your package of meat at the Butcher Shop, and I have it for you."

Slowly Molly peeked her head around the door as she opened it. "Glory to God, you brought it to me."

When Mickey saw her face he knew immediately that she had been upset by his advances. "Oh Miss Molly, I do apologize. I had no intention to offend you. Truly I am taken by you. Please come have a cup of tea with me and let me make it up to you."

"Maybe after work we can talk. Come by at five o'clock. We can have tea then."

"See you then," he said and handed her the package then turned on his heels and walked away.

Where was that ring? Molly asked herself. Was it in her purse? The ring might have power, but I don't like it at all. I must put it away some place where it will not cause me any more problems. This ring should be sent back to Mrs. O'Donnell to put an end to this misery and be done with it. She'd deal with it later and put an end to the whole thing.

Tea with Mickey was actually very pleasant. He was kind and funny, and she enjoyed it very much. He was working as an apprentice plumber with his uncle when Molly first saw him, and he was a student at the University and about to graduate. His conversation put her at ease, and she began to calm down as he talked to her. Oh to be a student at the University and make something of herself was her dream. She never intended to be a maid her whole life. Her mistress was very good to her, and she liked working for her, but she really wanted to be a writer. She loved to read, and she loved to write. The truth was that she hungered to learn all that she could. Mickey was hoping to be accepted into medical school after graduation. Such a fine future he would have before him. The apprentice plumber training was a fallback just in case med school did not materialize. She was beginning to like him more and more. However the likes of him would not be interested in the likes of her, her being a domestic worker and all.

Chapter 18

Who Is Molly and Who Is Mickey?

Molly had been a domestic worker since she was fifteen years old. She had worked for many years with her mother, learned the trade, and became a valued employee. She was extremely good with event planning and elegant dinner parties, as well as intimate gatherings. She knew how to arrange the tables, silver, dishes, and crystal. She was flawless in her serving skills and had been promoted to the post of training the rest of the staff. Due to her age, some of the older servants resented her instructing them. They felt they knew all that was needed to do the job sufficiently. As a result she was met with hostility and resistance when she tried to instruct them and was not very successful in her efforts. Molly was a shy person, and the staff's resentment had shaken her confidence. She was without question favored by Mrs. O'Donnell and tried very hard to live up to her expectations. This work was not the only work that Molly did. Many times Mrs. O'Donnell would lend her out to friends who needed a party planner. Molly was much cheaper than an actual party planner and always did a magnificent job. The friends were very generous in paying for her services, and it was a good way to make extra money.

Mickey was the son of the butcher, working part of the day helping his father prep the meats early in the morning. When he finished prepping the meat, he worked with Mr. Allen, learning the plumbing business. This was his safety net in the event that his application for medical school was denied. He was a big help to Mr. Patrick who would have loved for his son to join him in his butcher business, but young Mickey had his own ideas. He was very confident and loved life to the fullest. Even though Mickey helped his father, none of the customers were aware of this and had always assumed that he was in the plumbing business. That was of no concern to Mickey as he did whatever he chose to do without a second thought.

The games that people play when they try to impress others

are often misunderstood. Mickey was a straightforward type of person, and when he liked what he saw, he made no bones about going after it. Miss Molly was just exactly that. He liked what he saw, and what he saw was a lovely lady who had caught his eye and made him want to meet her. Molly, on the other hand, did not look for anything in particular. She put her nose to the grindstone and as a result, she was beginning to be known as a wonderful party planner.

When Mickey chose to pursue Molly, he was not discouraged by her rejections. In fact, he found it more alluring. He was planning to corner her at St. Patrick's Cathedral on Sunday and see what would happen when she saw he was serious about getting to know her much better.

Molly had become obsessed with the magic of the ring. All her thoughts were about returning the ring and getting rid of its curse. She was going to send it back to Miss Jenny and that was all there was to that.

Was there really magic in the ring? If it was truly magic, why did everything that was happening seem like a curse? Nothing seemed to be good. She had made up her mind that she would talk to her mistress. She would tell her the truth of how she found the ring on the floor by the luggage and picked it up. She would confess that she tried on the ring and couldn't get it off her finger in time to return it to the newlyweds. She foolishly believed the ring was actually magic. From that day forward everything that happened seemed to Molly to be very much a nightmare beyond understanding.

That afternoon Molly approached Mrs. O'Donnell shyly. "Pardon, mistress, would you have a moment to talk?"

"Of course. Let's sit at the kitchen table."

Mrs. O'Donnell led the way into the kitchen. White, lacy curtains were gathered back from large clean windows, allowing plenty of light into the room. The women pulled their chairs out and took a seat at the table. Molly rubbed her hands together nervously.

"What is it, dear?" Her mistress prodded.

Molly took a deep breath and began with the tale of how she came to find the ring and what had kept her from returning it before the young couple left for America. "I was so nervous and scared. When I couldn't get it off of my finger, I was certain that everyone would think I stole it."

The older woman nodded empathetically.

"Everything has changed since that ring be in my possession. I think it is cursed. I want to return it to Miss Jenny. Can you help me? "

"We will get that ring back to Jenny. Just leave it on the table here, and I will see to it."

"Thank you, Mrs. O'Donnell, thank you so much." It was as if a weight had been lifted off of her shoulders.

The mistress looked deeply into her eyes, "Molly, my child, there is no magic in this ring. It is just a ring and nothing more."

Molly nodded. Her mistress' reassurance calmed her a bit. "There is something else I need to talk to you about."

"Go on."

"Now, there be a young man appearing everywhere I go. He tells me that I've stolen his heart. " Heat burned her face as two crimson spots formed on her cheeks. "That can't be true. "

"And why can't it?"

Molly shrugged. "Try as I have to discourage him, he simply continues to show interest. Wherever I go, there he is. I fear going to the Butcher Shop. He always seems to be there."

Mrs. O'Donnell's sudden laugh shocked Molly. "Would the young man's name be Mickey?"

"Why yes." Molly answered in amazement.

"Well, then, of course he would be there. He is the butcher's son. He always helps him cut the meat for the day's customers. He's the one appearing everywhere you go?" Molly nodded with wide eyes. The mistress laughed again. "Molly, you should be pleased that he shows interest in you. He's a fine young man and comes from a good family. Mickey likes you because you are you and that is the truth. Now be gone with you and get your tasks done so you can go home early tonight. You've been working long days as it is. Off with you now."

Molly stood. "Thank you, again. My heart feels settled now that I've talked to you." She turned and left the room. Her problem with the ring was solved.

The difficulty with Mickey still needed to be dealt with. Was he really the problem she imagined? She did enjoy the attention he gave her. He was a very nice man, and it was very flattering that he was flirting with her.

Today was Friday, and she would have to go to the Butcher Shop to pick up the order for her mistress. Perhaps Mickey would be there. It seemed strange she was actually trying to run into Mickey.

As Molly walked to the Butcher Shop her heart raced. This is crazy, she thought to herself. Had she gone daft? One moment it was, she hated Mickey and the next, she couldn't wait to see him. This was going to drive her mad. The mistress said that Mickey was a nice young man, and her view of him changed very quickly. There was no magic ring that was needed to enchant this young man. He became enchanted on his own. Now Molly was finding that she was also becoming captivated. She could actually envision the two of them together. She entered the Butcher Shop and took a deep breath and looked around. Alas, there was no Mickey to be found. Mr. Patrick and she were the only ones in the store.

"Good afternoon, Miss Molly, and how you be this fine day?"

"Good afternoon, Mr. Patrick, would my mistress' meat order be ready?"

"I was just getting it ready. Would you like a cup of Irish coffee while you wait?"

"That would be lovely. Thank you very much." As Molly sipped her coffee while she waited, her eyes searched the room. She tried to peek into the backroom, but there did not seem to be anyone anywhere in the store but Mr. Patrick and herself. Molly's hope of running into Mickey was quickly fading. It was not going to be as easy to accidently run into him as she thought. She was too shy to ask Mr. Patrick where his son was. To show that much interest would be inappropriate for a young woman. There was a stool in the corner of the room, and Molly walked over to the stool and sat down and slowly sipped her coffee. Mr. Patrick set to work preparing Molly's order. A patron strolled into the store and walked up to the counter.

"Good afternoon, Miss Grace. I'll be with ye as soon as I complete this order."

"'Tis quite alright. I'll wait. Where is your handsome son today? He's usually in here to help you?"

"'Tis true, but he had tests at school and will be in when his class is over. I miss his help, I do. Today has been a very busy day. He must do well on his tests. 'Tis important for him. He wants to go to medical school and must have excellent grades to be accepted."

"He will do well. I know he is a good student. I was his teacher for two years."

Molly was very fascinated by this discussion of Mickey's scholastic standing. He was a good student and was also well thought of by his former teacher. These were all good signs of a good reliable man. She was very impressed and realized that she had underestimated him greatly. Embarrassment creep over her mind, and she was ashamed for the way she had acted toward Mickey. As Molly mulled over her thoughts, Mr. Patrick called out, "Miss Molly, happy you be to know your order is ready, it is."

"Oh thank you very much, Mr. Patrick, and be sure and tell Mr. Mickey that Molly said hello and good luck with his test." How shy Molly got those words out she could not say. She picked up the package of meat and was on her way.

Chapter 19

A New Journey–A New Home

"Where did the address go? I'm sure I put it into my desk drawer for safe keeping when Eddy and Jenny left for home. Now let me see. Everything is in such disorder. I should never have allowed the desk to reach this point of chaos." Mrs. O'Donnell was looking frantically in her desk drawer to find her address book, and it was nowhere to be found. She wished Molly would hurry back and help her. She began to take out one item at a time and place the papers in separate piles. Each pile was designed to organize the paper work in the desk drawer. There was one pile for paid bills, another for unpaid bills, and the last for odds and ends. The piles began to take shape and it became easier to recognize the contents of the desk drawer. Still no address book was found. Where could it be? She was mystified. She would have to call America and get the address from her newfound nephew, Eddy. That being settled in her mind, she set out to place the well-organized papers into the drawer. At this point of the project she promised herself she would never allow her personal desk drawer to ever get in such disarray again.

Molly came through the door with her arms full of packages from the Butcher Shop. She smiled at her mistress as she went into the kitchen to put the meat away. What a blessing it was to have Molly's help. The cleaning of the drawer had tired her more that she had realized.

She was going to have to call Eddy, so she picked up the telephone in the living room and dialed Eddy's number. The operator's voice announced that the number was no longer in service. What did this mean? Had something happened to the telephones in their small town? She decided to try again later in the day, after all, there was a six or seven hour difference in the time and that might have been the problem.

"Molly, please follow me upstairs. I need to find my address book. I seem to have misplaced it. We are going to start a reorganization project and get me organized today. This chaos is very hard to live with."

They ascended the stairway to the upper level. Molly was always ready to do whatever job was needed done. If organization was what she wanted today, that was what she was going to get. The small desk downstairs was just that, a very small desk with one small drawer. The desk upstairs, however, was much larger with four drawers on each side and a smaller drawer in the middle. It was full of all kinds of things. Molly thought it was going to be a big job. The mistress was already settled at the desk and was beginning to empty the center drawer. This was basically her pencil drawer, and it was full of pencils, pens, pads of paper, and such items. It was put into good order quickly. But the other drawers were a bit more complicated. They were cluttered and in disarray. It took some time to sort out the papers and try to get everything just as Mrs. O'Donnell wanted them, but there was no address book in that drawer. The next two drawers had the same result. After cleaning out and organizing all the other drawers the end result was the same—no address book. It was getting late and time for Molly to start home. She didn't realize the address book which the mistress was looking for was the very book that held the address for Miss Jenny and Mr. Eddy.

Mrs. O'Donnell tried Eddy's telephone number a second time. As destiny would have it, the out of service message was repeated. This disturbed her, and she decided to call Eddy's father. He picked up the phone on the second ring and was happy to hear from his cousin. When she asked about Eddy and Jenny, she was surprised to hear that things were not good between the couple. They had fallen on some financial problems and were not getting along very well at the present time. Eddy's father's voice fell from excitement to sadness, so she thought it best to change the subject quickly and explain the reason for her call and the missing ring that belonged to Jenny. She asked if he could give her their address so she could arrange to return the item. The address was given and the two bid each other goodbye and hung up.

Mrs. O'Donnell gathered the ring and the note she had written to Jenny and was getting ready to go mail it to America when she realized that she did not have the proper envelope to place it in so that it would not be damaged or lost. She would go to the post office in the morning and buy a small crush proof envelope that should work quite nicely. In the meantime she placed both ring and note into a regular envelope. While she was at it she would send Colleen, her niece, the Irish recipe book she had promised when she left for Greece a month before. Colleen was so homesick she wanted to cook some good old Irish stew.

Right on schedule the next morning, Mrs. O'Donnell made a trip to the post office to take care of her mail. Both envelopes were in her hand along with the addresses. She was not sure of the postage charge, but she was quite certain she had taken enough money to cover the cost.

Mrs. O'Donnell always looked forward to seeing the General Post Office in Dublin. It was one of Ireland's most famous buildings and always a thrill to see. She looked at the structure with admiration as she approached it.

She went directly to the window where she attained all the information needed. Hesitating for a moment, she collected her thoughts. First the crush proof envelopes, then the postage. That should do it. In exactly that manner Mrs. O'Donnell placed her order. The young lady behind the counter gave her all the information she needed and asked her to step over to the desk and fill out the addresses. At the desk, she proceeded to fill out the addresses and package up the items. No sooner had she started her task than Mrs. O'Malley came up to her and began a conversation about Miss Molly and her new beau, Mr. Mickey. Of course it took a little doing, but Mrs. O'Donnell finally convinced Mrs. O'Malley that there was nothing going on between Miss Molly and Mr. Mickey. After fifteen minutes of gossip, she was more than ready to finish her business and head home. She was going to meet two of her friends for tea early afternoon and was anxious to be on her way. Once Mrs. O'Malley bid her farewell, she continued addressing the envelopes. Sliding the contents inside, she sealed them and went to the counter again to pay the postage. Colleen's envelope would go to Athens, Greece and Jenny O'Donnell's would travel all the way to Riverville, Indiana, USA. It was strange that Jenny's envelope felt a bit heavier than Colleen's. It had to be due to all the confusion that was going on. She shrugged her shoulders. It was a small book and didn't weigh that much anyway. Everything was fine and the items were in the mail and on their way to the right people. The burden was lifted off her shoulders, and thank God for that.

Chapter 20

Jenny and Eddy

Life with Jenny and Eddy was not what it should be. There was constant conflict. Their relationship was very sensitive. There was very little conversation, except for the few zings they flung at each other. Eddy rarely came home before bedtime and stopped sleeping in the same room with Jenny.

It all exploded over the budget for the household and the extended hours for Eddy's Cool Deals. It was almost the same day that they had returned from Ireland. At first, Jenny had managed to gently stroke Eddy and win him over enough to lead him to believe that she was and had always been a loving, obliging wife. The game fell apart the moment Eddy let Jenny know that there was no extra money and that she would be on a strict budget and was going to receive an allowance which was to last her the entire month. Out of that allowance she was to pay for all the household bills. If there was any money left over she could shop for any personal items she might need. This was when Jenny's sweet talk and "I love you, honey" faded into an ugly altercation. As a result the two had never resolved any of the financial problems at hand.

Jenny had stopped cleaning the house right after the big blow-up. One morning, she woke up and looked around. Something brought her to her senses, and she decided that this was no way to live and started cleaning the house. She would never convince Eddy that she was sincere by acting the way she was and going on strike. So she began to clean first upstairs and then worked her way down. She began one room at a time and slowly cleaned up the entire house. Then she decided to wash Eddy's cloths which she did with reluctance. The thought of being a fool for Eddy really infuriated her, yet she knew that if something didn't happen to stop this entire situation she would never have any kind of married life with Eddy or anyone else for that matter.

It was a very nice three bedroom home with two baths upstairs and a very nice floor plan which flowed from room to room on the main floor, ideal for entertaining guests. She entered the kitchen and was struck with just how nicely the kitchen was designed. Because Jenny was fond of the color blue, she selected various shades of that color to paint the rooms. The effect was a beautiful. The house was a place that anyone would love to live. Yet here they both were totally miserable and not enjoying any of the things they had.

Standing in the kitchen wiping her hands dry after washing the last of the dishes, she walked to the living room and looked at the phone on the end table. She needed to talk with her husband. The last thing she wanted to do was call Eddy's Cool Deals. What if the receptionist answered the phone and wouldn't put her call through? This had to be done if any of the other actions were to do any good. After bickering back and forth with herself over whether or not to call, she found herself sitting at the telephone dialing the number to Eddy's Cool Deals. The voice on the other end of the line was indeed Maria, and surprisingly, she put the call through to Eddy.

"This is Eddy O'Donnell, how may I help you?"

"Eddy, this is Jenny, how are you?" She waited for an answer but received none. She continued. "I would like to get together with you and talk. Is that possible tonight?"

There was a long pause, and then he replied, "We don't seem to be able to have a conversation without a knock-down drag-out fight. I'm not up to that anymore. I think we should call it quits. I don't want to do this anymore."

As these words fell from his mouth, tears fell from her eyes.

"Eddy, please let's try to talk. You mean the world to me, and I just need to see you. A telephone break-up is not how this should end." These words came from her heart as she realized that Eddy was not interested in coming back to her but wanted to terminate their marriage.

"Meet me at the Corner Grill at 6 o'clock. We'll talk then."

Jenny hung up and dabbed the tears that had rolled down her cheeks dry. She knew Eddy had many reservations as to what good such a meeting would do, and that just made matters harder.

Things certainly weren't as easy to manipulate as when they first dated.

She looked around the house and cried. Her heart was weighted with great sorrow. Where did everything go wrong, she kept asking herself? Maybe she was a little too selfish with the wedding and house and honeymoon. Why did she not realize that Eddy was at the end of his rope? She thought that she could talk her way out of anything, and she was in real trouble now and would have to throw herself on Eddy's mercy and beg for a second chance.

She would have to face Eddy in one hour, and she had absolutely no idea what to say to him. He had been good to her she had to admit. She kept pushing for more and more, and she got it. She loved everything she had, but she found out that these things she loved and wanted were not really that important. They were not Eddy, and they did not take care of her.

The time had come to begin getting ready. She was going to make herself look as good as possible for Eddy. This was the most important meeting of her life, and she wanted to make the most of it. At 5:50 Jenny was on her way to the Corner Grill. She didn't want to be late.

Chapter 21

Can This Marriage Be Saved?

Eddy was running late but wasn't very concerned about it as he made his way to the Corner Grill. It was definitely a no-frills bar and grill. Even by Riverville's standards this place would not score well. The lighting was dim; one might think to hide the grunginess. The floor was bare to the concrete which was an ugly gray with a very worn-out look. The walls were old brick with paint flaking off to give an antique atmosphere as if it needed it. The Grill was what it was. Old and unkempt, but it had never stopped from being a preferred hangout. Above all the food was always good. Elegant would never be used in any description of this place. Jenny always wondered if the Board of Health paid regular visits to the establishment. The only comfort was that it had never been closed down for health violations.

Eddy turned the corner and walked into the Corner Grill, spotting Jenny sitting at a table in the back. He slowly walked toward her. She looked up and smiled, "Hello, Eddy."

Eddy nodded but made no move to give a greeting kiss or take her hand. This was going to be difficult. "You look very well."

"Thank you for coming. I know that this is not going to be easy for either of us. I'm only asking for a chance to put our marriage on the right track."

"It's a little late for that, don't you think? I'm weary of all the fighting, the quarrelling over money, and the lack of respect for my concerns with my business. It is all too painful to review. Then you went on strike and would not even keep the house clean. Did I deserve such treatment?"

In three short months she had managed to create a great deal of damage. She knew the charges. What she didn't know was how to fix things. "Eddy, please sit down. Let's have a hamburger and talk about all of this. I'm willing to change my behavior if only you would give me a chance."

"I don't have time for a hamburger. I've got to get back to the car lot. I'm open till ten o'clock tonight. I don't have anyone working except Maria, and she's been there since this morning."

"Wait, Eddy. Let me order two hamburgers and some fries to go, and I'll meet you at Eddy's Cool Deals, and we can eat and talk and you'll be able to catch every customer and Maria can go home and be fresh for the morning rush. What do you say, for old times' sake? After all, we have a life together. Can we give it a whirl?"

This would be called a hard sell. Eddy shrugged his shoulders and reluctantly agreed. He gave her a twenty dollar bill to pay for the food and left.

Jenny went to the counter and placed her order and waited for it to be filled.

When she heard, "O'Donnell," she jumped to her feet and paid for the food then left the Corner Grill with a positive attitude that things were going to work out in her favor.

The traffic was heavy and slow going as many people were heading home from work. A lot of the hometown people worked in the big city of Indianapolis and had a long commute home. She finally got to the car lot and parked the car. As she approached the office she saw Eddy and Maria laughing about something. Her positive mood started to fade. She felt the sting of jealousy. She could not remember a time that she and Eddy had had a good laugh together. What had happened to them? What went wrong? More tears came to her eyes, but she quickly recovered and remembered why she was there.

Jenny carefully entered as Maria was just coming out of the office. She braced herself to stay calm and be as jovial as possible. "Hi, Maria, it's been a while since I've seen you. You look great!"

"Thank you Mrs. O'Donnell. You look lovely tonight." She said almost warmly. Jenny moved on to her husband's office

"Eddy, dinner is served," she said as she walked through the door.

Eddy motioned for her to sit down in the empty chair. "Did you bring something for Maria?" he asked as she set the sandwiches down.

Jenny looked up in surprise. "I thought this was going to be a sandwich for just you and me," she answered, about to burst into tears. "You and Maria go ahead and eat. I'll talk to you later. I must have misunderstood everything."

"No, wait. Maria needs to go home to her family. She's been here all day already." With that said Eddy called Maria into the office and told her to call it a day and go home. He would take care of everything.

Jenny sat down and the two of them began to share the fries and hamburgers. They were really good especially since they were both starving.

"Look, Jenny, we've had a bad patch for the last four months. This is the first time I've spoken to you in a month. By the time I get home you're asleep and when I leave in the morning you're still asleep. As if that was not enough, I have to make a path just to keep from falling to and from the bathroom. I don't know what to do to please you except let you spend all the money you can for as long as you can. I tried to explain that we had to get a handle on our spending. The wedding was very expensive. The ring, the dress, the trip, all of those things added up and unless we get those bills under control, I would not be able to keep the doors of Eddy's Cool Deals open." Eddy paused to take a breath. "I have been able to begin paying down a lot of the bills a little at a time. The bank has been very understanding because I have always been a good customer and have always paid my bills on a timely basis. That has a lot to do with how the banking industry looks upon their clients and how much they are willing to loan them to help expand their businesses."

Jenny looked at Eddy with new eyes. "Oh Eddy, I know I've behaved badly, and I want to apologize for all my actions these past few weeks. I want to make it up to you. Please give me the opportunity to do whatever is needed to do to prove to you that I am sincere. I could help you here at the lot, maybe learn to sell cars or even take over Maria's job in order to save her salary until we are free of debt. Anything you need." Jenny herself could not believe what she was saying, but she really meant it. Eddy was quite taken aback by this little speech. He knew that Jenny was the master of manipulation and was very hesitant to believe her.

She always knew exactly how to push all the buttons that sent him in a lovesick puppy mode. He was not about to fall victim to her wiles. He must be strong and remain strong.

"Let's take this slow. You have to understand that Maria has been with me helping me hold this place together. I'm not terminating her to save the small salary that she makes. She needs that income to help feed her children and pay her rent. We need to start slowly and see where we are by this time next week. What do you say?"

This was a great plea that Eddy was making, Jenny was thinking, as she watched him in wonder. How could she have underestimated him so much?

"Eddy let me stay with you tonight and help you close the lot. We can go home together and have a dish of ice cream and just try to be friends."

"That all sounds great, but it will take a little time to get comfortable with each other. You can stay till closing, and we can have ice cream, but that's as far as it will go. I am still going to sleep in the guest room tonight. Is that agreeable to you?"

For the first time ever Jenny found herself humbled by the words that Eddy was saying. She realized that he had offered her a gift, and she was going to take it.

Just then a customer came into the office, and Eddy went out to help him.

The meeting was not all what Jenny had hoped for, but it was a start. They were definitely starting from a very different position than they had left off.

All of Jenny's efforts to clean up the house and put everything in order were not futile. As soon as Eddy stepped into the house he was not only impressed but also very pleased. "Wow!" Eddy said with a bright look of surprise. "This is amazing." That was as far as the comment went. However there was definitely approval in his eyes. Jenny being Jenny was not interested in being a maid, but for now she would go along with the mood which was being set. There was still much work to be done to get this marriage back on track. This was just a small peace offering.

The next day the envelope from Ireland arrived in the mail. When Jenny opened it, she found a cookbook from Eddy's aunt. She was puzzled at the gift of an Irish cookbook, but it was a sweet thing for her to do. She would send her a nice thank-you note.

Chapter 22

Colleen

At the same time Jenny received the cookbook, Colleen, in Athens received an identical envelope from Mrs. O'Donnell. She examined it very carefully and turned it over several times before carefully opening it. Not only was Colleen mystified by the envelope, but she was also shocked by it. When she had last talked to her aunt, she remembered mentioning an Irish cookbook, but there was no likelihood a cookbook could be in this crushproof envelope. Perhaps some recipes, but certainly no book. It would have been much heavier if it contained a cookbook. It was time to stop guessing and open the thing and see what it was. She reached for a knife and proceeded to open the well-sealed package. The seal finally broke open and out fell a note and a gold ring. What is this? She opened the note and read it very carefully. The note was addressed to a Jenny, clearly not her, and the ring belonged to her. Oh dear, Colleen thought. Her aunt had evidently mailed the two packets at the same time and mixed up the addresses. What to do was the question. She decided to do nothing unless her aunt discovered the mistake herself . The cookbook would have been nice but if there was one thing that Greece had was an abundance of delicious foods of all kinds. She had just arrived in Athens with her husband, Mimi, when she requested the Irish cookbook. That was well before she discovered all the amenities of Greece. Delicious food was certainly one of them. Greece was a beautiful country, rich with history and ruins. There was a taverna and a coffee house on every corner, along with beautiful old churches. The sun was always bright, and the night life was unbelievable. She had come to love the country almost as much as Ireland. Colleen looked down at the ring and thought that it was indeed very unique. It looked like some kind of a school ring. No matter what it was, she was keeping it unless her aunt requested it be sent back to her. Colleen slipped the ring on her finger, and it fit perfectly. That settled that. The ring would remain with her until such time as her aunt requested its return. It now appeared that the ring had a new owner and a new home.

Who would have ever guessed that this little class ring from Circle City High School would travel so far and find so many owners?

Chapter 23

What About Angie?

If anyone had asked Angie what had been going on in her life, she would most likely answer not much. This would probably be the understatement of the day. Two years had gone by since the graduation and dance.

Barbara was still her best friend and confidant. Jimmy was still a good friend, and Athena still wanted her to move out of the house. Baby brother, Bobby, was growing fast and soon would be going to preschool. Even though there was non-stop action going on around her, Angie still felt as if nothing much was happening. Then without any warning, Joey came home on an unexpected visit. Angie was so happy to see him. She ran and hugged him with all her might. Joey was home—what a treat.

Basil was also very happy to see him. "We didn't think you would get home until spring break," his father said. "To what do we owe this pleasant surprise visit? Come in. We're about to have lunch. Let's eat and then we will deal with whatever is on your mind. Angie come in with us. You're so busy these days that we never see you."

They all went into the kitchen. It was such a delight to have the whole family sit down and have lunch. Little Bobby climbed on Joey's lap and began to play with him. This is how it was when Joey came home, and it was wonderful. For the first time in a long time, there was a real family lunch.

After the meal, Athena took Bobby up to his bedroom and put him down for his nap.

"Dad I need to talk to you about something very serious."

"Alright let's sit down in the living room and talk. Is this a private matter or can Angie and Athena join us?"

"That will be alright, after all this is a family matter. Everyone needs to hear what is going on and help me make some decisions." Joey took several deep breathes before beginning. "Everyone knows that the future is very uncertain at the present time. The Korean police action is ratcheting up and there is talk of the Draft taking students out of school and sending them overseas. As if that is not enough, there is a lot of speculation that Vietnam will be needing help next. If this happens as they are predicting, everyone will be called up and drafted."

Basil looked at his son in silence as he was trying to understand exactly what Joey was saying. "Are you saying that you have been drafted?"

"Not yet, but I'm a senior this year, and my grade average is very good. More than likely I will be able to finish and graduate with my degree in Pre-Law. I have been offered a full scholarship to Harvard Law School. If I accept, there is a very good chance that I can avoid the draft for the next three years."

His father stood there silently. Then he said very calmly, "What do you need to do this?"

"I will need a five hundred dollar deposit and a lot of praying. The scholarship will be mine as soon as I pay the deposit. I will take a test which is to prove that I deserve the scholarship. Then I will be exempt until I graduate or my grades fall below the four point average which is the required grade average I must maintain. I wish I could say that I wanted to fight for my country, and I would if I had to, but I am not cut out to be a soldier. I would do more good by getting my degree and joining the military afterward."

"I have no problem with the five hundred dollar deposit. I'll write a check for you today. Is there an application I need to fill out also?"

"Yes, it's right here. I already filled out my part; the rest you will need to do. We must get it in by next week. Thanks, Dad. I'll try to do the best I can and be a good lawyer."

"I know you will. I have always known that you were capable of great things. This is proof that others have seen your aptitudes also. If you do not finish this degree now and are drafted you might never go back and finish your education. The war will go on and much as we all love and long for peace it has become increasingly difficult to achieve. Go forward and make something of yourself. We love you and support you all the way."

Chapter 24

The Tee-Pee Gathering

"Come on, Angie, I'm taking you out to the Tee-Pee. Everyone will be there tonight." Joey had already checked and all the old friends were coming.

The Tee-Pee was the same drive-in restaurant where Angie and Jimmy and Barbara and Chris had gone for dinner before the Grad Dance when they had double dated. It was a great place to eat and just hang out. Outside there were parking spots where you were served by the car hops. Most of the young kids, sixteen- to eighteen-year-olds liked to eat outside in their cars. It was always fun, and the car hop crowd loved driving around the parking lot to see who was there. The college kids went inside. That was the unwritten rite of passage to adulthood. The inside restaurant was very nice, and it always had great food and a pleasant atmosphere. An enjoyable mix of young adults and older adults would go for dinner or an after show snack. Of course, there was always the usual family dining. There was a dress code that everyone happily followed. There was never any trouble inside or outside the restaurant. It seemed that everyone respected and appreciated this meeting place and wanted it to always be around.

As they arrived, they saw Jimmy sitting at a table. He was home for the weekend and wanted to see Joey and especially wanted to get together with Angie.

Angie was so pleased to see everyone, but she really would have been disappointed if Jimmy had not been there.

She had been working hard to finish her two night school classes. It was evident to her that she would not be able to graduate in the timeframe she had hoped. At the rate she was going, she would not be able to go to nursing school for at least two more years. She had built a good steady clientele at the salon which stabilized her income. Stable money did make it much easier to pay for classes and just knowing that she could count on a steady amount of money every two weeks made life a lot less stressful. She had hoped that she would be able to double up and get more classes into her schedule, but it was too difficult to work fulltime and still make the grades. All the planning in the world could not make time stand still, and it was clear that many of Angie's friends would graduate from the University before she could complete her first year of study.

Angie noticed that Jimmy and Joey were in the corner talking very quietly. She started to walk over to say hi to Jimmy when she heard her name. She turned and saw Barbara standing by the door with her boyfriend, Chris. The two girls hugged each other. It has been a long time since they had seen each other; they began catching up on life immediately.

University life was an altogether different type of life from what Angie had been living here at home. The major difference was that Angie's social life was sadly lacking in excitement. When she heard Barbara talk about her sorority and the parties and dances that were going on, Angie suddenly realized that she would never experience this kind of campus life. Her goals were strictly academic; between work and school she was covered up and had almost no downtime. Angie did not even take time out to go to the campus and visit Barbara, even though she had been invited many times. She would lose too much money if she did not work Friday and Saturday. The weekends were two of the biggest days in the beauty shop. Everyone was busy all day. This was the plan she had set out, and it was essentially a good plan. The problem was that her timetable was off as to how long it would take to complete. While Angie was talking to Barbara, Jimmy came up behind her and covered her eyes. "Guess who?" He laughed. Angie turned quickly and literally fell into Jimmy's arms. Everyone laughed, but Angie blushed and tried to recover.

"I have been gone too long to let you go that fast."

"Jimmy!" She turned and planted a great big kiss on his lips, and he responded with equal enthusiasm. Everyone that was watching applauded.

Angie was mortified. How could she have been so bold as to kiss Jimmy? *And on the lips.* That wasn't her style, but then what was her style? Whatever it was, it was not all that successful. Perhaps it was time to step things up a bit. She had missed Jimmy while he was away at school, and she wanted him to know that she was very happy to see him again.

Jimmy leaned down and whispered into Angie's ear "Let's go to the table; I want to talk to you."

They both walked toward the table and sat down. Jimmy ordered a soda for Angie and him, and as they were sipping their drinks, Jimmy started the conversation. "I know we had agreed to be good friends and not be romantically involved. You have to understand that I really love you, Angie. I love the way you have worked hard just to send yourself through school, and I know that you will succeed. I love your loyalty to your friends and family. In fact, there is nothing that I do not love about you. I want you to know that my intentions are honorable and always will be honorable."

"Jimmy, I'm touched, deeply touched, but we're both still in school and need to finish and get our degrees."

"Angie, I've been drafted into the army, and I am waiting for my orders."

"Oh, Jimmy, I should have known. Joey came home and told us basically the same thing."

"Joey is lucky he is going on to graduate school, and with his grades he will be exempt for the next three years. I don't have his grade point average and will have to serve. I will possibly be sent to Korea or Vietnam."

"Jimmy, I didn't know that you were already drafted. Up to now there was only talk of the wars going on in the Far East. Now it hits home. You and how many more of our classmates will be going into the army? You will have to put your life on hold and hope that you can pick it up again when you get discharged."

"I will pick it up, and I will be a successful lawyer. That is my dream and will always be. I want to be a lawyer, and I will be. When I return, law will still be my career of choice. You are the one that I want to spend the rest of my life with. I want to marry you when I get back. I want to make all our dreams come true. It would be too selfish of me to ask you to wait. I will always have you in my heart, and when I return we will work on getting to know each other again. I'm sure that we will both be different. I'm also sure I could search the rest of my life and never find another Angie. Please just keep a spot in your heart for me."

"Jimmy, no matter what, you will always have a very special place in my heart. You will come back and maybe you will have changed your mind about me by then, but we will always be friends."

"That is the quality I love most about you, Angie. You plan far ahead and are willing to make concessions and give a guy space. Will you write me while I'm gone? I know that I am not the greatest one about writing, but I will do my best to keep in touch with you."

"I will keep in touch with you as long as it takes for your return," she replied.

"Hey you two, what are you up to over in this corner," Barbara was saying as she approached the table. She could see that the two were deep in conversation. They both looked up and saw Barbara and motioned her to sit down. She sat down and said more to herself than to anyone around her. "They have drafted Chris. He will be leaving for basic training next week."

It seemed that the news of the war and the young men being drafted was the big topic being discussed. Jimmy looked up and said, "Me, too."

Barbara began to cry. This was all too much for all them. Out of the ten young men who were at the Tee-Pee, nine were called to duty by the Draft Board, only Joey was exempt for graduate school. Joey felt guilty, but he could do nothing. His opportunity came because of his high grade point average and the fact that he was going into Law School. The others were either in Liberal Arts or did not have the grades to qualify for an exemption. It all seemed unfair and difficult to understand.

The United States had just finished World War II, and now they were embarking on what they called a Police Action. Many young men would be drafted and sent overseas to fight, but why? What was happening in the world that had changed so much? It had gone from the innocent times of high school and college to war and dying. During the peace process, they saw pictures of Roosevelt, Churchill, and Stalin taking a meat cleaver and chopping up Arabia, Germany, and many other countries. Never had a country come together and shown true patriotism as they did during WWII. Now instead of peace, there was a police action. Instead of being allowed to finish school, there was a mandatory draft in place. WHY, WHY, WHY? They were all young and carefree and now over half were off to war. When would it stop? These were all questions which would never be answered to anyone's satisfaction. Angie could still remember as a child sitting in church and seeing the young men in the community coming to church in their Army uniforms and going up to take communion before they left for war. It seemed that a great deal of time passed before we saw them again. Some never made it back. That was when their name would be added to a plaque which was hanging on the wall for all to see. The memory of the return of these fine young men seemed very much like a moving picture show. The difference was that they were looking at real life heroes and honored them in like fashion.

Angie recalled these events that happened when she was very young as she sat with her friends; memories which she would never forget. Imagine her shock when she realized that these heroes were not that much older at the time of their draft than Joey and Jimmy and all of the rest of the boys at the Tee Pee that very night. They were young men and women just graduated from high school when they were drafted. Now here goes another draft looming over the heads of all the eligible young men. When will all of this end? They all hugged each other and said goodbye for the evening, but there was a cloud over all of them that night.

As Angie and Joey were walking home, a flood of memories filled her mind and began playing like a movie. She saw herself walking down the street and looking from home to home. She was just a small girl, wondering why so many windows were displaying red banners with white stars. Other homes were displaying gold banners with one white star. What did that mean? She asked her mother what they mean. Rebecca explained that a red banner with a white star indicated that this family had a son in the armed forces, but a white banner with a gold star indicated a soldier lost his life. There were many white stars and too many gold ones.

As this movie quit playing, another began. The vision was Rebecca at the grocery store shopping. She was asked to give her rationing stamps, food and gasoline were limited, and everyone cooperated because it was war time. It was a time of separation and sacrifice. The song that was being sung was a song of hope for a safe return. You would hear them sing "Don't Sit Under the Apple Tree With Anyone Else But Me" and "I'll Be Seeing You." Heart-breaking, but all who heard these songs romantically awaited their sweetheart's return and for happily ever after to begin. How sad when one realizes that war does not solve anything. It not only takes lives of innocent people, but it also steals the soul and youth of a young soldier and turns him into a man far too early. When the war ended, all were joyous and stood ready to help in any way they could.

Tonight they had come full circle. The joy of victory in WWII still echoed in their ears. Here they were with another war—only it was called a police action. The best of the best were being called on once again into the service of their country.

Joey left to go back to school and prepare for the big test he was about to take. Jimmy left for school for an entirely different reason. He had to move all of his things out of the dorm and take everything home. He would return to school when all of this was over.

Angie continued to plug away at work and night school. Jimmy got his orders summoning him to Fort Knox for basic training. He called Angie and told her he would get in touch with her when he had his first furlough to come home. Angie was excited to hear this news as she really did not expect to see him for a very long time. This was the beginning of the waiting period, to hear news of Jimmy and what was happening. Time seemed to drag by with no word, until finally Jimmy called to tell her he was coming home for a week. This was great news.

Angie made sure to clear her calendar to have as much time with Jimmy as possible. There was only one day that would be a problem, but she felt sure she could work it out. She had received several letters from Jimmy while waiting for the first furlough. He had told her that none of the guys from school went to Fort Knox for basic training. He had made friends with several young men from the South but had no idea how they would form the division when it was time to leave basic training. He had applied for the

Military Police, better known as MPs. His second choice was the tank corp.

All this military talk was difficult for Angie to follow. All she knew was that Jimmy was coming home for a week, and she could not wait to see him.

Finally the day of Jimmy's arrival came. He entered into town very quietly. His mother picked him up at the bus station, and she cried, hugged and kissed him after he climbed off the bus. This was a huge event for all of them. Jimmy loved his family, and why wouldn't he? They were a great family. His mother had told Angie no matter who heard from Jimmy first to let the other know.

Jimmy called Angie as soon as he was free from the family and told her he would be over to see her. When she opened the door she was shocked when she saw Jimmy's G.I. haircut. They both had a good laugh which they both needed. They talked and made plans for the rest of the day. Angie's father came in and greeted Jimmy and told him how proud he was to have him serving in the army. Basil had always been proud of the US armed forces. He always said they helped all Europe and liberated Greece, among many other countries. He would always be grateful for that.

Jimmy was unquestionably different. He was always trim, but he was very fit now. Of course the haircut really made him look different. These were merely differences to his appearance. His manners were filled with yes, sir and no, sir. He seemed to be more edgy as of late. He looked tired. He was a little distant at first until Angie wrapped her arms around his neck and nuzzled her head into his chest. He began to relax. She looked up at him and kissed his lips. She knew this was not just a visit; this was goodbye for a long time. All of the words that had taken her breath away just a few months before were quickly fading. She had the feeling that Jimmy's desire to spend the rest of his life with her was beginning to fade and crumble. This felt like a final goodbye; her heart sank, and she was ready to cry. Angie found these words and before she could stop herself, they spilled out of her mouth. "You want to tell me something that is going to be hard to say. Right?"

"Angie, I, I don't know where to start."

"Let's make it easy, shall we? You have had time to think things over and don't want to be fenced in with any commitment to a high school friend. Is that how this conversation is going to start and end with we will always be friends, is that how it goes?"

"Not exactly. I want you to know that you will always be very special to me."

"Oh that's alright. You don't have to commit to anything. We are friends and that will always be so, but don't ever use the words very special or I love you to me again. Those are words that mean very much to me and not careless words which spill out of your mouth like water out of a glass. I'm too busy to be sidetracked by trivial phrases that are intended to seduce some desperate woman into bed. I am not that woman; I can guarantee that. Let's part friends and leave it at that. This can just be another one of life's lessons."

"Angie, I am being shipped to Korea Monday morning and will not be back for at least sixteen months. I had hoped to be ordered to some stateside camp or perhaps Europe, but I'm going into combat. Please don't give up on me now. I need your support more than ever now. If not as the love of my life, please be my friend." Jimmy was beginning to choke up at this point.

Sorrow sunk her heart. "Oh, Jimmy, I will always love you. You can count on that."

The two embraced, only this time it was a sad embrace which was also a goodbye for a long while.

"I will be back, and we will pick up where we left off; I pledge this to you."

Chapter 25

Let's Join Colleen in Greece

Colleen was getting very tense and was pacing up and down the living room of her condominium. It was part of a beautiful white stucco building trimmed with blue shutters and a flat roof which doubled as a terrace. It was also a wonderful area to hang wet laundry to dry. Laundry by day and terrace by night, it was a gathering place for all of the residents in the building. There were chairs to sit on and many would bring a cold drink, an iced coffee, or perhaps a glass of wine to help them cool off in the early evening. Then the conversations would invariably turn to gossip about the state of affairs in the world and especially Greece. The Greek people loved politics and could go on for hours.

The view from the roof was breathtaking. When the orange sun began to sink under the horizon, colors of blue and pink splashed across the sky until the sun disappeared for the night. It was a lovely time in the evening and most enjoyable. The inside of the condo had two bedrooms, a living room and kitchen with marble floors throughout. It overlooked the ocean and a private marina which was nestled in front of the seawall just below Mimi and Colleen's window. It was truly a beautiful sight to wake up to every morning and enjoy the whole day through. Their lovely condo was on the third floor, and their yacht was anchored at the marina. They both loved the sea and enjoyed sailing very much.

It had been a week since Mimi had been home and that long since he had called. He had gone to Crete on business and to visit his family. He was very angry when she had refused to go with him. Colleen had felt very uncomfortable with Mimi's family and relatives. She had gotten the message immediately that they were not very fond of the Irish or Ireland for that matter. Mimi had assured her that this was only a temporary thing, and they would love her as much as he does when they got to know her better. She had chosen to not expose herself to more of their scrutiny. Now she saw that she had made a big mistake, and they all took offence to her actions and were insulted by her boycott. This was even more insulting since this was the weekend of the Greek Orthodox Easter or *Pasha* as it was called there. Now that it was too late she regretted the whole decision. Mimi had not called her the entire time he was gone. He was to return that night, but she did not know when. What was she to do to make this a happy reunion with Mimi? The only good thing that happened was the arrival of the ring which certainly brightened her day. If the truth was known, it came to her by mistake, but still it came and she was thrilled.

Colleen set to work tidying up the home. When she had finished, she immediately began checking the kitchen pantry and made a shopping list for the market. One thing was certain, every Greek man loved to argue with his wife and to follow the argument with a great meal. The argument had already happened, and there was no winner, but it was followed with great regret. A good meal might be a good start to making peace.

She could have been part of the family Easter celebration which was always very special and meaningful. Easter was the most important religious holiday of the ecclesiastical year, and to this family her refusal to attend was an insult. This was a grave mistake. Her first order of making peace was with her husband; the very least that would be expected was a good meal. Thank goodness Colleen had been exposed to enough Greek culture that she knew many basic rules. It was much easier if you knew the rules of the game. That is not to say that there were not many surprises which were yet to be revealed.

Colleen knelt down and said a simple prayer for guidance in what direction she decided to take in her act of forgiveness. Sadly, the forgiveness of her husband was not going to be as difficult as the forgiveness of her in-laws. He loved her very much, of that she was sure. His mother, on the other hand, had not gotten to know her yet, and they had not even reached the point of acceptance of her as a good wife for her son. Mimi's father had died two years ago, and his mother had been left with all the responsibilities of the business and the home.

With this recent disagreement, the chance of just living in peaceful coexistence might be difficult. They say the Irish have a long memory, but the Greeks might be in the same long memory category alongside them.

Colleen decided at this point that to take one baby step at a time would be the best way to start the reconciliation. The first baby step would be to make her husband happy. Now off to the market to buy the makings of the wonderful meal she was about to prepare for her husband. If all went according to plan, Mimi should be home by six o'clock, which meant she had a limited time to get to the market and cook the meal.

Colleen loved to go to the market; there were so many wonderful open shops along the way. She especially loved the bakeries and novelty shops. There was the meat market next to the bakery filled with the most wonderful breads and rolls. Even more wondrous were the *Zaharoplastio,* or as the tourists called them, the sweetshops. They were filled with the most beautiful pastries anyone could imagine. Having lived in Ireland where sweets were not quite as special, this was a feast for the eyes. Colleen had promised herself that she would not only taste each one of these wondrous deserts but learn how to make them all herself. Mimi had told her that his mother was an amazing cook and knew how to make almost all of these desserts. "Now, no more daydreaming. Get along with yourself, young lady; you have a great deal of work to do before your wonderful husband comes home." She was talking to herself as she hurried down the narrow street. The plan for dinner shopping continued down the street as she picked up the items she needed from the meat market and the produce market then finally the sweetshop.

As she approached the condo, Colleen saw Mimi's automobile parked in front of the door. That cannot be Mimi's car she thought to herself; she had expected him to arrive at six o'clock not four o'clock. There was no time to make the dinner she had planned now, and it would not be a surprise that was for sure.

She hurried up the steps her heart beating like a drum as she made her way to the front door of their condo. "Mimi, darling, are you home so soon?" There was no answer. She called Mimi's name over and over and no one replied. She set the groceries on the kitchen table and walked to the window to see if by some chance he had gone out to the yacht to check on it. As she looked out the window she saw nothing but the usual activity of the marina. No Mimi in sight. Her heart sunk as she turned away from the window. All kinds of thoughts ran through her mind. The worst of which were that he had been killed and the body was somewhere perhaps in the car. She ran down the steps out to the car and was just about to open the door to begin her search when she felt a tap on her shoulder. She jumped in fear and turned quickly to be greeted by Mimi's smiling face. Tears streamed down her checks as she looked up and they kissed tenderly. "Oh Mimi, I missed you so much. I'm so glad your back." That was all she had to say and they were both on their way back into their home.

The truth was that there was no plan needed, just a sincere apology. Mimi directed Colleen to their bedroom. "One week is seven days too long to be away from you, love of my heart." They made love as if they had never made love before: gentle, loving and passionate, most of all memorable.

 Mimi looked into her crystal blue eyes and said, "From this day forward we will never fall asleep with an argument between us. I promise you this."

Colleen, without any hesitation, promised the same to him. This was the man she gave her heart to, and he also loved her in the same fashion.

"Well let's get down to business and get the wonderful dinner you were going to make for me together. I'll help."

"Oh you will, will you? Well off you go. No time for rest; we have work to do. Praise be to God I love you, and you have made me very happy."

Dinner was a wonderful treat, and the rest of the evening was equally wonderful. Now if only the apology to Mama would be that easily accomplished it would be magnificent.

Chapter 26

The Trip to Crete

The days were passing, and Mimi and Colleen had not yet come to any decisions as to how Colleen and Mama could bond together and be friends. The fact that Mimi had chosen Colleen as his wife was not enough to remove the hurt of not marrying in Crete and her not being able to attend the wedding. The fact that they married in the Catholic Church also added to the hurt. Mimi had promised Mama that they would have their wedding blessed in the Orthodox Church also; however as of yet there had been no effort to do this church blessing, and perhaps Mama thought there would never be any attempt to fulfill this promise. Perhaps Mimi had not explained to Colleen how important these matters were to his family.

There were many things that were done quickly, what with the passports and tickets having to be in order. The loose-ends and proprieties of how things were done in Greece were not as high on the list of things to be done as they should have been. Mimi was so anxious to marry Colleen that his mother and the family had been overlooked and put off.

Mimi had been living in Ireland for three years and working in the wool industry. He and Colleen had met two years before. They dated for a period of time, and when Mimi was to be transferred, he asked Colleen to marry him. Without thinking of the family in Crete, he went forward with the plan to marry in Ireland.

Mama was angry and had no trouble at all letting Mimi know of her displeasure in his impulsive action; thus an uncomfortable scene developed, and Colleen was victim of this oversight.

Mama was the matriarch of the family now that Mimi's father was gone, and was always informed of what was going on in the family. Mimi's marriage completely disarmed her, and she did not like it at all. What a mess this had all turned out to be. Mimi blamed his poor judgment on his some hurried decisions. One thing was certain and that was that this situation must be rectified if Colleen was to be part of his family. Colleen had to understand the problem and cooperate. The two of them had sat down and discussed this dilemma together and decided that they would go to Crete next weekend and present a plan to bless their wedding in the Orthodox Church and host a wedding party afterward for the whole family or even the whole island if that was that she wanted. Thank God Colleen did not resist his plan but rather was willing to go along with anything that would make this whole problem go away.

On Saturday morning the young couple was busy getting the yacht ready for the long trip to Crete. They were going to fly there but decided to make it a mini vacation. Mimi had hired a captain to drive the boat and a crew to help with cooking and cleaning the yacht. This was the first trip they had taken since they arrived in Greece, and Colleen was very excited. They were loading the last of their personal items and were about to board when Colleen remembered the ring and ran back into the condo to get it. She felt a need to have it with her as a bit of home in her pocket. At long last they set sail.

Crystal clear to the bottom, the Mediterranean and Aegean Seas were the most beautiful she had ever seen. Colleen had tears of joy in her eyes as they followed the Aegean Sea on the way to Crete.

The trip was beyond wonderful. Each port was more wondrous than the last, and Mimi was the king of the sea. He knew what was at every port and where to stop for a view of every must-see place along the way. For Colleen, it was a trip of magic and endless beauty. This was the best trip ever. She had sailed before but never like this. It was more like a fairytale than real life. Around lunch time they pulled up to a dock and dropped anchor. It was customary to have a big meal at lunch time and a light meal in the evening. Colleen knew this as she had lived in Greece for several months now.

They disembarked and went into a lovely taverna for lunch. The port was a typical fishing village. There was a huge half circle concrete pier leading to the seawall, and as you looked out over the pier, you could view all the sea crafts bouncing over the waves. It was a sight that belonged on an artist's canvas. Colleen stood there transfixed by the brilliance of the water and all of the sea crafts. This was the Greece she loved and admired.

Mimi came up beside her and kissed her tenderly on the head. "I can never get enough of this scene. This is why I bought the condo on the marina, so we could wake up and fall asleep with the sea beside us. O how I love the sea." The two walked slowly toward the taverna where they were served a delicious lunch of fresh caught fish, cooked greens, village salad, and a glass of wine. What more could anyone want?

After lunch, they all settled once again inside the yacht and continued their trip to Crete. It was quite a bit farther than Colleen thought, but then no one was in a hurry. The sea was a wondrous place and still very peaceful on a day like today. Colleen had managed to relax and completely enjoy the trip. She laid her head back onto the pillow on her chair and dozed off. Mimi was happy to see his wife finally relax. From the day he returned home from the Easter trip, Colleen had been a nervous wreck. This was the first time in a while that he saw her in peaceful sleep and was relieved. He had feared she would have a nervous breakdown.

Colleen awoke with a start when she heard from afar, "Crete just ahead. Radio the dock master to prepare for docking." She rose from the chair and shook her head to wake up completely. She looked over the ship's rail and saw the great city of Heraklion rise before her. They had arrived and very soon she would be facing her mother-in-law, better known as Mama. Let the drama begin. Keep telling yourself that you're doing this for Mimi and for a much better relationship.

Mimi came toward her and said, "Well, sweetheart, we are here. Let's get cleaned up and then we can go to Mama's house."

They both went to their cabin and began the process of getting ready for the afternoon coffee which would be awaiting them. It was much like the High Tea back home. It should be quite enjoyable and much needed after that nap.

Mimi went to get the car while Colleen finished getting ready. Once on their way, all was calm. Colleen had brought a gift of her favored perfume. She had painstakingly wrapped it to make it look extra special.

"We're here," Mimi said with anticipation.

They were greeted with much joy and warmth which made Colleen feel very comfortable. They sat down with Mama and ensued with harmless small talk. Mama was a well-educated lady and could speak English quite well. This made it very easy to communicate as Colleen's Greek was limited.

Mama's had a lovely home with a perfect view of the sea. She and Mimi shared the same love of the sea. For them, a house which hid the sea would never do. All the floors were made of marble. It was a stately home, and Mimi was obviously very proud of it. His father had worked hard to build it, and the business he left behind was for Mimi to step in and keep it at the same successful level he had left it. Papa had died one year ago, and Mama was still mourning his loss.

"Children, let us begin our plans for the wedding celebration. I understand you are Catholic, Colleen. Is this correct?"

"Yes, my entire family is Irish Catholic. Is this a problem?"

"No, of course not. Catholic and Orthodox are very close to each other. The problem is that you must be Orthodox to marry in the church. I know this seems very difficult, but it must be done."

"But Mrs. Poulos, I have always been Catholic and now you are saying that I must change my religion in order to marry Mimi when we are already married. I do not understand. I thought that we were merely having our marriage blessed in the church. Was I mistaken?"

"Mama, why are you making this process so difficult? We were in agreement that we would have our marriage blessed and have a small celebration, not a baptism. This is not necessary. I spoke to the priest, and he said as long as Colleen was baptized that was all that was necessary."

"Mimi, we are not here to fight, but I am thinking of your children and how they will be brought up."

"Mrs. Poulos, I can assure you that the children will be brought up as Mimi wishes. If he wants them to attend the Orthodox Church, then that is what will happen. I do not want to have a split up family. Then perhaps when all these problems are settled, I will become an Orthodox Christian and we will all worship as a family."

When Colleen said this, Mimi was shocked and very pleased at the same time. As for Mama, she simply said good that was settled and now on to the planning of the celebration. With this hurdle behind them the celebration planning was great fun and Mama was a very happy mother. She felt closer to Colleen and saw that Mimi loved her very much.

Colleen turned to Mama and said, "Mrs. Poulos, the celebration is to be planned at your discretion. I am honored that you wish to celebrate our marriage with the joy of a mother's heart."

"My dear girl, you know a mother's heart. I would like to purchase your dress if you will allow it."

"Of course. I would be more than honored that we can share this experience together."

She took the younger woman's hand. "Now, please call me, Mama."

Colleen smiled with relief and nodded. "Mama, it is."

With the agreements made the two women were happily ready to continue with the afternoon coffee and begin a new relationship with each other. Mimi was very pleased with the manner which Colleen conducted herself and felt very comfortable with the decisions which were made. All was well with the world.

Chapter 27

The Wedding

If Colleen had any doubts that Mama was the correct person to put in charge of the wedding reception, she certainly had none now. She was the perfect person to run the celebration. Before the week was over a date had been set, a hotel was booked for the reception, and the invitations were ordered. None of these actions were taken without the approval of the bride and groom. The list of guests was a mix of family, friends, and business associates. Mama was very aware of exactly what needed to be done to get the most advantage with both the family and friends and business connections. Even Mimi was amazed with what his mother was able to do. The very fact that all of these people would be in attendance was to his advantage, and he knew that he would be expected to take full advantage of this situation.

Now the time was approaching when Mama wanted the selection of the dresses for this occasion. Once the dresses were picked and the tuxedos ordered, there was the question of the flowers and the décor of the dining room. Mama wanted Colleen completely involved in the planning from this point forward. This was the second time Colleen planned a wedding. When the first wedding took place in Ireland it was a relatively small family affair. The guest list was made up of family, friends, and a few business associates. It was a lovely wedding, but Mimi's family was unable to attend; it was understandable that they were upset.

Colleen's Mum and Pa were not able to make the trip for this event. Journeys from country to country were difficult these days. World War II had ended, but travel was still restricted. The Korean police action was beginning, resulting in more travel restrictions. Greece still remembered the occupation it was under, and many were struggling to get back on their feet once more.

This wedding party would be among the first parties which would be hosted by one of Crete's well-known families. Mama was very careful not to flaunt her wealth before the people of Crete, but rather to show that an alliance was forming which would result in multiple wool industries reopening and jobs would be available for many. It was a careful balance of wealth and power.

Mama had made an appointment with the seamstress for Colleen and her to select the fabric for the dresses which they would be wearing to the wedding. This was the most exciting day yet. Colleen had decided not to wear her wedding gown but rather a lovely cocktail dress which seemed more suitable for this occasion. Mama, however, felt that the bride should be a step above the rest of the guests and led Colleen to a more memorable gown. She took Colleen's wedding dress and asked the seamstress to add crystals and pearls to the beautiful Irish lace. The seamstress suggested shortening the front of the gown a few inches making the train look even more magnificent. The last touch was to change the neckline by cutting the lace to follow the pattern into a V-neck, thus showcasing the original wedding gown of Irish Lace. Colleen had tears of joy in her eyes when she realized what had been a beautiful gown had become a magnificent gown.

The seamstress knew Mama so well that she understood exactly what she wanted. Mama was very happy with the experience and had no doubt that her daughter-in-law and she would be quite lovely on the wedding day. But best of all, Colleen would look like a bride—not only a bride but a sparkling jewel.

Needless to say the wedding party was a huge success, and the city of Heraklion was abuzz about the event. Many business alliances were made, and Mimi had much work ahead of him putting the wool plants back into working condition.

Colleen learned something also—that with every cause there is an effect. The effect which made changes in her life was the move to the island of Crete. Mimi had to be where the plants were. The result was that the young couple packed up their condo and began the process of moving to a new home. This was a happy move because they would be closer to Mama and the rest of the family.

Mimi and Colleen found that with the second wedding ceremony they both felt like newlyweds again and could not get enough of each other. They were always looking for opportunities to make love. Their favorite place to be romantic was the yacht. They both felt the freedom of the moment on the yacht. They would always start out with a glass of wine and conversation and before a sentence was finished the wine glasses would be down on the table, and Mimi would be kissing her tenderly as the sun started to set. The kisses would become more and more ardent, and his hands would fondle her breasts. The love making was something they both enjoyed, and it seemed to be desired more and more. They loved lying in bed and making love at night before they fell asleep, and in the morning just after they awoke, there was always morning desire. Love in the morning was a wonderful way to start the day. Colleen could not envision life without Mimi. He was all she wanted in a man and a lover. Life in Crete was wonderful. Mama was a loving and supportive mother-in-law, with the added bonus of being a skilled business partner for Mimi. She never intruded on the couple's privacy and knew well that they were completely in love.

When Mimi worked he was all business, and Mama was equally committed to the business. She had worked side by side with Mimi's father and knew the way the profession was intended to run. Colleen was also very accustomed to the ways of the wool industry, and the three made a good partnership. This made the move to Crete much smoother.

Chapter 28

Cause and Effect

Trouble came to the young couple shortly after the move. Mimi was notified that he was to be drafted into the Greek Army. This was a very sad moment for the newlyweds. Mimi had just began rebuilding the plant, and they were about to start production when the draft notice came. He had applied for an exemption, but as of yet he had not heard anything.

He received notice to report for basic training, and Colleen stepped into his role as head of operations and took over his responsibilities. She had enough experience as she had worked in the in wool industry in Ireland which was how the two of them met. Thus the cause and effect of the two young lives went on. Mimi was shipped out, and Colleen was running the plant.

Mama was coming in once or twice a week to help out. Now her participation in the business became much more demanding, and she began coming to the wool plant every day and would stay until closing. She knew the work and the employees very well. She was well respected and became Colleen's right-hand woman, which was a huge help.

Colleen discovered a few days after Mimi left that she was expecting a baby. Her joy and excitement was diminished by the fact that Mimi would not be with her through the experience of their first child. Without hesitation, she sent Mimi a telegram telling him the news.

The mixed emotions of joy and upset gripped his heart. A baby. Their baby was on the way, but why now that he was away? He looked for ways to get out of the service and return to his wife and his expected baby but ran into brick walls at every turn.

It was not long before Colleen was forced to move into Mama's home. Between morning sickness and trying to work every day, she had become very frail. She was not gaining any weight, and the doctors were becoming alarmed for not only Colleen's health but also the baby's development. Mama came to the rescue. She sent her maid to help Colleen.

Upon finishing basic training, Mimi was given leave. He rushed home to Colleen. Disturbed at how frail she looked, he didn't want to leave her side. He needed to check the plant. Mama assured him she would not leave Colleen unattended. "I won't be gone long." He said. He wanted to give every spare moment to his family especially now that his orders had come and he was to be shipped overseas to Korea.

He went to the wool factory and was pleased with the work that both women had done. That, however, was not enough to help the pain in his heart. He had become very depressed at the thought that more than likely he would not be present for the birth of his first child. Even worse than that he feared that he might be killed and never again return to these precious people who he loved with all of his heart, and his child would never know his father or know how much he loved him or her. He thanked God for allowing him to be with the two women he loved more than anyone else and knew he would make peace with everything else that he would have to endure when the time came. Soon there would be another person in their lives, and he already loved this baby. "Do not think that way," he told himself. "You will be back, and there will be peace once again. We will take the yacht out on the sea and breathe in the clean air as God predestined it to be. I will return and hold my precious Colleen in my arms once again. I will run and play with my children for we will have many. My love for them will be like a fountain which never stops flowing."

Mimi put his happy face on when he returned from the plant. He entered into the room to see Colleen to comfort her and give her courage for the hard year ahead. "We'll get through this, and you will return home safely. Mama has become like my own mother to me. She takes good care of me, Mimi."

Both women loved the same man and both would love the new member of the family when he or she arrived.

Chapter 29

Jenny Has the Cookbook and Colleen Has the Ring

Jenny was a nervous wreck, pacing back and forth in her home. She had received the Irish cookbook in the mail. Jenny had sent a thank- you note, and the mistake was discovered.

Mrs. O'Donnell called Jenny and informed her of the mistake and that she would return the ring as quickly as possible. She had encountered much difficulty getting in touch with Colleen. The phone had been disconnected. Her mother had mentioned that the couple was moving to Crete, and she was not sure what the phone number was. She assured Jenny that she would get word to Colleen about the ring and have her send it to the address she was given.

Colleen had her problems between morning sickness, the business, and not hearing from Mimi for two weeks now. She was more than a little concerned. Mama had not heard anything either. Colleen was back home. Mama had been so good to her, but she felt she would be imposing on her hospitality if continued to stay there. When the request for the ring had come, Colleen could not believe her ears. With all the troubles around her how could this foolish girl possibly want that ring so badly? Nevertheless, Colleen packed it up and had it sent out of the office. Good riddance was all she could think to say. That ring was no good to her.

The doorbell rang, and Jenny ran to open it. There was a small package left at the doorstep. Jenny quickly swept it up and ripped it open. This was the ring, she knew it. As the wrapping fell away the ring fell out and landed at Jenny's feet. She could not snatch it up fast enough even if it had been a million dollars.

Now maybe things will start going my way, were the thoughts that went through Jenny's mind. Now, wise guy, what are you going to do about it, was the second thing that went through her mind. It was as if an old friend had just come over to visit. Jenny quickly slipped the ring on her finger and was off to test its power on unsuspecting Eddy. Now we'll see who has the upper hand in this marriage.

Jenny had many axes to grind with Eddy. All of this year she had been forced to work to save money to pay off all of her personal charge cards. It was an outrage. He was her husband, and he should see to it she was given everything she wanted. When he was at his worst she agreed to help catch up all the bills from the wedding, but this was ludicrous; she had no money for herself at all. She could not get a job as a beautician in Riverville. There were only two beauty shops in town and no openings at either one. If she could drive into Indianapolis she could easily get a job, but good old Eddy said that it would not help enough because by the time the gas for the commute and lunches were paid it would be a break-even situation if not cost more than she could make.

He made her sick! Now she was working at Eddy's Cool Deals as the night receptionist/errand girl. It was humiliating. No more. Now that she had the ring things were going to be different. Mr. Eddy would not know what hit him.

She was speeding down the street and was hitting fifty miles an hour when the long arm of the law came after her and stopped her right in front of Eddy's Cool Deals. She was totally humiliated and very angry. Her timing could not have been worse.

From the front widow Eddy saw the whole thing. This was the last thing Jenny needed, another bill, a speeding ticket for one hundred fifty dollars, far from cheap. The whole affair had upset Jenny so much that she began to cry. As the police officer pulled away from the curb, Jenny realized what a humiliating event this was, she screamed, "I'll kill that bastard." This was incredibly bad timing, just when she thought that the tide was about to turn for her.

Eddy came out of his office and walked up to her car, looked at Jenny, and said, "What's next?"

"Look Eddy, I didn't do this on purpose. At least I'm keeping up with the bills and everything else I have to do in this crappy life I am living with you. You never said that I would never be out of debt. I didn't know that I would have to pay for the entire wedding, the ring, the dress, and the honeymoon to Ireland. When do you come into this debt responsibility?"

"Jenny, you're a child. You don't have any idea what it takes to live. Who do you think gives you money to buy groceries, who pays the mortgage payment, and who keeps the business solvent and the hundred and one other things I do every day? Don't bellyache about the bills you ran up with no consideration about cost and where the money was coming from."

"You pig! You never let up. I am not your slave, you bastard. Are you trying to kill me?"

"See you later, Drama Queen. Don't be late, or I will dock your pay." He turned quickly and walked back into the dealership.

What went wrong? The ring was supposed to work. Instead things could not have been worse, thought Jenny as she pulled away from the curb.

Chapter 30

What Do We Know About Eddy?

Eddy sat at his desk, and he was clearly embarrassed by the blatant spectacle of contempt which Jenny had just displayed. He was not ignorant of the fact that she had been very angry from the time the money problems occurred. He had hoped that as the debt was being paid down the tension would lessen, but instead it seemed to get worse. The fact that she had not been truthful about going to the University of Cosmetology was still a sore spot for Eddy. Even worse she lied about being pregnant. In truth, he was relieved. The last thing they needed to complicate matters was a baby. She had fabricated so many stories that it was impossible to know what the truth really was. It was hard to accept the fact that she really believed that this simple class ring was magic. It was too ridiculous to give it any credence. He had found out completely by accident when the ring disappeared after they left Ireland. She was so distraught that she let it slip that the ring was magic. She was actually frantic about the disappearance to the point of irrationally thinking she could go back and search Mrs. O'Donnell's home after they had arrived back at their Indiana home. After this most recent outburst everything seemed hopeless to Eddy. His plan was to pay down the debts and slowly begin to trust Jenny with a budget which would allow her to buy a few things for herself once again.

A year had passed since the wedding and the trip. Other than Jenny working, if that's what you wanted to call it, the debt was not nearly paid off. Her work was that of a teenager with no interest in anything she was asked to do. In the morning when Maria arrived, she not only had her work, but also all the work that Jenny left from the night before. Jenny never paid the bills on time that were her responsibility. Instead she paid late charges and almost nothing on the debt.

Eddy was very unhappy and felt trapped in a marriage with someone who lied about everything. He wanted some changes made in his life. He hated to say divorce but that seemed as if it was the only solution. He doubted very much if Jenny would mind. Their home life was no better than their public life. They had become roommates rather than husband and wife. There was rarely any love making between them, and when there was it was very quick and without much feeling. Sex had become merely a fulfillment of a need on both of their parts. There would never be children; she didn't want any, and he didn't want her to have his children. It was a dead end no matter how you looked at it.

In one year of life with Jenny, Eddy had gone from Great Expectations to No Expectations. The only thing he had not tried was marriage counseling. He didn't want to throw in the towel without at least trying that. One thing was certain, he didn't want to live like this anymore.

Chapter 31

Marriage Counseling

That evening after they closed Eddy's Cool Deals, he suggested that they go get a bite to eat. "Would you like to go to the Corner Grill? You always liked their hamburgers?"

"That sounds great. Let's go."

They had not been to the Corner Grill since that fateful day when Jenny decided to make peace and start again. That was when love making was an adventure and not a chore. When the sky was the limit as to what length they would go to try to make things work. Eddy held the door open for Jenny to enter the Corner Grill. She looked tired. The whole day seemed to be an effort.

The waitress greeted them and led them to a table. They both laughed when they realized that they were sitting at this same table the last time they came here. They both ordered the hamburger and fries dinner plate. Jenny had ordered a cup of tea, a habit she picked up in Ireland on their honeymoon.

"Jenny," Eddy began, "things cannot continue this way any longer. We must get hold of ourselves and at least make an effort to make a go of this marriage."

Jenny looked up in shock to hear these words come out of his mouth. "I'm sure you think that all of this is my fault. I know everyone thinks I am a terrible person. I feel as if the world is closing in on me, and I cannot escape. What do you want from me? I try, but it's not working." Jenny's eyes were filled with tears.

"I think we should see a marriage counselor. Perhaps counseling might help us to find the path to happiness. We should at least try."

"Let me think about it. I have never been much of a believer in counseling. I agree that we have to do something. I do not want to give up on us. There was a time when we were madly in love.

I would love to be back to that time again. Let's try." Jenny was very reluctant and agreed with great reservations. She was very confident that a marriage counselor would not help. She was also afraid all of the sessions would end up in a blame game where she would be the bad guy. How did this marriage end up this way? Jenny had to admit that she entered the marriage with the idea that Eddy was rich. Apparently rich is relevant to what your particular definition for rich was. She was afraid that her definition was unrealistically based on the fact that money was no object. Eddy's definition was, what was his definition? She never really understood what it was. He was making money on the used cars he sold yet he never expanded his business. It had been the same today as it was when he first started. It wasn't until they returned from Ireland that he hired a receptionist. He would not have done it then except for the fact that he was furious with her for all the money she spent on the wedding and the trip. He should have told her there was a limit on the whole thing, but it was easier to blame the whole thing on her. She would give the counseling a chance, and if it did not work out, they would have to decide what the next move would be.

Eddy had long ago forgotten his dream of building the business and having children to leave a thriving company to. Jenny would be a disaster as a mother, he was fairly sure. She had long since infuriated his family. His mother and Jenny were barely speaking. He had tried over and over to mend fences between them but to no avail. Jenny refused, as did his mother. Her parents were out of the picture altogether. They never even came to the wedding and up to now had not even tried to be civil to them. Jenny had tried to have them over for dinner numerous times only to have them back out at the last minute. Her mother was willing, however. She and Jenny did see each other from time to time, but only if her mother was certain that her father would not find out. That family situation was an impossible mess. Eddy wished he could feel sorry for Jenny but all of the other problems had toughened him, and he could not even empathize with her. They really had done a lot of damage to their marriage, and he was not sure it could be helped. He did not want a divorce because he was Catholic and the church did not allow it and because he did not want to be the first member of his family to fail at marriage.

Time passed, and the crucial day of the counseling appointment arrived. They had not made any progress on their relationship but nevertheless they kept the appointment. Jenny had long since given up hope that the magic ring which she had counted on so heavily was going to be any help.

Jenny and Eddy met at the car lot and rode in one car to the counselor's office. They were both very edgy as they drove a short way to the office. The councilor was a man, and this made Eddy a little more comfortable. Jenny, however, was even more anxious than ever. They both wanted to get off on the right foot.

The session consisted of a lot of questions about the history of the marriage and what each expected from the other. This was the usual information which anyone would need to know if they were going to help solve any problems. While answering the questions they also discovered new things about each other. This was indeed a surprise on both of their parts. However, one of the first things they discovered was that they really did not know each other very well. This was an unexpected surprise to both of them. Perhaps this was not going to be as big a waste of time as they had both thought. After a question–answer session they were given an assignment to do on their own and come back to the next session with the results.

They both had to admit that it was not as bad as they expected. They promised to work on the assignment and return for the next session. This was one of the few times that they had both agreed on anything in a long time. Hope runs eternal, and hope was what both of them had. Hope for a new start and some answers to a lot of questions that they both had.

Eddy had decided to concentrate on his business and see if there were ways he could expand his operation to reach the next level.

Jenny was trying to decide if she was as unhappy working for Eddy as she thought or was she disappointed that she did not go on with her career as a hair stylist as she had planned when she went to beauty school.

Chapter 32

What Happened to Molly?

Molly had very happily turned the ring over to Mrs. O'Donnell. This was probably the best thing she had ever done. She felt that a huge weight was lifted from her shoulders. She was happier than ever and was glad that the ring was back to its rightful owner.

Colleen had graciously forwarded the ring to Jenny; the mistake was taken care of.

Molly was still working for Mrs. O'Donnell and happy to be there. Mickey was still very smitten with her, and the two were happy sweethearts. The outside world was closing in on Ireland as news of a police action in Korea had come. Oh surely not, we just finished a War; it couldn't be true.

What was it that Colleen had written the mistress? Oh yes, she said that Colleen's husband, Mimi, was called to duty in Korea. Oh please God, don't take me Mickey away, was Molly's prayer. Trouble all over the world; who would have believed such a thing could happen. There was talk that the lads would soon be called to duty once again. Even Mickey was afraid that he would have to serve. The whole world was upside down. All Molly could think about was please Lord don't take Mickey away; I love him so much. These were extremely troubling times. Mickey and Molly were talking about their future together, and now it seemed that no one dared to make any plans. Perhaps this would pass, and life would go on as usual. Life did not go on as usual, and Mickey was called to duty. Their plans for the future were set aside for the time being. This was the state of affairs for now and for the next few years it seemed. Molly was thankful for her job and her mistress. She was such a kind woman which made everything Molly was about to face a little less painful.

Mrs. O'Donnell had told Molly that Colleen was facing the same situation, but poor Colleen was pregnant and her husband off to war. Praise God that she had such a wonderful mother-in-law.

There were rumors that Colleen might come home to Dublin for a spell to be with her family. For the time being she was in Crete and getting along very well.

The police action was taking a toll on everyone around the world. Somehow it seemed more like a war to all who were affected. Molly swore to pray every night for all of this to end very quickly. The fact that both girls had had the ring at one time or another gave them an extra bond to each other. Molly began to write letters to Colleen to encourage her while Mimi was away, and Colleen would answer her letters. The girls became pen pals and formed a friendship that would last a long time.

Chapter 33

Angie and the Police Action

Angie was getting ready to start the day when she was very suddenly overcome by grief. Tears began to pore from her eyes and before she knew it, she was sobbing. She was in her bedroom which even though small in size was very cozy. Her walls were light peach, and pictures of all her friends and family hung on them. She had lacey curtains and a peach and white spread on her bed. There were two windows and a door that lead out to the roof top above the laundry room below, but Angie called it her balcony. A very girly room, and she loved it. She had also placed a picture of her mother on the wall. Athena was never happy to see that picture, but it was Angie's room and she did not make a big fuss about it.

Unfortunately the relationship between the two of them was no better. All of the disagreements between her father and Athena were still about Angie and her comings and goings. Perhaps the tears were caused by the picture of Rebecca, but Angie knew that it was more about the picture of Jimmy and her at the Grad Dance. They both looked so happy and full of hope for the future. The future that was expected was not the future that was at hand. Angie had anticipated that she would be in her third year of college by now, but she was only finishing up her first year. She had actually managed to get good grades but was far from any hope of graduation and entry into nursing school. She had a good following at the beauty salon and made a decent amount of money which allowed her to pay for her classes. No way could she mange to move out and still continue to pay for entry courses for nursing school. She wanted to specialize in emergency room care or surgical nursing. On the brighter side she was getting closer, and as soon as she could enter nursing, she would move out of her home and into the nursing dorms, but that was still quite a way off.

Jimmy had been shipped overseas to Korea six months ago, and she had not heard from him once in all that time. He did not even let her know where he was, and it was very upsetting. They had parted with a good understanding of what was ahead for them both. She definitely felt it was a no strings attached parting. They had said they would write each other, but not one letter had come from Jimmy in all these six months. Suddenly Angie's eyes filled up with tears, and she began to sob. Did Jimmy mean more to her than she had realized? He seemed to always be around. Even at times when no one knew where she was going he would be there. The night that she had gone to the Tee-Pee for a soda he happened to be there and they sat together. When she had no date for the Grad Dance he was available and took her as his date. What a wonderful evening that was. Now he had been gone for six months, and no one had heard from him. She dried her eyes and looked in the mirror. She looked a fright, but she decided to call Jimmy's mother and see if she would give her his address. He must still care about everyone here. She finished getting ready and ran downstairs for breakfast. Athena was sitting at the table with little Bobby.

"Hi there, little fella," Angie called out to Bobby.

"Good Morning, Athena, has Dad gone to work already? "She asked.

Athena looked up and glared at her with real contempt. "I would greatly appreciate it if you would stop expecting to eat breakfast here every day," she began. "I am sick of seeing you in this house. As far as I am concerned, you are an intruder and belong somewhere else. Your father has coddled you long enough. I want you out of this house or paying room and board before the end of the week."

Angie was at a loss as to what she should reply. She just looked at Athena in disbelief and turned and left the room. This was not a good morning for her, and she had a long day ahead. She decided to walk to the bus stop and go to work. There was a vendor in the parking lot that sold breakfast items. She could pick up some cinnamon toast there. Tonight she would have to talk to her father to see if he was in agreement with Athena. Even little Bobby was saying mean things to her like she was a very bad girl. It was always amazing how good she was, bringing him candy. Poor

Sammie gets it all day long.

The day turned out all right in spite of the way it started. Angie called Jimmy's mother, and she asked Angie to come to the house. She had wanted to talk to her for some time now. This created new anxiety for Angie as his mother had never shown any interest in chitchatting with her before. Nevertheless, she told her she would be over right after her class was dismissed that evening.

Angie arrived at Jimmy's house about 8:30 p.m. His house was about five blocks from hers, so it was not that much out of her way. As she approached the home she noticed that the front door was opened as if she was sure that Angie would arrive soon. Angie cautiously drew near the steps. As she reached the door Mrs. Jordon greeted her.

"Come in, Angie," Mrs. Jordon said. "I'm glad you called me today. I've wanted to talk to you for quite some time now."

Angie was taken off guard by this comment. She had never really had a conversation with her and up to this point this was the most words they had ever exchanged. However, since they were on a roll, she thought she should take advantage of it and see what she could find out.

"It's been six months since Jimmy left for Korea, and I have not heard a word from him. I was becoming concerned and thought perhaps he had written you, and you could give me his address so that I could write him." She said all this without taking a breath of air.

"Angie, I am sorry to say that I have not heard from him either. When he left he was not allowed to say where they were sending him. He said something about special training and that he would know in six months what would happen, and we would hear from him at that time and not before. I am quite concerned about him. He seemed very tense when he left. He told me that he had more or less broken it off with you. Something about you deserved better than he could give you. Yesterday, I received a note from his commander saying he would be home on furlough in two weeks. I am going out of my mind wondering what's going on and why all these top secret overtones."

"He didn't volunteer for any special forces, did he? He wouldn't have done that, would he?" Angie's heart was racing at the thought of Jimmy going into even more danger than he would be in the regular army, and it had frightened her beyond words. "Oh Mrs. Jordon, I am very afraid for Jimmy. If he does come home soon, will you please call me? I would really like to see him."

"I'll get in touch with you as soon as I find out anything. Thank you for coming by this evening, Angie. I know that you care for Jimmy and are as concerned as I am about him." The two women embraced each other and said a goodbye. Then Angie left.

As she walked down the street toward her home she was suddenly overcome by sadness. Jimmy was a peaceful young man not really cut out for Special Forces yet it seemed like the only logical answer. What else could be going on with him? She rounded the corner and saw her house in front of her. She climbed the steps and reached for the door which was locked. She rang the bell and her father came to the door. "Hi, Dad, how are you tonight?"

"What are you doing Angie? Why are you so late coming home? Athena told me you and she had a disagreement, and she wants you out of the house. I've asked you to please not make trouble and what do you do? Start trouble all the time. Why, why do you do these things?"

"Dad, I did not do anything. I just said good morning to Bobby and Athena, and she told me that I could not have any breakfast and was to move out of the house or start paying room and board. I just left and went to work. Dad, I just paid for my classes and don't have any money to pay room and board. I will not get paid for another two weeks. Please don't put me out. You know I have tried to keep up my end of the agreement and work my way through school. Athena wants me out, and if I leave I will never finish school. You know that. I swear I did not try to make any trouble. If you want me to clean house on the weekends, I will. I will do whatever you want. Please let me finish school."

By this time she was sobbing and Athena came in the room. "You should stop all this acting. You think you are some kind of a martyr. Well, I am getting very tired of you, young lady, always trying to place a wedge between Basil and me."

Angie retreated into the hall and was about to go back outside when Basil told her to stay, and they would work things out.

That night a huge fight broke out in Basil's and Athena's bedroom. Angie heard Athena threaten to leave, and Basil told her to go ahead; he couldn't take it anymore. At that moment she fainted and Basil, in a panic, ran downstairs to fetch a glass of water for her. After that things were very quiet on the home front.

Chapter 34

Athena

The stress of not knowing what was going to set Athena off again was making family life very tentative. Athena was quite annoyed with Basil for not supporting her on her pronouncement that Angie should get out of the house or pay room and board. Because he did not have enough nerve to stand up to his daughter did not mean that she had to put up with her. At this the point, she could barely tolerate Angie or Sammie. As for Joey, she would be very happy if she never had to see him again. Every time Basil would say how proud he was of his son and all of his accomplishments, she would become very annoyed.

She had tried very tactfully to find out all she could about Basil's first wife. Of course, no one was going to tell the truth. They were all very respectful of her memory, but Athena could easily read between the lines and knew they were lying. She could not believe how they went on and on about how wonderful the children were and stepped right up and helped Basil with everything around the house when their mother was taken to the hospital. Athena bet that was a fairytale. None of them knew anything about how a house was to be run until she came on the scene. Oh, it was nice enough to hear, but Athena was sure that nothing of the kind was true. If these children have any resemblance to their mother, then Basil was a fool to have ever married her. Just look at Angie. She couldn't stop bellyaching about everything. She was a plain Jane, and it would take a ton of makeup to just make her presentable. All she did was work and go to school, and she was pitiful at both. She rarely went out and there certainly were never boys breaking down the door to take her out. She only went out when Joey came home and took her with him. How pathetic was that? The way Basil makes over her you would think she was a princess. Athena was convinced that the best thing that happened to Basil was when she came on the scene. She started to straighten these animals out, and that was not easy.

When little Bobby was born, Basil got to see what real joy was with his new son. He is a prince, and Basil loves him more than any of the other children who have burdened his life and made it miserable. Whenever Athena saw her little Bobby get excited and light up with joy when he saw Angie come into the room, she got angry. Angie had no right to try to steal his love from her. What does a baby know about character anyway? If she had her way she would kick them all out. It was high time Basil got rid of these monkeys on his back, she vented. The more she thought about it, the more her anger intensified. By the time Sammie came through the door, she was furious.

"Hi, Athena. Jeff asked me to come over and play ball for a while. I have most of my homework done. Do you mind if I go for an hour?"

"Why don't you go and never come back!" she screamed at him. Poor Sammie was so stunned he dropped his books.

"What did I do? I just got home."

"Don't question me. I am not feeling well and all of this conflict is making me ill. Go to your room and don't come out until I call you."

All he ever wants is to play. He can cool his heels for a while and maybe then he will appreciate playtime.

She walked into the kitchen and poured herself a glass of wine to calm down before Basil got home. This tirade she was having had to come to a stop. The children had not done anything wrong. The problem was that they were always there, and Basil couldn't understand that she needed some downtime away from this family she inherited.

Basil had no right to treat her the way he did last night. She was the lady of the house and what she says should go. This was not a boarding house for Angie, and she wanted to put a stop to her coming and going at will. She must think of a way to get her out of here. She was formulating a plan which she thought would be the best way to deal with this situation. It would take a few telephone calls to set this plan into action. As for Basil he would pay for that little outburst last night. She would make him pay.

Chapter 35

Money Troubles

Time was going by, and Angie was upset with the little progress she had made with her work and studies. She had never expected to make a lot of money in the beauty business, but this was getting ridiculous. The cost of the classes kept increasing. At the rate she was going she would not be able to start nursing school before her twentieth birthday. She had to think of a new strategy. She was only two courses away from having all the pre-requisites for nursing school. Unfortunately, these were difficult courses and required a lot of study time, which meant less work time. This would cut her income down substantially, resulting in not enough money to pay for the first semester of nursing school.

Although life had been quiet at home, Angie was not optimistic that Athena would abandon her plans to get her out of the house, and she knew she could not afford school if she had to pay room and board. This was a stark reality that she had to face. A new plan had to be made with more unknowns figured in the equation. Her income, even though better than when she started, was far from satisfactory to pay all her bills and continue school. She had to think of a new strategy, but what? She had a year's worth of credit hours. She would have to go to the counselor's office to check on the cost of each course and that would help a lot in making decisions. If she could manage to take the two courses, she would have to work four days a week instead of six. This would cut her income considerably. That is if she was accepted with only one year completed in college credit hours. On the other hand, she would still have to complete the required courses. There really was no way out of one more year in night school. She could not give up working and still pay for all the courses she still needed.

If Athena would only stop trying so hard to throw her out of the house, things would not be as bad. She was going to have to talk to her father. Perhaps he could put a stop to some of these demands which Athena had placed upon her. Her plan for making money with college girls as customers was a pipe dream. It turned out that most of them were even more broke than she was, and the last thing they would spend money on was a hair style when a dressed up pony tail worked just fine for them and was a whole lot cheaper. If she couldn't work something out, then all her efforts would have been for nothing.

Chapter 36

Family Vacation

Angie was ready to talk to her father and try to reason with him about how she would get through the next two months and by September be able to enter the School of Nursing. If he would agree with what she proposed, everything would be great. She would try to sit down with him tonight and see what would happen. She would even invite Athena to join them to ensure that she was aware of the plan.

Meantime, Athena was busy cooking up her own agenda. She sat down by the telephone and began to dial her friend's number. It had been quite some time since she had talked to Nina, and they had a lot of news to catch up on. This was a brilliant plan, she thought as she was dialing the number. Nina answered the phone and both women began talking about old times and had a wonderful conversation which was filled with memories and new events that were happening. As they were talking, the conversation turned to the beach and summer vacations. Nina talked about her sons Ted and Steven. She was having a lot of problems with Ted who was twenty-five and would not settle down. He was very fond of music and wanted to promote his band which at the present time was playing in bars and cheap dives. He was always drinking and running with a fast crowd, and she was very concerned. She would love to find a sweet young girl to marry him and make him settle down. This was music to Athena's ears. A sign from God, exactly what she wanted to hear but was not sure how to approach the subject. She had heard the rumors that Ted was a real problem, and they were desperate to find someone to settle him down.

This was the exact time that Athena mentioned that her family was looking for a nice beach resort for the family to spend their vacation. Was the beach where they went nice and family friendly? Of course it was and why didn't Athena and her family join them. It would be great fun. This was exactly what Athena wanted to hear. Unfortunately for Angie, this was a scheme by both mothers to get the two unsuspecting young people together. The problem was that Ted was twenty-five and Angie was nineteen. She was too young and too inexperienced to manage a relationship with an older man who was already living a life of bands, bars, and women. That made no difference to Athena. This was her master plan to marry Angie off, and if the marriage failed, she would have to deal with it on her own. She would make sure that Basil thought that Ted was a very wonderful young man who would take good care of Angie and if anything went wrong it would be Angie's fault. This would be the best way to ensure that Angie would not ever return to this house again. It was the happiest moment that Athena had had in a very long time. The best part was that she would be located far enough away from them that visits would be hard because this guy spent money like it was going out of style. She would not be able to buy a coat let alone make a trip back here.

The trip plan will be the next order of business. Athena was looking for an opportunity to corner Basil and get him on board for this trip. After that everything else would fall into place. This was the best plan ever, and everyone would thank her for getting the two kids together. What a success this would be.

Just as Athena predicted, the trip to the beach was not hard to sell, and everyone was very excited to go on a family vacation. Even though Angie didn't want to lose the money, she really needed a vacation and was glad she was asked to join the family. Joey got home just in time to come with them. It was so much fun driving to the Wildwood, New Jersey seashore. It was a great trip, and even more unbelievable, there were no disagreements and no one got upset. When they got to the beach, they found the guest house in which we were to stay. Joey unloaded the car and carried the luggage up to the rooms, and they began to explore the area.

The first stop was the beach. The sand was a beautiful tan color and felt good under their feet. This was going to be fun. The area where they were staying was made up of old guest houses. These were groups of houses which devoted the first floor to a dining room and kitchen where the guests were served home-cooked breakfast, lunch, and dinner. There was a schedule posted stating the serving times for meals. On the second and third floors there were long halls with rooms on both sides of the halls. There were two bathrooms at each end that the guests shared. This was the very first time that Angie, Joey, and Sammie were ever in this kind of a guest house, but this made it a real adventure. The house itself was a quaint old-fashioned home. Angie loved it. They had arrived in time for lunch and were told where to sit. Much to the kids' surprise, Athena's friend and her family were already seated at the same table. The two women greeted each other with genuine affection and turned and introduced their families to each other.

Ted and Steve were both older than Joey and Angie but seemed very interested in getting to know both of them. Right after lunch Angie, Joey, and Sammie wanted to put on their bathing suits and go to the beach. Steve and Ted told them to slow down; they would be out to join them in a minute. That was the way the vacation started, and it was already a hit. Ted seemed to be very interested in Angie and was always trying to get close to her. Angie, being Angie, was so intent on swimming that she didn't even notice. They swam and dove into the waves and played as if they had not ever seen water before. Of course, they always had fun at the pool, but the ocean was so much more thrilling. Finally, they all decided to take a break and made their way back toward the beach umbrellas where the parents had made a great place for them to sit and rest before the second bout with the ocean. Suntan lotion was making its rounds, and everyone was slathering themselves with it to attempt to avoid a sunburn. There were really two groups of people—the younger ones and the older ones. Bobby was so engrossed in all of these new things around him that he wanted to be part of it. Angie walked over to the little guy and picked him up and began to carry him down by the beach. She let him splash his little feet in the water, and he laughed and kicked his feet all the harder. Athena kept very quiet during this time as she did not want to start anything. After all it really was a help to her not to have to chase him around the sand. She was very tired now and needed a nap.

The sun finally began to set, and it was time to pick up the beach towels and all of the beach equipment to take back to the guest house until tomorrow when they would haul it all out again. Ted stayed back to help Angie and Joey pick up the stuff. If this was a preview of things to come this was going to be one of the best vacations they had had in a long time.

Ted managed to sit next to Angie and spent the entire dinner dominating her, which seemed very strange since Angie had always liked to mix with everyone, not just one person. Joey was thinking that it was about time that Angie got a little attention, especially since Jimmy dumped her and didn't look back; at least that's the way it looked. Maybe this will build up her confidence again. She had worked herself to death trying to get through school all because the old man would not pop a cent to help her. The whole thing made him sick.

The week went on, and Angie and Ted became a couple. Everyone spent the day together as a group, and at night Ted would always take Angie for a walk. Joey was a little concerned that Ted was too old for her. He seemed too smooth and experienced. What was he trying to do with a girl like Angie anyway? Joey was afraid she would get hurt. Even Basil was beginning to show a little concern by the amount of attention that Ted was paying Angie. His concerns were essentially the same as Joey's. That evening Basil talked to Athena about the situation. She reassured him that Ted was a very nice young man.

"Just take it easy and enjoy the fact that for the first time since graduation she is having some fun."

"OK. I'll take it easy, but I just don't like this guy as much as you seem to. He seems to be too advanced for a girl like Angie."

For right now he was just watching, but if he saw anything out of the ordinary he would be all over it. Athena was not too worried about it. She was sure Ted would sweep her off her feet. She hoped they would elope before anyone knew what happened. Basil and she would not have to pay for a wedding nor take any responsibility in the outcome. This was an excellent plan she told herself.

The rest of the week flew by. Angie was having a little innocent summer romance. That was all it was to her. They laughed and joked and played in the waves and were inseparable. Steve tried to intervene and break up the intensity, but Ted just chased him off.

Finally it was the last evening on the beach and that was when Ted made his move to seal the deal. He suggested that they take a long walk after dinner down to the dock where they could be alone. Ted was well aware of Athena and his mother's scheme to get the two of them together, but he never indicated that he knew. As far as he was concerned, she was a decent girl, was lots of fun, and young enough to be manipulated into his way of thinking. She had no clue as to what his lifestyle was, and that fact would make it much easier to convert her to his way of thinking. It would most certainly get his parents off his back, and he would have someone to take care of him. She was a hard worker and there would be no reason for her to stop. He could sure use the extra money, and it would bring respectability to their relationship. If they got married, no one would question his actions. He could continue his life as always, get his band in gear, and she would be the dutiful wife. She would never know about his girlfriend, the backup singer for the band. He could see her as much as he wanted, and this poor innocent girl would never know what was going on. Now for the hard sell.

He took Angie's hand and stopped. Turning her toward him, he looked into her eyes. He could feel her anxiety and thought he would calm her with these words. "Angie, I love you." He leaned into her kissed her with hot passion.

She had never been kissed this way before and was shocked when he opened his mouth and his tongue went into her mouth probing, searching, tasting her at the same time his hands began to wander under her blouse and touch her breasts. Angie jumped away. "What are you doing? Stop that right now. Who do you think you're messing with?"

He looked at her in shock. Could it be that she was still a virgin?

"Oh! I just want to have you be mine. Don't tell me that you're still a virgin?"

"Is there something wrong with that?" she yelled at him, "I am not an easy piece of ass, just waiting for Romeo to come along and gratify her sexual desires. You can bet your sweet life it will never be included as a goodbye to the end of a summer romance, if that is what this was supposed to be."

This took Ted aback a little. He had played this game before with a whole lot of cooperation and gratitude. Did this girl think she was someone really special? The time had come for his final proposition. "I wanted you to come to Washington D.C. I would set you up in an apartment, and we could get to know each other better. We could get engaged and plan a life together."

Angie was shocked to hear such a proposition. Did he not hear anything that was just said? Was he not listening when she told him about her plan for her education and career? Was she talking to the wind? "I'll tell you what. Let's give ourselves some time to think. We can write to each other and meet again or you could come to Indianapolis during Thanksgiving break. We can see how we feel and maybe then we can make a better decision."

"I don't want to wait that long before we see each other again. We can write to each other and then I could come and see you on a weekend and we could see how we feel then." They both agreed to try this. When Ted kissed her goodnight, it was much gentler. As Angie walked away she was very aware that there was a lot missing in this kiss. The whole evening had fallen short and was very troubling. The passionate kiss and all the tongue and wandering hands were far from thrilling. In fact, she didn't appreciate or enjoy any of it. What was going on? Why did this man want her to move to Washington D.C. when she told him over and over that she was working and taking classes to enter nursing school? She felt very uncomfortable about the whole thing.

Just then Steve came up beside her and said very quietly, "Hi, Angie, I was just walking on the beach when I saw you and Ted. Please don't take this wrong, but I have been watching you and Ted, and I can see that you are one in a million as far as girls go. It's for this reason that I feel I must caution you to please be careful when it comes to Ted. He's a great guy and a wonderful brother, but he falls short on the commitment side of a relationship. I've heard you talk about your work and school and how focused you are on getting into nursing school. Please don't do anything crazy where Ted is concerned. He's always looking for conquests but very rarely manages to fulfill any of his great promises. He loves the game but chokes when it comes to the finish. With all the effort you have made to complete your studies you deserve to achieve your RN and do the work you wish, don't be diverted by a smooth-talking Romeo who will more than likely leave you high and dry. You deserve the best that life holds for you."

Angie looked at Steve and said, "Thank you, Steve. I appreciate your concern and I will not do anything foolish. The world is full of foolish men and women who have made terrible decisions and end up with nothing. Tonight you have not only been a friend but a guardian angel, thank you. All I wanted from Ted was a friendship. I knew that I was not ready for a serious relationship with anyone."

As Ted was walking back to the guest house he was muttering to himself. He was angry that this girl had not only resisted his advances but cooled him with one sentence. He knew that his mother and Athena were trying to fix them up, and he went along with it in the hopes that he could use her as cover to get them off his back. Well that fell through, but he'd fix her. She'll land in hot soup as soon as I give Athena my sob story, he thought with a vengeance. That's all she needs to hear to tear into little Virgin Angie.

Chapter 37

Summer Ended but the Memory Lingered On

Early the next morning the Demetrious family was busy loading up the automobile with luggage and preparing the car for the long drive home. Joey and Angie were busy with the luggage and Sammie was washing the windows. Basil and Athena had gone to the table and began ordering breakfast for the family and were reserving the table for the whole family. Nina and her family had not come down for breakfast yet. As the food began to come out, Basil ran to call the rest of the family in to eat. It was very curious that Nina's family had not come down yet.

Finally, Steve entered the room and sat with the Demetrious family sipping a cup of coffee and visiting with them. They all said goodbye and hoped to see each other again very soon. The family climbed into the car and, with Joey behind the wheel, were on their way back home. The summer vacation was over, and now it was time to get back to reality and back to the daily routine. This was the end of another chapter in all of their lives. Angie seemed to have escaped the trap that Athena had attempted to set and was none the worse for it. Thank God Steve had warned her about a man who had begun to steal her love. She had narrowly escaped without a broken heart. Ted really showed his true colors—the creep.

The drive home was much easier than the one going to the seashore. Perhaps it was because they knew where they were going on the return trip.

After fourteen hours with three drivers and a picnic lunch on the roadside, even Athena enjoyed the trip home. Basil, who had not taken a vacation for several years, looked the most rested he had been for a very long time. Even better they were all getting along and that in itself was a good thing. They pulled up to the house and everyone jumped out and began to unload the car. Athena supervised the work and everything went smoothly.

The next day was Sunday, and the family prepared for church and the start of a new week. Angie felt comfortable with everything that had happened on the vacation and with the way Ted and she had parted. She hoped he would never write her. The truth was that she did not like the way he had acted that last night. He was not very nice, and she had lost respect for him and she was sure that he had never respected her.

She was very anxious to find out if Jimmy had come home as his mother had expected. She would run down to his mother's house and talk to her and find out what was going on with him. If he was in Special Forces she might never see him again or at least for a very long time.

As life would have it, it was time for Athena to probe and find out what had happened between her and Ted. This was a subject Angie would like to avoid. However, she was going to try to delay this until after she found out about Jimmy.

"Angie, please come to the kitchen. I want to talk to you." Before Angie could get out the door, Athena appeared in the kitchen doorway. "I don't think you heard me. I said I wanted to talk to you. Come into the kitchen now."

Angie walked into the kitchen and sat down at the table which had long since become a place to be reprimanded. Athena came into the room and closed the door after her. Her stare made Angie squirm.

"What's wrong, Athena?" was all she was able to get out before everything fell apart.

"I told you that Nina was one of my dear friends, and her family is very special to me. You on the other hand went out of your way to alienate Ted and upset him a great deal. Last night before you came in he stopped and told me that you were very rude to him and hurt his feelings so badly that he would never get over it. What were you thinking? How could you humiliate me and our whole family that way? I am very angry, and it will be a long time before I forgive you for embarrassing our family. What do you have to say for yourself, young lady?"

"Athena, I don't know what Ted told you, but I did not embarrass the family. You must believe me. Ted tried to proposition me by telling me he loved me and wanted me to move to an apartment in Washington D.C. for us to get to know each other better. He didn't consider all the time I have put into my education. He did not even consider that it would be very inappropriate for me to do such a thing. I tried to explain that I would not dishonor my parents by doing such a thing. Then he tried to convince me that I should give it a try and kissed me in a very bold and unacceptable way. I asked him to stop, and he was very angry." Angie did not tell Athena anything about Steve and what he had said, but she could tell that Athena did not believe her. Why was she so upset about all of this anyway? It didn't affect her at all. She refused to humiliate the family by living an immoral life with a good-time Charley. In fact, she was mortified that he had the nerve to even ask such a thing. What kind of girl did he think she was? The big payoff was that she was in trouble for making a good decision. She just couldn't win.

Athena looked at her coldly and said, "You just ruined an opportunity of a lifetime. Ted is a wonderful young man, with much promise. He is really too good for you. You are a loser and always will be.

By this time tears were in Angie's eyes and she replied, "I'm sorry you're displeased with me. I should have known that it was too good to be true that we could return from this wonderful vacation and just savor the great time we had. I will try very hard to finish this last course at night school and see if I can enter nursing school. That way I will be out of the house and perhaps that will be the only thing that will make you happy. I will never be with someone who laughed at me because I was still a virgin. I will never give that up for a quickie on the beach."

As she finished and started to turn to leave, Basil walked through the kitchen door. "What is going on in here?"

"Oh nothing much. Just the fact that your stupid daughter has wrecked the best opportunity of her life, and she will probably never get another opportunity like this ever again."

Angie could not take any more. She turned and ran out of the room and straight out the front door.

"Angie!" Basil called out but to no avail. She was gone.

"What was going on in here?" asked Basil in a very angry voice. "Can't you back off for five minutes? We just got home, and you couldn't even wait for the girl to take her suitcase up to her room before you unloaded on her. I'm getting sick and tired of all this bickering. What did she have time to do to merit all of this? Tell me now and tell me the truth."

Athena was about to open her mouth to tell Basil what a fool Angie had made of herself and the family.

Before she could continue Basil cut in and said in a no nonsense tone of voice, "I've told you over and over again, Angie is not leaving home until she gets married or gets established in her career, which by the way she is paying for in full by working her tail off. If you think that Ted is such a great catch, I think your judgment is clouded by your friendship with Nina. That man is a drinker and a player, but worse than that, I did not like the way he was trying to take advantage of my daughter the whole trip. Thank God she had enough sense to dump him when he tried to make his move. Do not ever try to set up something like that again. My daughter is too precious to me to watch her walk into a disaster." Basil was so upset that he got up and went outside for a walk to cool off.

Athena began to cry, but with Angie gone and Basil off for a walk, she had no choice but to put little Bobby to bed. The way she felt, in her present state of mind, she knew it would be difficult putting herself to bed let alone putting Bobby to bed. Somehow she managed, and the little guy had no problem falling asleep with no understanding of what had just happened.

Athena paced for nearly an hour hoping Basil would make it home before she gave out. This did not happen. Neither Basil nor Angie came home. This made Athena even more nervous than she already was. It was almost midnight before she heard the front door open. She ran to the head of the stairs to see who it was. Then she heard Angie and her father talking. She started to go downstairs when she heard Angie say, "I don't want to make any trouble for you and Athena, Dad, but I cannot keep going on like this. I am tired and cannot keep worrying about what Athena will be upset about the next time she's in a bad mood. If I could just stick it out until I finish this night school class, I will apply to the School of Nursing to see if they will accept me with only an associate degree. I know I will not be able to become a surgical nurse, but I don't think I can make it for a whole year. Athena will hate it."

"You have worked too hard to take second best just because we have some problems at home. We will work them out, and you will finish school as you intended. I will speak with Athena, and she will have to understand that this is what is going to happen and she is to stop harassing you. This is your home as much as anyone's."

Athena heard the words and was stunned by them. Her plan had not only gone poorly but it was a complete disaster. This would be hard to recover from. She turned and walked quietly into the bedroom, got into bed, and pretended to be asleep. As she lay there in bed she heard Angie tiptoe past the room and go into her bedroom. No Basil appeared. After a while fatigue took over and she fell asleep.

Chapter 38

Tension

The atmosphere in the Demetrious household was tense. To say extremely tense would not be an exaggeration. Athena was trying to find a way to justify herself and make up with Basil. However, he was not going to be an easy person to reason with. Exactly what the reasoning would be was not clear. Athena had been caught in a lie, and the circumstance of her involvement was that she was attempting to broker a marriage between Angie and Ted with no concern for the feelings of either of the two parties involved. Ted was well aware of the situation. It was Angie who had no idea what was going on. Ted fully expected Angie to be swept off of her feet and willingly fall into his arms. Angie did not have marriage on her mind, and the way Ted made his move was very insulting and a far cry from romantic. It was inappropriate and a major turn-off.

Basil still had the other children to consider. It would be only a matter of time before she would start on Sammie and Joey to get them out of the house. This troubled him greatly because he had a deeper fear that if he were to die little Bobby would also be in the same situation with Athena wanting him out of her way and on his own, and he would not have anyone to protect him except his brothers and sister. It was a huge worry which he kept pushing into the back of his mind. Basil was becoming more and more troubled about the situation and was seriously contemplating seeing a lawyer to make a will and set up some arrangements for the children. Angie and Joey were fast reaching the age of adulthood and would more or less be on their own. It would be very difficult for them to take care of the two younger children. He did not know what to do.

Chapter 39

Trip to the Lawyer

Basil very rarely used a lawyer and did not have much knowledge about how things were done where wills and guardianships were concerned. He only knew his business and how he would take care of it, but when it came to his children, it did not seem to be quite as easily decided what would be the best solution. He did not trust lawyers very much, yet here he was trying to work out some kind of a plan to ensure that his children would be taken care of in the event that he should die, God forbid. To leave Athena as sole executer at this time, the way she had conducted herself where Angie was concerned, was a very bad choice. It seemed that Angie and Joey would be the best guardians of Sammie and Bobby. This made him feel very sad because he felt as if he were betraying Athena and his marriage promise to love, honor, and cherish her. Here he was actually trying to make arrangements with a lawyer to place his children in the care of someone other than his wife. This seemed too radical a step to be taking. He was becoming very confused and guilt ridden when it came to actually sitting down and working out a plan. Here he was sitting in a lawyer's office, allowing this man to write out a plan. Was this what he really wanted to do? Basil's first mistake was that he had no real trust in lawyers and their conclusions. This was a very big problem. Essentially the first meeting was not good. Basil left the office and decided to make peace with Athena and live with the situation even though not ideal, there was nothing that he heard from the lawyer that made a better alternative.

Chapter 40

Make Peace and Go On

Basil called a truce with Athena with a promise to never try to get Angie or any of the other children out of the house until they were finished with their education and were able to support themselves adequately. She agreed happily to the promise because she was very upset with the way things were going and saw nothing to be gained by continuing this war. Angie made herself scarce once again. She would leave early in the morning and return at night every day. It made it very difficult to make peace with her when she was never at home. Angie really didn't want to make peace. The things her stepmother had said were mean and hurtful. It only proved how little she thought of her. If she had really fallen for that guy she would have a broken heart by now. If anyone was taken advantage of, it was her. Ted knew what the score was, and she was like the lamb to the slaughter. If Steve had not talked to her she would have gone on believing that he really loved her. Ted was actually angry when his plan was rejected. She was surely going to put that into her book of life's experiences. Not Good!

This whole thing had gotten her off track. She was worried about Jimmy and with the entire hubbub it had blown right out of her mind. She needed to get in touch with his mother to see if she had heard from him. Ted was in the past and that was where he would stay.

Her class had just ended, and she was going to stop by Jimmy's mother's house and see what she could find out. She was getting hungry and wanted to get home to eat something before Sammie ate all the leftovers. Athena had been careful to leave a plate of food for her every night, and it seemed to please her dad a great deal. She would have to thank Athena and make peace for everyone's sake.

She arrived at Jimmy's house and rang the bell. His mother came to the door and greeted her. "Angie, I'm glad you came by. I've been thinking about you. I got a letter from Jimmy, and he is shipping out soon. He couldn't tell me where he was going, but he's getting a one week furlough before he goes. I think it's best to let him get in touch with you on his own. The letter sounded very detached, and I don't want to push him on anything."

Angie looked up and nodded her head in agreement and said, "If he would like to see me, I'll be very pleased. If not I'll understand." She thanked his mother and said goodbye and headed home. Time to make peace and stop being a jerk. There were real battles to fight, and they weren't family feuds.

On the way home her thoughts were full of Jimmy. The answer to her prayers was that he was all right and from her conversation with his mother, all indications seemed to point to good news. He would be home soon, and she felt certain that he would get in touch with her.

The front door to the house was opened when she got home, and the family was waiting for her. She greeted them and walked to the kitchen and was happy to find a plate of food waiting on the warmer for her. As she sat down to eat her dinner Athena came into the kitchen. Angie looked up and thanked her for having a warm dinner waiting for her. Athena smiled, looked at her stepdaughter, and said that she wanted to put the past behind them and start a new page in their relationship. Angie looked up in surprise. This was a miracle. Athena had made her apology very easily and the two women hugged each other and put an end to the feud once and for all.

"This is your home, Angie, and I want you to know that. You must complete your studies, and we are behind you one hundred percent. It's important for you to know that and not worry about anything concerning where you will live. This is where you will live for as long as you need."

"Thank you, Athena, for putting my mind at ease I really appreciate it. I will never forget this gift you have given me tonight."

Chapter 41

The Furlough

Summer was coming to an end, and Angie made the decision to take the two courses she needed and enter nursing school the following year. She was excited. Nursing school was just around the corner. She was confident that she would do well and would be able to take an entrance exam for surgical nursing. This was what she had been working for all this time.

As Basil sat down to read the daily paper, the doorbell rang. He got up from his easy chair and opened the door. He was greeted by Jimmy. The two men exchanged a warm handshake, and Basil exclaimed, "Jimmy, my boy, welcome home! It's good to see you."

"Thank you, Mr. Demetrious; it's good to be home. Are Angie and Joey home? I thought if they hadn't eaten yet we could go to the Tee Pee and grab a sandwich. Believe it or not, I've really missed the Tee Pee's food."

'I'll bet that you will have no problem talking them into it. I'll call them. Wait just a moment."

It was no time at all before both Angie and Joey were bolting down the stairs. "Jimmy, how it is going buddy?" Joey was the first to come into the room and he gave his good friend a giant hug.

Angie was a little more reserved saying, "Hi, Jimmy."

Jimmy took Angie's hand and gave it a squeeze and did not let go right away.

"I wanted you guys to go to the Tee Pee and grab a sandwich with me."

"Say no more; we're ready to go," Joey said. The three of them were on their way. It was like old times except it was not old times. It was new and uncertain times for all of them.

Angie's heart was racing, and she could hardly control her joy at seeing Jimmy again even though part of her wanted to give him a hard time for not writing. She was too happy to complain about anything.

They were just pulling up to the Tee Pee when Jimmy said, "This is my dream. I've been thinking about coming home and going to the Tee Pee with you guys for months. I can't believe it's finally happening."

This was a very special moment for them all. They were all together. Even better, they were about to chow down on a delicious Big Chef double-decker hamburger with everything on it and a creamy chocolate milkshake. As they were enjoying their food, Jimmy started telling them what he had been doing over the past few months and why he had not been able to get in touch with them. What Angie had suspected was in fact true. He was in Special Forces and was receiving secret training. He couldn't talk about his mission, but he did know that it was dangerous and he was being shipped to Korea as soon as he returned to the base. All he could say was that he would be on the Thirty-Eighth Parallel. No one would hear from him during that time and if anything happened to him only his mother would be notified.

It was a lot to take in. Though Angie suspected Jimmy was in Special Forces, she was not prepared to hear it. Not only did it sound dangerous, but it was dangerous. The two of them begged Jimmy to be careful and told him he would always be in their prayers.

"Hey, come on, let's lighten up a little. Sure it's dangerous, but that's what all the special training is for, to keep us alive. This will be over soon, and then we can all pick up where we left off. I'll finish at the university and start my career. Everything will be normal again."

This all sounded good, but there was still the fear in all of their hearts that nothing would ever be normal again. Life as they knew it had changed, and it would forever be changed. Joey knew that Jimmy and Angie wanted to be alone for a while so when he saw some friends come into the restaurant, he excused himself and went over to their table.

There was an awkward silence for a few minutes and then Angie said, "Jimmy, I must admit I didn't realize what you were doing was so dangerous. I was a little angry when I didn't hear from you. I know you were very clear about not wanting any strings attached when you left and I agreed, but I'm not sure I really meant it. I hoped you would write. I understand now why you couldn't, but at the time, it was very hard."

It seemed to her that he owed her an apology, and it seemed to him that there was no need for any apology or explanation. What he was doing was secret and he was not able to tell anyone. The fact that she knew as much as she did was already more than she and Joey should have known.

"I did not dream that you had volunteered for Special Forces and were training for a special mission."

"It's okay, Angie. I know I was pretty rough on you when I left. We went from sweet romance to bittersweet parting. I have no right to hold you up with your life and don't expect you to promise me anything. You're free to go out and see whoever you wish. I only ask that you give me a fair chance when I come home."

"You promise me that you will at least give me a fair chance also. After all, you're the one going away. I'll be here until you return.

All in all the evening was a good one—actually one of the best in a long time. Jimmy asked if he could see her again tomorrow night. She told him that as far as she was concerned the week was reserved for him. This made him happy.

He gave her a gentle peck on the lips and said goodnight. "I'll see you tomorrow."

This was a very special evening, and it meant the world to Angie.

The week was a whirlwind of activities. Angie and Jimmy went out every night and had a lot of fun. She already knew that she was in love with Jimmy, and this week sealed the deal. As the day of his departure crept closer, Angie felt herself feeling melancholy at the thought of his leaving. It was more than she could bear. She knew this day would come, but everything was so perfect that she could not stand the thought of not having Jimmy around. She was beginning to slip and felt herself falling more deeply in love with him.

Up to this time there was no heavy petting and no mention of sex, but it was definitely on both their minds. On the last night of the furlough they were carried away until they both were ready to lose control when Angie wanted Jimmy and Jimmy wanted Angie even more. All the loneliness that had overtaken her during the past few months became too much for her. She had loved Jimmy since the Grad Dance and nothing had changed. It was the same for him. How they had managed to deny those feelings was a mystery to both. Angie was ready to give in when Jimmy stopped and looked deep into her eyes and said, "No, Angie, not like this. When we do this it is not going to be in the back seat of a car as if it was loveless sex. What if you would get pregnant? No, let's stop this now. This is not the way we want our first child to be conceived. We'll be married in our church with our families and friends present. You'll wear a white wedding grown, and I'll wear a tux. Best of all we'll have a first night on our honeymoon that we will remember the rest of our lives, and it will be spectacular and we will love each other the rest of our lives. I will wait for you forever. We both know how we feel. I'm not wise enough to say our love will never change, but I do believe that if it changes it will be for the better."

They parted that night feeling they had something to work toward and knowing that the bond between them was strong enough to get through the immediate future. However, it was not going to be easy.

Angie was accepted into the school of nursing, and at last she was able to begin her education for the career she had wanted for so long. She didn't hear from Jimmy. She knew this would happen, but she didn't realize how difficult it would be to wait and not know. Her father tried to make it easier for her by saying no news was good news. Even Athena tried to comfort her, but it was impossible to forget that Jimmy was in constant danger and could be killed.

Angie was glad that the school of nursing was consuming so much of her energy. The work and classes took up all of her time. She was forced to take a leave of absence from her job in order to meet the demands of her classes. Fortunately, all her hard work the previous year had not gone unnoticed, and she was awarded a scholarship that covered almost all of her tuition. Basil reassured her he would help pay her other needs. He felt she had proven herself, and he was willing to help her reach her goal.

She thanked God for this promise. She prayed every night that Jimmy was all right.

Chapter 42

What Happened to Eddy and Jenny?

Eddy and Jenny were at an impasse. Neither one really wanted to change. Eddy gave in and told Jenny to find a booth space and give the beauty business a try. She immediately jumped at the chance and went to the city to check on the possibilities that might be available.

With Jenny out of the office, Eddy could finally relax and reassess his business. His problems with Jenny had made everything seem impossible. He no longer knew if he really loved her or if his business was worth salvaging. Worst of all, he had begun to believe he really was a world-class loser as Jenny kept telling him over and over again. There was no denying the fact that all these ugly words and accusations had taken a huge toll on him. He had to force himself to kiss her; sex was almost nonexistent, and he had no desire to even try to change that. Jenny was an uncontrollable force, and he was worn out. The only good thing that came out of all the fighting and ugliness between them was due to his relentless demands that they pay their debts. They were at last debt free.

He could at long last consider taking his business to the next level and begin the expansion which he had put off for so long.

Eddy decided to hire a salesman on commission-only basis to help increase the sales. This was a huge step for him, but somehow he felt that it was a good move.

Jenny found a decent booth space where she felt that she could build a good customer base. She signed a lease and made a shopping list of supplies she would need. She liked the people who were working in the shop and for the first time in a long time, she felt good about this decision. She placed her order and set out to check the rest of the area where she planned to begin her new career.

Jenny had never really found peace in anything she had done. She was barely speaking to her mother. The more she thought about that, the worse she felt. After the wedding, her mother had made many attempts to make up with Jenny, but they never did manage to find a convenient time to meet. She was overcome by sadness; she missed her mother. Deciding that a call was long past due, she picked up the phone and invited her to have lunch sometime. It was not much, but it was better than nothing.

That evening Jenny met Eddy for dinner before his night shift. She was excited about the progress that she had made with her life, beginning a career as a beautician and taking a step to mend the relationship with her mother. She wanted to share the news with Eddy. At last something was going right. In all the time they had been married she had never wanted to reveal any of her plans to him. For the first time ever Eddy and Jenny were not only ready to share their news with each other but were actually excited about doing it. This was a real revelation.

First Jenny told Eddy all about her booth space and where it was. She also told him that she felt quite sure that the shop was doing a great deal of business and that she could do well there. She showed him the lease agreement she had signed and the order for supplies needed. She would be up and running in four days. The joy that she felt beamed from her face. Eddy could not help but smile. Then she told him the best news of all; she had called her mother and they were going to have lunch together the next day. Too much time had passed without seeing her, and she really missed her very much. She wanted to repair the relationship.

Eddy listened with mixed emotions. He could not believe what he was hearing. Jenny was really making strides in her life. He was happy for her and wondered if he had been wrong in his judgment. Maybe he was too hard on her about the debts she ran up. He should have been more understanding.

They both had started out on the wrong foot and the result was a miserable marriage. Was it possible for them to turn things around and be happy?

Now it was his turn to share his new plan. He told Jenny about the new salesman he hired to help him expand the business. He wanted to wait about six months and then build an auto repair shop in the rear of the office. That way, he could not only sell the automobiles but also service policies which would increase his income quite a bit. He was thinking of hiring a night girl to take care of the phone lines and give Maria a break. This would give her time to help with more of the office work since Jenny would no longer be at Eddy's Cool Deals.

"Why haven't we talked like this before tonight, Eddy? I feel as if I have never really known you at all, and we've been married for three years now."

"I feel the same way, too, but let's not rush anything. We've been on a very rocky road, and I personally cannot trust you to not go back to your old ways. I can't take that anymore. Let's see if we can really get along and then when we are both confident that we can handle our relationship, we can move into a real marriage."

"I understand what you're saying, and I'm willing to try. I've said some very terrible things to you, and I know you will have trouble forgetting them, but we can both at least try, don't you think?"

Eddy smiled and moved close to her. "Let's seal it with a kiss." His kiss was full of hope for a brighter future.

The two of them threw themselves into their respective businesses and began to enjoy the adventure of starting over and making a success of what they were doing. Eddy's Cool Deals was expanding, and Eddy was doing great. The new salesman worked out to be an asset. As a result, Eddy added another salesman to help and for the first time since he opened, he had much more than he could handle.

Jenny opened her booth space and began accepting every walk-in that came through the door. Her clientele began to grow as did her profits. She made many friends there at the shop and was content with her booth space. The only thing that really troubled her was the class ring that she had taken from Angie. When her mind went back to that day at beauty school, she could not believe she had done such a thing to that poor girl who was so focused on her education. Angie loved the ring, and Jenny knew it. She had been foolish enough to believe that the ring was magical. It held no more magic than any other ring. I wonder what ever happened to Angie, she thought. She seemed to have disappeared. No one in any of the shops around her area had ever heard of Angie

Demetrious. Perhaps someday their paths would cross. Who knows? One thing she did know was that she needed to get her marriage back on track and the two of them make this joy she felt last forever.

One day Jenny was working on a new customer—a teenager who wanted a special hairdo for the senior prom. They were talking when the subject of her senior class ring came up. The girl mentioned she didn't get a class ring because of the expense and had really regretted it. This was like an arrow into Jenny's heart especially because it brought back the whole class ring incident. The grip of guilt strangled her like cold boney fingers around her neck. As they were chatting, Jenny reached into her uniform packet and pulled out the ring and handed it to the teenager. "I know this is not from your school," she said with a catch in her voice, "but wear this Circle Center senior class ring and pretend it's your school. Think of it as a graduation gift. It's yours"

"Oh! Thank you so much, but I can't take it. This is your ring, is it not?"

"No dear, it's a ring I found and have had for many years. I'm giving it to you and keep it as long as you like, and if you wish you, may pass it on to someone else. How does that sound?"

"I love it. It will be perfect, and I'll always treasure it. Thank you."

With that action the Circle City class ring had a new owner and Jenny was no longer under its spell. Maybe everything else in her life was going to change. Who knows?

Chapter 43

Colleen's Baby Is Born

Life in Crete was as good as it could be considering that Mimi was in Korea with the Greek army and Colleen was great with child. Her time to deliver was getting close. Mama had made things much easier for her, especially when she insisted that Colleen move into her home temporarily, or at least until Mimi returned from the army. She was still working at the wool factory every day, but it was becoming more and more difficult to continue this heavy load. The baby's due date was in one month give or take two weeks. At this time, it was what the doctor estimated. It was going to be a normal childbirth. Because Mimi had been away most of this time in Korea, he had missed all but the first month of the pregnancy. She was well aware that he would not return before the birth of their child. In three months he would have been gone a year. Colleen was not prepared for the emotional stress that the pregnancy would cause and how depressed she would get without Mimi's support. Mama had been wonderful to her. They had worked side by side in the wool factory attempting to bring it back to the level of excellence of its former reputation. Mama had an exceptional mind for business and many of the former experienced employees returned to work for her. They were both sure that Mimi would be pleased with the results. The salesmen were busy writing orders for the factory, and Mama and Colleen were trying to get the shipping department prepared for the orders to go out. Colleen was seriously thinking of going home to Ireland to be with her mother for the birth of her baby. Even with Mama as wonderful as she had been, she was becoming increasingly sad and missed Mimi and missed her family in Ireland desperately. She wanted to see them especially now that she was going to bring a new life into the world.

The plant was running smoothly, and the manager of production was very competent. Mama had a good group of employees, and she could rely on them to take care of everything. She could even come to Ireland with her and be present when her first grandchild was born.

Colleen considered all these things as she was trying desperately not to think of what was really in her heart. She could not stop crying from fear and loneliness. Mimi was in Korea, and she had only heard from him sporadically for the last few months. He was stationed close to the front lines, and it was difficult to get letters out. He sounded upset because he could not be with Colleen for the birth of his first child. He seemed unhappy, and it was very clear that he felt that war was *hell*. He never asked about the wool factory and how things were in Crete nor had he ever written the words I love you from the time he was shipped out. She had to stop thinking about this. It just made her sadder and sadder. With her sorrow came the tears. She found herself often crying alone. She didn't want to upset Mama. She was already worried enough for the safety of her son. Colleen was about to write a letter to Mimi telling him that she was going to go to Ireland for the baby's birth. When Mama came into the room to check on her and found that her daughter-in-law was crying and looking very forlorn. She had known for a long time that Colleen had been heart sick with Mimi gone, but she had hoped when the baby was born it would make her happy. Deep in her heart she knew that nothing would make her happy except seeing Mimi again.

Mama handed her a handkerchief. As Colleen dabbed her tear streaked cheeks, she discussed the trip to Ireland. The older woman, lit up. "I would love to go to Ireland with you, but first, we must receive the doctor's approval. This would be a long trip and there may be many risks. We also need to make sure that your mother has a skilled doctor to deliver the baby when the time comes," Mama instructed. Colleen's time was so close that she feared for Colleen and the baby. Mama said that if the doctor did not approve for her to make such a long trip, she would have her mother come to Crete to be with her and to see her first grandbaby born. "How does that sound?"

Colleen nodded happily as newfound smile met her face. She went to the telephone to call the doctor. Mama stayed with her as she made the call, but the news was not what the young mother-to-be wanted to hear. As Mama had thought, he was uneasy about Colleen traveling to Ireland. He didn't want her to take any chances. He was familiar with her case and was afraid of a breech birth because the baby was very active and kept turning. Her heart sunk with disappointment, and her eyes filled with tears filled once again.

"Please don't cry, my child," Mama said trying to comfort her. "We'll call the airport and see if any flights are available for your mother to come to Crete. If not, we will check the ships. It would take a little longer for her to arrive, but we will not give up."

Mama got on the phone immediately and called the airport. She was able to get a flight out next Tuesday. "Now let's check with your mother and see if that would work for her."

Colleen picked up the phone and called her mother to see if she was willing to come. It was amazing how Mama was always able to solve problems which seemed insurmountable. She was so happy to hear her mother's voice that she started to cry again – only this time her tears were that of joy. As Mama had predicted, her mother was thrilled to come to Crete. So the two women once again became a team and began working on making reservations and plans for Colleen's mother to come to Crete for the birth of the baby. For the first time in months, Colleen was smiling. Her mother was going to come to Crete to see her and to be with her when the baby was born. She would arrive on Tuesday; this was wonderful.

The excitement had exhausted Colleen, and Mama made her go to bed before she became sick. After working with the young woman all these months she knew very well that she would work continuously until she could barely place one foot in front of another.

Colleen went to bed for a short rest and fell fast asleep. She didn't wake until the housekeeper came into the room with a tray of food for her. "Mama has given strict orders that you are to stay in bed and get some much needed rest." The housekeeper looked for somewhere to put the tray. "Where would you like this?" she asked. Colleen motioned toward the table. She set the tray down close to the bed and quietly left the room. Colleen ate her dinner and once again lay down. Before she knew it, she was sound asleep once more. Exhausted, she slept till morning. When she awoke, she felt like a new person. It's amazing what a good night's sleep will do for you.

After breakfast Colleen sat down at the table and wrote a letter to Mimi telling him the news of her mother coming to Crete and of all the help that Mama had given her. She wrote how much she loved and missed him. The letter went on about the many systems that had been put in place in the factory and how well everything was going. She emphasized what a brilliant business woman his mother was and how she had come to love her as if she was her own mother. As she wrote these words her eyes filled with tears as she had never expected to have such feelings for anyone but her own mother.

The days passed and finally her mother arrived from Ireland. What a glorious day that was. Mama wisely left mother and daughter alone to catch up on family news. It was no time at all before the three women had bonded and became fast friends. Colleen's mother was filled with happiness and thought her daughter was fortunate to have such a thoughtful and kind mother-in-law.

It was not long after her mother's arrival that a letter came from Mimi. Colleen held the letter to her heart as if by doing so she would be closer to him. If only it were that easy. He was answering a letter which she had sent a month ago. But she didn't care how old the letter was. It was from him, and she loved it. She kissed the writing and kept hugging it. This was as close as they could get to each other. Oh how she missed him and loved him. Words were not adequate to describe what she was going through and if her eyes could see across the ocean she would see that he had done the same thing to her letter when he received it.

Two days later, the labor pains began. The two mothers readied her and took her to the hospital. The two grandmothers and the mother were now prepared to meet the new little baby. Was it to be a boy or a girl? Nothing more to do now but wait until the little one decided to make an appearance.

The hours passed and still no baby. The grandmothers were pacing the floor and wondering if anyone would come out and tell them anything. It seemed as if a century had passed since they had brought her to the hospital. Mama had gone to the desk many times now to inquire as to the well-being of her daughter-in-law, but no one seemed to have any information. What was the problem? The waiting was making them wonder if there may be some sort of problem. Of course the waiting and not knowing was nerve-wracking.

Finally after five hours the doctor came out and told the ladies that a very healthy and beautiful little boy had arrived. He weighed 7 pounds and 8 ounces. Then he said it would be about an hour before they would have Colleen in her room and that they had plenty of time to go and get some lunch. The two of the new grandmothers hugged each other with great joy then grabbed the doctor with so much happiness that their first grandchild had arrived and was healthy and a boy. Mama knew that Mimi would be very happy when he heard the news. Mama decided to send a letter along with a picture to let him know that he was now a father of a baby boy and that the baby and his wife were both well. Because Mama was a very thoughtful person she felt that it would be best if she mentioned this to Colleen and her mother first. That afternoon when they went to visit the mother and child, she asked Colleen if she would object if she sent a note to Mimi announcing the arrival of the baby boy.

"Oh, Mama, yes, of course we need to tell Mimi. He needs to know." Colleen smiled. She wished he was there. "He will be so happy. I wish I could see his face when he gets the news that he now has a son." It had been a long time since she had heard from him, and it was becoming increasingly more and more difficult to include him in her world. She was very disappointed in his lack of interest in how she was and what was going on in this little world of hers. Nevertheless, she really needed to notify him that he had become the father of a beautiful baby boy. She asked Mama to bring her some note paper to write this announcement on, and she would take care of it tomorrow as soon as she got the paper and envelope. The thought of writing this announcement to Mimi made her very nervous. She had begun to feel that he had no interest in what was happening back home. It was almost as if his home had become the army barracks and his family was his platoon. This was silly of course. They would be his family now that his life would depend on these men around him. This was war. She would write the announcement as soon as Mama brought the note paper and pen. Making peace with the fact that Mimi was at war and wasn't in charge of what was happening to his life made her feel much better. When her mother and Mama were preparing to leave Colleen asked if Mama would bring the camera tomorrow and take a picture of her and the baby to send to Mimi. Mama was very pleased that she had asked and reassured her she would.

Chapter 44

Mimi in the Army

Evening chow had just ended and even though it wasn't roasted lamb and potatoes with a village salad, stewed green beans, and a loaf of village bread, it served its purpose. The day had been brutal and many men were injured and a few had lost their lives. The meal was something to thank God for even though He seemed to be very far away in this God forsaken country. But even with all the war going on around you, Mimi still knew God was near. The Yanks were across the way and were very friendly men. They were a generous and good-hearted group, always inviting the guys over for a beer. They were the kind of guys you wanted by your side when you went into battle. He had to take time out to write Colleen a letter. He had owed her one for a long time now but didn't really want her to know how bad things were there. He realized that the baby's due date was very close, and he wanted to be there to share in the joy of the arrival of his first child. Mama would be fussing around getting everything ready. Thinking about all of the preparation for the new baby made him very sad. This was a time of joy, not a time of separation. In this Hell Hole there was not much joy and certainly not a lot of celebration. He had to stop thinking in this manner or he would go mad. Once again he put off writing to Colleen. What could he say? Today he watched a fellow soldier get his head blown off, and he's still shaking in his boots. Better still his battalion just inherited three new house boys. All three are orphans who are trying to survive by cleaning up the barracks and doing the laundry in exchange for a little food and two dollars. Two of them had younger brothers and sisters who were depending upon them for everything. There was no one else to help these poor kids; it was all left up to them to help each other. He would not even have considered writing these kinds of truths to his love. She would be so very upset to think that these children were left to their own resources to survive. Now that would be a great thing to tell a woman who was expecting their first baby any time now. He'd wait a few more days and then write her a letter.

One month later a note came from Colleen announcing the birth of their son. He was a beautiful baby boy weighing seven pounds and eight ounces. She hadn't name him yet because she wanted him to be a part of this event. She told him that she was well and his Mama was a tremendous help. Also her own mother had come to Crete because of Mama's generous heart. She closed by sending all her love to him and hoped he would be home very soon. "Please write me," was her plea. "I miss you very much. If you don't say anything other than you are well that would be enough to make me happy for months."

Mimi's eyes filled with tears as he read these words. He had a son, his wife missed him, and all she wanted to hear was that he was well. He immediately picked up a pen and began writing the letter which he had put off for too long and poured out his heart to his love and expressed his joy over their new son. Before he knew it, he had written a letter filled with love and caring for her and his family. He closed the letter by saying they should name their son after his two grandfathers.

Chapter 45

As Time Goes By

Colleen was busy working from home and taking care of the baby at the same time. Mama had insisted that she stay with her, and of course, her judgment was correct. With the help of the housekeeping staff, the burden of staying on top of the everyday responsibilities of keeping house and taking care of the baby was lifted from her. As a result, she was able to recover from the delivery much sooner. It also allowed her to help Mama with some of the bookkeeping responsibilities, which she had been doing while she was expecting the baby.

By all accounts it was a day very much like every other day. She had finished feeding the baby and was about to lay him down in his crib to take his morning nap when the doorbell rang. This was not such an unusual thing to happen in the morning. The mailman was always very thoughtful and would bring the mail to the front door so that Colleen or Mama would not have to go out to the mailbox to retrieve it. The people here on the island were very kind and considerate to her. He handed her the mail. "I hope there is a special surprise for you today," he said with a knowing smile. Since he said that nearly every day she did not pay any attention to what he said. She placed the mail on the table and went back to laying the baby down for his nap.

The little guy was snuggled in his crib sleeping soundly, so she went back to the mail. She would separate the bills from the personal. As she picked up the mail and began that process, she noticed that one of the envelopes was different from the rest. She quickly pulled out the odd envelope and saw a letter addressed to her from an army P.O. box. Her face flushed and her hands began to shake. It was a letter from Mimi. Her heart skipped a beat, and she felt as if she would faint. The envelope was addressed to her and the writing was Mimi's. Her hands were shaking so much that she could scarcely open the envelope. She finally managed to open it and pulled out the contents. Her heart was racing by now, and she felt tears come to her eyes. She was afraid that she might die as she was having trouble breathing. She must be strong. Her baby was depending on her to take care of him. She glanced at the first page and began to read his words.

My darling Colleen,

You are the love of my life. I have missed you desperately and could not bring myself to write you for fear you had grown weary of waiting for me. This war has taken its toll on all of us here at the camp. I could not bring myself to write about all the horrors I have known for the past few months. There has been human suffering and death all around me. I could not write to you of the terrible things that I have had to suffer here on the front lines. When my battalion gets back to camp, we try to forget what is going on all around us. Everyone here is suffering, but the children are the most seriously affected. At the present, time we have five orphaned houseboys in our barracks who work cleaning up our facility in exchange for food. One of the children has two younger orphaned siblings, and there is no one to help them. We try to send blankets, towels, and as much food as we can. This is not how children should have to live.

My dear wife, my heart is breaking watching these things happening. I am so grateful that I am able to help these children although I wish I could do more. With God's help and guidance we will be able to give them a better life.

I am counting how many months, weeks, and days that are left until I return to you and our son. My heart breaks when I think of all the things I have missed and will miss because I am here. I want to be home for our baby's first tooth, first word, and first step, but I know these things will come and you will witness them without my presence. I promise that I will make up all of this lost time and slowly we will both forget that once there was a war in far off Korea and we were separated by it; but we will be together again and our love will only grow. When I think of all that, I have already missed it breaks my heart. I should have been the one to take you to the hospital. My eyes should have been one of the first pair of eyes to see our son. Don't misunderstand me. I am very grateful for Mama and your mother being there with you. If I could not be there I am so glad that they were and that you were not alone with no one to help you through this experience. All I can say is that war is hell and my wish is to come home as soon as possible.

Please, name our son after his two grandfathers, Constantine Patrick. Ask my good friend, Theo, to be godfather to our little Costa. I know you will want to baptize our son soon, but I beg of you please do not baptize our son until I return, please do this for me.

I promise I will write you often and please send me pictures of our son so that I can feel that I am part of his life even if I am far away from Crete. I will be home soon.

Give my love to your mother and Mama. I love you more than you could know. Kiss little Costa for me and please tell him his father loves him very much.

All my love to you. I long to hold you in my arms again.

Your

Mimi

As Colleen finished the letter she crushed it to her heart and began to sob uncontrollably. About that time, Mama was coming home for her lunch break. As she entered the house she saw Colleen sobbing. Her heart filled with fear. She saw that her daughter-in-law was holding a letter to her heart and she feared the worst had happened. She raced to her side. "What is it? What is wrong? Is it Mimi?"

Colleen looked up. "Everything is fine, Mama." She reassured. Mama put her hand over her heart. "I'm having a cry of joy due because of this beautiful letter from my husband."

Mama calmed down and began to ask questions about what Mimi had said. This was all normal as she just wanted to know that her son was well. Colleen kept saying he loves us all and wishes to be home. Both women were pacified just by talking about Mimi and knowing that he was alive and well. Somehow the letter had brought calm to the household.

The time seemed to both stop and fly by at the same time. When Colleen was watching the baby change day by day it seemed that the time was going too fast. Mimi had been correct when he had written that he would miss many firsts with little Costa. He had finally begun to sleep through the night. This was indeed a blessing. For the first time since he was born she was able to sleep through the night, too. It was wonderful. The first night that it happened she thought that something terrible had happened to him. She was terrified to look into the crib for fear that he had caught some unknown disease and was gravely ill. When she discovered that he had just slept through the night she was overjoyed. Then came the time he turned over in bed by himself. These were major thresholds for her baby and Mimi would only hear about them in her letters and her pictures which by now could fill an album.

He would answer her and tell her just how much he loved her letters updating him on their son's progress and the pictures were always in his pocket so he could look at them. He especially loved the ones where she was holding little Costa in her arms. They were the most beautiful sight in the world. He always begged her to be sure to show Costa pictures of him so he would not be a stranger when he came home.

Mama tried very hard to keep up the pace which was required to run the factory, but she had reached the point of complete exhaustion and was ordered to complete bed rest. The time had come when Colleen and little Costa needed to move back to their own home. She had been a wonderful support all this time, but now she was ill and did not need her and her baby there. She knew that no matter how much she would try to keep Mama quiet, she would get up and fuss. Colleen had to move back to the home which Mimi and she had. Mama was very upset that they had to leave but she herself knew that she was no longer able to work at the wool factory. She asked her housekeeper to send a competent maid and nanny to Colleen's home as she would have an increase of multiple tasks at the Wool Factory to say nothing of the responsibilities of the baby. Therefore, Colleen and little Costa moved back home and were accompanied by a housekeeper, nanny, and a cook. Mama was an angel to think of all the things which she would need. She had asked that as soon as the baby was settled and the staff had been given their orders for her to return so she could update her on the Wool Factory's status. Everything was going smoothly at home, and Colleen was going to shop for some basic things that were needed. It had been many months since anyone had lived at the house.

The cleaning supplies were current as Mama had a crew go to the house and freshen it every week. She had everything recorded in an outline and when Colleen arrived she was ready to go over it in detail. Colleen had not been away from little Costa since he was born and to say that she was nervous would be an understatement. She called the house to check on him, and the nanny reported the little guy was sound asleep. Therefore, the meeting between the two women went very well, and Colleen promised to report to Mama anything that deviated from her plan of action.

The next morning Colleen went to the factory and began her work. The nanny had taken over little Costa's care and now she faced the same feelings that Mimi had. Someone other than the parents would be present when the baby got his first tooth, took his first step, and many other firsts, but she had to step up and do her part until Mimi could come home and take over completely. At this time, the most important thing was for Mama to get the rest she needed and be returned to good health once more. As a result Colleen was thrust into the managerial tasks at the wool factory.

The months flew by now with all the work at the factory and the baby at home. She had been able to set up a good schedule so that she could spend as much time with Costa as possible. There were some days when the nanny would bring the baby to the factory. Colleen would feed him and enjoy some mommy time with him. She managed to keep up her communications with Mimi and her family in Ireland, but she was beginning to get very tired. As she viewed the calendar, in three months Mimi should be eligible for honorable discharge. Little Costa was now nine months old and as of yet he had not done more than stand up in his playpen. Perhaps Mimi would be home before he took his first steps. He will be so proud of his son. Costa looks very much like Mimi and Mama. He had Mimi's eyes and dark wavy hair and Mama's lips and chin. There was not a lot of Irish in him except for his light skin. She missed Mimi so much that she was skipping months hoping to get him home sooner.

Mama was much better. The doctors did not want her to return to work, but she was back helping and allowing Colleen to go home earlier to be with Costa anyway. Although it was not known to Mama, she had arranged the work load in a way that she had little to do. There was no need for her to become ill just because she wanted to help.

At last the time for Mimi to come home was very close. He wrote a short letter saying that he was due to be shipped out of Korea but would not be able to get in touch with any of the family until they actually arrived in Athens. This was indeed glorious news. Colleen began a clean-up, fix-up at their home. It had been a while since any real work had been done. Their home was a very comfortable place for two but a little tight for three. The baby might have been small but his needs were many and the equipment which was required took up a lot of room. The spare room which was now the baby's room was completely filled with a baby bed, a changing table, a diaper pail, lots of toys, and a stroller. The nanny had attempted to find a place for everything, but it became an insurmountable task to organize all these items. Today Colleen was determined to complete the job. When Mimi came home he would find his cozy home waiting for him with his wife and child inside.

The homecoming had become a real team effort. Between Mama and Colleen the houses were ready for a celebration. Everyone at the wool factory was on their best behavior to make as good an impression as was possible.

It took Mimi almost three weeks of travel time, paper work, and the debriefing from the department of the army before he had reached the last step of his discharge. One thing he had learned after being in the service of his country was patience. It was all about hurry up and wait. He had done it for what seemed like an eternity. He saw no reason to worry or get impatient at this time. When you reach this point in the process, you learn nothing is gained by being impatient. Then at last, he was discharged and out of the army. Somehow he thought he would feel different and yet he felt just as he always had. He hurried to catch the ferry boat to Crete and then it hit him, he was going home. Soon he would be with his wife and son. He was very tired by now and fell asleep in his seat as the ferry sped toward Crete. When the boat reached the dock, it jolted him awake. It took him a few minutes to realize that he was home in his beloved Greece and his home island, Crete. He gathered his belongings and looked out to see if anyone had come to pick him up. There on the pier he thought he caught a glimpse of Colleen, but when he looked again he did not see her and believed his eyes played tricks on him. He started down the gangplank and realized his eyes did not play tricks on him. It was Colleen. He started toward her quickly. Before he knew it, he was running straight into her waiting arms. They hugged and kissed with a hunger for each other that could not be denied. This was the beginning of the second chapter of their lives.

The trip home was the most anticipated of all. His heart was beating so hard he was sure everyone could hear it. Colleen was chattering about the latest news on the island and Mama and the baby. They were getting close to Mama's house when Mimi suddenly clutched Colleen's hand and became very nervous and wanted to put off seeing anyone. She put his mind at ease and calmed his anxiety. They walked up the steps to Mama's house and when the door was opened there stood before him all the family and his friends welcoming him home. The first thing he saw was his little Costa and as he approached the child very slowly to not alarm him, little Costa looked at him and said *"Baba"* (the Greek word for daddy). Colleen had been showing the baby his father's picture and saying the Greek word for daddy to him. The joy in Mimi's eyes was the most beautiful sight of all. Now he was once again with his family. He felt calm, joy, and peace come over him. He was home at last!

Chapter 46

Molly and Mickey

As time passed, Mickey and Molly fell more and more deeply in love. They spent as much time as they could together, and an engagement announcement seemed inevitable. Unfortunately, in the midst of their happiness, Mickey received a draft notice and was ordered to report for duty in thirty days. Molly was heartbroken and frightened at the thought of Mickey going off to war. He had known the day would come, but he had hoped he would already be enrolled in medical school by then. Once he could prove he was a full-time student, a deferral might have been possible. But luck was against them. The decision was reached that they would marry before he left.

Mrs. O'Donnell tried hard to discourage this impulsive marriage. Molly was as dear to her as a daughter, and she was aware of the difficulties faced by wartime marriages. She personally had witnessed many unhappy endings to such weddings. However, love won over caution. And the two were married three days before Mickey shipped out to basic training.

Molly and Mickey were both very happy; however, they did not fully comprehend the reality of the coming separation. For now they were newlyweds, but very soon they were going to be separated by thousands of miles and a lot of uncertainty. They made the most of their few days as husband and wife, but the date of departure came quickly. As Molly kissed him goodbye, she said a silent prayer that the conflict would be resolved before he finished basic training so he would be returning home to her within a few weeks' time. Her hope never became a reality.

The war lingered on, and Molly continued to work for Mrs. O'Donnell. She found that her party planning skills were very much in demand as more and more of Mrs. O'Donnell's friends asked if she would help with their upcoming events. Before long, she was receiving calls from all over the county to cater and plan events for families and businesses. It all worked out very well for both women. Mrs. O'Donnell no longer needed Molly's services every day. She was not entertaining nearly as much as before. She was relieved that Molly had a supplementary income. She was still coming to Mrs. O'Donnell's home once a week to clean, change the bed sheets and towels, and do the laundry.

Mickey continued writing Molly regularly, but he was not the same Mickey that had left Ireland. His joy seemed to be gone. There were no little jokes and endearments as there had been before. He seemed to be more reserved and serious. There was very little detail about what was going on and certainly no stories of Korea and its people. Molly mourned the loss of Mickey's fun-loving heart and hoped that he could find it again when he returned.

She forged ahead with her business, eventually having business cards printed with the phrase: "Molly's Catering and Party Planning. Call us to make your event extraordinary." She slipped one in an envelope she sent to Mickey, asking what he thought of her plans. Sooner than she expected, she received a note back that said simply, "I LOVE IT. I can't wait to get home to help you."

Beyond work, letters were much of Molly's life. She wrote to Mickey every day, but she also exchanged letters with Colleen several times a month. The two girls never seemed to run out of things to say to each other. Molly knew all about Colleen's pregnancy, her work, and Mimi's Mama. Colleen had offered many suggestions for Molly's catering business. The women consoled each other in their loneliness and bolstered each other's spirits when they started feeling low. In addition, the letters gave Colleen another link to her homeland. Colleen loved Crete, but Crete without Mimi was not really home to her. They promised each other that one day when the men returned home they would visit one another. Colleen was always telling Molly that Crete would be an excellent destination for a romantic honeymoon. Molly thought that was a wonderful idea. Crete for a honeymoon would be a dream come true.

One day just as Molly was preparing a letter to Colleen, the postman came and delivered a letter for Molly from Colleen. Her friend had just given birth to a beautiful baby boy. Molly was overjoyed. The good news made her heart leap from happiness.

Good news was rare these days and this was indeed good news. Molly sat down immediately and wrote Colleen. When Mickey returned from Korea they would plan a trip to Crete to meet her Mimi and the baby. It would be wonderful.

Finally the news came that Mickey was coming home. Molly thought she would die of impatience waiting, but instead she worked even harder to make sure she had everything ready for his return. The catering money she had earned was enough to rent a cottage and buy furniture for their home. She wanted everything to be perfect when he arrived in Ireland.

One day, there was a knock at the door, and Molly was greeted by a tired Mickey holding a red rose. "Hello, my lady fair, I've brought you something almost as beautiful as you are," he said with a twinkle in his eyes.

"Oh, Mickey, I love you and have missed you so much." Molly jumped into his waiting arms, hugging her husband with all the love in her soul. He bent down and kissed her sweetly before scooping her up and carrying her into their new bedroom.

Molly was too happy to even think coherently."This is true; it is my Mickey's arms that I am in. This is real. He has returned to me and is well."

He kissed her tenderly and touched her face with his hand and then her golden-red hair. It was all as he had remembered and even more than he had hoped for.

The reunion was wonderful. The two worked together for a few weeks to tie up all of Molly's catering obligations, but then they told all of their customers they were taking some time off. Finally, they were going to get that honeymoon they had both dreamed of those many months they had been apart. As the boat for Crete left the dock, Molly looked into Mickey's eyes and saw that all would be well.

Chapter 47

What Happened to the Class Ring?

The class ring was last seen in the possession of a young lady who received it from Jenny. The ring was never a big deal to Judy, the young teenager who thought it was nice of the hair stylist to give it to her, but it was someone else's class ring, not hers. When the stylist gave it to her, it was almost as if she wanted to get rid of it and didn't care who got it. She always felt creepy about the whole thing. However, it was still hers, and she took care of it. She couldn't just throw it away; she felt that was not the right thing to do. She placed it in her jewelry box and rarely wore it.

What was Judy's story? Her mother had worked with battered women and their children as the intermediary of sorts. She had made arrangements with many shelters in the area where these women could go and stay for a time. This would give them a chance at a new start. It had become common for two or three women to show up on her doorstep looking for shelter. Most were terrified and in need of protection. Judy's mother knew where to send them and would make arrangements to get them securely to a safe haven.

One evening, a husband of one of the women followed her to Judy's home. The mother would not open the door to him, so he forced it open and charged inside. Judy watched in terror as he beat her. Rushing to the phone, she called the police. The baseball bat was right by the door where he was beating her mother. If she could get over to that, she could hit him in the head with all of her might and get him off of her precious mother. As she ran to help her mother, she heard the sound of police sirens. The man didn't let up. Thank God he didn't see the bat or would have probably used it. The police rushed in and pulled him off of her mother. He had beaten her within an inch of her life. Judy rode with her mother to the hospital shaking the whole way. The man was arrested, and the woman was taken to a shelter.

Her mother was hospitalized for almost a month. When she

returned, she closed the door to all of those desperate women. It was safe to say that she retired her position as an intermediary and began to live a quiet life. Judy, however, was never quite comfortable in the house again. After her graduation, she packed her suitcase, making certain to include the class ring with her belongings and left home to find her way in the world.

She had worked at a drugstore soda fountain after school for two years and managed to save five hundred dollars. This was what she hoped would support her until she found a good job. Of course her mother was very upset over her leaving, but she realized that much of this was her fault. In her desire to help unfortunate women, she did not protect her own daughter. The result was the loss of her daughter. Judy assured her mother she would keep in touch. Her mother would always know where she was, and she would call her regularly to make sure she was all right.

This was the way Judy's life continued for several years and many jobs later. She missed her mother a great deal and decided to return home and attempt to continue her education. Without a degree she had reached a ceiling on any career she might pursue. She learned this truth the hard way after reaching many dead-ends.

On the trip home she spent the night at a motel which was just off the main highway. It was one of new motels which were beginning to appear all over the country. They were simple but clean and seemed safe enough. They served coffee and doughnuts in the morning, so she would not have to stop for breakfast along the way. She was about four hundred miles from home when she stopped. She was certain she could be home by early afternoon the next day. Just the thought of home made her heart beat a little faster.

The next morning she ran down to the lobby to have a cup of coffee and a doughnut before she began the last leg of the journey home. As she was sipping her coffee, she noticed a young mother with two small children. The woman had a close resemblance to many of the women who would show up on her mother's doorstep looking for help. The woman came up to Judy and asked her to help with her children while she got a cup of coffee. Judy nodded yes and while she was distracted by the children, the woman left to get a cup of coffee. She returned with a doughnut for each of the children. By the time the confusion had calmed down and Judy turned to pick up her belongings, she discovered her purse was gone along with all her money, her car keys, driver license, and everything else that she needed. Believe it or not, the class ring which had been given to her by Jenny before her high school graduation was also in the purse. It was almost like losing a friend. The money, driver's license, and car keys did not upset her nearly as much as the lost ring.

Judy had no choice but to phone her mother for help. Her mother wired some money to her and soon she was safely on the road heading toward the home of her childhood.

The ring had once again found a new owner and a new home. It was no longer Judy's concern, but there was still a part of her that felt guilty about that ring from the day it was given to her right up to the day that someone took it from her. She often wondered what happened to the woman and her children.

Chapter 48

A Rocky Road

The sneaky thief at the motel was indeed a desperate woman running for her life from a brutal husband who had beaten her mercilessly and left her penniless with two small children ages one and two. This was how Judy found Patty at the motel. She was without resources or hope. Patty felt that stealing Judy's purse was a quick solution to her desperate situation. Daniel, her so-called husband, had fooled her from the beginning. She believed everything he had told her, and now she found herself becoming a thief just to feed her babies and get to safety. She made a promise to herself to return the handbag and money as soon as she was back on her feet once more.

Patty was an only child and quite spoiled by her doting parents. She grew up to be a rebellious teenager, and her parents couldn't control her. Her behavior continued to worsen. One day she left home, and they did not hear from her for weeks. When she finally surfaced once again it was to tell them she had found the love of her life, and that was the last they would hear from her.

When she first met Daniel, he was a smooth-talking guy with lots of personality. He could charm birds out of the trees. His charming front and ambitious plans for success disappeared quickly. She was just eighteen, full of a self-inflated image of how smart and beautiful she was. No one could tell her anything. She knew where she was going and she called all the shots. Patty never accepted any advice that anyone gave her. She was going to set the world on fire. Her problem was not her dream, but rather where she went to find it. Cheap bars and dives where guys and girls would go to be picked up was where she hung out as she attempted to get free drinks. She mingled with a crowd of individuals looking for excitement, easy money, and instant gratification.

There could be no good outcome to this story. It was at one of these places that she fell for Daniel's smooth lines and big promises. They met at a bar that they both frequented, and she was so gullible that she not only fell for him hook, line, and sinker, but she foolishly bragged about a trust fund that her grandfather had left her. It did not stop there. To make sure that he believed her, she imprudently told him details of her bank account. She even went as far as to show him the bank book. She truly believed that showing off like this made her look cool.

She was ahead of those squares that were all afraid of their own shadows and would never dare go to any of these pick-up bars she was frequenting. Not knowing that all the time she was falling into the trap that Daniel had set for her.

The atmosphere in these bars resembled a motorcycle gang hangout. It was a rough crowd, but that didn't scare her one bit. If only it had then perhaps she could have avoided a great deal of misery.

Daniel was not only a good-looking smooth talker, but he had great skills picking up girls. He had made an art of it—pick up the girl and make her believe she was the only girl in the room. That was always the first step. The second was to convince her that he was smarter and slicker than anyone else. They were quite the handsome couple, or so they thought. She was dazzled by what she viewed as his sophistication. She never once doubted that he was everything he claimed to be. Needless to say nothing could have been further from the truth. Her biggest mistake, as if any mistake could be bigger than her trying to hang out in this environment and believe she would escape unscathed, was telling Daniel that she had money in the bank.

Before she knew it they were an item, and she began running with his crowd which was the worst of the worst. He never forgot for a moment that she had money and was making a plan to access it. Then in a moment of passion, which she mistakenly considered true love, he said let's get married.

They ran away and got married that night. Things were considerably worse from that day on. The marriage was not legal, and the license was bogus. Patty was too humiliated to go back home so she decided to make the best of things and immediately became pregnant with her first little girl. Daniel was not at all interested in hanging out with a fat sick girl who had become a millstone around his neck.

She was too sick with the pregnancy to notice that he was staying out later and later every night. The small apartment where they lived was just that, a small ugly place in desperate need of painting. The stove was hit-and-miss, mostly miss, and the refrigerator never got cold enough to even make ice cubes in the freezer section.

When he was home he demanded that she have this dump clean and tidy. He wanted all his clothes washed and ironed and a hot meal on the table. She did the best she could, but how clean can you get a place with just a broom and dust pan? He never left her any money to buy groceries which made hot meals a problem. He usually would slap her around when he was unhappy with her. That was the way it usually started and would accelerate into a fist and then God help her. She tried to not let him know how much he was hurting her because if he thought she was in pain it would trigger him to become even more violent in the beating. So far he only used his hands and feet, but he had threatened her with a frying pan and a lamp when she made a whimper.

She only had two maternity dresses and was rotating them every other day. Sometimes she would wear his shirts as tops. The baby was born shortly after one of the beatings. As if that was not enough, she had a very difficult delivery to add to her misery. She had applied for help for unwed mothers and received some aid. There was constant fear in her life. If the baby cried, as all babies do, he would get so angry that he threatened her. "Keep the kid quiet, or I'll throw her against the wall and that will shut the brat up for good."

Then he would punish Patty by slapping her around and knocking her down to the floor where he raped her viciously over and over until he got bored then would leave her there bleeding. Of course it would follow that she became pregnant again. This time she went to the bank to get some money and check her balance. She wanted to know how much money she had so she could make a withdrawal. To her astonishment there was nothing left. She saw papers that showed that Daniel had signed her name on the account and withdrew all of the money two weeks before. Once again she was forced to stay with him and hoped that she could find out where he had put the money.

She realized too late that he had put the money in his personal account, and he was not giving her a dime. He told her she was too stupid to have money anyway. Once again he beat her mercilessly and left. She went into labor and nearly died from the beating and the delivery. Lucky for Patty the woman in the apartment next door heard the screams and came to her aid. She took the baby girl and Patty to the hospital where the new baby was born prematurely. Both of their lives hung in the balance.

Thankfully they both lived. It was many weeks before mother and baby could leave the hospital. The kind neighbor took care of the little girl during that time. Daniel never asked if anyone knew where Patty and his daughter were. He was just delighted to have her money and not to have to deal with her anymore.

Patty came home to nothing. Daniel had moved from the apartment and had thrown Patty's entire wardrobe, along with the baby's things, out in the trash. When the good neighbor was sure Daniel was gone, she went to the trash and managed to rescue some of the things. She cleaned and packed them so that Patty would have them when she returned home. The young mother was not surprised when she found that Daniel was gone. She was actually relieved not to have to deal with him any longer. She never got over the fear that he would come upon her in her sleep and beat her to death. After she was a little stronger, she decided to leave her friend who had helped her so much and head home. She knew that her mother and father were very angry. It would be difficult for them to forgive her, but she needed them now. She wanted to apologize to them for her actions and rebellion. She wanted most of all for them to meet her babies. That was how she ended up at the same motel as Judy. Even though she knew it was wrong to steal Judy's purse, she was a desperate woman, just as Judy had suspected. She swore an oath to herself that as soon as she had two hundred dollars she would pay Judy back and send the purse with all the contents to her.

Her mother was very sympathetic but did not trust her anymore. Sadly, Patty had become a street person and would do anything to survive. Her mother felt she was too old to try to help her with her problems. Her father had felt betrayed and was unforgiving. They both said, because of the children, she could stay with them for a short while but that was as far as they could go.

It was a very hard lesson to learn, but Patty understood what they were saying. They had gone through a very difficult time with her and now that they were older and could no longer deal with any adversity. They just wanted a quiet life. They would love to see the children for short periods of time, but would not be babysitters while she worked. She had worn them out and that was all they would do for her. They were not rich people and did not have the means to give her any money. She was surprised at just how well she understood what they were saying to her. For the first time, the realization of what her actions had caused was revealed to her, and she was ashamed.

She picked herself up and went to the shelter which was in town and found work and a place to call home. She cleaned, washed the laundry, and stocked the food pantry. It was hard work and in her weakened condition, she became exhausted easily. Nevertheless, she was determined and desperate enough to work harder than she had ever worked before. She was able to save two hundred dollars which she immediately sent to Judy along with the purse which she had taken a life time ago. She kept the ring as a reminder of what terrible mistakes she had made and the dark and ugly direction her life had taken.

Chapter 49

Angie Is in Nursing School

Angie had registered for her classes and was on her way to the student housing. She had already met her roommate and really liked her. She was sure they would get along. However, she was a bit surprised by how small their room was. There wasn't much room for personal items, and she could see at a glance only minimal clothes would fit. The realization that she would have to leave most of her clothes in her closet at home was going to be a reality. This could become quite troublesome. The room really needed help to make it a little more fun.

Her roommate was already moved in and had taken most of the closet space. Angie made up her bed and placed the few things she had in the remaining space. As she stepped out in the hallway she saw a community bathroom at one end of the hallway which was shared by all the students on the floor. At the other end of the hall there was a study corner with a couple of tables and chairs. Thank goodness for that because it would have been very difficult to study in the dorm room. All in all, she thought she could manage to get along here with no problem. After she had found a place for all her things she went to the auditorium for orientation. All of the nursing students had gathered there to get instructions for the beginning weeks of school. Immediately after orientation she went to the bookstore to buy her books and supplies. As often happens after making this purchase, the student leaves the bookstore suffering from sticker shock. The books were quite a bit more expensive than she had expected, especially when compared to her night school classes. She would have to work part-time to make ends meet. Before she started job-hunting, she would talk to her father and see if he would help her with part of this. Of course there would still be the problem with Athena allowing her to leave most of her clothes in her room. She probably already had other plans for that room. Problems of details and money were always present and kept getting in the way of a smooth transition. She would go by the house tonight and tell them that she would have to leave most of her clothes there in the closet. She didn't know what she would do if this wouldn't work out. It would be terrible to have come this far and not have this problem solved.

The day flew by, and Angie began gathering her books and things to head home. She would not begin occupying the dorm room until tomorrow. The bus was running late so she got home much later than usual.

As she approached the house, she suddenly felt very apprehensive. She opened the door and was surprised to see the entire family sitting in the living room. They were anxiously waiting to hear about her first day.

"Angela, come sit down and tell us all about your first day," Basil said after greeting her with a gentle kiss on her cheek.

She was more than happy to give them all a full report. She asked if she could leave her clothes in the closet because there simply was not enough space in her dorm room for another thing.

"I'm using that room as a sewing room. I need all of that space for my things." Athena announced.

Angie didn't realize she no longer had a room in the house and was dumbfounded by the announcement. Basil looked at Athena angrily. "Forget the sewing room. You managed without a sewing room all this time. Angie will need a room when she comes home during breaks just like Joey needs his room." Angie feared what might follow this small disagreement, but everything remained calm in spite of the rage which was rumbling beneath the surface.

Athena puffed and folded her arms across her chest as the features in her face became hard.

"That settles it," Basil said. Pride for his daughter's accomplishments beamed on his face. "You can leave whatever you wish in your room and come and go as you need."

The first week of classes was a whirlwind. There was so much to learn and retain. In no time study groups were formed and the tables at the end of the hall were abuzz with activity. She was working hard to keep pace with the group. Much like any class in any school, some students were way ahead of the curve, and some way behind. The study groups really helped a great deal, and she was glad to be part of one. Each day brought a new challenge. It was very exciting, and she felt right at home in this atmosphere. She was really looking forward to getting out on the hospital floor and getting some practical experience. This was what she had worked so hard to achieve, and it was well worth it.

The weeks were flying by and before she knew it, three months had passed. It was time for her to decide what direction she was going in nursing. Angie had become increasingly interested in becoming a surgical nurse. It didn't take much thought on her part. These past three months only served to reinforce this selection. She still wanted a degree, Bachelor of Science in nursing. She had worked too hard to accomplish all of this and would not allow anything stop her. She had thought long and hard about become a surgical nurse. The big bonus was that she would not have any trouble finding work in the field of surgery. She had placed her name on the list as a volunteer for surgery. This worked very well; she received many opportunities to actually work and observe many surgical procedures.

Her roommate, Liz, was also trying to get into the surgical program. The pace was brutal but even so there was always time for a little fun. Most of the girls liked to go across the street to the Barbeque Bar and Grill. Angie would go with them for the fellowship but had never been a drinker and would end up drinking a coke, not a beer. It was a break for the nursing and medical students to go there and relax. It was a nice change of pace, too. They would exchange gossip about their superiors and whatever other hot topics of the day that came up. It was fun, and no one seemed to notice that all Angie ever drank was cokes. It was understood that either before study table or right after study table everyone would meet at the Barbeque Bar and Grill, or as everyone referred to it as, The Bar.

Jack was one of the med students. He took a shine to Angie and would hang around her and talk. She thought he was nice and was flattered by his attention.

Jimmy was still her guy, but she was trying hard to think positive thoughts when it came to him. She knew that he was not able to write, but she was always afraid that he might have gotten hurt or worse. This friendship with Jack and the attention she was getting was just to take her mind off of worrying about Jimmy. Not hearing from him was much harder than she had imagined it would be.

When she closed her eyes, she could envision Jimmy laughing, joking with her, and giving her a quick a kiss. It was always a careless kiss, one that was given with the expectation of many more kisses to come. Oh, if only he would write, it would mean so much to her. The war was still going on, and she was becoming very lonely and felt as if he had abandoned her. Merely a note that he was okay would have done wonders. It was no surprise that she was flattered by the attention this second-year med student was giving her. They would sit and talk and trade surgery stories with each other. It was innocent enough, yet it was becoming more and more important to her to sit and talk to him. Jack seemed to feel the same way. Whenever Angie would go with the girls he would always seek her out. It had been almost a year since she had seen or heard from Jimmy, and she could not deal with this silence. What was it he said to her that night at the Tee Pee? Oh yes, something about top secret, and she already knew more than she should have, and it was dangerous for her to know anything. Oh why did he go into the Special Forces? It was too risky. She thought she could deal with it, but the truth was that she would never get used to the fact that he might have been hurt or even worse, dead.

It was just small talk with Jack. They were friends and nothing more. It was not as if she was sleeping with him. God knows there was plenty of that going on around there.

That evening at The Bar, Jack asked her if he could walk her back to the dorm. They pushed away from the table where they sat and walked into the cool night air. The walk back was slow and steady. Jack was a serious student and did not goof around with his studies. He loved the profession, and he came from a family of many generations of doctors. He was in his second year of med school, was one of the top students in his class, and was working hard to be an excellent surgeon. Angie had been in the operating room with him a few times. In that respect, they had a lot in common. She was about to begin her second year and in six months would receive her cap. It was quite an honor and one she was looking forward to since she had decided to be a nurse.

Jack turned toward Angie as they walked along the well-lit street. "I enjoy talking with you at The Bar; it just gets so loud that it can be a strain just to hear. You could barely hear yourself think let alone hear what anyone was saying."

With that remark, she began to laugh, and they both had a good laugh, something they both needed badly.

"Hey, come on, let's go over to Union Hall and get a bite to eat. I'm hungry, and they're still serving in the cafeteria."

"All right, that sounds like a good idea. It's still early, and I haven't eaten either," Angie replied as they headed in that direction. "I'll still have time for my study group after we're done." This was a turn of events which was totally unexpected but was a very pleasant surprise. Even more surprising, she didn't feel guilty about getting a bite to eat with Jack. It was very natural and innocent and somehow she felt that Jimmy would want her to have a little fun. After all, they weren't firmly committed to each other and even though he mentioned marriage, he never asked her to wait for him nor did he use the word engaged during the time he was home on furlough. He said he didn't want her to be committed to him, because it wouldn't be fair to her. He wanted her to be free to do what she wanted to do, and when he returned, they would pick up where they left off and get reacquainted. All he asked was for her to give him a fair chance. Now almost a year had passed and many of her friends who were drafted about the same time as Jimmy were being discharged, but he was still silent. She was close to giving up and beginning to feel that perhaps he had found someone else. This was a futile way to think. He had told her more than once he wanted no strings attached because it was not fair to her, but he wanted a fair chance with her when he returned. That was all he asked. Enough of that kind of thinking. It only led to sadness and dark thoughts of what might be happening when no one really knew what the truth was. Jimmy had always been honest with her, and she had no reason to think otherwise. She was in the moment now with Jack. It was just a walk and a bite to eat.

Jack walked her back to the dorm; they said good night and that was it. No big deal. What in the world was she fretting about?

She had to continue to live and also enjoy herself a little. The study group was going when she arrived and most of them saw her leave with Jack and began to tease her about it. They were all laughing and enjoying poking a little fun at her. Of all the people on the floor she was the most serious and most unlikely to be with Jack. So it was absolutely time to razz her a little after all, "all work and no play makes Angie a dull girl." To Angie's surprise, she rather enjoyed the razzing done in good natured fun. It broke up the seriousness of the hospital routine.

All the nursing students were doing practical training by this time and dealing with many heartbreaking illnesses. The pediatric floor was the most upsetting of all. No one wanted to see small babies and children sick. However, if that was what your specialty was going to be, you had to get toughened to it or you would never be able to help the sick recover. They all knew it was going to be hard and the training was all about knowing what needed to be done and doing it. So a good laugh now and then was a good thing.

That night, as Angie was preparing to go to bed, she was deep in thought about the events of the evening and Jack and Jimmy. A year was a long time to go without a word, and she was tired of always being on edge because she didn't know where and how he was. For all she knew, he might have gotten involved with someone else and was not interested in the dull girl from home who was pining away for him. What a laugh he might be having at her expense although that was not like Jimmy, and she didn't want her imagination to run away with her and create a scenario which did not exist because she wanted to justify her hanging out with Jack this evening and enjoying it so much. She was only human and deserved a little fun. If Jack asked her to hang out again she would go out with him. He was fun, and he was here.

That very night Angie sat down at her desk and began writing a letter to Jimmy. She was not sure if he would receive it, but she was writing one anyway. Enough was enough. One year was ridiculous. If she made a fool of herself, so what.

Dear Jimmy,

It has been a very long time since I have had any word from you, and I am becoming increasingly concerned as to your well-being. I know that you are very busy with all of your missions, but you must realize that I too am busy and need a little peace of mind. Please confirm that you are all right. I would appreciate it very much. I am about to be sent to the VA Medical Center and do not want to go there and see all of those young men recovering from wounds and whatever else they might be suffering from and thinking of you lying injured in some unknown country without anyone caring for you. Please, I beg you, send word as to your status.

Many of our friends are now retuning home and picking up where they left off— going back to school or beginning new jobs. I love you too much to stay angry very long, but I would like to know something about how you are.

All my love always,

Angie

That was all she could write, and she placed the letter in an envelope, wrote the address, a military P. O. box which he had given her just before he left. She was still mystified as to why she had not written him sooner. It was just a note, but it was enough to make her feel as if she had taken a step to bring him closer to her and to end the silence between them.

Chapter 50

The Veterans Medical Center

The VA was to be Angie's next assignment in the rotation system. She had just completed six weeks in pediatrics and was now facing twelve weeks in the service of the VA. This was a good opportunity to study all kinds of injuries, rehabilitation, post-traumatic stress syndrome, amputations—the list goes on and on. It was one of the longest rotations on the schedule. They wanted all the medical teams to be able to deal with anything that came through the emergency room door. The first step in the rotation was to tour the area and get familiar with all of the surroundings. To Angie's surprise, on the tour she saw not only young men injured in battle, but also much older men from World War II and World War I with a variety of ailments. In many ways it was a very educational tour. It also made the nurses much more comfortable with the men, and the men more comfortable with the new nurses. Some of the men greeted the new group of nurses with wolf whistles and welcoming smiles which was always returned by the young nursing students. For these girls this would turn out to be both interesting and challenging. Of course it could also be heartbreaking.

Angie, who was beginning to think she was creating her own stresses, was constantly afraid that she would see Jimmy lying in one of the beds gravely injured. This was so stressful that she was getting ready to request a transfer out of this hospital. However, after careful consideration, she decided it would not look good on her record to have this rotation become a total washout. She stayed and was glad she did. She learned much more than she believed she would.

After a month of waiting for a reply to the note she had sent to Jimmy, she returned to her room to find a letter on her bed. Her heart began to beat like a drum and her hands were shaking so badly that she was ready to faint. Somehow she managed to get a hold of herself and ripped open the envelope. A letter fell out. She gazed at it lying on the bed for some time before she picked it up and began to read it.

Dear Angie,

I am writing this letter from my barracks, and I am still in Korea. This is the worst Hell Hole I have ever seen in my life. I could not write before now as I have been in a grave situation which I cannot discuss. Some day if I ever get out of this place I will tell you all about it. Or on second thought it's something that would be very hard to tell you. We grew up in a different world and were totally ignorant of the kinds of things I have had to witness. My wish is never to deal with war and violence again. I understand how this must have looked to you not hearing from me for so long but orders were orders, and I could not communicate with anyone until I was removed from Special Forces. I am now officially free of that service and will be up for discharge in six months. I am counting the days; I cannot wait to see you again. Thinking of you is all that has kept me going. Please, I beg of you, do not give up on me. I will be home and then if you wish we can begin to get reacquainted once again. You have taken a new career path, and I have had many of life's experiences which no one should have to endure.

I still love you. I have carried the picture of us at the Grad Dance with me always. I am sure that we both have changed in many ways. All I have ever wanted was to spend the rest of my life with you, and my hope is that you feel the same way.

I will write to you regularly, and I hope you will keep in touch with me. Don't be angry because I have not communicated with you sooner. You will never know how much your letter meant to me. Now that you have heard from me please keep writing. If you have found someone else, I will understand, but give me a chance, that is all I ask.

I hope to hear from you soon. I love you.

Yours,

Jimmy

Angie dropped the letter and fell on the bed. She could not help the tears from flowing. She had heard from Jimmy. He was alive and uninjured. She was sobbing uncontrollably by the time her roommate entered the room. Liz was alarmed and sat next to her on the bed trying to comfort her. After a few deep breaths, Angie got control of herself. Liz grabbed some tissues for her. "You want to talk about it?" she asked softly.

Angie shook her head. "Not just yet. I'll be okay. I'm not quite ready to talk."

Liz nodded and sat down on her bed. "Well, whenever you're ready, I'm here."

Angie managed a weak grin. "Thanks."

Chapter 51

Where Is Jimmy?

Jack and Angie were still hanging out together, mostly in groups, but occasionally would go out to dinner or lunch together. He respected her commitment to Jimmy and understood that they were going to give their relationship a try when he returned home. They went out as good friends. Jack was not pushing her to be more than good friends, at least not until it was clear that nothing was working out between Jimmy and her. He was not going to interfere by working on her emotions and the loneliness which she felt. He knew very well that she was totally vulnerable at this time. Besides that, he was not looking for a serious relationship with anyone until he had finished his internship. By then perhaps she and Jimmy would be kaput. How she could be so unaware of the depth of his feeling was a mystery to him. It was perhaps better that she didn't have that added pressure on her at this time.

Even though Jimmy was now writing her more often, it was never with any specific information. This was certainly not what she had thought he meant when he promised to write more regularly.

She was now beginning her last year of nursing before starting her specialty training. She would be doing only surgery and learn all there was to learn. It would be very difficult, but that was what she always wanted to do.

Jack was now entering his last year of medical school and would soon become an intern, working exclusively in the operating room. It was an exciting time for them both. They were both preparing to enter the final stages of their specialty training.

The gang met at The Bar that evening. There was live music that night, and it was lady's night. They all assembled at their favorite table and were taking their seats when Jack and Angie came in to join them. It was a lot of fun and the evening was enjoyable. Three or four of the girls had dates and left early.

Jack and Angie had stayed behind to enjoy the music and just relax. They had no pressing assignments to complete and had not had time to just sit and talk for what seemed to them a long time.

Angie actually found herself fantasizing what life with Jack would be like. She had to force herself to stop this daydreaming, or she would be in Jack's arms and only God would know what would happen. A thought of Jimmy flashed through her mind. Suddenly, she felt ashamed of her fantasy. Guilt and disloyalty gripped her heart. She actually wanted to run and hide in shame. It was wrong for her to feel this way. Jack was there next to her; Jimmy was God knows where. Should she feel guilty because her imagination was running away with her? Why was all this happening? She really wished that Jimmy was here fighting for her love and honor. She wanted the warmth of human companionship, not a struggle over right and wrong. What was she to do?

As if sensing Angie's struggle, Jack asked, "Is something bothering you?"

She was too embarrassed to admit that she was visualizing the two of them in an ardent embrace which she was enjoying much more than she wanted to admit. But she answered generically, "Oh no, nothing really. I'm just tired." That seemed to satisfy him, and the subject was dropped. The conversation turned to their elective specialty, surgery. She barely realized another hour passed. They decided to call it a day and go back to their rooms. As they were strolling back towards the dorms Jack sensed the tension Angie was feeling. "Have I done something to offend you?" He asked with caution. "If I have, I'm very sorry."

"You've done nothing to offend me." She reassured. "It's me. I'm a little nervous about the future."

He nodded assuming she was talking about the specialty she was about to enter into, and she was possibly afraid she might be making a mistake. He chuckled, "I think I know you better than you know yourself. You will be great in the operating room."

She dropped her head and muttered a thank you. They said goodnight and went to their respective dorms.

As she went up the steps, she said a little prayer that Jimmy would jump into action and sweep her off her feet and added to please let him make it quickly, before she made a move that would be unwise.

Chapter 52

There Is No Place Like Home

A letter from Jimmy had arrived at last. It was full of a lot of can't wait to see you and it will not be long now. What troubled Angie was what he was not saying rather than what he was saying. She was looking for something more that might unlock the mystery of what was going on in his mind. She was beginning to feel he was holding back something that was very important. Something had happened, and he was not sharing whatever it was with her. She herself did not know exactly what she wanted to hear, but she knew that what he was saying was not what she wanted to hear. There was some reference to the future but for some reason she did not feel it was her future. It was both upsetting and puzzling at the same time. She had been waiting so long and this was a real letdown. She wanted to go home for a visit.

Joey was there now; maybe he could help her unravel this mystery and see what he thought about the whole thing. Besides, there was going to be a get-together of the old gang at the Tee Pee on Saturday. She wasn't working that weekend and was looking forward to going. Her father had been great. He'd paid for her nursing school and the burden of finances was off her shoulders. She was definitely going home for the weekend and that was that. Jimmy had jerked her around long enough. She was now entering shaky ground with him. He almost sounded as if he was about to spring something on her, and she did not like it at all.

She called Jack and told him that she was going home for the weekend and would see him on Monday for lunch if he was available. He was, and it was a date. The rest of the day flew by, and she packed a few things and took some of her books with her in case she had a few minutes to do some studying.

It had been a while since she had been home and was really looking forward to seeing everyone. Sammie was in high school now and little Bobby was going to grade school; the boys were growing up fast. Joey was at law school, and she had not seen him since his graduation. Where did the time go? It was unforgivable to be so busy that you lose track of your own family.

Basil came by the hospital and picked Angie up to take her home. He was very happy to see her. He hadn't seen her since she received her cap. That was a true "Kodak moment," and for her it was a milestone on her path to being a nurse. He was very proud of her. She had more than proven her determination to become a nurse. He was sorry he did not help sooner. You cannot look back and regret what you did not do, but rather look forward to what you can do.

They chatted all the way home, and she caught up on all the family events. She had no idea when she entered nursing that the program was so intense and required so much time, but she loved every minute of it and was glad to be part of it. They were pulling up to the house when Bobby ran out and jumped into Angie's arms. What a welcome that was. Even Athena was happy to see her again.

That evening Joey came home, and for the first time in a year the whole family was together. Sammie was busy telling Joey and Angie about his high school adventures and how well he was doing. All in all everything was going well, and Angie was happy to be home again. To sleep in her old room was wonderful. The room was as she had left it, as had been promised. It was so peaceful, and she was completely happy tonight.

She was up early the next morning as had become her habit. She had not been able to sleep past six o'clock in the morning since entering the nursing program. She went into the kitchen and was assaulted by the memories of many a battle fought in this room. She had to come to realize she was quite a handful and could admit it now, but she supposed that it was all part of growing up. She was busy making coffee when Joey came into the room. The aroma of freshly brewed coffee permeated the room, and one by one the family members wandered into the room stopping by the coffee pot to pour a cup. The preparation of breakfast was well underway and of course another fresh pot of coffee was being brewed. It was good to be home. Breakfast was a grab and run affair in the hospital. At home it was an event. After breakfast, Angie asked Joey if she could talk to him when he had time, and they set a time to talk after they got showered and packed their overnight bags. "See you later," they both said at the same time and went off to take care of their individual rooms and overnight bags.

They were both done about the same time. Angie came down first dressed in her blue jeans and a sweatshirt. Sammie was already downstairs dressed almost the same way. The laughter started when Joey came down dressed in, you guessed it, blue jeans and a Harvard University sweatshirt. This was too funny to keep them from having a good laugh.

"Come on, Angie, let's go for a ride. I want to show you something." So they got into the automobile and started out. "Where do you want to go for our talk?"

"Somewhere we can be alone and no one can hear us."

"I know the perfect place." They drove over to the Fire House Café. It was a small little café off the beaten path which was usually empty around this time of the morning. As Joey had expected, the place was empty. It was basically an early morning and early lunch place. They were pretty safe as far as people dropping by went. There would be no one before eleven o'clock.

"Alright, what's on your mind that brought you home, wanting to talk in private with me?" asked Joey.

"I am very troubled concerning Jimmy. First of all, I had not heard from him, not a word, *not one word*, do you hear me, for almost a year. Special Forces or not, that is not acceptable. That's nothing but a lot of thoughtlessness! When I wrote him a letter with an ultimatum he answered with the usual I love you stuff, but something is just not right. I know that he has been through a lot, but this is different. It's as if he is not telling me everything. He kind of drops hints but not enough to make any sense. Almost as if he is talking to me and leaving out every other word in each sentence which really distorts whatever it is he's trying to say. I have been true to him this whole time and believe me it has been tough going. The other night a group of us had gone across the street from the hospital to a bar to hang out for a while when I essentially had a fantasy about Jack, the med student that has been hanging out with us and has been very attentive to me. I saw us in a passionate embrace and kissing. It was so real that it was disturbing. I was embarrassed about the whole event and felt that everyone present knew what I had just experienced. As if that was not enough, when I returned to my room that evening I found a letter from Jimmy waiting for me. This was way too much for me to handle, and when I opened and read the letter, he indicated that he would be returning soon. Of course he could not say exactly when, but he would explain everything when he saw me and he was sure I would understand. Now what kind of double talk is that?" By this time as Angie was relating the story to Joey she was getting more and more upset. "I feel that whatever it is that I am supposed to understand is not a good thing. I think I have been wasting my time being true to him. I feel I have been nothing but a total fool waiting all this time," she said sadly.

"Now Angie, don't go jumping to conclusions. Give the guy a break. He's been away at war for a long time. He may be a little shaken and not have it all together yet. If he said that he was going to be home soon then I am sure he will be coming home anytime now. When he comes home he'll be able to explain everything to you, and you will understand what has been going on. Simmer down and stay focused. As far as having fantasies, who hasn't had illusions at some time or another? That doesn't mean you're committing a sin. After all, you've been waiting for Jimmy a long time. I'm surprised you haven't been tempted much sooner than now. As far as I'm concerned, he's been thoughtless about your feelings for too long. Give him a chance when he gets home to explain himself. You two have had a good and respectful relationship, and I am confident that it will always be that way. He is possibly a little shell-shocked right now and is not sure if he can fit into the civilian life again."

It was so like Joey to logically build a case for Jimmy that would be impossible to challenge. Okay, that was fine for now. He'd be coming home sometime soon and then she would see what was going on. Meanwhile, she came home to enjoy the weekend and that was exactly what she was going to do.

That evening Joey and Angie went to the Tee Pee get-together. They were looking forward to seeing all of their old friends. Many had just returned from active duty in the army and were once again enjoying civilian life. Secretly, Angie was hoping that Jimmy would be there waiting to surprise her. Oh, how she wished that would happen. She knew, however, that it would not happen, because Jimmy was still in Korea. Still the hope lingered on.

By the time Joey and Angie arrived, many of the old gang were already there. Of course there was no Jimmy, and she knew he could not be there. She saw a lot of her old friends. Barbara ran up to her and greeted her with a big hug. As usual she was full of excitement and news. It was not Barbara's style to hold back, especially with Angie. She couldn't contain herself. She blurted out to Angie in one quick sentence, "Chris and I are engaged!" Before Angie could recover from the wonderful news, Barbara continued, "And I am having a get-together at my house next week, and you better be there. You are to make it a top priority to attend or I will be mad at you. I'm calling it, 'Coffee, Tea, and Wine.' Don't you love it?"

Angie smiled and replied, "You're engaged? Congratulations! A party? It sounds like great fun; you can count on me. It's wonderful news about you and Chris. I'm so happy for you."

The rest of the evening was filled with wonderful exchanges of what everyone had been doing and how their lives had changed. It was a great evening, and Angie was glad to be there. It was different from her routine at nursing school and the hospital. This was a real change of pace. What was really an eye opener was how different she had become from the rest of the gang. She attributed a lot of it to dealing with life and death situations every day. Everyone there brought a little something different into the reunion. Joey and she were the only ones still attending school. Joey was in graduate school, working on a law degree, and Angie, in nursing. This was the first time that she became aware of the differences in everyone. They had all come a long way since Circle City High.

Chapter 53

Coffee, Tea, or Wine

The fun of the weekend was over for the time being. Angie was a little disappointed. She felt she had entered a world that her old friends had no understanding of. She foresaw that there would be a gradual separation occurring between them. Their paths were going different ways. Perhaps it was just her this time, but there was definitely a lack of understanding of the difference between college and nursing. She could not even begin to explain what she was doing in the emergency room and the operating room. Most of them could not stand the sight of blood let alone what went on in an operating room.

Barbara's Coffee, Tea, or Wine party was a reunion of sorts with the old gang from Circle City High School and a few mutual friends from college days. It sounded like fun at the time and worked with her schedule. Luckily Thursday was her only day off, so she was free to attend. She had to admit that it was fun catching up with everyone's life since graduation. Her life had been so unbelievably busy that if it had not been for Barbara, who was a great organizer, she would have become a dim memory to all of the others in this group of friends.

Thank heavens for Barbara. Now she and Chris would be getting married and Barbara had asked her to be the maid of honor. Angie felt it was a special honor and was very happy. True, they were all living in different worlds right now, but they were still good friends, and they wanted her to be part of theirs even though they were traveling on a different path at the present time.

It was romantic the way Chris had given Barbara her ring as soon as he was discharged from service. It was ironic that Chris, who never left the states, was discharged and home before Jimmy who had served in Korea and was still waiting for his discharge orders. Life was a mystery with nothing but curves in a road filled with many road blocks.

Life went on no matter how upset Angie was about Jimmy. The work was piling up in her everyday life. She found herself in scrubs, face masks, and hair nets most of the time. The operating room was a busy place, and the fast pace was therapeutic to her. Tomorrow she was to be doing surgical prep. This was the real thing, not just observing, and it was exciting.

She was actually looking forward to going to the Coffee, Tea, or Wine party Barbara was hosting Thursday when she would meet the girls. It would be a nice break and would get her away from the hospital and Jack, who was becoming a huge distraction. She needed to be free of distractions for a while and hoped that Jimmy would get home soon so she could decide once and for all was she really in love with Jimmy or had Jack moved into that special spot in her heart.

Finally word came from Jimmy saying he would be home the end of the month. He was coming from Korea via a Victory Ship and only God knew how long that would take. They were all being shipped to Seattle, Washington. There was a base located there for debriefing and discharge. It would be difficult to know just how long this would take before he was actually able to head home. He would call as soon as he had definite information. He said to say hello to everyone and that he couldn't wait to see her. That was it? All this time and that was it? I'm going to have a talk with him as soon as I see him, thought Angie. It seemed that Jimmy was unquestionably lacking in communication skills. Strong and silent didn't cut it anymore. She was at a low boiling point right now, and it was unpredictable how long it would last before she exploded.

Today, she was looking forward to seeing her old friends and putting men out of her mind.

After a long pout she came to the conclusion that there was no way she would greet Jimmy with such a rotten attitude. She set her anger aside and got over it. She continued her regular routine as if she had never received his message. It was much easier to deal with everything with a positive attitude.

Thursday was here, and Angie was excited to see everyone. Barbara was a good friend, and she had become the self-appointed keeper of the friends. She always made certain that the group stayed in touch with each other. If it had not been for her always pulling Angie back into the group, she would have lost touch with everyone who was a real friend. Now she had to check her closet to make sure she had something to wear. She had been wearing scrubs so long that she forgot that she needed to pick out a dress.

She took a shower and got dressed. Kathy was coming by to pick her up, so she had to hurry to be ready on time.

The girls reached the house in plenty of time and were getting ready to knock on the door when Barbara threw open the door and gave them both a big hug. "Come on in. You are in for a real surprise."

"What are you talking about? You have me completely baffled. Come on Barbara, you've never been able to keep a secret. What can it be?"

They both laughed as they entered the living room. The room was familiar to Angie and brought back a rush of happy memories. This was where they all met to go to the Grad Dance, Barbara and Chris and Angie and Jimmy. All dressed up like kings and queens. Flash bulbs were going off as happy times filled with dreams for the future. It was an inviting room filled with warmth. You could walk from the living room right into the dining room, and Angie remembered looking into the room on that night of the dance and seeing the side board filled with glasses of soft drinks and potato chips. The memory made her smile when she saw the side board today with glasses of wine and cheese balls and crackers. What a long way they had come.

Angie knew everyone in the room and was busy greeting them, when to her surprise she heard a voice behind her call out to her, "Hey Angie, you look great, how are you?" Angie turned, and to her complete surprise there before her stood Jenny from beauty school.

"Jenny, what a surprise. It's good to see you again. It has been forever."

Barbara came up to the two women and said, "I see you two have found each other. Is this a small world, or what? I met Jenny looking for houses in the very same housing development that Chris and I were looking for a house. We were talking and somehow your name came up."

"Oh really. I didn't know that you and Eddy were moving into Indianapolis. Doesn't he still have his Eddy's Cool Deals?" Angie asked.

With that Jenny preceded to tell her all about herself and how great everything was. Of course Eddy's Cool Deals was still going strong but neither one of them could stand to live in that hick town any longer. She had booth space in Frankie's High Styles and was doing very well. It only made sense that they move in closer to where she was working. It was high time that he did a little commuting himself. She asked if Angie had ever made it to nursing school. Of course Angie took great pleasure in telling her that not only did she get to nursing school, she was now a surgical nurse in training and would be a registered nurse by the end of the year. After the brief update they joined the rest of the girls, took their seats, and chatted with each other. Barbara set a beautiful table filled with all kinds of pastries, cookies, fruits, and nuts. It was a lovely spread. In no time the girls headed for the side board for a glass of wine and cheese and crackers. It was not long before the side board began dwindling quickly of wine and snacks.

Barbara came into the room with a tray containing two bottles of one white and one red wine and began serving everyone refills. She told them all, "More refills are in the dining room. Help yourselves."

The wine actually acted as an icebreaker, and the girls now relaxed and began to gossip openly about themselves, their husbands, and lives in general. Soon what began as a little harmless gossip became quite an interesting discussion. Barbara sat down and the girls all started to talk about everything under the sun. Many of the married girls openly talked about their husbands, and much to Angie's surprise, some were very unhappy. Some were shocked by the realization of the responsibilities that came with marriage. Of course not all the married girls were unhappy. It seemed that the some were disillusioned with their career choices. Jenny was one of the unhappily married girls, and she talked very openly about what a jerk Eddy was.

She revealed they had tried counseling but that was a bust. They finally decided to move up here to Indianapolis and bought a house. They were moving very soon, and she was sure that things would be better here.

As the conversation turned to high school days, one of the girls started talking how those were the best years of their lives. Angie was surprised to learn how many agreed with her statement. Angie was stunned by this declaration. She could not believe that was where these girls thought their lives stopped being happy. Of course there was some talk that echoed Jenny's sentiments. This was very sad to hear and more than a little discouraging.

Angie would've loved to tell them about some of her experiences in the cold, cruel world but backed off and thought better of it. She realized these girls were just talking off the top of their heads and not from real life experiences.

Barbara, in an effort to change the subject, just happened to mention the class ring that Angie had lost. Everyone in the room picked up on that and remembered how upset she was when the ring was lost.

Jenny then joined in the conversation, "I know," she said and went on with her rendition of the story. "I was right there, remember, Angie? You were a real wreck the night the ring disappeared. Angie was so upset she nearly tore the room apart looking for it."

They all laughed at the story. Everyone but Angie thought it was funny. She could have laughed too if she wasn't so sure Jenny had taken the ring.

The entire conversation was upsetting to her. She laughed with the rest of them, but it hurt her deeply. It brought up a lot of old feelings that she had put to rest. Unfortunately, the memories of that night came rushing back while they were joking about the class ring and that memory upset her the most. She had all but forgotten about that ring. It happened so long ago it didn't matter any longer.

The subject changed several times that day and covered many subjects, but the discussion of Angie's class ring struck a nerve which really hurt her feelings. She always thought Jenny had something to do with it, but she never had any idea why anyone would want that ring.

After coffee and dessert the party began to break up. Everyone said their goodbyes and left.

Jenny said, "Let's get together sometime soon."

Angie answered, "Sure, sounds good." The party was over. It was fun but she still didn't like Jenny and she told Barbara to be cautious of her.

Barbara asked Angie if she had heard from Jimmy yet, and she answered, she was expecting him to get home sometime soon. She also said she was getting very discouraged and wished he was coming home tomorrow. As was Barbara's style, she reassured Angie saying he would be back soon and everything would be great. Angie was hoping that this was not wishful thinking on everyone's part.

The two girls hugged each other before they parted. Barbara asked Angie if she thought Jimmy would be one of the groomsmen at their wedding. Angie said that she was sure he would. Barbara was happy to hear that Jimmy would be in the wedding party.

Angie and Kathy were walking to the car and not far behind them was Jenny. Jenny was in her own world now. She was furious with herself for coming to this party. She was out of place and should never have come. These were women from a different world than hers. What a bunch of stuck-up women. Angie was right there going right along with them. There was a name for that kind, and it wasn't nice.

Chapter 54

Just One More Delay

The end of the month arrived and still no word from Jimmy. This was a joke—a horrible cruel joke. She was finding it hard to breathe. For some unknown reason she had chosen to believe that he would arrive on the last day of the month. Breathe, she kept telling herself, breathe. This was absolutely the last straw. She was going to Seattle, Washington to the base where he was supposed to arrive and get to the bottom of all of this nonsense. This was the worst day of her life. She felt as if she had been abandoned. She had not worked in over two years and was totally at her father's mercy when it came to money. How would she even manage to take a trip like that? Stop it! She told herself, this was insane. How could she go to Seattle with no money and no information and no time off from the hospital? This was a bad idea and at the present time she had no alternative, except to wait a few more days to hear something. After all she had waited this long. What are a few days more or less? She managed to calm herself down and prepared for the worst while she hoped for the best.

She continued with her normal routine and tried to give no thought to Jimmy and this whole mess. All of her other friends had simple reunions with their boyfriends. At least that was the way they told the story. Everyone envied Barbara because she and Chris were engaged, and they were planning a wedding. The others looked unhappy. It was hard to say what it was about those girls that troubled Angie. They should be happy. All the guys were home, and they were together, at least that's how it seemed. Barbara had said don't believe everything you hear. Trust me, it's not all true. One day we girls should get together and exchange stories. This was something Angie didn't want to miss.

She came back to her room after a grueling day in the surgery service. She tossed her cap on the bed, pulled off her shoes, and started to undress to take a shower. She felt as if she was covered with disinfectant and whatever else she had to handle throughout the day, and it had been a long one at that.

She reached for her robe and toiletries when she noticed the telegram lying on her bed. She quickly reached for it and tore it open. The note was very brief and it read as follows:

Angie,

Sorry for this message stop Our ship has been delayed indefinitely stop Will wire as soon as departure is known stop

Jimmy

Well that was short and sweet. I guess he had to send the message quickly and didn't want to add a bunch of mushy stuff, she thought to herself. She had become accustomed to these sorts of disappointments and refused to let it bother her any longer. She would go with the flow for now. Mentally she couldn't go through any more emotional turmoil. It would make her sick or cause a nervous breakdown. She already knew she was close to one a few days ago. She had gone to the staff doctor and asked for some tranquilizers, and he told her to calm down or she would make herself a candidate for a king-size nervous breakdown, and she was too good for that. Everything would work out in time, he told her. Please stop trying to speed up something that simply cannot be changed. That was perhaps the best advice she had received yet. That day she decided to quit all this apprehension and think positive thoughts and if she was disappointed, she would have to get over it. The days turned into weeks and weeks turned into a month before she heard from Jimmy again. Once again his message came in the form of a telegram. She didn't get excited nor did her heart beat harder or hope ring eternal. Standing there looking at the telegram as if it was a piece of meaningless paper, she tossed it on the table and walked out to the study room to study for her last exam of the term. She had to get a good grade and was sure she would. They all went across the street to The Bar for a drink after study table. Angie didn't need a drink, but wanted one of their grilled cheese sandwiches and fries. She was starving because she had eaten only a small breakfast. Nevertheless, she followed them to The Bar and had a Coke, grilled cheese, and fries. The Bar was simple, clean, and inviting, with a grill behind the counter in plain sight of all the customers so you could actually watch your order being made. It was really cool. The rhythm of the cook was a fascinating show in itself. Angie sat mesmerized watching the process. You could actually taste the food as you watched it being prepared. The BIG attraction was that they served beer and wine if you chose an alcoholic drink. Thus the name, The Diner, became The Bar, and the legend was born.

Angie was so famished when her food arrived that she began wolfing it down as fast as she could. When Jack suddenly appeared and sat down beside her, she was shocked to see him sitting there. She had tried to avoid him as much as possible for the past few months, but tonight she was taken by surprise and could not hide from him this time.

"What's up with you anyhow?" he began. "You've been dodging me for months now. Have I done something to offend you or do you just simply not want to be around me?"

"I, I don't know what to say," she stammered. "There is no problem with you at all, the problem is with me. I was beginning to like being with you very much, too much, actually. I was looking forward to seeing you more and more and that was the problem. I feel very disloyal to Jimmy when I am around you. It's just that simple."

He looked at her very thoughtfully and responded, "If that jackass was treating you the way he should, you would never have gone with me in the first place, and we would not be having this conversation at all. I don't have to tell you what is wrong here. You know better than anyone what is wrong. The guy is bonkers. Something happened to him over there, and it scared him to death. I don't know what it could be, but I'm not sure you're ready to take on this kind of problem. I'll give you some time after he returns to see how it goes. Perhaps by then you'll have come to your senses, but if you still feel the same way about him, then I'll disappear from your life, and that's a promise."

Before Angie could reply he got up and left The Bar. She was too shaken to even finish her dinner. She took a few sips of Coke, paid her bill, said goodbye to her friends, and left. As she reached the door she realized that she was crying. Tears were streaming down her cheek, and she couldn't control them. Jack had issued an ultimatum, but he had also given a diagnosis of what Jimmy's problem might be. Both of these declarations were extremely troublesome. Even beyond that, he indicated she couldn't handle this problem; she wasn't sure what all of it meant. Jack was saying that he would wait until Jimmy returned, but she had to make up her mind. If she decided to continue to try with Jimmy, Jack would be gone. She didn't want him gone from her life. Yet she wanted Jimmy to be part of her life, too. How was it possible to solve a problem as important as this one in one week?

She had just reached the hospital when she remembered the telegram which was in her room. She rushed back and leaped up the steps to her room. With haste, she entered the room and hurried to the table where she had left the envelope. Picking it up, she tore it open. It read as follows:

Angie stop

The ship has been repaired stop Unit will be boarding sometime tomorrow stop Not sure when will dock in Seattle stop Will call first chance stop Cannot wait to see you stop

Jimmy

Her lip quivered. She read it again and sighed. Then the tears flowed. Only this time she was sobbing uncontrollably. At last he would be coming home. They would be able to sit and talk face to face and understand what was going on between the two of them. She pulled herself together and set out to prepare for this new turn of events. At this moment there was absolutely no doubt there was still a great deal of feelings left in her for Jimmy. That last night together flashed by her eyes, and she saw a gentle, kind young man pouring his love and kisses out to her. She became flushed when she remembered exactly how she felt at that moment. If he had been a different kind of man he could have had his way with her. She knew that he wanted the same thing that she did at that moment but instead stopped and whispered to her, "No not this way; our first time will not be in the back seat of a car. What if I get you pregnant? Our first child will not be conceived this way. We will be married in our church with our parents present. You will wear a white gown, and I will wear a tux. We will have a first night which will be magnificent. This I promise you."

Remembering those special words made her cry even more. She felt like an emotional mess. She couldn't help herself. She was so shaken that she felt she would faint. Please God, return this man to me as he was with his kind heart and loving ways. I loved him then, and I am sure I will love him again. She fell on top of her bed and fell asleep from exhaustion, clothes and all, and didn't wake up until the next morning.

Chapter 55

Things Change

Now there appeared to be a set schedule in place for Jimmy's departure. Angie felt she could at long last expect to see him sooner rather than later. At least she had something tangible to hold on to. She still didn't know when exactly, but this time she felt it was much closer than ever before. A second real fear began to arise, and this fear began to replace the concern of when he would be home. A new reality had taken root in her mind. The words that Jack had said in anger had struck a nerve. Would Jimmy be different when he returned? This was an apprehension which she had pushed way back into her mind and held there in limbo for a long time. The words that Jack had used, "He's gone bonkers, and something frightened him. Whatever happened to Jimmy could have triggered an adverse reaction." Sight unseen she had already determined that some very big changes had taken place in Jimmy. The kind of changes that sent chills up her spine when she forced herself to think about it. She knew she had also changed. She was no longer the same young girl struggling to make it to the School of Nursing. She was a much younger Angie then. An Angie who loved to have fun and went to the Tee Pee to hang out with her friends. Now she had been exposed to life and death situations caring for sick patients, some critical, some not so serious. Every decision was deadly serious; one wrong choice could mean a patient's life. She had experienced a taste of knowing that there were other men who could be very interested in her. This fact alone made her think: What were her real feelings for Jack? Did she want him in her life? How would Jimmy feel if he knew she had these kinds of thoughts about another man? What about Jimmy? Had he been tempted to stray from her during this time? Maybe he might have had a romance or two while he was overseas. Who knows what other issues there might be. Issues that had not even crossed her mind yet. Stop! Don't think this way, she told herself. This kind of thinking will not have a good ending.

Her real fear, however, was perhaps the changes which had taken place in both of their lives would not be pleasing to either one of them. Why was she making problems now? He wasn't even home yet. Nothing had happened to even indicate that any problems existed. More than likely there weren't any issues at all. Perhaps she was more concerned she wouldn't have the capability to deal with any personal problems that might occur while he was adjusting to civilian life. Or was that simply her nature to look for trouble where there was none? What a fool she was. She should be enjoying the news of his upcoming arrival. Was she searching for reasons to have things go wrong? It had been so long since she had seen or had any kind of conversation with him that she was lost as to what to even say to him after, "Hello Jimmy, I really missed you." Then what? She had to stop and settle down and prepare for her big test in an hour. She decided that since she had a free day after the test, she was going home to visit with her father and Athena. It had been too long since she had seen any of the family, and she needed to check up on Sammie and little Bobby, too. Perhaps her father could give her some encouraging advice.

Suddenly she remembered the prayers her mother had given to her to pray regularly. She had committed them to heart. She began to pray them. Her heart was comforted as she did.

Angie finished her work and packed a small overnight bag and set out for home. It was a short ride on the bus, and it barely gave her time to think about all the concerns which had nagged her for over a day now. How could she explain them to her father? He had always lacked the disposition to understand her anxieties. As far as he was concerned, as long as she was healthy everything else would work out. She had exhausted herself to such an extent that she actually fell asleep and was awakened by the sudden stop of the bus. She shook her head and looked around, trying to get her bearings. She woke up in time for the next stop where she had to get off. The walk was short from the bus stop to her front door. It was a good thing she had called home to tell them she was coming over to spend the night and visit or they might not have been home. She opened the door as she had done so many times before. "Hello. Is anyone home?" she called as she entered the house and was greeted by a whiff of the most delicious fragrances of a home-cooked meal she had smelled in a very long time. The aroma of a home-cooked meal was totally foreign to the hospital cafeteria. Something told her she was in for a real treat.

"We're in the kitchen. Come on back," was the reply. Sammie came running out to greet her with a big hug.

"Come on, Angie. You're just in time for dinner."

She followed him into the kitchen and was welcomed by the rest of the family. Little Bobby ran and jumped into her arms and gave her a great big kiss.

"Come in and sit down. We'd just about given up on you it was getting so late," her father said, as she entered the room and sat down at her place setting.

Even Athena seemed happy to see her. They all looked at her for a moment, when her father commented that she had lost a lot of weight, and asked if she had been eating.

"Yeah, I've been eating, but nothing good like this food." Angie smiled and smoothed her dress. She couldn't wait to sit down and eat. After a blessing of the meal, they all enjoyed the wonderful food which Athena had prepared. Even Athena commented as to how much she had missed her visits. It had been over a month since she had been home. It seemed a little strange to hear she had been missed. Before Angie left for nursing school all Athena would say was how soon are you moving out? I want your room for my sewing room. All Angie could say was that she had been very busy and could not leave because she was working at the hospital much more now. All of the rest of her day she was either in class or the study group. It had been very hectic, and she simply could not break away. It was good to be home, and she really wanted to see everyone and this was the first opportunity she had to come home. After dinner she helped Athena clean up the kitchen and then they went into the living room to have a cup of coffee and talk. Sammie had to get his homework done so he went straight upstairs to complete his assignments. Bobby played with his toys while Basil, Athena, and Angie sipped coffee and chatted.

After a while Angie brought up the subject of Jimmy's retuning home. She told them both that after a long period of no communication, he finally informed her that he was boarding a ship and would land in Seattle, Washington for the processing of his discharge and debriefing. Then he was coming home. He sounded as if he expected everything to be just as he left it. This concerned her greatly, and she needed to talk to them both and see what advice they would give her. It was now over two years, closer to three since he left, and she was troubled by the thought that they both had changed a great deal during this time. There had been long gaps of time when she never heard a word from him, and when she did it would be a short, nonspecific type of communication. She excused this lack of writing by rationalizing this was his way of keeping in touch without revealing any information of his mission for the Special Forces. She knew that he couldn't disclose anything he was doing. Now he was coming home, and she feared he had changed more than she could imagine. She was certain she had changed much more than she realized. What if they didn't like these new changed people they had become?

Basil looked at his daughter with loving eyes and simply said, "Angie, no one who has been away at war, even if they were in the infantry, let alone in Special Forces, come back the same person they were when they left. You have got to face that fact. The problem is that the two of you have gone too long without seeing and talking to each other. He really doesn't know what you've been doing, and you don't know what he's been doing. This is a difficult situation. I personally don't want you to trap yourself in a situation where you feel you have a responsibility to him and become committed in a relationship that will bring you nothing but heartbreak."

Athena nodded in agreement with him. She felt it was wrong for Jimmy not to have sent some sort of communication in all that time, if for no other reason except to let her know he was safe. All of this was just talk. The truth was he didn't contact her and now he was coming home and her heart was on the line.

"Do you think the best thing to do is to see him and see what happens?" Angie asked. "The worst thing that could happen is I get upset still one more time, but it will be easier to get over that kind of hurt than to try to make a hopeless relationship work. His past actions have already hardened me to that kind of heartbreak."

"Angie, you look exhausted. Go up to bed and get some rest. You work too hard under normal circumstances, let alone this. Get a good night's sleep, and we will talk again in the morning. Things will be clearer then, and we will all have a chance to sleep on it before any decisions are made," her father said.

He kissed her, and she went up the stairs to her room. As soon as she got to her room her heart softened and her mind went back to times when things were simpler and problems which seemed gigantic where actually not nearly as enormous as they seemed. She changed into her PJs and climbed into bed and fell asleep very quickly. Somewhere between three and four in the morning she awoke suddenly and sat up in bed. She looked around her and saw that she was in her own room at home and laid back down and went back to sleep. She slept until eight in the morning. By the time she took a shower and got dressed it was too late to see her father; he had already left for work. She packed her bag and went downstairs. To her surprise, her father was still at home. She entered the kitchen and saw the whole family. What was going on, she thought? They all greeted her with a grand good morning and a great big smile.

"Good morning to you all. I can't believe you are all at home. Why aren't you at school Sammie, and Dad, you aren't at work yet. Is it a holiday that I don't know about?" she asked.

"Today is Angie's day, and we have taken the day off. We wanted to spend more time with you. Do you feel better this morning?" her father asked.

"Yes, I do. It's the first time in a long time that I feel rested," she said as she sat down to a cup of coffee.

Athena brought over some scrambled eggs and bacon for Angie to eat along with toast and orange juice. This was a feast for Angie, and she actually began to cry she was so over whelmed by all of this attention she had received. "I guess I'm a little emotional this morning. Thank you all for everything. This is so special. I love you so much." She said wiping the tears from her eyes.

Shortly after breakfast she began to prepare to leave when her father stopped her and said, "Please don't try to solve this problem with Jimmy alone. We have all known Jimmy for years. He has been in and out of this house as if he were one of my own children. However, please bring him home when he gets back, and let's all assess Jimmy and see just how much he has changed. What do you say to that?"

"I think that is a good idea and will do just that. I'll call you as soon he gets into town. Thank you, Dad. I've always loved you, and I certainly appreciate the concern you are showing for me now."

She picked up her bag and headed out the door to go back to the hospital when Basil said, "Wait. I'll take you back to the hospital. You don't have to hassle with the bus today.

Chapter 56

Let's Not Forget the Class Ring

For some unknown reason Angie had a flash back to the day her class ring disappeared. Why the thought of that day came to her was unclear, except for the fact that the girls at Barbara's party had talked about her class ring. It had been a long time since that ring had been lost. She had never forgotten that the mystery of its disappearance was never solved. She could still see the ring on the tray of her work station that day. There was no one else around who had the opportunity except Jenny. What other explanation could there be? She had looked in every corner of the room, and it was no place to be found. When Jenny offered to help, Angie had noticed her halfhearted effort in the search she had made. In retrospect she really made little to no effort at all. It was almost as if she knew it would never be found. There was also the mention of a magic ring she possessed on the day that she announced that she and Eddy were engaged. It could be that this flashback was just a result of the fact that Angie and her friends which included Jenny were talking about the incident, and it all came back to her. She had not given the ring a second thought after her graduation from Circle Center High. Yet today it kept bugging her, and this made the whole incident almost seem as if it were a recent event.

What was unknown to Angie was that her suspicions were correct. Jenny had in fact taken the ring and convinced herself that it was magic and the reason that Eddy had asked her to marry him. Sadly, there was no magic in the ring. Eddy had asked Jenny to marry him because he truly loved her very deeply. The misery of the situation was that she had treated him dreadfully and used him to get what she thought she wanted and credited the "Magic Ring" for the very things that Eddy had worked very hard to get for her. Their marriage had been a miserable episode filled with horrible accusations and hateful language which resulted in a very poor relationship. What had emerged was sadly the death of a love that would have brought her joy and happiness. The love that Eddy had for Jenny had faded into a loathing which even though they had tried to work out their problems, it became impossible to forget the ugly words which were hurled at each other. Their relationship had turned into a cold war which never resulted in having a family or any kind of normal relationship between them. Eddy had long since moved out of their bedroom and into the guestroom. He and Jenny had ceased to have any sexual relations and had not slept in the same bedroom for quite some time. This had been the state of their relationship for too long now. He was Catholic and did not wish to have a divorce on his conscience. Even though it had taken much longer than Eddy had originally thought to accomplish, he finally managed to pay off all of the bills Jenny had carelessly run up, but now he was lonely and needed the comfort of a loving woman. He gave it one more try in an attempt to resolve their problems, but after much counseling it led to no resolution of any problems. It seemed that whatever the marriage counselor advised Jenny took as a direct assault on her and accused the therapist of taking Eddy's side. She finally refused to go to anymore sessions, and the whole thing fell apart. The end came when Eddy, quite by accident, made the discovery of a secret lover who Jenny had been with for quite some time. This discovery was the straw that broke the camel's back. He was left with no alternative but to call it quits. There was nothing left to salvage and even if there was, he was not interested. She begged him to forgive her, but he saw nothing left for them. She became desperate to hang on to him, but the only reason for her motivation was that her lover was a deadbeat who was constantly hitting her up for money. So the chapter of Eddy and Jenny was permanently closed.

As his last obligation to her, he set her up in a small beauty salon where she could support herself and bought her a house presented to her with deeds to both properties and bid her good luck, goodbye, and was gone. His hope was to move on to a better life, with someone who would love him and give him children which he wanted very badly.

Angie of course was never aware of any of these facts. Not that it made any difference to her at this stage of her life.

Chapter 57

Now Is the Hour

Finally after three weeks Jimmy sent another telegram which read as follows:

Angie,

I am leaving Seattle tomorrow stop Arriving via Train Saturday Nine AM stop Please meet me at station stop Cannot wait to see you stop

Jimmy

Short and sweet seems to be the way all the communications had been running. What will we talk about? He had not told her anything that would give her a clue as to what was going on. She would have to see what happened at the train station. She'd get her schedule changed so she could go to the station to pick him up. There was just one tiny problem: she had no car. Where would she get a car to pick him up? Maybe her father would let her use his car for a few hours. That might be a good way to get Jimmy over to her house so the family could see him again. She would call him now.

Basil was more than willing to lend Angie his car that day. It was actually the first time since high school that she had used his car. It was strange, now that she was a grown woman, to ask to use the car like a teenager would.

As the time for his arrival approached, she became more and more nervous. The prospect of the reunion was totally unnerving her. Then when she realized that she had not even thought about what to wear, she went into a panic and nearly fell apart. *She had to look her best.* A quick search in the closet did not reap anything special. After much thought she decided to go low-key and picked a nice blouse and skirt. Simple, but nice, she loved the idea and how it looked. All she had to do now was to settle down and keep busy and wait for tomorrow to come.

At the crack of dawn Saturday morning, Angie was dressed and ready to go. She looked great as she arrived at the train station. She found a parking spot and walked into the depot to wait for the arrival of his train. Everything was going according to schedule. The train was fifteen minutes late, but it arrived. She walked to the gate where his train was coming in and waited anxiously as passengers came down the steps from the train. She was trying desperately to remember how Jimmy walked and talked and even looked. Fear gripped her when she thought that she had actually forgotten everything about him. Settle down, she told herself, he has dark brown hair, is six feet tall, has olive skin, and what color eyes? Think, what color were his eyes, blue? No brown, or is it hazel? I can't remember. I won't know him. I know I won't. Then suddenly someone tapped her on the shoulder and said, "Hello, Angie, remember me?" She turned and looked into this beautiful face with dark brown eyes, and she felt herself get lightheaded.

She recovered and said, "Jimmy, it's you, it's really you. Thank God you're back." She stepped forward to hug him when he took her in his arms and kissed her as if he had not kissed anyone for a long time. It was a hungry kiss, yet yearning, and best of all it was passionate, filled with love. Angie almost collapsed from the joyfully serene effect it had on her. Without realizing it, tears of relief and happiness where forming in her eyes, and when she looked up at him, his eyes melted her into his arms even more.

"I thought you wouldn't be here," he whispered in her ear. I have dreamed of this day from the time we said goodbye a lifetime ago. Now at this very moment I am holding you in my arms, and I still cannot believe we are together again." With that he kissed her once again, a little less hungry kiss, a much gentler kiss, but still made no mistake it was a kiss filled with love and caring.

Angie gently pulled away and said, "Let's get out of here and go someplace where it is much quieter. Have you had breakfast yet?" she asked. "I know a great spot. Come on. Follow me." He grabbed his bag and followed her orders.

As they approached the car she turned to him and he kissed her again. "It has been too long," he said.

He put his bag into the car and got into the passenger's side as she got behind the wheel of the car. She drove straight over to the

Firehouse Café. There the two of them had a great breakfast and had a chance to talk a little without being interrupted. They talked about a lot of things and of course she gave him an update on all his friends who had recently returned from service. She told him about Barbara and Chris getting engaged. Barbara had asked her to be her maid of honor, and they wanted him to be a groomsman. Angie was very excited about that. They were making wedding plans and looking for a house to buy at the same time. Then she turned to him and said, "Of course the biggest news of all is that you are home at last. Please tell me why you never wrote me? I thought you had forgotten me all together."

He looked at her squarely in the eyes and said, "I could never forget you, Angie. You were the only thing that kept me going during this dark period of my life. At times I thought that I would never see you again. I was captured by the North Koreans and taken to a prisoner of war camp. They kept me there for six long horrible months. I actually thought I would never live to see you or freedom ever again. Then by the grace of God, the Special Forces came and rescued us, me and my fellow prisoners. Some were Special Forces as I was, but most were just unlucky infantry men. I thank God that we were rescued. Most of us made it back to our battalions, but some were too sick from hunger, the injuries, and diseases they suffered and did not survive. You have no idea what it meant to me to know you were here hanging in through thick and thin. I have never loved you more than I love you this very moment. Please don't respond now. I know I have put you through enough anxiety for a lifetime. Let's give ourselves time to get our feet on the ground. If you still feel the same about me as you did, then we can take the next step. What do you say?"

"I say that I have waited this long, waiting a little longer to make sure we are right for each other would be the sensible thing to do."

He paid the bill and they left the diner and headed home. "Did you get in touch with your mother?"

"Yes, she knows that I was coming in today. She is looking forward to seeing me as soon as possible."

"Do you mind dropping by my house to say hello to my family for a moment?"

"No, not at all. I would love to. I've always been fond of your family. They have always treated me as if I was part of their family. Is Joey home?"

"Joey is still at school although he has gotten a little crazy lately. He wants to drop out of school and hitchhike across the United States with his roommate, Digger. I think he has lost his mind." Angie looked very concerned as she related the story to Jimmy.

"Why is Joey thinking of quitting school when he is so close to graduation? Doesn't he realize that he could still be drafted as soon as he leaves school? He's not thinking straight. Maybe I should talk to him. Do you think it would do any good?"

"It might, or at least convince him to hitchhike the U.S.A. during summer break. I don't know." Angie threw up her hands in surrender over this situation.

While still walking to the car Angie asked him what he planned to do now that he was back. Was he planning to go back to school or get a job? He shrugged his shoulders and said he had several options but wanted to have a little time to think. Right now, more than anything, he needed to get his feet on the ground and get some rest.

He still had to get reacquainted with civilian life again. Once he did that, he could make a more sensible choice about his future. He had a lot of catching up to do on all the time he had lost with her. Too much time had been lost, and he didn't want to waste any more time being separated from her. He was not concerned about a career right now. He had plenty of options, but there was only one Angie.

By this time they had reached her house. The whole family was waiting to say hello to Jimmy. Even Joey had made a surprise trip home and was standing there with the rest of the group. They had coffee and cake waiting for them. It was a very pleasant break and made Jimmy very happy to see the effort that had been made to welcome him home. He asked Joey to join Angie and him for dinner that evening. Angie looked up with a surprised look on her face as this was the first she had heard of the plan for this evening. Joey jumped at the invitation and set the time for eight o'clock. Jimmy wanted to get a little sleep first as he had traveled all night and had only catnapped a little and was exhausted. He and Angie left shortly after they had the coffee and cake and headed to his house. His mother would be waiting for him and he didn't want to worry her. She had experienced enough anxiety over him already.

As Angie and Jimmy approached the house, the front door opened and Mrs. Jordon and his brother and sister raced out to greet him. They were so excited to see him after all this time. They pulled the two of them into the house and made them right at home. It was a happy reunion, and a peace fell over the family as they thanked God for bringing Jimmy home safely. After the family had a loving reunion Angie had to excuse herself; she had to leave for classes. She was also to work a short shift and needed to be on her way. Jimmy walked her to the car but stopped to check out his car. His car really looked good to him—still in the garage at home. He told her to be ready at 8 o'clock and he'd pick her and Joey up. She told him to pick her up at the nurse's quarters at the hospital. She would be out front at eight o'clock.

"By the way, I really love the outfit you're wearing. You look sharp," he said.

"Thank you. I thought it would be appropriate for this occasion."

"You were right—I love it, but I really love the girl wearing it even more." He kissed her again and went into his home. Angie watched in disbelief. This was really happening, wasn't it, she asked herself. Then she thanked God in heaven for bringing Jimmy home safely. As she drove away, the reality of what he told her sank in and the realization that many prisoners of war did not survive the rescue mission. That was why he didn't write all those months. She felt ashamed that she had gotten so angry with him for not writing. War was not a joke—it was deadly serious business, and she would never take it lightly ever again.

The rest of the day flew by. She was finishing up her shift and was about to check on the last patient under her care, when Jack came up behind her. They both were checking on the same patient. She had not seen him and gave a start when she turned. "Oh! I didn't see you, you startled me. Is Mr. Johnson your patient?" she asked.

"Yes, I just wanted to make sure he was resting comfortably and all his vitals were normal," Jack replied.

"Well that is what I am here for. I was about to take the vitals, and I'll have a report ready for you in just a moment," she said as she began taking care of the patient. "How are you feeling, Mr. Johnson? I'm going to take your vitals now. Are you having any discomfort?" she asked as she proceeded to take his blood pressure. When she finished her work she turned to Jack and handed him her report.

He looked it over and said everything was looking good. He asked Mr. Johnson if he needed any pain medicine. The patient nodded, yes, and Jack motioned for Angie to place a request for pain medicine for Mr. Johnson. After Angie left the room Jack continued his examination of the patient. He checked the incision for infection. "Everything looks good," he declared. He bid the patient goodnight and left the room.

Angie also finished her report and left the floor and headed for the nurse's quarters. She was walking toward the elevator when Jack caught up with her.

He stepped into the elevator and looked at Angie with enquiring eyes. "Well did your G.I. Joe make it home yet?"

Angie looked up at him annoyed by his comment. She thought to herself, what is he is trying to prove by harassing me, but answered in an even tone, "Yes, he came in today. I'm going to meet him shortly. Please give me some space will you?"

He lifted his hands in surrender. "I'll give you all the space you need. You will not see me around after next month. I've been offered an internship at a trauma hospital in Chicago for the next two years, so I will not be around and probably will finish my residency there also. It's a great opportunity, and I have decided to take it. I didn't want to leave without saying goodbye. I wanted you to know that I am still hooked on you and would be back in a heartbeat if you would say the word."

"Jack, I like you too, but I have to see if there is anything left between Jimmy and me. He's been gone for a long time and has been through a lot. I owe it to him to give him a fair chance. I appreciate your honesty. If you could give me a little time to make an honest assessment of my situation, then I can truly know that

I have made the right choice. Please stay in touch with me when you leave. You have an amazing opportunity. Congratulations!"

"That's all I need to know. Rest assured that I will write you when I get settled, but in the meantime, I'm going to be here for a month and perhaps we will see each other here in the hospital from time to time."

They said goodbye, and Angie hurried off to get ready to meet Jimmy. How could she make any true assessment of this situation with all the pressures that were being placed on her? Yes, she liked Jack, but like and love are two totally different feelings. Jimmy had melted her heart when she saw him at the train station. She felt all of the old feelings come rushing back. However, she recognized that Jimmy definitely had issues that would need to be addressed. Her plan was to try to understand what was going on with him, one step at a time. A plan was forming in her mind. One thing was unmistakable and that was she still had a lot of feelings for Jimmy. As for Jack, she had already given that friendship a lot of thought and came up with nothing. She finished getting ready and ran down to the street level to meet Jimmy.

She was just in time to see him pull up to the curb and park, preparing to wait for her. It had started raining and Angie had come running out to avoid getting wet. She went straight to the car door of Jimmy's car and opened it.

Joey was sitting in the front seat, but jumped out to allow her to sit next to Jimmy.

"This is just like old times." Jimmy said. The rain had begun to intensify as they drove away from the hospital.

"I thought we could go over to the Huddle Cave. That's always been a good place to eat, or is it still in business?"

"It's very much in business. That's a great idea. Let's go," Joey chimed in.

"I haven't been there for ages and you're right, it's a good place to eat," Angie added

They drove along quietly when Jimmy finally broke the silence by pointing out the changes he had noticed in the city since he had been gone. He was a little disturbed that some of his favorite buildings had been demolished and replaced by modern skyscrapers. It seemed sad that they didn't preserve some of those old buildings. He had always thought they were beautiful and full of character. "Oh well," he said, "out with the old in with the new. That's progress I guess, although I did like the old a lot better."

"Things and people change, Jimmy. That's the way the world is. Even Circle City High has changed. They've built a very large addition on the west side of the building and added two parking lots. The new football field was started a few months ago," Angie added. "It made me sad to see the old football field turned into a parking lot. It was hard to accept because I always thought of it as a landmark."

"What about you, Joey, how do you feel about all the changes?" Jimmy asked.

"Personally, I haven't noticed. Change is happening all of the time. It's part of progress or so they tell me. I feel like I need to make a few changes myself. When I first started going to college, I had one mindset, but now that I'm going to law school, I have completely changed to another mindset. It is as if I have no understanding of what I am doing, or why. Nothing makes sense anymore. Everything has become a huge confusion and my mind cannot accept it any longer. Digger, my roommate feels the same way. That's the real reason we want to hitchhike across the country to see what's going on in other places. Perhaps if I had served in the army, I would have more answers," Joey replied.

"Trust me. You do not want to serve in the army. You have a brilliant future ahead of you so why wreck it? Your summer break is coming up next month. You can start your hitchhiking adventure during your break. Have your fling in the summer. Get it out of your system and go back in the fall to finish your degree and be none the worse for wear," Jimmy suggested. "As a bonus perhaps you will get some answers to your questions and begin to understand just what is going on around you. I'm sure you'll be better for it. You'll be an outstanding lawyer, of that I have no doubt.

"That's a great idea. I thought that I would need more time than a summer, but a summer would give me just enough time to see if this is really what I want to do," Joey thought out loud. "Hey, do you guys mind if I don't join you for dinner tonight? I really want to go home and get hold of Digger to see what he thinks of this plan. I think we can swing it for the summer, but I don't know how he would feel about this new plan. You're right Jimmy. If I drop out now, I'll lose my scholarship, and it would not be easy to qualify for a new one. Thanks, buddy. You're a real friend."

Jimmy turned the car around and drove Joey home and dropped him off and said, "Joey, don't do anything foolish. Trust me. You don't want to be drafted. Get your education. Call me before you leave for school." Joey nodded and ran up the steps into the house.

Angie and Jimmy headed for the Huddle Cave in silence. "What just happened?" Angie asked. "I talked to him till I was blue in the face and didn't get anywhere. You make one suggestion, and it became the solution in nothing flat."

"Nothing really happened. Joey heard what I said and it made what you had been saying to him make a lot of sense. He'll be alright. He's too smart to give up the opportunity that he has for a whim."

"We've been talking about all the changes that have taken place while I was gone. It made me realize that we can't go back, Angie. We can only go forward, or we'll go crazy," Jimmy continued. "The past is the past. What you and I have been through these past two and half years is the past. You have your past and I have mine. Good or bad, that's the reality of the whole situation. When I returned and held you in my arms, it was as much of a test for me as it was for you. Neither of us knew how we would feel at that moment. I fully expected you to be cold and unresponsive to me. I realized one thing, not only were you responsive, but you were as responsive as I was. I loved you when I left, but I love you even more now that I'm back. For the first time, I'm able to understand why I fought so hard to get back to you."

Angie was dumbfounded by his words. He said he loved her more now than he did before he left. Could this be true? We just now got back together and how could he know he felt that deeply already? This was very worrisome to her.

She carefully replied to his statement by saying, "Jimmy you're swept away by feelings, and we can't trust these feeling right now. We have to give each other time to get acquainted once more. I've changed and so have you. At this very moment, I love you very much, but I want to be sure as you should want to be sure that we are truly in love with who we are, not who we were before we were separated by this war. Let's make certain I'm not one of those old buildings full of character with age and you aren't one of those brand new skyscrapers, new and different. We want our love to last, not a love ready for the wrecking ball. After some time has passed, we may discover we are not really who we thought we were."

They continued to drive toward the Huddle Cave in silence as they both contemplated what they had just discussed. The rain was getting heavier, and Jimmy made the comment that in Korea there was always hard cold rains that would chill you to the bone—one of the many things Jimmy hated about Korea.

The Huddle Cave was an all-American restaurant which had been in business since 1940 and served basic American cooking— breakfast, lunch, and dinner. It was a white building trimmed with neon lights. One row red and one row blue, the sign outside read, "Stop Eat and Recharge, the Food is Great!" at the Huddle Cave. When you stepped inside, the first thing you saw was a tidy black counter with bright red stools for customers wishing quick service. On each side of the room were tables and chairs and booths, which were also in the bright red and black theme. The walls were white and displayed pictures of the various items which were featured on the menu.

The rain had stopped when Jimmy pulled into the parking lot. Surprisingly, it was quite busy this evening. The hostess led the two of them to a table. She handed them a menu once they sat down. Several of Jimmy's old friends were there having a bite to eat and when they saw him, they came over to the table and welcomed him back home. Jimmy was very touched by their warm enthusiastic welcome. Angie was happy to see how many of their old friends were glad to see them and welcomed Jimmy so warmly. The whole place was filled with nostalgia.

Once they were alone, they looked at each other and took a deep breath. It was wonderful to know so many old friends were there to say hello. Jimmy felt reassured when he realized he was not forgotten.

"I had no idea so many of our old friends would be here. Remember when we thought that this was a place for old folks to come and eat? Well I guess we're the old folks now. This day has been amazing.

"Jimmy, I want us to last," began Angie, "I want us to have good times and share bad times together. We are a lot more mature now than we were when we parted. We have both been through a lot and we need to put it all behind us, before we go on to a more serious relationship."

"I know that, but why can't we put these things behind us together? Is there someone else in your life?"

"Jimmy! No absolutely not. I have been here waiting for you and trying to finish my training. How do I know that you haven't met someone else and want to get her out of your mind by marrying me?" This was her completely unexpected answer.

"You cannot seriously be thinking about such a possibility? I have thought of no one but you this whole time. Now you're making me mad here. I'm telling you how much I love you, and you're accusing me of having someone else. How could you think that? You've got us heading for a wrecking ball, and we're just now getting together."

"I'm suggesting the same scenario you've suggested about me." By this time they were both angry. Then suddenly they both came to their senses and began to laugh at the same time. They both realized that this was a ridiculous conversation.

The waitress came to the table and took their order. They looked at each other, but with guarded eyes, which weren't there before.

"Look, Angie, I don't want to go through the drama of what I did or did not do while I was away from you over and over again. It was bad enough going through it in the first place and having an instant replay is not my idea of a pleasant walk through memory lane. The only woman I had any contact with was the nurse who took care of me when I was wounded after the escape. She saved my life and was very good to me. I was in grave condition when they took me to the hospital and when I saw her I thought that God had sent an angel down to help me. I cannot begin to explain to you how much her care meant to me. I loved her for what she had done. I know I'll always have feelings for her for that very reason—especially after the horror of the prisoner of war camp I was in. I loved her the way a child would love his first teacher navigating him through the first, second, and third day of school and calming the fear of being away from his mother for the first time. She never took the place of you in my heart and never will. I know, however, if I had stayed any longer there might have been something more between us. But she was not you, and you are the one I have always wanted."

"Oh Jimmy, I've been terrible to you. I don't know what has gotten into me. I've been a wreck waiting for you and now that you are here, I'm actually picking fights with you. You never told me that you had been injured. How serious was it?"

"I almost lost my leg. I still have some shrapnel in my hip. It wasn't removed in Korea. They didn't think I could survive the surgery at the time. I'm going to the Veterans Medical Center here to have an evaluation next week and hopefully be scheduled for surgery. They made an appointment with a surgeon, when I arrived in Seattle. It's Monday morning. I'm afraid they might still think the leg will need to be amputated."

"Don't worry. They won't take your leg unless it has become infected. I know most of the doctors that are on the VA surgical teams because I had to work with them during my rotation training."

Jimmy, please forgive me. I do love you, but I don't want you to take me for granted. I, of all people, should know that patients fall in love with their doctors and nurses all of the time. I know a lot about that sort of thing. You get the patient at his most vulnerable point. Perhaps he has just survived a horrific accident or illness. Those things happen all the time. I thank her for taking such good care of you and sending you home safely. I'll always be grateful to her."

"Don't worry. I never have taken you for a fool. Here comes our food. I'm really hungry."

"Me, too. It's been a long day. You're the same wonderful guy you always were, and I don't know what I was worried about. I don't care if you loved your nurse because she helped you when you were too weak to help yourself. I have had many a patient become attached to me for that very same reason. I understand this very well."

They ate their dinner and laughed and talked about old times and they both began to relax with each other. He looked into her eyes and smiled as if all he ever wanted was to be with her. He had been honest with her, now she had to be just as honest with him. It was her turn now to tell Jimmy about Jack.

She was searching for a way to begin. "Jimmy you've been honest with me, and I need to be honest with you. I've found myself in an awkward situation. There is a small Bar and Grill across the street from the hospital which became a student hangout—a place to get a drink or a snack and unwind. My study group would go to the bar after we finished studying and I would join them for the fellowship. You know I was never much of a drinker. I was the one who would always have a Coke. They would sit around and exchange stories about their superiors and indulge in some innocent gossip. It was fun and a nice change of pace. The med students began to join the group and contribute to the gossip. It was always fun, no couples, but sometimes some of us would want to get something more to eat than a snack. One night Jack, one of the med students, asked if I wanted anything to eat, and I said, yes. We went to the Union Hall, not exactly a secret rendezvous, to have a sandwich, and we walked back to the dorm together. He was very nice and became my friend. After a while, going to the Union Hall for something to eat became a kind of routine. He was aware of my feelings for you. I made it perfectly clear that I was waiting for you to return from Korea, but at some point, he thought our friendship should be more. There was a major disagreement over this misunderstanding, and he more or less issued an ultimatum which really angered me and proved how naive I really was to think we could be just friends with each other and not expect that at a certain point, it might turn into a romance. I told him he was totally out of line and that I wouldn't give up waiting for you until you proved to me that we were finished. Jack had said that it would never work out. He wanted me to give him a chance to prove how he felt. It all ended badly, and I've been avoiding him as much as possible."

"When I saw you this morning, I knew that I would always love you."

Jimmy looked at her and said that he knew she was always true to him. She was that kind of girl, and it only made him love her all the more knowing that someone else saw just how special she really was. After dinner, they began to make plans. He wanted to see her again tomorrow and every day after that. For the first time in many years, Angie was happy and felt as if a huge weight had been lifted from her. Jimmy was home at last.

Chapter 58

No More Secrets

As a prisoner of war, Jimmy was the target of repeated and relentless brutality by the hands of his captors, especially once they found out he was with Special Forces. Their goal was to break him down to get important information from him. After much torture and at the point of great weakness, he broke. He gave old information of maneuver which had already happened, but it never ceased bothering him that he broke down. He was never able to deal with the reality that he did in fact break down and give up some information which might have caused injury to many men who were involved in a certain operation. He could never forgive himself for his failure to protect the information. The result was constant guilt and recurring nightmares that continued to haunt him. This was a nagging fact that he had deliberately ignored telling Angie. He did this because he feared she wouldn't be comfortable being with someone whose discharge was delayed three times due to Post-Traumatic Stress Disorder. She had no idea that he had asked for an evaluation and treatment for this condition while he was in the hospital for the surgery on his leg.

He knew he had to tell Angie; it wasn't fair that she did not to know. They were like two peas in a pod.

The surgery went well, and Jimmy had a quick recovery. He was on his feet in no time and more relaxed and opened to talk.

Not long after recovery, Jimmy pulled Angie aside. It was time to get this burden off of his chest. His dark brown eyes penetrated hers. "Angie, I have something to tell you." He took a deep breath and continued, "One of the reasons it took so long to get transferred home was because I was being treated for Post-Traumatic Stress Disorder. They kept me back to treat me. I was getting better, but I seemed to be slipping into that dark cloud again."

Angie was shocked. "We have to get you help!" The fact that she said "we" gave him confidence to tell her that he had already taken care of returning to treatment. He felt as if he had been dishonest. When he had an opportunity to tell her the truth, he had opted to ignore that one fact. He was afraid she would leave him and think he was crazy. He looked into her eyes and said, "Angie, I love you so much that I didn't want to take a chance of losing you forever."

"Jimmy, you can always be honest with me. When two people love and wish to pledge themselves to each other they have to be open and honest. Nothing less will do," was Angie's answer. "You don't need to worry about me not standing by you. If you have any doubts about that then you really don't know me very well."

Jimmy looked at her and felt ashamed to have ever doubted her. Now they could start to face some of the issues they would have to deal with.

Chapter 59

On to Civilian Life

One of Jimmy's duties in Special Forces was to work with the JAG branch of Special Service. Because of JAG, Jimmy became interested in the justice system. He had always wanted to be a lawyer, and this was a great opportunity for him to have some hands-on experience. Now that he was home, he began to research what opportunities were available to him if he sought a career in the legal field. He discovered his training with JAG coupled with his previous education would place him in about fourth year of pre-law, with testing, and the GI Bill would pay for any education he would need to become a lawyer. He had mentioned his plan to Angie and explained what his interests were. She was very supportive of whatever educational choices he made. She still had two more years to finish her specialty, no matter what he decided to do. In truth, Angie had placed all of her energy in attaining her nursing degree and waiting for Jimmy's return.

Her reality had become a world filled with doctors, nurses, patients, operating rooms, hospitals, sickness, health—all the things that she was doing day after day. She had been so busy with that that she had not taken any time to consider what Jimmy might want or how that might affect her. She had taken it for granted that he would go along with anything she wanted. Now that Jimmy was home, she had to rethink all of her long-term goals and include him and his career plans into the equation of their future if she wanted a successful relationship. This was easier said than done. It would necessitate her actually taking her desired goals, adding his desired goals, and coming up with a practical solution as to how to reach them without one of them sacrificing their career choices and education needs.

Now that he was a civilian and they had become an item among all of their friends, she was desperately trying to understand what all of the undercurrent and tension she was experiencing really was. She should have been happy, but it was high school all over again. Selecting a university, filling out applications, tracking down grade transcripts—but the real problem was with both their birthdays coming up, Jimmy would soon be twenty-three and she would be twenty-one. This made her ask the question over and over again. Do we really want to go through all of this school stuff again? She kept telling herself that she would do it for Jimmy if that was what he really wanted to do.

The sad fact was that her disposition had changed. She was no longer able to go with the flow. She would get irritated easily and actually found herself unable to concentrate on her class work. Even the study group was frustrating her and that certainly was not helping. It was evident now that she needed to get hold of herself before she flunked out. None of this made any sense. She still loved Jimmy, but he had become too high maintenance for her. She had become accustomed to coming and going at will. Now it was as if she was required to get permission for every move she made outside of class.

Jimmy had not formally asked Angie to marry him, and there was no engagement ring presented yet. The unasked question was looming there between them—an unseen enemy sitting, teasing, and taunting mercilessly. Angie wanted to hear a real proposal come out of his mouth. She never put pressure on him to commit to marriage, but she wanted him to commit to her. He was constantly dancing around it, always avoiding any dialogue concerning this matter. He made more of a commitment to marrying her before he left for the service than now when the time was right. He had become very possessive, and she didn't like that at all. It was as if he didn't trust her. It had been several months since his return and they had been marking time. He would get very passionate and was ready for more than just petting. As far as Angie was concerned, however, on a day not that long ago, Jimmy said they should not take a chance on her getting pregnant by having premarital sex and that they would have a church wedding. He had said that just before he left for duty overseas. She decided she would never be carried away by that kind of passion again. She was not about to be an easy lay for him or anyone else for that matter. She was going to protect her virtue until the day she married and that was that. No one was going to use her to relieve sexual tensions and then get up and walk away when he was done. Jimmy set the rules then, and now she was beginning to feel as if she was being used. She didn't like that at all. The time was fast approaching for a showdown. Right now, she was busy with finishing up her registered nursing degree. He, on the other hand, was checking out his options for pre-law. Tonight they were supposed to go out. She wouldn't wait another day to know where she stood. He'd been setting the pace since he returned from Korea. Now it was her turn.

She wasn't happy and she had a suspicion he was as unhappy as she. They were beginning to drift apart. She felt the separation. They were on two separate paths. She realized that she was "just Angie" to him. Not the love of his life, or the person he wanted to share his life with. It would break her heart for them to go their separate ways, but she knew steps must be taken if anything positive was to take place. He had changed quite a bit since he returned from Korea. She expected some of the changes, but her hope had been that they could move on and start a new life. None of this had happened. If anything, he escaped deep into his own little world where no one was allowed to enter. He was feeling sorry for himself and all he had missed because he had been drafted into the army. He felt the army had taken his life away from him and replaced it with the army life. It was a temporary change—an unexpected detour in his existence. The detour, however, was not to some exotic destination filled with historic sites and beautiful landscapes to photograph for an album of memories, but rather an ugly landscape filled with suffering and death. This new course which his life had taken was not one that anyone wanted. In fact, many had no idea it was even happening. Once he entered this world, no one could reach him. It was as if he had lost interest in the future, the past, and everything around him. This kind of depression could not continue any longer. It had consumed him and made him very unhappy. The mood swings he was having would go from happy to sad in an instant. He would go from hot and heavy to cold and indifferent. She thought that he needed to go back to therapy.

She loved Jimmy and wanted to marry him, make a home with him, and have his babies. Was that wrong?

Joey, of all people, got confused when he was on the verge of graduating college. He almost destroyed his chances to complete his law degree and was on the verge of losing his scholarship to finish school. He and Digger hitched across the country and after having survived many close calls, came to their senses, returned and finished school.

She had to laugh when she thought of the day they both showed up on the Demetrious' doorstep. They were hungry, dirty, broke, and a sight for sore eyes. They resembled refuges from a third world country. The family considered sanitizing everything they owned or at the minimum, spray them down with a disinfectant. What an adventure they must have had. Secretly, Angie had always wished she could have gone on such an exciting adventure. As if life itself was not exciting enough.

Time was drawing near to either stand up and fight or collapse and quit. Tonight she and Jimmy would confront the ghost who was standing invisibly between them and kill it once and for all.

Chapter 60

A New Beginning

Jimmy came by as usual and met Angie in front of the nurses housing. He was in an unusually pleasant mood that night. She was confident about what she was about to do. She wanted to hold out until after dinner was over before she approached the delicate situation with him. The Huddle Cave had become their personal kitchen, and they both felt very comfortable there. It was clean, friendly and best of all, the food was good. They called it their restaurant as a running joke which made them both laugh. At least that was what Angie thought it meant to both of them. The question was, how did Jimmy like their restaurant? As they pulled up to the Huddle Cave he made a caustic comment half to the air and half for Angie's benefit, which came at her like a knife thrown directly at a target and the target was her.

"Well here we are once again at the Nut-House Cave where you can order your usual double hamburger and grape limeade. You should be overjoyed at that prospect of eating your favorite sandwich and drinking your favorite drink. Yum, Yum Good."

When Angie heard these words her blood ran cold, her face turned red, and anger ran through her entire body. She turned to him and said in a confrontational voice, "What are you trying to prove with a crack like that? Jimmy, you better get your act together and watch it or this will be the last time that you will ever see me!"

Remarkably, Jimmy was taken completely by surprise. He stopped the car and looked at her with somber eyes and said, "You cannot be serious; what in the hell has come over you?"

"You really don't know do you? This kind of thing has gone on long enough, too long in fact. Your moods have been swinging up and down, and round and round like an elevator with all the cables broken. I never know what to expect anymore. You're never happy about anything. You find fault with everything. May I ask what is wrong with you this time? Take me home right now. I want to end this evening immediately if not sooner! What do you want from me anyway? I'm getting tired of this whole attitude you have. You are never happy about anything anymore. One day you're excited about starting school soon, the next you're angry and depressed. I think you need to go back to your therapy sessions. You were making a lot of progress with your therapist. I really felt he was helping. You can beat this thing; I know you can. I have tried to be sympathetic, but that has not gone anywhere. Whatever is bothering you, it's tearing us apart. I don't know what happened to you or what you saw while you were in Korea, but I do know something has to be done."

Surprisingly, Jimmy was receptive to the tough love words that Angie was throwing at him. "I know that I have been a little touchy lately, but you don't give me a break. Don't threaten me like this ever again. You're everything to me. I don't think I could have made it this far without you. Maybe you're right. Perhaps I should seek more help from the psychotherapist again." Then he turned and looked at her with a very sincere question, "Have I really been that difficult. Do I always hurt your feelings and give you a hard time?"

"Look, Jimmy, between the two of us, there is enough blame to go around. The important thing is to get some help and get you out of this dark place you have been in. I miss the old Jimmy. We were happy together then. Now every other word is an accusation or a slam."

"Please, help, I really need you and want you with me. This whole thing is holding me up in everything I want to do." He shook his head and looked straight ahead. "I have nightmares and wake up in cold sweats almost all the time. I hear guns and exploding land mines screaming in my ears. Sometimes the noise doesn't stop, and I have to run and hide I am so afraid they are real. I feel as if I've lost my mind." He turned toward her. "I look forward to seeing you and when the time comes to pick you up I start shaking for fear that someone will throw a hand grenade at me the minute I step outside. I know in my heart it's not true, but the fear is still there. Please don't throw me off your team. I can't get along without you."

"I'm not going any place. We're going to lick this thing together.

Just hang in there, and you will beat this thing."

He nodded and gave her a big hug. When he pulled away, a smile lit his face with hope. "Now let's go in and eat—I'm starving." They jumped out of the car and walked into their very own restaurant to eat the great hamburgers and delicious grape limeade with a new hope in their hearts. They even laughed and joked the rest of the night.

Chapter 61

Jimmy Fights his Demons

Jimmy's treatments were going along very smoothly, and he was showing marked improvement. This made Angie very happy as she saw a real change in him. The doctor had requested that she come to the next appointment with Jimmy. He felt she should be updated on Jimmy's progress. She agreed and the next day they went together. Jimmy was a little worried about her being there with him. He was embarrassed, too. She might think him weak and lose respect for him. He couldn't bring himself to say this to her, but it was there between them mentioned or unmentioned, nothing could change that. She did, however, see him now with different eyes. She always loved the way he was, tender and caring. Today she saw glimpses of him returning to the way he used to be before Korea and all the horrors he had experienced during his tour of duty. She had many fears herself. Her biggest fear was that she would lose her Jimmy and everything she loved about him forever. She dreaded that this whole exercise would prove they were not meant for each other. She of all people should know that this counseling was the only thing that would help Jimmy return to a normal place. As they waited to be called, they didn't talk to each other but thumbed through magazines to kill time. Jimmy had been going to therapy for six weeks now, and she was sure that the treatments had helped. He was able to concentrate on his application to the university and even began work on his presentation letter. This was a big step for him.

The therapist called for a conference with both Jimmy and Angie. He began to talk to them both and explained the situation. Jimmy had heard a lot of this already, but Angie was hearing it for the first time and was a little stunned by some of the facts that were being revealed to her. She knew Jimmy had some bad war experiences, but she couldn't believe that he had suffered to the extent to cause him such serious trauma. The doctor continued to explain the results of all of these incidents had forced Jimmy to retreat into a safer world where he did not have to deal with the problems of war. The fact that she was there to act as his support had been an enormous help in keeping him in touch with reality and for that he thanked her. He was going to be all right. However, he would need to continue with therapy indefinitely. He didn't think it would be forever but at least for the rest of the year. He told them both that the sessions help work on many of these problems. By working together, he felt very strongly that Jimmy would be back to the man she remembered. It was a great relief to hear those words and tears came to her eyes.

They both thanked the doctor and left the office.

As they stepped outside, Jimmy offered to give Angie a ride over to the dorm. "That would be great." They walked silently to the car – just her presence was enough company for him. Jimmy said he would be back to pick her up later to go to the Tee Pee that night. She said, "I'd love that." She waved goodbye and turned to go to her next class. For the first time in a long while, all was well with the world once more.

After a great deal of psychotherapy and much tender loving care from Angie, the old Jimmy began to emerge once again. He seemed calmer and happier. It was impossible to forget what had happened in Korea, but he had learned to live with it. He felt less guilty that he had survived when others did not. The truth of what had happened was revealed to him, and he was at last able to accept it. Now he felt ready to take the next step and begin a new life.

He wanted to marry Angie and build a life with her. Before he could ask her to be his bride, he first had to be able to support himself and her. It was time to gather all of his information and meet with an advisor to learn just how much more schooling he would need after his army training and his earned hours at the university before he was drafted would count towards his degree. Thus Jimmy began his exploration. He researched all of his possibilities and discovered that he was a lot better off than he had imagined. He began to look for a law school and once again began the process of applying. This whole process made him feel alive again. His mother was happy to see a little joy in his face. He had been staying with her since he had returned from service. For the first time since he returned from Korea, his mother and Angie both felt that he was once again on track with life and were filled with hope for him. He was once more on solid ground. Angie liked Jimmy's mother a great deal. She had always been wonderful to her. Now that things were moving in a positive direction, they were both more at ease.

A month had passed before Jimmy got any replies concerning his applications. He had received several letters of acceptance, and he reviewed them.

Angie had received her RN degree and was now preparing to enter her surgical training at the Medical Center. She was happy about that. Her father was pleased to see that she was doing so well. Now it was Jimmy's turn to get going.

Angie was home for the weekend to get some more of her things and prepare for her last phase of training. At long last, she would become a surgical nurse.

Still Jimmy had made no hint of their future together. The relationship was friendly and loving, but not committed. She was not going to push. If Jimmy wanted a committed relationship with her, he would take the next step. Maybe he just wasn't ready yet. She wanted to marry him, be his wife, have his children more than anything, but only if he wanted the same. Patiently, she continued to wait.

They had plans that evening. Jimmy was coming by her house to say hello to her dad and Athena then take her out to get a snack. Just as she was thinking he should be arriving soon she heard the doorbell ring. She walked to the door and opened it. Sure enough there was Jimmy with a bunch of flowers in his hand. He walked in and handed her the flowers before she could get a word out. His face was beaming with a big smile. He seemed very sure of himself as he walked across the room. "Hi, gorgeous," he said as he bent down, gave her a kiss, then handed her the flowers. His entrance was overwhelming. She stared at the flowers with her mouth slightly ajar.

Basil came through the dining room and into the room where Angie and Jimmy stood. He looked at the flowers and greeted him with a cheery hello and a hand shake. Angie was frozen in amazement. This was not Jimmy's usual way. He was always much more reserved and quiet. She gave herself a little shake and invited him in to sit down as did Basil almost at the same time. Angie said she was going to put the flowers in a vase of water and be right back. She went to the kitchen with her nose buried in the beautiful bouquet.

When Jimmy was certain she was out of earshot, he turned to her father and said. "Sir, I want you to know that I have nothing but honorable intentions toward your daughter. I love her very much and have for a very long time now. I want to ask her to be my wife, with your permission, of course."

Angie's father was so impressed with this young man and the respectful way in which he asked for his only daughter's hand in marriage that he could not possibly refuse his request. He thanked Jimmy for the respect he paid him by asking for his daughter's hand in marriage. "If Angela accepts your proposal, you have my blessing," he said happily.

"Thank you, sir." Jimmy shook Basil's hand just as Angie reentered the room. She was a little taken off guard by the two of them but tried to act as normal as possible by setting the flowers on the table.

"These are just beautiful."

Just then Jimmy turned to her and said, "Angie, I have just asked your father for your hand in marriage, and he gave us his blessing."

Angie's eyes widened. She couldn't believe her ears.

"Angie," Jimmy continued, "I love you and want you to be my wife. Will you marry me?"

Angie stood there stunned. This was not how she had imagined a proposal to be. She thought it would be a lot different. Although it was quite proper and certainly pleased her father a great deal, most of all, it showed a great deal of respect for her and her father who felt very strongly about propriety and placed a great deal of value on it. His actions showed more than just love and respect but also created the most unforgettable event of her life. She looked him straight in the eyes and said, "Yes, Yes, Yes!" Jimmy pulled out a ring and slipped it on her finger and kissed her right there in front of her father. With a tear in Basil's eye, he also kissed her.

Jimmy and Angie were engaged. He had made the commitment which she had wanted for so long, and it came straight from his heart.

Basil called all the family still at home into the living room to announce the engagement of Jimmy and Angie. Athena, Sammie, and Bobby came running into the room. It was unusual for Basil to call a family meeting. Joey was still away at school and would not be home until the end of the semester. As they all assembled in the room, they couldn't help but notice that Basil, Angie, and Jimmy were all beaming. The boys looked at each other and back at their father. What is going on, was the unspoken question on everyone's mind. Basil broke the silence and announced with great joy that Jimmy had asked for Angie's hand in marriage and they were now officially engaged. Everyone was happy except for Sammie and Bobby. All they could think of was that Angie would be leaving the house to make her own home away from them, and they would not get to see her as often. She was away enough since she had started her nurse's training, but now she would be gone. There would not be a bedroom in this house for Angie. Jimmy was going to take their Angie away from them. Angie sensed that they were upset and instantly hugged the two boys. "Don't worry. I won't be far away. My new home will always be open to you."

This made them happy, and they were relieved to know that she was not vanishing from them forever. They were smiling again in no time at all. Jimmy was also smiling knowing that this extraordinary woman who he had fallen in love with was even more special than he had even imagined. He was now confident he had made the right decision.

Basil opened a bottle of wine to toast best wishes to the newly engaged couple. There was a glass of wine for each of the adults and Coke for the kids. "Long and happy lives to the newly betrothed," and they all repeated "To the newly betrothed." Jimmy and Angie were truly happy.

"We must now go to my house to tell my family," said Jimmy. They both thanked Basil for the toast and left to tell Mrs. Jordan the news.

The door at the Jordan home was opened, and the couple walked in. Mrs. Jordan was a typical Greek mother always thinking about her family and was enthusiastically preparing supper for the family. Jimmy's brother and sister were getting ready to sit down to eat the small Greek feast their mother had prepared.

"Come in, come in," she said as she motioned them to come sit down and eat with them.

"Mom, Angie and I have something to tell you," Jimmy stated. "I have just asked Mr. Demetrious for Angie's hand in marriage. He gave me permission to ask her, she said yes, and now we are engaged."

His mother rushed over to them and hugged them both with tears in her eyes. She said, "It's about time. I'm so happy for you. Sit down. Let's break bread together and celebrate. It's not a fancy meal, but it's good."

They both sat down and ate together with the family and shared some of their plans for the future. This was truly a very happy day for them both.

Chapter 62

How Did Angie and Jimmy Feel About Their Future?

Mrs. Jordan was entirely devoted to her family and had made her children the first priority, especially after her husband passed away and she was left alone to raise the three of them. She'd worked hard to support her children and give them all the educational opportunities they needed. It was no surprise to Angie to find an evening meal prepared when they walked into the Jordan house. She would always prepare dinner for the family no matter how tired she was. It was her joy to take care of her kids. Jimmy loved her and would do anything for her. After he was drafted into army she felt great anxiety not knowing how he was. All the time that passed with no word from him caused her a great deal of suffering. Jimmy's lack of communication took a great toll on her. Angie was very familiar with that silent period. His mother and Angie had leaned on each other for support. Now she was going to be her future mother-in-law, and Angie could not be happier. She helped his mother clean up the kitchen and made some coffee for them. The kids had to get their homework done, and it was time to leave.

The events of the day resembled a dream. Today that dream became a reality. She had no idea that Jimmy was going to propose. The fact that he had asked her father (who was a typical Greek father) for his blessing on their engagement was the most significant thing that Jimmy could have ever done. Her father felt strongly about decorum, and Jimmy had set the bar for propriety very high tonight. It had earned him a place in her father's good graces for life. This was for certain. This level of respect won him Angie's heart forever. She loved him more than even she had ever imagined she was capable of loving anyone. In all of the excitement, there were no details discussed—no plans, nothing but this burning love.

This was a serious lifetime commitment looming before them.

Both thought they knew what to expect, but as with any union there were many stumbling blocks ahead for them. On the plus side, they both were Greek and that in itself was a common denominator. They went to the same church which solved the religious question. Angie was having second thoughts about the timing of this huge move.

Both of them still had at the very least a year before they would be finished with their education. Were they really prepared to get married? This was forever and neither of them really knew what forever was. She had watched her mother and father in their loving relationship and the deep devotion to one another. He was steadfast during her long illness and ultimately her death. When Basil lost Rebecca, he lost his world.

He and Athena didn't have the same kind of relationship. She always thought that Basil should do everything to please her no matter what he might need. Angie had questioned their happiness many times. It almost seemed as if he was going through the motions but whatever it was that she wanted, it was not acceptable nor did it satisfy.

There was no need to dwell on Athena and Basil when Angie was trying to anticipate her own problems. She wasn't going to think foolishly that none of those things would ever happen in her life. She knew there would be many obstacles along the way. She was not laboring under any delusions that she would have no problems. She had no delusions thinking that she and Jimmy would go sailing on the wonderful sea of love with nothing but sunshine rising and roses blooming for the rest of their lives. She recalled so many conversations with her friends when they were walking to school, back in the day of carefree problems. The end of the world was when you didn't make the team or weren't asked to the prom. When they talked about how certain of the parents hated each other, the conversation usually ended with the girl's solution, which was like this, "That is never going to happen to me. I know what a man needs, and I know exactly how to make him happy." The question always was, what did a man need that he never seemed to be getting? They always knew what he needed and were quite sure they could give it to him, but they were never able to explain what it was. It always made her laugh to hear such silly statements. The truth was that none of them had any idea what it was that made happiness. It was one of life's mysteries— the undefined answer to the ever asked question. Perhaps there was no answer to this question: how do you make each other happy? The trick seemed to be to think you know, but end up not knowing any more than you did when you first asked the question.

She had been living in a nurse's dorm across from the hospital for nearly three years now. She would go home to visit when she had time. Most of her things were still there, but she had never had her own apartment. She never had to furnish anything in her life. She had not the slightest idea how to go about planning a wedding. When she thought about the task of planning the wedding, she realized it was a complete mystery. She had no idea where to start. For a moment, she wished Rebecca was there to give her advice and help make all the plans. She knew however, she could always count on Maude to give her advice and suggestions about flowers. She would love to help Angie make plans.

At the present, neither she nor Jimmy were earning any money. If there was one lesson that she had learned in her struggle to get through school, it was that everything took money. If Basil had not stepped in and given her a helping hand she would have had to drop out of school and start working again to pay for her tuition. She could never have reached the specialty training for another three years. It's a hard fact, but you need *money* for everything you do, or you simply aren't going to make it.

Oh stop! This line of thinking was counterproductive. The more you think, the higher the mountain gets, and at this point, it has become an impossible mountain to climb. Think productively. She would go out to buy a bride magazine that would start educating her on how to plan a wedding. Just maybe she would find a killer dress in the magazine that would make her look like a million dollars. After all, there is nothing wrong with looking good is there? There was probably a planning list somewhere in that magazine. That settled it. She would not only look like a million dollars in a killer dress, but she would learn all she needed to know about planning a wedding and all for the price of a magazine. You sure could not beat that!

Jimmy, on the other hand, knew exactly what he wanted. He knew

Angie well enough to sense her hesitation about the future. Before he ever thought of giving her an engagement ring and making a commitment of marriage, he had thought the entire plan through very carefully. He was certain that she was at this very moment going slowly out of her mind. She probably thought he hadn't even considered anything regarding the future. She also would have been very wrong. He had spent much time researching all of his career options. He was certain that he would be pursuing his interest in the legal field. He had researched the prospects and had gathered a great deal of information. He knew that he had earned many credit hours toward a degree from his Special Services training in JAG. He had a list of all the things he needed to research before any career decision could be made. He was afraid perhaps he jumped the gun a little by asking Angie to marry him before he had done all his investigating. But he did not jump the gun at all. He was feeling Angie slipping away from him. He acted badly while he was in Korea, when he didn't communicate with anyone for such a long time. One night he had sat in his room and realized deep in his heart he could look the rest of his lifetime for someone to share his life with and never find anyone who would come even remotely close to measuring up to Angie. She was the best as far as he was concerned. He knew that he was the luckiest guy in town to have a girl who was this great. He loved her from the first time he kissed her and an electric current raced through his body. At this very moment he loved her even more, if that was possible. The past was the past, and he wanted to leave it behind him. Now it was time to look to the future. He would never forget how she stood by him throughout his ordeal and helped him rise above it. Now it was his turn to stand up and take control and get the future in order.

As a result of all this soul searching, Jimmy realized that he had no time to lose. He began immediately by placing a call to the local School of Law and then he called the Office of Justice. He had made the second step in his leap of faith and began for the first time since his return to plan for the future in earnest.

As he gathered pertinent information an actual plan began to form in his mind. He discovered that not only had he managed to earn credit hours toward a degree, but he had actually earned a Bachelor of Arts degree. He was eligible to enter law school at the beginning level and take a placement test to determine where he would be placed. He had received a lot of training in his service with the JAG offices. He was actually surprised just how much he had learned there. All of this information gave him a lot hope for the future. The time had come to determine how much he had learned. This was good news indeed and meant that he and Angie could get married sooner than he had dared to hope.

He called the university to inquire about the testing process. He was sending the wheels of progress into motion.

Chapter 63

A New Day and a Beautiful Life

Jimmy had received a call to come to the school office and fill out the application. After it was reviewed, he would be notified, and his placement test would be scheduled. It was still weeks from the end of the spring semester. He hoped he could take a few courses during summer school to catch up on the courses he had missed. Angie was completely unaware that any of this was happening. He wanted to know all the facts before he told her of his plans. The last thing he wanted was to elevate her hopes only to have it turned out to be a disappointment.

Of course, Angie being Angie, she had begun a little different type of research herself. She had begun to think about apartments, school tuitions, and even the cost of groceries—all of which would have to be budgeted into their finances. She was now in the process of creating an itemized list of all of their expenses and testing an idea which she called the envelope system. This was something her father had taught her years ago when she was beginning her dance and piano lessons. Every week she would get an allowance. In that allowance was lunch money, dance lesson money, and piano lesson money. If there was any money left she could use it to go out or buy a treat for herself or save it for whatever she wanted at the time. She would call it her Mad Money envelope. The end result would be enough money in each envelope to pay the bills when they were due. This was her idea of a fail-proof budget. There were no great expectations of a huge Mad Money envelope—only a hope there might be something left over. She was going over her notes when she had a brainstorm and for a very brief moment thought about a part-time job, but on second thought maybe that was not such a good idea. She'd be worn out and probably not be able to perform well as a surgical nurse in training, or be any fun as Jimmy's girl. Of course, all of this speculating was premature as there was no date set for the wedding yet. By this time, she was kicking herself for thinking about these things at all. She was not giving Jimmy credit for being capable to manage anything.

Jimmy was not some immature teenager without any sense at all about money; he knew how to survive. He would blow his stack if he even thought that she was thinking about solutions as if they were desperate. She needed to give Jimmy a little credit for being responsible enough to have thought many things through before he ever asked her to marry him. She had better begin thinking positively and have more confidence in her Jimmy. After all, he did manage to survive the POW camp, worked in Special Forces, and came home in one piece. She was not being rational; they were not getting married to each other to live in poverty. They were both going to work together and build a future with each other.

Angie had been so engrossed with her own concerns that she had lost sight of what was most important. She had noticed a definite change in herself lately and had become extremely edgy with each passing day. Her nerves were out of control. In an effort to calm herself down, she had purchased an expensive *Brides* magazine. She sat down on the bed in her dorm room and lost herself in a sea of wedding fantasy. There were white satin gowns trimmed in sequins, crystal, and lace. Cinderella shoes with one pair more beautiful than the last. She saw some of the most beautiful china and crystal she could imagine. It was everything bridal. This was certainly a temporary escape into a "happily ever after" world. It worked beautifully. She didn't have one thought about Jimmy and how they would survive, except to think of how great he would look in his tux.

Lately she was having a recurring dream, and it was becoming increasingly disturbing. She didn't know if this dream had an intended meaning or if she should just interpret it as wedding jitters. Whatever it was, it distressed her enormously. Her dream always started well but it would always reach the point where it got so troubling that she would wake up in cold sweats. It was always Jimmy and her out having a wonderful time talking. His arms would be holding her close to him. She wanted to push him away, but the more she tried, she simply couldn't bring herself to make him stop. She was overwhelmed with desire and lost all sense of what was taking place. She began to cry out and would wake up abruptly in a cold sweat in tears and completely perplexed. She was embarrassed and ashamed of herself. The dream was so real that she would look around the room to see if Jimmy were there.

Why was all this happening to her? She and Jimmy had agreed that they would wait for sex until their wedding night, but now she was more than willing to jump into bed with him and throw caution to the wind and satisfy both their desires. She actually wanted to go ahead and break their promise to each other and have reckless sex together, with or without a wedding.

One night after one of their dates, they had gotten a little too passionate. They were both on the edge of the cliff, when suddenly she said let's go ahead. Who will ever know? We're getting married anyway, aren't we? He stopped suddenly and looked at her and said, "We will always know. We can wait. Our wedding is coming, and soon we'll be married, and we will make love the rest of our lives. We promised each other we would wait, and I love you too much to spoil this for us. We both wanted this to be very special."

Was this a fantasy that she wanted to live out? Many of the other nurses were engaging in casual sex and had had numerous sexual encounters and talked about them quite freely. They actually boasted about the performance of different men. They talked about casual sex as if it were a game with them. They would even trade partners and later compare notes as to how they rated their performance. Angie was very shocked when they spoke of their conquests. She was actually completely confused by the way they didn't have any emotional ties to any of the sexual partners. The most shocking part of all was that they never even thought of sex as an intimate act between two people who loved each other.

Now that Jimmy and she were engaged she suddenly wanted to experience this great thing called sex. It had become an obsession with her since Jimmy had gotten control of his Post-Traumatic Stress Disorder and returned to being the old Jimmy she had always loved. She had to stop all of this mania and appreciate the respect she and Jimmy had for each other. She didn't want to have a string of meaningless conquests; she just wanted to have Jimmy. In all of her dreams all she ever wanted was Jimmy. To be in his arms, have his lips on hers, kissing her lovingly, fondling her as if she was a precious gift and treating this gift with loving care. He was everything in the world she wanted. He was all she needed and soon her dreams would come true.

Jimmy and she loved and respected each other. They would have sex on their wedding night. The problems which seemed so enormous now would all be answered, some before the wedding, but most of the solutions would begin after they married and were working as team Jordan.

Chapter 64

When Will the Wedding Bells Ring?

Athena was becoming increasingly restless over the uncertainty of the young couple's cautious planning. Basil, on the other hand, was pleased they were being careful and not rushing into marriage. He felt they were both being wise to take all the possibilities into consideration. They wanted to complete their schooling and then at the very least have a job waiting for them. Angie seemed to be fairly secure as far as employment went. When she completed her training, more than likely she would be hired by the hospital. Jimmy, on the other hand, still had a way to go. Unless he received a paying internship he would be dependent on Angie for financial support. Knowing this young man as he did, he was certain that Jimmy was too independent to allow that to happen.

Athena had her own plan. She wanted to move to Greece and had a timetable as to when this huge plot would be implemented. Basil knew she wanted to go back to Greece, but thought it was wishful thinking on her part. After all, he had a business to think of. He didn't want little Bobby to have to leave his home and make a big adjustment in what would be to him a foreign country and foreign schools. Athena was relentless in her demands that Angie and Jimmy set a date and do it soon. She was already upset because the wedding would be an expensive event.

Six months had passed since the couple had become engaged and in that time both Angie and Jimmy had done everything they could to get on solid ground in order to take the final step of setting a date. A very solid offer from the law firm which he had an internship with before he entered Law School had been presented to him. Of course he would have to pass the battery of placement tests before he could begin Law School. The position which was offered was a part-time, but it was a good and might lead to more after he passed the bar exam.

They did not want to set a date for the wedding until some of these things were confirmed. Basil thought perhaps it would be helpful to sit down with the young couple and have a heart-to-heart conversation with the two of them to speed up the process and possibly set a date for the wedding. This was contrary to Basil's natural instincts, which were never interfere or attempt to influence his daughter and her fiancé by pushing them to set a date for the wedding. Basil was uncomfortable meddling, and it was obvious he didn't want to get involved at all. Athena was behind this entire meeting. It made no sense. What could be her motivation? Angie knew that Athena was already upset about the cost of the wedding even though no plans were made yet and no prices quoted. If Basil refused to host the wedding, his good name would be destroyed in the entire Greek community. Athena had made it quite clear that she wanted this wedding date set and soon. It was no concern to her if Jimmy and Angie had financial security or if they ever completed their education. Let them struggle. She could care less if it was a hard path with no money. As long as she got what she wanted that was all she was interested in. She wanted to get to Greece soon enough for Bobby to start school there. What she wanted only included her happy little family which consisted of only Basil, Bobby, and her. She was going to leave Sammie in Angie's care and Joey would have to take care of himself. The longer she had to wait, the harder it would be for her to move.

Angie and Jimmy shared small talk on their drive to meet with Basil. They had no idea what was on his mind, but the reason for this get-together was the number one thing on her mind. She was trying with all her might to avoid the subject because she didn't want to be tense when they arrived. Jimmy was still in the mindset that everything was great and had no misgivings about anything. Angie knew this kind of meeting was coming more from Athena than Basil. There was nothing to be gained by worrying about what might happen, better to find out what actually was going on and then deal with it. They arrived at the house. As they entered, they saw Basil sitting in the living room alone and looking forlorn.

"Hi, Dad," Angie said trying to sound happy. Jimmy nodded a greeting.

Basil got up from his chair and waved the two of them into the living room. Basil stammered around trying to start the conversation, but it was painfully difficult for him. Angie thought it would put everyone at ease if she mentioned how great it was to be home.

But unfortunately before she got anything out, Basil began an attack which threw both of them off base. He demanded to know why they had not set a wedding date yet. Then he continued to make it clear that his good name was being questioned by their friends due to the way the two of them were carrying on. Jimmy was shocked to say the least. He was wondering where all of this came from. He and Angie were being perfectly proper, and he had treated her with the utmost respect. She certainly did not act loose and easy. Her actions were anything but improper. What was all of this about? Before he could say anything, Basil was on the attack once more. He asked for an explanation why the wedding date was not set. He insisted it be set as soon as possible. Both of them were dumbfounded. This was an unbelievably shocking display. Why was Basil so worked up? Angie was trying to ask why he was so angry. She thought that he understood that she wanted to finish her surgical training and Jimmy was still taking placement tests.

"I do not care what your plans are. I want a definite date set and a wedding planned." By this time he was white with anger.

Angie was not only shocked but also upset that he had taken such a disrespectful position with them. She had done everything to keep things calm and had no idea why the wedding date was so important.

Jimmy looked Basil in the eyes and replied in a very calm voice, "Sir, I assure you that there is no unsavory relationship going on between Angie and me. I respect Angie. I love your daughter and treat her with the great respect. I would like to know who it was that insinuated that we were acting in a disgraceful way. It is vindictive gossip and totally untrue. I thought that you understood that we were trying to complete our career goals first so we could plan our financial future."

Basil's face turned from white red. He felt more than a little embarrassed. Deep down inside, he knew that all of this talk came from Athena's girlfriends. They were jealous and their gossip was intended to harm his daughter's reputation in the community. From the time that Angie was able to finish nursing school their tongues were wagging. He suspected that Athena was encouraging this gossip, and this thought enraged him. He pulled himself together. Shaking his head he said, "Please forgive me for this outburst."

"Of course, Dad." They all hugged each other and promised to put this outburst behind them and not hold it against each other.

Angie could not stop herself from asking, "Why had Athena allowed such talk to take place in her presence and not defend my reputation? It makes me very sad."

Basil dropped his head in shame. Once again Athena had told him stories that were lies. Why had this woman been so manipulative about something that should have been a very happy event? Now it would be hard to repair this episode with his daughter and Jimmy. The shame was too much for him and he broke down. He asked them for forgiveness again and begged them to put this ugliness behind them.

Athena heard this and her heart dropped. That girl wiggled her way out of this. Now what was she to do to speed up things? The trip to Greece would go on. She would see to it. The difference was that she must proceed with caution from now on.

Chapter 65

A Wedding for Me and My Girl

Finally, Angie and Jimmy decided to set a date for their wedding. It was a long struggle, but they were both on firm footing career-wise and wanted more than anything to get married. Jimmy had his law degree and was preparing to take the bar exam. He had been working in a law office as a paralegal while he was attending classes. That job gave him invaluable experience in the world of law. The job had helped establish him in a well-known law firm which was something that would have taken years to achieve.

Angie had completed her training as a surgical nurse and was fast becoming one of the best surgical nurses in the hospital. Many doctors requested her as their operating nurse. The couple was happy, and it was time to settle down.

Angie had to move back home because she was no longer a student.

Jimmy continued to live at home with his family while he was a student. It was much cheaper and also allowed him to help his mother with the expenses of her home. Now the time had come for both Angie and Jimmy to find a home for themselves. They were looking for a house or apartment where they could live after they got married. Jimmy would move in first and begin to settle in. Angie would join him after the wedding. This seemed to be a very logical plan. They would work on the house in their spare time and see what necessities they would need after the wedding gifts came in. Then there was the matter of furniture. They decided to get the bare necessities to begin with. It would be a slow process, but they both had begun setting aside a little money as soon as they began to earn a salary. They left the student life and began to actually make some money. Jimmy had been working part time and had managed to save some money along with the army pay which he had put into a savings account. He felt confident they would be fine financially. Even though he helped his mother with some of the utility bills, he still was able to save some money. They would get the necessities a little at a time.

The meetings with the priest to book the date for the wedding went very well. The couple was preparing to leave when the priest requested they remain a little longer because he wanted to be sure that they knew what they needed to do in preparation for the wedding. He had a list prepared and handed it to them to look over. He asked them to check it very carefully to be sure they had all of the items necessary completed before the ceremony took place.

They were quite shocked at just how little they actually knew. This list was exactly what they needed to complete their to-do list. The priest had explained many things during this meeting, which was extremely helpful to both of them.

Basil could at long last take a sigh of relief and move forward with planning the wedding. Athena was at last satisfied with the news of a wedding date.

Basil had his own ideas concerning the wedding reception and where it should be held. When they came home Basil announced to the couple that he had booked the reception in one of the nice hotel ballrooms downtown. He was very pleased with himself. He wanted to take them to the hotel to see the ballroom. Angie was relieved to hear that her father had taken the initiative in booking the reception hall. He had lifted a heavy burden off her shoulders. He really wanted to do this because he would invite the entire church community, as was the tradition of the time. After all, he had already attended many weddings, and this was his opportunity to reciprocate to his friends with an invitation to his only daughter's wedding.

There was an endless guest list that, between Jimmy's mother and her parents' guests, was getting longer every day. Of course there were still their personal friends, many of whom were not from the church. A Greek wedding ceremony was relatively long, but the celebration was always great fun. There was plenty of food and drink and endless dancing. Everyone loved to dance the Greek dances. They were lively and joyful, and you never needed a partner. You merely joined a line and followed the leader. It was fun for everyone, and the bride and groom were no exception. This was a festivity for the bride and groom. By the time the wedding celebration began, they would hopefully have put all of the nervous jitters behind them and be ready to have fun. As always, her friend Barbara stood at the ready to help whenever Angie might need help.

Both Athena and Basil were happy with the date the couple had set. Athena, of course, was very clear as to what her role was to be, and it was definitely not the mother of the bride. She was happy with the role of stepmother. She told her step daughter in no uncertain terms that she was not entertaining any of the out-of-town relatives and guests that would be invited to the wedding. She said it was not her responsibility. Angie refused to be upset by the announcement her stepmother made. She knew instinctively that Basil would take care of those matters and would not allow her to embarrass him in any way when it came to their out-of-town relatives and friends. He would see to it that she would entertain the relatives whether she liked it or not. These were small details which Angie need not worry about.

There was some serious shopping to do, and at the top of the list was the wedding gown. This was definitely a job that her friend Barbara would have to help with. Angie was on the phone with her to set up a gown shopping date immediately. This was the kickoff of the search for the most beautiful dress with the best price. Must fit like a glove and above all it had to make Angie look like a million dollars. A piece of cake. These two girls were pros when it came to shopping, and now they were about to begin their search for the greatest wedding dress ever. "Come on, Angie, let's see what the bridal shops have to offer," Barbara said as the two started on their excursion. One thing they did not expect was the endless display of wedding albums, invitations, thank-you notes, and the much-needed wedding photographers. These were three items that were totally forgotten but promptly placed on the to-do list. Today the dresses were at the top of the list in this whirlwind of wedding decisions.

Basil had already made it clear that the flowers for the wedding would be done by his friend and colleague, Mr. Stephanos, who owned the Athenian Flower Shop. Well that was one less decision to worry about. When Basil was paying the bills, he ruled completely.

Angie and Barbara had gone to ten different bridal shops and did not find anything they liked. After they left the tenth store they decided to call it a day.

Angie needed to concentrate on the pre-wedding party. The party was in two weeks, so she had to get busy and get a dress for that occasion. The two girls said goodbye and went their separate ways. It seemed strange but true that sometimes the most unexpected events take place, at the most unbelievable times, and today, was one of those days. Angie decided to walk home from the bus stop and accidently made a wrong turn and came upon a strip of shops which must have been new as she had never seen them before. She hadn't heard any one of her friends mention any of these shops, but there they were, as big as life. There was a window display in one of the small boutiques that caught Angie's eye. She instantly fell in love with the dress on display. It was the perfect dress for the pre-wedding party. Without any hesitation she entered the shop to take a closer look at this unbelievable dress she saw. Looking around the shop, she was overwhelmed by the extensive variety of dresses on display. Even the big department stores didn't have this kind of assortment available. She immediately saw three dresses she really liked. Angie asked if she could try them on to see how they looked on her. The sales lady led her to the dressing room. She asked if she could find anything else for her, but Angie wanted to see how these dresses looked before she got any more. It was no contest when she donned the gown that had originally caught her eye. It was a two-piece outfit. The top was a wide V-neck made of light brown taffeta with a matching skirt which was a full skirt of print on winter white taffeta with brown and tan swirling leaves outlined with sparking browns, gold, and reds. It looked beautiful on her, and she was sold. As she began to put her own clothes back on, a clerk came to the dressing room to check on her customer. She wanted to see if there were any other dresses or different sizes she could show her. Angie was so thrilled by the styles this boutique had that she asked if they had any wedding gowns. The sales girl answered that they had quite a nice selection to choose from. She took Angie to the back room full of gowns. Of course she loved them all but one really took her fancy above all of the others. The clerk brought the gown back to the dressing room and helped Angie get into the dress and needless to say the wedding dress looked beautiful on her. She asked if they would hold the dress for a day. She and her friend would be back then to see it. She wanted to get her opinion. Naturally they were more than happy to hold the dress until then. It is safe to say that that day both the pre-wedding dress and the wedding dress were selected. She told the clerk that she loved the dress which had been the main reason she came into the shop in the first place, and she would take that one with her. She paid for the dress and was a very happy girl as she continued on her way home.

Athena was becoming increasingly unhappy and very sensitive with anything that concerned Angie and the wedding. Whenever Basil displayed joy and pride in his only daughter marrying such a fine young man like Jimmy she would feel herself freezing up and wanting to strike out in some way. Lately she had been upset with all the money that this party and the wedding was going to cost. Everyone stayed out of her way because she was like a firecracker ready to go off. Basil finally stepped in and told her that she was to settle down. It was their party and their reputation at risk if they did not do right by this wedding. Everyone in the Greek community would be gossiping behind their backs. It was essential for them to host the best party and wedding for his only daughter. As was said earlier, when Basil pays, Basil rules, and Athena understood it perfectly. No more was said about the event. The planning of the wedding and reception went on with the cooperation of all the participants involved. Angie took a sigh of relief and decided to enjoy every aspect of the wedding.

The pre-wedding party was great fun and was held at the Demetrious home which was overflowing with about a hundred Greek families feasting and dancing, and wishing the young couple *Kala Steffanna*, which literally translated from the Greek meant, "Good Wedding Crowns," or wonderful marriage. However they said it, the meaning was a blessing on the betrothed couple. Both Angie and Jimmy were unbelievably happy.

Jimmy's mother was overjoyed with the festivities, and Basil, knowing her financial situation, made it clear to her that he would take care of all the expenses. She was very relieved and saddened at the same time that she had been left in such a position. Jimmy insisted he buy all of the flowers as was the tradition.

This gesture on Jimmy's part touched Basil very much and once again reinforced the fact that his daughter had made a good choice in a husband.

Chapter 66

The August Wedding

At last the wedding day had arrived. The Demetrious house was vibrating with activity. Joey was home and ready to serve as best man to his sister and soon-to-be brother-in-law. Sammie was to carry the wedding crowns, Jimmy's little sister was to be the flower girl, and Bobby and Jimmy's little brother were the ring boys. The couple did a good job of including all of the children in both families in the wedding party. Friends and family took their places as bridesmaids and ushers. This was indeed a very handsome wedding party. Basil was wearing a black tuxedo and Athena looked beautiful in her mother of the bride dress. The bridesmaids were all wearing cocktail length pale blue dresses and the groomsmen were dressed in white tuxedo jackets and midnight blue trousers. It was a bitter sweet day for both Jimmy wished his father could be there to see him get married and Angie would have loved for her mother to see her now. She knew Rebecca would be proud of the way she turned out and the man she was about to marry.

There was no time for retrospection now. The time for a new beginning was approaching. The bridesmaids were arriving with dresses in hand, and everyone was busy helping each other with their dresses and the bride with all her preparations. It seemed as if the whole house had temporarily lost its mind. The men in the family decided to go to the groom's house to escape the insanity.

Jimmy's home, unfortunately, was not much different. Joey was there along with all of the ushers doing their level best to make Jimmy a wreck. It was a joy to watch, and they were all having a hilarious time at Jimmy's expense. Jimmy had been through war, and it was not as chaotic as this. His mother had taken the kids to Angie's house to get ready so that they would not be exposed to this display of good natured fun because they were still much too young to understand that kind of horseplay. The grand finale as they were heading for the cars was when they all were singing in harmony, "Please, please get me to the church on time."

The girls' departure was not quite so dramatic but it was still filled with drama. They all managed to get to the church where the flowers were distributed to the wedding party and everyone looked marvelous. Concerns were slowly vanishing and calm had settled over everyone.

The church was a small one-room building with a small annex. The annex was actually a small house that was occupied by the caretaker of the church. His duties were to keep the building and grounds clean, and the annex in good condition. He was also to safeguard the contents of the church from theft. The church had a capacity of about one hundred fifty people, but if no one was watching they could get two hundred in with standing room only. The guest list was two hundred and fifty, and they were crowded into the balcony and every single space available. It was indeed a sight to behold. The Athenian Flower Shop and Mr. Stephanos did an outstanding job of transforming the church into a wondrous sight of beauty. Each aisle was decorated with white candles on candle stands accented with a bouquet of white roses and bows of the same color. Two huge matching bouquets of white roses were placed in front of the church. It was a beautiful transformation of the church where both of these young people had attended all of their lives. The organ was playing softly in the background as the guests assembled in the church and took their seats. The ushers were busy seating the guests.

A hush fell over the crowd as the mother of the groom was ushered down the aisle by her young son, followed by Athena, ushered by Joey. Then the organ thundered the beginning of the bridal march. The best man walked the groom to the front of the church followed by the groomsmen. Then each of the bridesmaids marched down the aisle one by one. The little flower girls and ring bearers brought smiles to the guests' faces as they walked down the aisle, only getting sidetracked once when one of the ring bearers waved at his grandmother.

The moment finally arrived. The music changed, and everyone rose to their feet. Angie stepped into the aisle with her hand hooked securely on her proud father's arm. This was a much more powerful moment than Angie had imagined it would be.

The realization of what was happening came down on her full force. They were standing in the house of God to take each other as man and wife for the rest of their lives. This was a very serious step, and it was the first time that the full understanding of what she and Jimmy had done by protecting their virtue for only each other really meant.

With glistening eyes, Jimmy stepped down and Basil gave his daughter's hand to him. He took her hand. With a slight bow, he bent down and kissed Basil's hand as a sign of respect and a promise to take care of his daughter. This, too, was a moment of a powerful exchange between the two men. Jimmy took Angie's hand, they took their places, and the ceremony began. At the conclusion of the ceremony they were introduced as Mr. and Mrs. James Jordon. The guests clapped as the bridal party turned and walked down the aisle and the wedding was completed. Now it was party time.

It was quite a wonderful party, and everyone present enjoyed it. Basil could not say enough about just how wonderful Jimmy was. Joey toasted the couple, and although he felt sad that Angie would now be starting a new life away from their home, he was happy that he had gained a new brother. Sammie was happy. He no longer worried that he was going to lose Angie. He was happy that he had gained not only Jimmy, but also Jimmy's brother and sister.

After the eating and drinking was over, the dancing began and a wonderful party followed. The cutting of the cake was done, the bouquet and garter were thrown, and the bride and groom slipped quietly away to have a moment to themselves.

The wedding reception was coming to an end, and Angie and Jimmy were preparing to leave for home. The last dance was played and goodbyes and best wishes were given. Then it was off to home to change clothes, pick up their suitcases, and begin the honeymoon. As they were leaving, a crowd of well-wishers surrounded them and showered them with rice. This was such a wonderful day, and tonight would be a wonderful night.

Chapter 67

The First Night

Jimmy and Angie stopped at her house first. They were laughing as they climbed the steps to her house. The door swung open and before she knew what happened, Jimmy had swept her up in his arms and carried her over the threshold and into the house. He was kissing her as he did this and they both had their eyes closed. When they heard applause, they realized that they had an audience. Jimmy's cheeks flushed and Angie buried her head in his shoulder. Caught in the act of the moment, with camera flash bulbs going off all around them, they realized that they had been on candid camera and recorded for life. They would look back on the moment with grateful affection, especially to the ones clever enough to capture it.

Jimmy put Angie down, and she ran up the stairs to her room to change into her going away outfit. She carefully hung up her dress and changed her clothes. Her suitcase was packed and by the time she came downstairs, Joey had managed to fill the house with friends and family alike, and all were ready to continue the party. The groomsmen carried in wedding gifts brought to the reception. Jimmy was on his knees looking over the gifts. Angie joined him and they both proceeded to open some of the gifts. Everyone loved seeing what was in the boxes, and faithful Barbara was there with a pencil and paper recording the gifts and who had given them. She knew that tags would go missing and just wanted to help the couple's job of writing thank you notes a little easier. Even Athena joined in the fun and was actually serving drinks to all the guests in the house. She seemed to be happy and really enjoying the entire wedding. Mona Jordan was there, filled with joy for the young couple. The kids that had been in the wedding now laughed and played. Of course they were the center of attention and probably had a better time than anyone else at the wedding.

Basil looked at his son-in-law and nodded. "It's time for the newlyweds to be on their way."

"Thank you all for everything." Jimmy said as they began their goodbyes to the guests. Basil hugged Jimmy and kissed Angie.

"Thank you, Dad. This wedding was more than I ever dreamed it would be."

"I love you, Angela." He said with a tear in his eye.

As they started down the steps, the children were waiting and began showering the bride and groom with rice and waving franticly as they pulled away.

The excitement began to die down and the realization hit Angie; she had been so nervous she had not eaten any of her dinner. Now, she was quite hungry and needed to eat something. So Jimmy made a quick stop at his house to change and pick up his suitcase; then headed the car towards the Tee Pee to get his love some food. She was hungry!

It was truly a day for the bride and groom for as they entered the Tee Pee, a group of friends who had attended the wedding were inside having a midnight snack. They jumped up and began serenading the newlyweds with a song that they had called "their" song from the first day they began seeing each other, and it was the song that was played when they danced their first dance at the reception—"Tenderly." Jimmy began to dance her around the restaurant, and even though Angie did not want to admit it, she was thrilled. The dance ended with a kiss and everyone sat down together at the long table. Angie had her double hamburger with a grape limeade and was content. The friends were teasing the couple and urged them to get going. After all, it was the first night of their honeymoon.

It was not long after the teasing started that the couple was once again on their way to wherever Jimmy was taking her. He hadn't said where they were going; it was a surprise. They drove along and reached a small motel where they stopped for the night. Angie asked Jimmy if he had made reservations and Jimmy began to laugh. It was a nervous laugh.

"I have to confess; I forgot all about booking a place for us to stay. I hope you're not mad at me for forgetting to make arrangements.

Angie began to laugh and answered, "I sure hope they have a room because I'm not going back to my house and admit we forgot to make any reservation."

Luck was with them tonight, and they did find a room. Angie realized that she and Jimmy were about to go into a motel room for the consummation of their marriage, and for the first time in this long courtship, they would make love. The thought frightened her. She was suddenly embarrassed when the second realization hit her that she would not be going home. It would be Angie and Jimmy from now on. It seemed surreal that after all this time she was on the threshold of beginning her life with Jimmy as husband and wife. He picked up her overnight bag and led the way into the motel room. As they approached the room, Jimmy stopped and looked at Angie and said, "This is not exactly what I had envisioned, but I'm still carrying you over this threshold, and we're going to have an unforgettable night."

With that said he swept her up in his arms and carried her into their room and kissed her gently. He set her down and kissed her again. Suddenly, all the dreams of the past years were coming into reality, one by one. They both were helping each other out of their clothes and were overtaken by the passion which they had controlled all this time. They had completely surrendered themselves to each other, and the freedom was beautiful. Jimmy's gentleness made Angie even more passionate than even she knew she could be, and it all ended in sweet love that was so worth waiting for. They made love several times again before they fell into a sweet sleep. They were two happy people, sleeping peacefully in each other's arms. When morning came, they once again resumed their lovemaking. The intensity was different now as they were both so in love that it seemed normal and natural that they should be making love and their hunger for each other was one of true love.

This was a celebration of what was to be their future life together. This they pledged to each other.

They had breakfast and began the first leg of the trip to Florida to bask in the sun and to rest and recuperate.

Chapter 68

Back Home Again

Angie and Jimmy had a great time on the honeymoon, but as in all things, the time had come to return to reality. Too soon they were packing and preparing to return home to their new apartment and to tie up all the loose ends from the wedding. Angie had already begun a list of things that needed to be done as soon as they returned. Just moving all of the wedding gifts from Angie's house to their new apartment was going to be a job. They were more than a little excited about getting their new home together. Jimmy never had time to move into the apartment as the original plan had been. There was just too much to do for him to make the move, and it had taken much longer to get the lease signed than they had expected. Angie still had to move all of her things from her father's house to her new home. The move was normal, and they did not foresee any unexpected problems. They were happily preparing for the long drive home. The beach and the sun had been what the doctor ordered and they both had a chance to relax and enjoy the restful trip.

They began their trip back home right after breakfast. Life has a way of playing strange tricks on you especially when you think everything is going well. This seemed to be exactly what was happening today. While driving back home, they had the misfortune of being stopped by a traffic policeman who issued them a speeding violation. Jimmy made a stop at the courthouse and paid the ticket immediately to avoid a penalty charge. The traffic ticket wouldn't have been so bad if it hadn't been for the fact that the same evening they were stopped in Tennessee for another speeding violation. This time the officer forced the couple to drive back to the judge's house for a judgment on the ticket. Angie was getting a little nervous and the fun of the day was beginning to fade from her mind. As things turned out, Jimmy was able to pay the fine, and they were once again on the road. That was a good thing, but the traffic violation fines had been so expensive that they were short on money and decided to drive on home which was still a long way from where they were. They were both young and were able to share the driving duties and made it into the city by dawn.

They pulled up to Angie's house where they hoped to get some sleep. This was when the cruel truth of life hit them both right between the eyes. The locks on the house were changed, and they couldn't get in. They knocked on the door, but no one opened it. They then decided to go to their apartment and see if they could get some sleep and deal with all of the rest of this later. Of course, there was no bed set up nor were there any blankets or pillows available. Everything was at Angie's house. So they cut the paper away from the mattress which had been delivered just before the wedding. They lay down and fell fast asleep. They woke up around noon and began the move.

They had to move their things into the apartment and get the new home organized, and that is exactly what they did. Little by little they got the job done.

They made a conscious decision to not mention the locks having been changed. There was no need to start any discussion. Little did anyone know that there would be plenty to say before the night was over.

As Angie was packing up her personal things, she went to the attic to get the box that contained the few articles she kept of her mother's. To her complete amazement, the box was gone. She rushed down the stairs and asked her father where the box was. Athena was sitting there as quiet as a mouse as Angie asked what happened to her mother's box of things. They both claimed ignorance as to the existence of such a box.

"Oh no, it's all I had of her," Angie cried. The box held only a few of her mother's favorite items, the sheets of paper with prayers and instructions from Rebecca, along with the long braid of her hair which she had placed into the handbag, and now they were gone. Jimmy tried to console her, but he knew she was heartbroken over this. They gathered up all they could, and Angie told her father they would be back to get the remaining gifts the next morning. She was still crying when they left.

The next day they returned to the house to complete the move.

Angie went up to her room to finish with her personal things only to discover that the box she had in her closet containing the last doll she got from Rebecca was gone. This only confirmed the contempt Athena had for Angie and her mother's memory. To take her mother's things and now to throw out her last doll; it was too much. She very carefully packed her wedding gown and took it with her. There was no way that she would leave the gown behind only to find that it would have disappeared in the same manner her mother's box had. As they pulled away from the house, tears were rising in her eyes. She knew that this was the closing of one life and the opening of another. A new life filled with love, hope, and joy.

She loved Jimmy, and he loved her. This was all that mattered right now. If the boys ever needed a home she promised herself that her home would always be their home also. Jimmy reached over and squeezed her hand. He was fairly certain he knew what she was thinking. This too will pass.

Shortly after the wedding, Basil, Athena, and Bobby left for Greece for a short trip. Sammie came to Angie's house and stayed with Jimmy and Angie until they returned. Joey went back to school, and life went on.

This became the routine for the next three years. With each trip, Basil and Bobby became more and more distant. Sammie had been taken on the third trip, but after that it was as if he was not one of Basil's children at all. On the fourth year, they moved all the furniture and their belongings to Greece. Basil loved Jimmy very much and was always very respectful to him, but he would act very distant with Angie.

As the years passed, Angie and Jimmy had started their own family. Angie had a little baby boy and two years later a little girl. She stopped working to raise her children. Jimmy was doing well with his career. Sammie was now in college and lived on campus. Basil decided to return to Indianapolis on what would be his last trip. It was a nice visit, and he was there in time to witness baby Basil born. When he came alone, it was always a pleasant visit. But alas, the time came too soon for his return. Angie and Jimmy's home was full of love, children, and activity.

Life rushed by and when Angie had all of her children in school, she returned to work part-time. Jimmy was an excellent lawyer who opened up a firm with his brother-in-law, Joey.

One day the phone rang in the early morning hours. Bobby was calling from Greece to tell the family that Basil had passed away. It was an unexpected call, and Angie was unprepared for this news. Five months earlier Athena had passed away after a long battle with cancer. Now with Basil gone, it left Bobby all alone. Jimmy insisted that Angie go to Greece to see what could be done for Bobby. As much as Angie did not want to go, she prepared to leave for Athens to bring Bobby back with her. This was indeed a very sad day for the whole family.

Angie was gone for two weeks, and for the first time in her life she was in the country of her parent's birth. She met their brothers and sisters who up to this time were aunts and uncles who had been nothing but pictures. Before her very eyes they became flesh and blood and a life-time bond was formed with this family across the ocean.

Bobby was a big boy of fifteen. Standing in the airport with Basil's brothers, Bobby saw Angie as she stepped off of the plane. He could not control his tears when he saw her. He ran to her and hugged her with all his might. "I have missed you so much. I wish you stay here with me and not go back." He cried. Angie's heart broke as she held her brother.

The time flew by, and Angie was unable to resolve many of the estate problems. Joey and his wife came to help, but they were equally unsuccessful in the endeavor. Bobby's aunt, Athena's sister, was not willing to allow Bobby to return to the United States. In the end, Bobby stayed in Greece with Athena's relatives, and Angie and Joey returned home with very little resolved.

Time went on, and Angie had the added responsibility of traveling back and forth to Greece to check on Bobby. Bobby was not happy, but was afraid to return to the United States with her so it became a routine that she traveled to Greece to check on him.

Chapter 69

Life Goes On

Years passed. The children were growing up, and Jimmy and Angie were happy in spite of all of the ups and downs that life dealt them. One day as Angie was working at her desk she received a strange telephone call. The voice on the other end of the phone was searching for an Angie Demetrious. Angie was taken aback by the question. She had not been called that for years. She answered, yes, that was her. The lady informed her someone had found a high school class ring they thought might belong to her. As she heard the words, "might belong to her," she was shocked. She could not believe what she was hearing.

"Have you lost your class ring from Circle City High School?"

Angie had not thought of her class ring for years. She had long since lost all hope that it would ever be found. It had been almost fifty years since it went missing.

"Goodness, it has been at least fifty years since I lost my class ring. I couldn't imagine that it would ever be found. Why do you think this is my ring?" Angie asked completely dumbfounded. "It went missing shortly after I left Circle City High for beauty school, and I never saw it again."

The voice on the other end of the telephone introduced herself as the president of the Circle City High School Alumni Association. She was from the class of 1972. The association now had developed a website, she explained, and they were attempting to transfer all of the records from each class into the database. At the present time they had only gone back as far as the class of 1963. It had turned out to be a much bigger job than any of the committee could have imagined.

A week ago a young woman had called the alumni association's office asking how she could find the owner of a class ring who she believed had attended Circle City High. She then proceeded to describe the ring. It was a woman's gold ring with a blue center where a stone would normally be. The school name, Circle City High School encircled the blue area. On either side of the name of the school were the numbers of the year 19 on one side and 55 on the other side. At the bottom were the student initials A on one side and D on the other. The woman said she had located Circle City High through the Internet. With the use of yearbooks they were able to find a Sam Demetrious in the class of 1963. After making a call to Sam's residence they learned that Angie was his sister, and she had graduated in 1955. After checking the 1955 yearbook they discovered that there was only one A.D. in the class of 1955, and it was her.

Angie was in shock. After all this time to have something like this happen was bizarre.

"Where in the world was the ring?" Angie asked.

"It was found in Rocky Mount, North Carolina," replied the lady.

"How in the world did it get there? I've never even heard of it before now."

"Let me fax you a picture of the ring so you can verify it is yours."

When the picture came through there was no question about the ring belonging to Angie. But how did this happen? It had been fifty years since the ring was lost and even more difficult to explain was how it ended up in Rocky Mount, North Carolina.

Let's go back in this story, shall we. We will go back to the time that Judy had the ring and Patty stole Judy's purse at the motel. The ring was inside that purse. If you recall, Patty was desperate. She had two very small children and no money. She was running for her life from a cruel, abusive man who had beaten her and left her and the babies.

She tried to go back home, but her parents couldn't trust her and wouldn't take her in. She went to a shelter and found employment and stayed there with her children. As time passed she got herself back on her feet, but things never went very well for her. Try as she might, she couldn't get out of the hole she was in. Her children became unruly and life was too much for her. Deciding to move on, she hitchhiked across the country; she wanted a change of scene. More bad luck awaited her in North Carolina. As she was walking away from a job she had just lost, she passed a park. She reached into her pocket and found the blasted class ring which only reminded her of what a loser she was. In one more desperate effort to break the string of misfortune she was having, she took the ring out of her pocket and threw it as far as she could over the wall surrounding the park. The ring lay resting in a mound of fallen leaves , without an owner for the first time.

Patty ran as fast as she could away from what she considered her misfortune. She was a new person now and would not be under the spell of a stupid class ring ever again.

What became of Patty is still unknown.

The president of the alumni association gave Angie the name and e-mail address of the lady who found the ring and was searching for the owner. She felt that the two of them could make their own arrangements as to how it could be returned.

Angie could not believe that this was actually happening, but she e-mailed the woman named, Amelia Dixon, and asked how the ring was found. Amelia was anxious to tell the story and called Angie. She had gone to a great deal of trouble to find the owner. She explained that her husband was the head of the parks department in Rocky Mount, North Carolina, and a crew was getting ready to turn the leaves to mulch when someone in the crew saw the ring in the mound of leaves. Her husband retrieved it and brought it home to Amelia. She did some detective work on the Internet and found Circle City High School's Alumni Association and got in touch with them. The rest of the story is now history.

Angie was so touched to learn that in this day and age when everyone was in such a hurry, someone would take the time to search for the owner of a class ring which had been missing for fifty years and put the ring and owner together. This was indeed very special. Arrangements were made for mailing the ring to Angie, making a happy ending to a very long story.

Amelia placed the ring in a gray velvet ring case and sent it back to Angie. The special effort she gave to getting this ring back to its rightful owner meant so much to Angie. Amelia would continue with her busy life and Angie would continue with hers, but this deed of kindness and consideration would live in both of their lives forever. An act of kindness and unselfishness that brought two strangers together in an effort to return a class ring for no other reason than to put it into the hands of the rightful owner. Angie couldn't stop smiling. The ring had so much meaning to her during the time she was working so hard to get through beauty school and night school classes, and it was found and returned to her. The kindness and consideration that this stranger displayed only proved to Angie that there were people in this world who made life worth living, and she had the good fortune to have someone like that come into her life.

She took the ring out of the gray case and slipped it on her finger. She just loved it and smiled as it dazzled against her skin like a golden bond.

Epilogue

Angie felt as if she had been given back an old friend after receiving her class ring that had disappeared so many years ago. Though she never knew about the various travels the ring took, she was always puzzled at how it managed to get all the way to Rocky Mount, North Carolina. To this day that remains a mystery to her.

Angie and Jimmy raised their four children and lived to see them grow, love, and marry. They enjoyed grandchildren and great-grandchildren. Angie continued in her field of surgical nursing, and Jimmy was a successful lawyer. The law firm of Jimmy Jordan and Joey Demetrious grew to be one of the most successful in the city.

Sammie became a very effective physiatrist specializing in traumatized children and adults. Angie, Joey, and Sammie remained close. The boys looked up to Angie as the matriarch of the family—a position she never sought, but it remained as part of her legacy. Both boys married lovely young women and had beautiful families.

Jimmy and Angie never stopped loving each other and never regretted any of the struggles and hardships they had faced together.

Jenny was never heard from again. Although rumors emerged that she was still working as a hair stylist in a small salon in Riverview.

Eddy did find a good woman to marry, and they had three beautiful children. He had at long last found real love and happiness.

Colleen and Mimi continued to live in Crete and had many children. Mama was always a part of their family. Once or twice a year, Mimi, Coleen, and their children traveled to Ireland to visit Colleen's family. Her parents were wonderful grandparents, and the children loved them very much.

Molly and Mickey were happily married and lived in Ireland with their three children. Molly's catering business expanded across the city. She was always busy, employed many, and was never in need of business. As a doctor, Mickey was outstanding and highly sought after. He never forgot to bring Molly, his loved one, a red rose home every day of the week as a reminder of his love.

As for Judy, she settled down with her mother and began work on a shelter home for battered women.

Patty continued to work hard and tried to pull herself out of the hole she had dug. Surprisingly her children had become an inspiration to her and at long last she made peace with world.

Little Bobby, not so little any more, remained in Greece and made a life for himself as an English translator. His sister, Angie, would make the trips to Athens regularly to visit with him and to make sure he was alright. She loved him very much. As he grew older, he would come to Indianapolis to visit his brothers and all of his nieces and nephews. It was not ideal but at least they remained in touch with one another, and in a few years the travel back and forth would become a regular part of their lives.

It goes without saying that the class ring retired and spent a peaceful life in its little gray velvet ring case, brought out on occasion by Angie to wear and admire. The ring enjoyed a quieter life and was happy to never hit the road again.

***

The characters in this book have no resemblance to anyone living or dead. They are created from my imagination. The town of Riverville is a purely fictitious town.

Elaine Jannetides